MIST

MIST

SUSAN KRINARD

A Tom Doherty Associates Book

New York

MIST

A Tor Book
Published by Tom Doherty Associates, LLC
175 Fifth Avenue
New York, NY 10010

www.tor-forge.com

Tor® is a registered trademark of Tom Doherty Associates, LLC.

ISBN 978-0-7653-3208-0 (trade paperback)
ISBN 978-1-4299-5568-3 (e-book)

Tor books may be purchased for educational, business, or promotional use. For information on bulk purchases, please contact Macmillan Corporate and Premium Sales Department at 1-800-221-7945 extension 5442 or write specialmarkets@macmillan.com.

First Edition: July 2013

Printed in the United States of America

0   9   8   7   6   5   4   3   2   1

To Serge, with love

In the time of Ragnarok, the Twilight of the Gods—
As darkness descended, and Loki's horde beset the Aesir;
As the Alfar fell and Fenrisulfr opened his jaws, Odin to consume;
When the World Tree shuddered and
Surtr set the Rainbow Bridge aflame;
Thus spake the All-father:
To you, my servants, Valkyrie, Choosers of the Slain,
I entrust the greatest Treasures of the Aesir:
To Horja, Gridarvol, the Unbreakable Staff;
To Eir, the Apples of Idunn,
without which the gods cannot survive;
To Hild, Eight-legged Sleipnir, Swiftest of Horses;
To Bryn, Freya's Cloak, giver of the power of flight;
To Olrun, the lost Sword of Freyr, which needs no hand to wield it;
To Regin, Mjollnir, the Hammer of Thor, Mightiest of Warriors;
To Rota, that glove called Jarngreipr,
to which the Hammer must return;
To Skuld, Megingjord, the Belt of Power;
To Hrist, Bragi's Harp, whose voice charms all creatures;
To Kara, the Gjallarhorn, Summoner of Warriors;
To Sigrun, Gleipnir, the chain that cannot be broken;
To Mist, Gungnir, my own, the Spear that can never miss its mark.
All these you must hold, by your Oaths, untouched,
Until the Aesir come again.

MIST

PROLOGUE

"Just a little further, *skatten min*," Mist said, helping the little girl to her feet. The ramparts of snow to either side of the narrow path were as high as the child's hips, but Rebekka had refused to stay on the trail Geir and Horja had broken through the nearly trackless wilderness. Snow was falling more and more thickly, reaching down like a smothering hand and flattening the dense forests into shadowy silhouettes.

"I'll take you back to your uncle," Mist said. "Do you think you can hold onto my pack if I lift you up?"

The girl gave Mist a scornful look from beneath her close-fitting hood and woolen cap. "I don't want to stay with Uncle Aaron," she said. "He talks too much. Where is my papa?"

Rebekka should have been born a Valkyrie, Mist thought. She had the spirit, the strength, and an excellent judgment of men in one so young.

But the days of open, honorable battle, when the bravest fighters were chosen to join the gods in their great hall, Valhalla, had gone long ago. Once Mist and her Sisters had swept over blood-soaked battlefields on elf-bred steeds, selecting the victors and sweeping up the souls of valiant warriors to live on forever as Einherjar, the army of the Aesir. Forbidden to join in battle themselves, the Valkyrie had borne the trappings of war but never hurled their spears or bared their swords. They'd had to be content with basking in borrowed glory.

No more. Now a handful of Odin's Shield-maidens carried Sten guns with the Norwegian Resistance, creeping and skulking and striking from silence without warning, shooting down the murderers of women and children like the dogs they were. Killing them—not with magic, but with the skill of their own hands—and making sure at least a few of the Nazis' victims escaped.

Rebekka stared at up at Mist expectantly. "I want to stay with you until Papa comes."

The girl was too young to understand. She would likely never see her father again.

"You know your papa has gone a different way," Mist said, kneeling to help Rebekka remove her skis. She tied them onto the girl's pack and waited while Rebekka scrambled up onto her back. The child let out a little puff of excitement as she settled into her lofty position astride Mist's shoulders.

"How much longer?" she asked.

If they were lucky and the weather got no worse, they might reach the Swedish border before dark. But it was not hours Mist was thinking of. It was the years ahead, long years in a world that no longer held any memory of her kind except in myth.

Mist fingered the talisman pendant hung on a sturdy leather cord around her neck, the one Odin All-father had given her before the Last Battle.

"You will go to Midgard," he had said. "You and each of your Sisters will bear a weapon that must not fall into the hands of the evil ones. As long as you live, you will guard them. Until . . ."

Mist had never seen him again, nor understood why the All-father had sent the Valkyrie away when there would never be anyone to wield the Treasures, let alone steal them, when the Last Battle ended. Evil would die along with the Good.

And yet Mist's duty remained. Until the German invasion of the Northlands, her only reason for existing was to carry her burden through eternity.

This war, among all the countless that had come and gone in two millennia, had ended her self-imposed exile. She had found a new purpose, and it resided in this little girl and hundreds like her. Rebekka would know an end to conflict and a life that, for all its smallness, would find meaning in simple pleasures, in love, in future generations. All the things Mist had learned to live without.

The guttural cry of a gyrfalcon overhead pulled Mist from her thoughts. White against white, her Sister Valkyrie, Bryn, was only a flicker of motion in the colorless sky, almost invisible. As Mist watched her circle, Bryn faltered as if caught by a noose and pulled abruptly toward the earth. Her wings trembled, and a shower of pale feathers fluttered down amid the snow.

"What is wrong with that bird?" Rebekka asked, following Mist's gaze.

Mist caught a puff of white down and clenched it in her fingers. From the beginning of the war Mist had refused to accept that, even with the gods so long dead, the Valkyrie were still forbidden to use the Treasures. It was she who had suggested that Bryn take advantage of the magic cloak she had vowed to protect.

So far, it had been invaluable. But lately Bryn had been giving disturbing reports, claiming that it was becoming increasingly difficult to put on the cloak and change her shape.

"It's as if it doesn't want me to wear it," the dark-haired Valkyrie had said at their last camp. "As if Freya is punishing me for my blasphemy."

Mist had scoffed. "Blasphemy for using it to aid *her* people in their time of greatest need?"

Bryn had shivered and shook her head. "The Treasures were ours to guard, not to use. We have no right."

They had spoken of such things, Mist and Bryn and Horja, when they had found each other after Minister-President Quisling had taken control of the Norwegian government under the German Reich. All three of the Valkyrie had been living in solitude, apart from each other; none knew what had become of the other nine guardians, or why any of them had survived when Asgard, the realm of the gods, was no more.

"There must have been a reason," Bryn had said. "The All-father would not have entrusted the Treasures to us if he knew no one would return to claim them."

But Mist had only laughed. "Odin was blind," she said, "and now he is gone. He condemned us for nothing. We could have died honorably instead of holding to a meaningless oath. Now we have the chance to fight again."

Bryn and Horja had been shocked at her casual sacrilege. Horja, who guarded Gridarvol, Thor's unbreakable staff, had joined Bryn in protest.

But Mist hadn't listened. With the staff, Horja could not only fight but clear paths through the deepest snow. Freya's cloak would give Bryn an invaluable edge in spotting enemies. Gungnir, Odin's spear, would find its mark when all other weapons failed. The gods would never return to punish Mist or her Sisters.

Now, as if to prove Mist right, Bryn recovered, spread her wings, and cried out again before darting toward the fringe of woods that ran parallel to the trail. Mist knew there was no more time to waste.

"Hold on tight, Rebekka," she said, pushing off on her skis and falling into the steady rhythm she could maintain for days without rest. Snow drove into her face and stung her eyes, but she didn't slow until she was in sight of the other refugees.

Aaron Fischer, who had taken up the rear, turned awkwardly to face her.

"Rebekka!" he said, the word catching on the wind. "Where have you been?"

"She's all right," Mist said. She reached behind her and swung the child to the ground, setting her on her feet. "Rebekka, you must stay with your uncle." She met Fischer's shrouded gaze. "Can you carry her? I must go back."

Fischer grunted agreement, and Mist lifted Rebekka onto her uncle's shoulders. The girl glanced back mournfully as Fischer lowered his head and set off again, too weary to ask where Mist was going, or why.

Jumping up onto the snowbank, Mist raced alongside and ahead of the straggling line of refugees, her skis driving through the soft upper layer of new-fallen snow to find the harder pack beneath. A raven circled overhead—the symbol of Odin's two avian advisors, Thought and Memory—scenting the violence soon to come.

Within minutes she had caught up to Geir, who was closely following Horja and using his skis to flatten the snow in her wake.

He saw her and half turned without slowing. "Mist?" he said.

She signaled for him to stop, jumped back onto the trail, and bent her head close to his. Her breath melted the rime crusting his ginger brows and the week's worth of beard on his chin. His hazel eyes were little more than slits nested in a web of creases, and his face was haggard with worry. He had never looked more beautiful to her.

"Germans," she said. "I'm going to help Bryn deal with them."

Geir put his hand on her arm; even through layers of gloves, coat, and sweater, she could feel his warmth.

"How many?" he asked.

She grinned, making sure he could see her expression. "Don't worry about me," she said. "You know I can handle them."

And he did. At first he'd been skeptical that any woman, however brave or skilled with weapons, could keep up with trained

Resistance fighters. She'd proven him wrong on their first mission, and when Horja and Bryn had joined them he had supported their participation wholeheartedly.

Of course, he didn't know what they were. But he'd never questioned her, and she had seen the pride in his eyes. Pride, and something she had never thought to see in any man's face.

She began to believe he might one day accept what she was, that they might remain together, even though she would not seem to age at all over his entire lifetime. It was a hope she nurtured like a fragile flame in the icy darkness.

Geir searched her eyes, his fingers squeezing her sleeve. There was no question that he had to remain with Horja; if the Germans broke through and attacked the refugees, he would be needed here.

"Take care," he said, and seized her head between his hands. They kissed, a rush of heat that brought the blood surging like the giant Surtr's fire through Mist's veins.

"Are we stopping?" Mrs. Dworsky said, catching up to them. Her voice was thin, but there was no complaint in it. "Is it time to rest?"

Geir broke away to face her. "Not yet," he said. "We must keep moving a little while longer."

Mist didn't stay to hear Mrs. Dworsky's reply. She leaped onto the snowbank and raced back the way she had come. As she neared the woods she stopped, planted her poles, and unslung the Sten gun from over her shoulder. She pulled off her gloves, checked her Nagant revolver and made sure Kettlingr was within easy reach. To the eye of the refugees and the enemy, the blade was no more than a knife any woodsman might carry, but with the right spells it became the sword she had kept at her side since her coming to Midgard.

Shrugging off her pack, she removed Gungnir from its cloth wrappings and secured it to her belt. Like Kettlingr, the Spear's true shape was masked by spells only Mist knew. Its grip hummed against her skin as if it were calling for the blood it had been denied so long ago.

In all her time with the Resistance, Mist had never wielded Odin's spear. The others had made use of their divine weapons, as she herself had urged, but she had never found the need to draw Gungnir or chant the Runes.

The thought filled her with a strange foreboding that shamed her. She had laughed at Bryn's worries, and now she laughed at her own. If today was to be the day, she would use Gungnir without hesitation. It was a tool, nothing more.

Bryn emerged from the trees, naked save for the feathered cloak wrapped around her shoulders. Her legs sank deep into the snow with every step.

"Where?" Mist asked as the brown-haired Valkyrie joined her.

"Close." Bryn's labored breaths shaped streamers of condensation that came far too quickly. "Horja is still with the others?"

Mist nodded, searching Bryn's eyes. "Are you all right?"

Bryn cut the air with her hand, dismissing Mist's question. "We must hurry. There are six of them, and they are coming fast."

"Can you fly again?" Mist asked.

Bryn's hesitation was brief. "I will do what must be done."

Without another word she turned back for the trees, Mist on her heels. Bryn's clothing, pack, and weapons hung on a low branch just inside the border of the wood. She ignored them and ran on, threading her way among the stands of birch, maple, and pine. By the time Mist reached the other side, Bryn was gone.

But the enemy was very much present. Most of their kind were loud and clumsy, blundering through the snow like blind, pregnant cattle. Their dark uniforms were foul, ugly streaks of filth in the purity of the wilderness.

These men were different. There were four, not six, but they were alert and watchful, crouched low and constantly scanning the land around them. They were expecting a fight. They might even be worthy opponents.

Mist removed her skis, knelt behind a thick screen of young birches, and waited for Bryn to reappear. The falcon burst from cover to Mist's right and winged skyward, calling out to catch the Germans' attention.

Aiming the Sten gun, Mist raked the soldiers with a spray of bullets. Two of the men fell flat on their bellies. A third collapsed in a halo of blood. The fourth remained standing, returning fire with calm precision.

For the first time since she had joined the Resistance, Mist felt the sting of a bullet slice through her clothes and bite into her flesh. The shock of it knocked her off her feet. She rolled onto her stomach and pulled the trigger again.

The gun jammed. She tossed it aside and yanked her Nagant from its holster. Her first shot missed the marksman, who dropped and continued to fire. The other two men opened up on Mist, pinning her to the ground.

Bryn shrieked, diving at the first shooter's face with claws extended. He batted her away, his shots going wild. Bryn swooped up again, but her course was erratic, broken with strange dips and starts. Mist jumped up and ran toward the soldiers, snapping off the remaining six shots in rapid succession. She rolled into the scant cover of a depression in the snow and reloaded. When she came up, Bryn was diving again.

Not diving, but falling, her wings hugged to her sides. Mist emptied the cylinder at the German running toward her. He staggered, and Mist dived back for the depression. Flames engulfed her right hand. She lost her grip on the gun, and it flew out of her reach. She felt blindly for Kettlingr's hilt with her left hand, but her fingers, slick with blood, couldn't find purchase. She chanted the Runes as she tried again, praying it wasn't too late, and tugged the blade free just as it began to change.

Bryn lay sprawled on the ground near the German's covert, her body half covered by the cloak. Mist screamed and raised Kettlingr high as she charged the two soldiers who remained on their feet. They stared, caught by the bizarre spectacle of a woman attacking them with a sword.

But the weapon refused to obey her commands. There was something wrong with the hilt; it was too long, impossible to swing.

Because it wasn't Kettlingr at all. She held Gungnir in her fist, the spear that could never miss its mark. Her feet tangled under her. The breath seized in her throat. She hesitated for a single second, and during that second one of the Germans aimed his Schmeisser at Bryn and brought her down in a flurry of blood and feathers.

There was no more thinking then, no fear. Mist flung Gungnir, impaling Bryn's murderer. The German who had stood to face her at the beginning hardly blinked. He finished replacing his magazine and took aim.

If luck and skill had abandoned Mist, rage had not. It carried her across the space between them, driving her body like a Panzer tank to smash him down. She wrapped her bare, bloodied hands around his neck, watching his disbelief with savage satisfaction as she snapped his neck. She pried his Schmeisser from his dead fingers and plunged toward the fallen soldiers.

Only one was still alive. She finished him off, dropped the gun, and threw herself down beside Bryn's body. If Bryn had been human, she would already have been dead. But she was breathing in spite of her terrible wounds, gulping air into punctured lungs and bleeding from the mouth. Her eyes were glazed and unseeing.

"Mist?" Bryn lifted her hand, clutching at the air.

"I'm here." Mist clasped Bryn's hand gently in her own unwounded one and smoothed the dark hair away from the Valkyrie's forehead.

"Did we win?"

"Yes. Because of your courage."

Bryn tried to shake her head. "I failed. The cloak . . ." She gasped, and Mist lifted Bryn into her arms.

"I failed, *venninne min*, not you."

Fresh blood bubbled over Bryn's lips. "Take the cloak. Swear you will . . . guard the Treasures. Keep them safe, as we were meant to. They will . . ." Bryn sighed and closed her eyes. "Swear."

Mist swore. Denying Bryn's unwavering faith was beyond her power. When she had finished, Bryn released her hold on life, as surely gone as if she had lived no longer than an ordinary woman.

Mist bowed her head. There would be no one to carry this warrior to Valhalla. If some other afterworld existed, it would be a cold one where valor and pride and loyalty had no meaning.

The sun was sinking below the trees, and Mist knew she had no time to commit Bryn's body to the fire. Carefully she untied the cloak and slid it free from beneath Bryn's shoulders, her injured hand aching in the cold. She brushed stained snow from the feathers, draped the cloak over one arm, and selected a fallen twig lying nearby, sketching Runes of protection in the bloody snow to ward scavengers from Bryn's body. The raven circled overhead, watching for a chance at a fresh feast, but even it could not pierce the wards.

As the Rune-staves slowly lost their shapes beneath the steady snowfall, Mist chanted a second spell. The cloak seemed to fold in on itself, growing smaller and smaller until it was nothing but a bundle of feathers. Gently Mist tucked the bundle into its silken pouch and hung the sturdy cord around her neck.

Yanking Gungnir free from the German's chest, Mist cleaned it and returned it to its sheath. She had just retrieved one of the Schmeissers when she heard the gunfire. Without stopping for her skis, she ran back through the woods, leaping like a stag through the deep snow and jumping onto the broken trail as soon as she reached it.

Her vision adjusted to the dark as easily as a cat's, but in that moment she wished she were blind.

The utter silence warned her before she found the trail's end. She saw Mrs. Dworsky first, lying facedown in an uneven circle of blood-blackened snow. The others were scattered like seeds carelessly tossed from a giant's hand, sprinkled with a dusting of white like fresh earth from a spade.

Mist picked her way from body to body, searching for signs of life. None had survived. But Rebekka was not among the bodies, nor was Geir, or Horja.

Without hope Mist continued on, her heart pumping steadily, her breath moving in and out as if her body insisted on living long after her mind had lost the will. Someone croaked her name. She stopped and looked at the figures hunched together in the lee of a stunted pine.

The first thing she saw was Geir's face, pinched with pain and grief. Rebekka crouched huddled in his arms, her head cradled in the hollow of his shoulder. Horja lay on her side, one broken half of Thor's staff still clutched in her right hand. She, too, was alive.

The last of Mist's strength drained from her body. She forced herself to continue until she'd reached the pine and fell to her knees. The bodies of two German soldiers lay a few meters apart a dozen paces away. The ones that hadn't been with the others Bryn had told her about. The ones she'd forgotten.

"There was an ambush," Geir whispered. He stared through Mist, his eyes reflecting the horrors of massacre. "We couldn't . . ."

"Rebekka?"

"All right." Frozen tears glittered on Geir's cheeks. "But the rest . . ."

Horja tried to push herself up. The piece of carved wood she held fell from her fingers. "It snapped," she said with a strange, almost childlike bewilderment. "Where is Bryn?"

Mist swallowed and shook her head. Horja fell back with moan of despair.

"Why?" she cried. "How could this happen?"

They stared at Mist, man and Valkyrie, as if she held the answers. And she knew. She knew why this had happened, why the divine Treasures had failed, why they had suffered defeat at such a terrible cost of lives entrusted to their care.

Pride. *Her* pride, in believing she and Horja and Bryn could be more than mere guardians, that they could intervene in the fate of men, that they could wield the Aesir's weapons with impunity. Her bitterness, insisting that they owed nothing to gods who were dead and gone, who had imprisoned them with a hopeless duty.

Bryn and Horja had warned her. She hadn't listened. But it was all the others, not she, who paid the price.

She crawled closer to Geir and touched Rebekka's shoulder. The girl flinched and turned her head, one eye visible above the scarf wrapped around her nose and mouth.

"Rebekka, I—"

"You left us!" Rebekka said, her voice rising in a wail. "You ran away!"

Mist let her hand fall. It didn't matter whether or not she had done what Rebekka accused her of. She was still to blame. She met Geir's haunted eyes.

"Are you all right?" she asked.

He nodded, his gaze sliding away. "I couldn't stop them. I shouldn't be alive."

Echoing anguish roughened Horja's voice. "I wasn't strong enough to protect the mortals. Forgive me."

Mist sucked in a frozen breath. "Can you walk?"

"Yes. But Gridarvol . . ."

"Take the pieces. Perhaps someday . . ."

It can be repaired. But she knew it wouldn't be. No one lived who could do it.

Somehow she shaped the ravaged fragments of her thoughts into a semblance of order. "The most important thing now is to get Rebekka across the border," she said, looking at Geir. "Can you do that?"

Geir searched her eyes. "You aren't coming."

It wasn't a question. He knew her too well. "I left Bryn and four dead Germans on the other side of the wood," she said. "I'll watch for pursuit. When I'm sure you're safe, I'll look after her . . ." She closed her eyes. "Her body, and these people's as well."

Geir shook his head slowly, like a man waking from a dream indistinguishable from reality. Horja got to her knees and rose, waving away Mist's offer of help. She stumbled toward the nearest body.

"Mist—" Geir began.

"Listen to me. This is where we must part. We—" Her heart contracted until she couldn't feel it anymore. "We will not see each other again."

His voice rose. "You aren't to blame. I—"

"I brought this down on us." She cut him off before he could speak again. "Don't ask me to explain."

"You think I don't know?" he shouted. Rebekka whimpered, and he lowered his voice again. "You and Horja and Bryn. You're not like the rest of us."

"No. I should have been wiser." She willed him to understand. "We couldn't stay together. I could never give you what you want."

"You know nothing of what I want!"

"*I* want you to live, all three of you. You'll have to care for Rebekka now." She began to shiver. "I'll find where you've taken her and send money. Promise me you will see to it."

Geir said nothing for a long time. She saw him gathering protests, arguments, denials . . . watched his beloved features contort with anger and grief and unspoken pleas, settling at last into acceptance.

"Where will you go?" he asked.

She wanted to fight. She wanted to kill every last German in Norway with her bare hands.

But she was cursed. She could never again risk bringing that curse down upon those who were ready to sacrifice everything for freedom.

"Don't worry about me," she said. "*You* survive. Build this country again when the enemy is gone. Make a new world, Geir. Find someone like you, someone . . ."

He reached out and grabbed her hand. "There will never be anyone else."

Horja returned, carrying both halves of Thor's staff in her arms. "The snow has stopped," she said. "We should cross while it's still dark."

Mist eased her hand from Geir's grip. "I'll cover your tracks," she said, "and make sure no one is following." She removed both the raven pendant and the leather pouch from around her neck.

"This is for you, Rebekka," she said, holding out the pendant. "It will always protect you."

The girl stared at the crude, carved image and the Rune-staves carved on the flat stone. She met Mist's gaze without anger or fear.

"How can it protect me?" she whispered.

"Because it once belonged to someone very powerful, and all his strength is in it. Now you will have that strength too, in your heart."

Slowly Rebekka took the pendant, and Mist helped her pull it on beneath her hood. She sketched an invisible Bind-Rune on Rebekka's forehead and got up to face Horja.

"I have something for you as well," she said, offering the pouch to her Sister. "Bryn would want you to keep this safe."

"For what?" Horja asked. She thrust out her hands, showing Mist the splintered ends of what was meant to be forever unbroken.

"You were right. There are no gods to reclaim them. The Aesir have forsaken us."

"Bryn had faith," Mist said. "Keep that faith for her, Horja. And if you ever meet the other Sisters, let them keep the faith as well."

Horja bowed her head, and Mist settled the cord around her Sister's neck. Then she turned back to Geir.

"Live long, *min kjæreste*. I will not forget you."

Holding Rebekka tight, Geir got to his feet. Tears leaked into the sun-etched creases that framed his eyes. "*Farvel, elskede min.* Until we meet again."

Mist pulled her hood low over her face and stood unmoving until he had followed Horja out of her sight. The raven—or another like it—croaked in a pine somewhere to the east. She listened for a moment, counting her breaths, and then set out after the others. They wouldn't see her, but she would be sure they'd made it before she left them for good.

Long before dawn, Geir, Rebekka, and Horja were safely across the border, and Mist was on her way back to lay Bryn to rest.

The Valkyrie's world had ended. When Geir and Rebekka and Rebekka's children and grandchildren were gone, the Valkyrie might finally be permitted to join the Aesir in oblivion.

—an ax age, a sword age
—shields are riven—
a wind age, a wolf age—
before the world goes
headlong.
No man will have
mercy on another.

—*Prose Edda*
Snorri Sturluson
Translated by Ursula Dronke

1

The sword sliced the air inches from Mist's face. She swung her own spatha to intercept the blow, bracing herself and catching her opponent's blade in mid-stroke. Metal clanged on metal with glorious, discordant music. Her adversary bore down hard for several seconds, his furious gaze fixed on hers, and abruptly disengaged.

"One of these days," Eric said, his face breaking out in a grin, "I'm going to beat you."

Mist lowered her sword and caught her breath. Perspiration trickled from her hairline over her forehead, soaking the fine blond hairs that had come loose from her braid, and her body ached pleasantly from the workout. She grinned back at Eric, who sheathed his sword and reached for the towel draped across the bench against the wall.

"You're good," she said. "Almost as good as I am."

He grimaced and scrubbed the towel across his face. "I outweigh you by eighty pounds," he said. "I don't want to think about what you could do to me if you were my size."

Size had nothing to do with it, though Mist hadn't yet found a way to tell Eric why he'd never be able to beat her. She'd even thought once or twice of letting him win, male pride being such a fragile thing, but instinct was too strong.

Mist sheathed her sword and ran her thumb over the engraving etched into the hilt. *She* had no right to pride of any kind. She'd lost that right long ago, as she'd lost her honor and the only man she had ever loved.

And yet Eric had unexpectedly roused her from the despair of one who waits for redemption that will never come. Like Geir, he wasn't afraid of a woman who shared his strength. He'd taught her to laugh again. And when she looked into Eric's face—the face of a true warrior of the Norse, broad and handsome and fearless—she knew he was safe. Safe because he would never demand more than she could give. Safe from her mistakes.

But there would be no more mistakes. She had made sure of that.

"I'm headed for the shower," Eric said, catching her glance and giving her a sly look in return. He padded toward her, remarkably graceful and light on his feet, his bare chest streaked with sweat. He lifted a loose tendril of her hair, rolling it between his fingers. "Care to join me? I'll wash your back if you'll wash mine."

His meaning couldn't be clearer, and she was eager enough to join him in bed after his long absence. But she dodged aside when he bent to kiss her.

"I'm really tired tonight," she said, smiling to take the sting out of her rejection. "Long day at the forge. I promise I'll make it up to you tomorrow."

Eric frowned and rubbed his thumb along the edge of her jaw. "You okay? You've seemed a little preoccupied ever since I came back."

She covered his hand with hers. "It's nothing. I missed you, that's all."

"Have you?" He nuzzled her neck. "Show me."

"Soon. I promise."

Eric let her go and winked. "My sword is always at your service, m'lady." He strode toward the door that connected the gym to the loft's ground-floor living space, throwing another wink over his shoulder, and Mist was left alone in the echoing silence of the gym.

Her wrist was aching again. The red tattoo encircling it—still as bright as the day she'd had it done—seemed to squirm on her skin, an endless chase of wolves and ravens, the animal symbols of Odin All-father.

You used your wrist too much today, she told herself. But that didn't account for this strange restlessness, which even Eric had noticed in spite of her best efforts to hide it.

With a sigh Mist returned the sword to the rack at the opposite end of the gym and followed Eric into the long hall, pausing at the door to the master bedroom. She could hear Eric singing in the shower.

Not in the mood to wait for her turn—and another invitation to bed—Mist threw on her leather jacket, pulled on her gloves, and went out to the garage. The temperature had fallen thirty degrees since the warmest part of the day, and the cold seemed to crackle in the late December air. Even the tart, briny scent of the Bay a third of a mile to the east seemed subdued by the frigid weather.

Her Volvo was ancient and often unreliable. It usually rumbled and complained like the great hound Garm whenever she needed it to operate smoothly, refusing to respond to even her most coaxing spells . . . such as they were. Tonight the car leaped to life almost immediately; it almost seemed to Mist as if it, too, felt her restlessness.

Dogpatch was far from quiet even at this time of night, in spite of the unseasonable cold; the Muni light-rail ran right down the center of Third Street, and the whole neighborhood, once an industrial area packed with warehouses, was becoming fashionable with young professionals who frequented the growing number of clubs, restaurants, and galleries. Colored lights festooned the old houses and shops, and someone had set a decorated Christmas tree on the roof of the recording studio across the street.

Without really thinking about her destination, Mist turned north on Third Street and left on Sixteenth Street toward Golden Gate Park on the other side of the city. It didn't surprise her that she'd ended up here; it had the closest thing to woods as anywhere in San Francisco, and it made a nice change from the tiny, half-dead scrap of lawn behind her loft.

She parked along Lincoln Way, got out of the car, and entered the park from Nineteenth Avenue. It was near midnight, and the park would officially be closed to visitors in a few minutes, but Mist had no trouble finding an unobtrusive way in. The only other people in the park were the homeless and vagrants who spent their nights huddled in tattered blankets under the bushes. There would be no Christmas for them.

Christmas. Yule, as it had been known before the coming of the White Christ. The solstice had never really been more than an excuse for celebration, an end to the darkness and the coming of a new year. If this bizarre, unseasonable winter ever ended.

A few gentle snowflakes drifted down to melt on Mist's hair as she walked along Martin Luther King Jr. Drive and headed toward Stow Lake. There was a breathless quality to the frigid air. Dense fog began to settle over the nearest trees, turning the park into a ghostly realm of indistinct shapes and ominous silence.

Fog. Mist stopped, lifting her head to smell the air. Fog like this came in the summer, when warm Pacific winds blew over the colder waters along the coast.

A sudden chill nipped at Mist's hands and face. Strange weather or not, there was nothing natural about the icy vapor that stretched probing fingers along the ground at her feet, slithering and hissing like the serpent Nidhogg bent on devouring everything in its path.

Disbelief shook Mist with jaws of iron. She knew the smell of the vapor and what it had portended when the Last Battle began.

But it wasn't possible. The Jotunar, the frost giants, were as extinct as the great sloths or mastodons that had once roamed the North American plains.

Mist encircled her left wrist with her right hand, trying to soothe the unnatural, burning agony beneath the glove. She *wasn't* going crazy. There was a perfectly logical explanation for the hallucination. This was the old, rejected world's final attempt to hold her bound in the chains of guilt and self-contempt and loneliness, to abandoned oaths and a way of life she had discarded years ago like ash-soiled rags.

She needed to go home, go to bed, wake up to find Eric beside her—ready with a grin, an invitation, and a reminder that her life was normal now, had been normal long before she met him. Turning on her heel, Mist started back for the street.

A low, rasping chuckle stopped her in mid-stride. She spun around. A face emerged from the vapor, rising two heads above Mist's generous height. A broad face, heavy, filled with anger and fell purpose.

Pale, cold eyes met hers. The mouth, with its rows of teeth filed to points like daggers, gaped in a grin.

"*Heil*, Odin's Girl," the giant said in the Old Tongue, his voice deep enough to shake the ground under Mist's feet. "Or can it be that I am mistaken? Is this what the Valkyrie have become, mountless and dressed no better than thralls?"

No hallucination, no illusion, no madness. The truth took Mist by the throat and shook her like a child's doll.

This was real. This was death. And everything she had come to believe, everything she had tried to make of her life, was a lie.

Instinct, rusty as an ancient blade left to molder in a salty bog, brought Mist back to her senses. Her Swiss Army knife, the one she'd carried since World War II, was of no use against a Jotunn. She peeled off her gloves, dropped them on the ground, and began to search for a long stick, a fallen branch, anything she could use as a weapon.

"No sword, Valkyrie?" the giant asked. "No spear?"

Mist knew she had to keep him distracted. He was obviously the type who enjoyed playing with his victims.

"A little out of place in a modern city, don't you think?" she said, slipping back into English as she backed away and swept her foot across the ground.

The Jotunn either didn't know English very well, or he preferred the drama of the ancient language. "A pity you embraced this mortal world so completely," he said. "It will be your undoing."

Mist's boot struck something solid that rolled under her foot. A weathered bit of branch—likely rotten and not as thick as she would have liked, but she didn't have time to look for something better. She snatched it up and held it behind her back with her left hand while she reached for the knife attached to her belt with her right.

"So you are not without your defenses after all," the Jotunn said with a low laugh.

"What are you called, Jotunn?" Mist asked, forcing the archaic words through the constriction in her throat.

"I am Hrimgrimir," the giant said. "I know you, Mist, once Chooser of the Slain."

And she knew *him*. Hrimgrimir was the frost giant who guarded the mouth of Niflheim, the frigid realm of the goddess Hel, where all mortals but the greatest heroes went after death. Mist had assumed that Hel and her dead minions, like all Loki's evil forces—along with the gods and *their* allies—had been destroyed in the Last Battle.

Except one of them hadn't.

"From where have you come, Frost-shrouded?" she demanded, carefully flicking open the blade. "From what dream of venom and darkness?"

Hrimgrimir chuckled. "No dream, Sow's bitch." He blew out a

foul, gusty breath. "A pity you chose *her* side. You might have lived to see the new age."

Keep him talking, Mist thought. "Whose side?" Mist asked, scratching a crude series of Runes into the branch with the tip of her knife.

"Are you stupid as he says?" Hrimgrimir asked, advancing on her with a slow, heavy tread. "The Sow is your mistress."

"Freya?" Mist said, angling the blade to slice the pad of her left thumb. "I served Odin, but all the gods were your enemies."

The giant sniffed. "What are you doing, bitch? I smell your fear, but—"

Mist smeared her blood into the shallow Runes, dropped the knife, and swung the branch out from behind her back. She breathed a quick spell, and the blood began to smoke.

Too late, Hrimgrimir recognized what she had done. He reared out of the vapor, huge hands curled, his power and giant-magic swirling round about him like ice-forged armor.

Mist felt his assault in body and soul, and her bloody fingers almost slipped on the branch. But she had been stricken by the battle fever that had driven her through World War II. There was no chance she'd back out now.

She tried a second spell, and this time the magic obeyed her. She stumbled backward as the branch began to change, the end in her hand forming a grip that perfectly fit her grasp, the other end broadening and sharpening into a blade.

"Is that all?" Hrimgrimir said with another grating laugh. He waved his hand as if he were batting away flies, and his fist connected with the branch-blade.

But the wood was no longer wood at all. It flashed in the faint ambient light reflected by the clouds overheard, a blade like the one she had carried so long and laid to rest with all the other reminders of her past.

Hrimgrimir howled as the edge of the sword connected with the side of his hand, slicing a ragged gash in his tough flesh. He took a step back, giving Mist the chance to shift position. She lifted the sword and crouched, legs tensed to lunge forward. Hrimgrimir bellowed and raised both arms, leaving his midsection vulnerable, and she struck at him, aiming straight at his gut. He tried to block her attack with one arm, and cold, blue blood splattered over her as her Rune-spelled blade sliced him to the bone.

Mist jumped back, ready for another attack. It never came. The vapor fell like a curtain in front of her, a writhing wall of maggots sheathed in ice. She swung again, but her sword whistled through empty air. The vapor began to recede as quickly as it had come, crackling angrily and leaving a crystalline film on the grass.

Shaken, Mist let the battle fever drain from muscle and nerve and bone. A cold sweat bathed her forehead and glued her shirt to her back. The burning sensation in her wrist was nearly gone, and so was her shock, yet the sense of unreality remained.

A giant had come to Midgard, bringing with him an evil no child of Mist's adopted city could imagine. Not even the Nazis, or any of the tyrannical regimes that had come and gone since, had possessed such power. *They* had been human.

Flexing her fingers against the ache in her left thumb, Mist dropped her temporary sword and retrieved her knife. Almost instantly, the branch assumed its original form, the Runes burned away along with her blood.

But her thoughts continued to boil with questions. Where had Hrimgrimir come from? Even if she had been wrong about Ragnarok, the Last Battle, and the utter destruction of the world she had known millennia ago, she was certain she would have discovered the presence of other survivors long before the appearance of this one.

Certainly no Jotunn could walk Midgard unnoticed for long,

even in more modest size. Had she been drawn to the park tonight because she had felt his presence?

She didn't have to ask herself why he'd tried to kill her. Though there had always been a minority of Jotunar who had been friends and allies to the Aesir, few giants could meet a servant of the gods without enmity.

But why now? He had known not only what but who she was, and his attack had seemed very personal. He'd been waiting for her. For *her*.

Mist stared blindly at the trail of blackened grass Hrimgrimir had left in the wake of his retreat. Hrimgrimir had threatened her, but he'd given up as soon as she'd wounded him. Something about that hasty retreat bothered her. Carefully she reconstructed the Jotunn's words, parsing them for any meaning she could have missed in the heat of battle.

"You might have lived to see the new age."

Her heart stopped, and the fine hairs on the back of her neck stood rigid as a new-forged blade. The Prophecies had foretold a new age after Ragnarok, one of peace and plenty. That age would hardly have been one friendly to the dark forces. Few Jotunar would welcome its arrival, even if they survived to see it.

Unless the "new age" Hrimgrimir spoke of was very different from the paradise that had never come.

Skita. All Mist wanted now was a warm bed and Eric. But she had to have answers to this mystery before she could ever hope to have a normal life again. She had to find Hrimgrimir and make him talk.

Moving quickly, Mist followed the Jotunn's trail, her boots crunching on the frozen grass. The park was still silent save for the bitter wind in the treetops and the distant roar of a motorcycle on Fulton Street. She had gone only a few hundred feet when the track disappeared completely. No trace of the giant remained.

And yet, as she stood still and opened her senses to the unseen, the feeling of something out of place began to grow again.

She looked for another piece of wood. She was long out of practice, and she, like all Valkyrie, had possessed only enough Galdr and basic Rune-lore to perform her duties. She'd been lucky the first spell had worked and that it hadn't weakened her. This time the magic might fail or even turn against her.

Still, she had to try. She found a piece of firm bark, opened the knife again, and held the bark against the trunk of the nearest tree. The Runes sizzled as she cut them into the wood, simple yet powerful symbols formed of short, straight strokes: Uruz, Thurisaz, Ansuz.

It was too dangerous to use blood again so soon, so she closed the knife, withdrew a lighter from her jacket pocket, and set fire to the bark.

In three breaths it was consumed. The ashes fell to the foot of the tree in the pattern of an arrow, facing west.

Without hesitation Mist turned onto a narrow, dusty path that wandered among a dense grove of Monterey pines. Her search brought her to a heap of discarded clothing spread over the pine needles, half hidden under a clump of thick shrubbery.

Mist cursed. The magic *had* turned against her, mocking her meager skill. She was about to leave when the pile of rags heaved, and a hand, lean and pale, reached out from a tattered sleeve. A low groan emerged from the stinking mound. She smelled blood, plentiful but no longer fresh.

Against her better judgment, she knelt beside the man. She expected an indigent, perhaps injured by some thug who found beating up helpless vagrants a source of amusement. But the hand, encrusted with filth as it was, appeared unmarked by the daily struggle for food and shelter, more accustomed to lifting golden goblets of mead than sifting through rubbish in a Dumpster.

She started at the thought. Mead had been the most favored beverage of gods and heroes and elves.

This one certainly didn't look like any kind of hero. Hesitantly she pulled the blankets aside. A tall, lean form emerged, dressed in a torn shirt, trousers too short and wide for his body, and hole-ridden sneakers. He lay on his belly, legs sprawled, cheek pressed against the damp, chilly earth.

And his face . . .

Mist had seen its like countless times in Odin's hall, Valhalla, regal and stately among the carousing Aesir and warriors, fairer to look upon than the sun. It had always been accepted that the most beautiful of all creatures were the light-elves of Alfheim, allies of the gods.

This man was not so beautiful. His face was a mask of gore and mud, one eye swollen shut and nose covered in blood. Yet his features could not be mistaken.

A frost giant had come to Midgard from gods-knew-where. Now one of the Alfar had arrived as well, against all reason. Against every "truth" she had known, believed for so long.

Mist touched the elf's shoulder. "Can you hear me?" she asked in the Old Tongue.

He moved his hand, fingers digging into the soil, and spoke in a voice rough and raw with pain.

"Who . . ." he croaked, opening his one good eye. "How . . ."

There was no doubt, no doubt at all, that he was speaking the Old Tongue with the accent of the Alfar. He was every bit as real as the Jotunn had been.

"Rest easy," she said, shrugging out of her jacket and laying it over him. "You're safe."

The eye, so dark a blue as to be almost black amid the red and brown of blood and dirt, regarded her with growing comprehension. "Safe?" he whispered. With a sudden jerk he rolled to his side, pushing her jacket away. "The Jotunn . . ."

"There is no giant here now," she said, pushing him down again. "Lie still, man of the Alfar. All is well."

The sound he made might have been a laugh. He eased himself back down, inhaling sharply, and looked into her face. "Who . . . are you?"

Mist hesitated. The laws of Midgard—the natural, mundane laws she had accepted for centuries—had been broken. She didn't know what the rules were anymore or whom she could trust, including herself.

But he was of the light-elves, who had fought and died alongside the gods. Even if she'd never had much use for the lofty, superior aesthetes who had been much too grand to spare so much as a glance for a lowly Valkyrie, she badly needed answers.

"My name is Mist," she said.

In a burst of speed his hand shot out and encircled her wrist, long fingers curling around her tattoo. It seemed to catch fire again, and she wrenched her arm out of his grip. He closed his eye and released a shuddering breath.

"It is as I hoped," he said.

Mist was too angry and startled to wonder what he'd hoped. "Whoever you are," she said, "don't do that again."

He rubbed at his swollen mouth with his other hand. It was shaking. "Where is the frost giant?" he asked.

"He fled."

"He did not . . . harm you?"

"No. I think I scared him off."

"You fought him?"

"He attacked me. I didn't have much choice." She leaned closer to the elf, studying his face in search of anything familiar. "What do you know about him? Where did he come from? Where did *you* come from?"

Wincing, the elf pushed himself up on his elbow. "I will . . .

answer all your questions, Mist of the Valkyrie," he said, his voice regaining a little of the melodic cadences of his kind. "Is it safe?"

Mist shivered as if Hrimgrimir's icy vapor had sunk deep into her flesh and muscle and bone.

"I don't know what you mean," she said.

He stared at her, his sole visible eye filled with mild contempt. "Do not pretend ignorance. It is not plausible."

"I don't much care what you find plausible. Who *are* you?"

"I am . . . Dainn. Dainn Far-seeker."

Dainn. It was not an uncommon name for elf or dwarf. There were two most famous among the Alfar. The first was Dainn Rune-bringer, who had given the Rune-magic, the Galdr, to the elves, as Odin had brought it to the Aesir after days of bitter suffering. Mist had never seen Dainn Rune-bringer in Asgard, and it was no wonder: that Dainn was said to have vanished many ages before the fall of Asgard.

And then there was the *other*. Memories of the Last Battle flooded into Mist's mind, images of bloody conflict and hopeless courage. She and her Sisters had only been present at the start of the fight, but she knew that the Alfar, though they never lifted a single weapon amongst them, had fought bravely with their potent magic. All but one.

He, too, she had never met, but she knew all about him. Dainn Faith-breaker, slain by Thor for the foulest treachery against Odin and the forces of good.

The Dainn before her was as ordinary as any elf could be . . . which would have been dazzling enough if he hadn't just come out of the wrong end of a fight.

"Dainn Far-seeker," she said. "The Jotunn attacked you?"

He nodded and gingerly touched the lump on his forehead. "It was not my intention to let him catch me."

"He was after you, too?" she asked. "Why? What did you mean when you said—"

He held up a grimy hand to silence her. "Do you still have it?"

His voice had taken on an imperious note, which might have been more convincing if he hadn't been covered with filth and rags that probably hadn't seen anything resembling soap for years. He obviously wasn't going to let her get away with playing ignorant again.

Simple, everyday annoyance began to wear the edge off Mist's shock. "Odin gave me no leave to speak of it to anyone," she said, "not even the Alfar."

"You can trust me."

Sure, Mist thought. But even if an elf had improbably gone over to the dark side, he couldn't break the warding spell.

"It's concealed and shielded with magic devised and gifted to me and my Sisters by the All-father himself," she said. "And now I think you'd better start explaining—"

"What did the Jotunn say to you?"

"You seem to know that already," she said, lapsing into English.

"You said nothing that could lead him to it?" he asked, his own English like something straight out of an Austen novel.

"No, I didn't," she said. "And no Jotunn could get through the wards. It would take a god to do it.'"

"And yet you have clearly been unprepared for any attempt to take it from you."

"I didn't exactly expect to meet a Jotunn or an elf when I got up this morning."

He shook out his long black hair—the feature that all Alfar took most pride in—as if he might shed the leaf-litter and dirt that matted it almost beyond recognition. "I cannot fault you for holding true to your duty."

"I don't know *what* I'd do if you disapproved of me," she said with a heavy dose of sarcasm. "Now maybe you'll deign to tell me how you and Hrimgrimir managed to survive the Last Battle."

Dainn rolled onto his knees and tried to stand, a little of his

Alfar's natural grace returning, then sank back down again with a very unelvish grunt of frustration.

"The Last Battle?" he said. "Is that what you thought it was?"

There was no mistaking his mockery, blandly delivered with that oh-so-superior elvish attitude. "It's been centuries since Ragnarok," she snapped. "Since none of us heard from Odin or any of the Aesir in all that time—"

"You naturally assumed that the gods had met their final destruction, as the Prophecies foretold."

"What are you talking about?" she demanded. "What in Hel's name is going on?"

Dainn sighed, staring out into the darkness. "The Seeress also foretold a new existence of peace and harmony after the gods met their final end," he said with exaggerated patience, as if he were dealing with a naïve child. "Look around you. Does it seem to you that the world has been reborn?"

She knew cursed well it hadn't. When she'd moved to San Francisco some fifty years ago and found Odin's sons, Vidarr and Vali—two of the handful of Aesir foretold to survive Ragnarok—she'd quickly learned that they had no more idea what had happened than she did. In fact, they didn't even remember how they'd come to be in Midgard in the first place. But that didn't mean Ragnarok hadn't wiped out the residents of the other Eight Homeworlds.

So she had told herself long ago. So she'd had every reason to *believe*.

"Midgard is as it always was," Dainn said. "The Sword's Age never ended. Not for this world."

"Tell me something I don't know," she said, getting to her feet. "What's your point?"

"My point is that there *was* no Ragnarok."

In a way, Mist was far less startled by his answer than she should have been. But she wasn't ready to concede just yet.

"Before I and my Sisters were sent to Midgard," she said, "I saw everything happen just as it was supposed to. Baldr murdered. The Wolf loosed. Loki—"

"There was an ending, yes," Dainn interrupted, looking up at her. "But not the one we expected. Paradise never came because the Aesir and their enemies did not perish."

2

___

It was the revelation she had been bracing herself to hear, and yet fresh shock pumped through her body and settled in her gut, roiling and churning like worms in a bloated corpse.

"They're still alive?" she asked. "How? Where are they?"

"Odin believed he could forestall Ragnarok. He failed, and all but one of the Homeworlds—*this* one—were destroyed. But before the Aesir, Alfar, and those they fought could destroy each other, they were thrown into Ginnungagap."

"The Great Void?" she said, feeling her way through a morass of thoughts as sluggish as stagnant water. "Nothing lives there. Nothing can."

"It is simply another plane of existence. Not entirely physical as we know it, but it maintains life." Dainn rotated his right shoulder. Something popped, and he winced. "The Aesir and their enemies have been trapped there in a form of stasis since the Last Battle."

She scraped her hand through her hair, nearly yanking half of it out of her braid. "Who trapped them?"

"That is a discussion for another time."

Of course it is, Mist thought, *just a minor detail, after all.*

"What does 'stasis' mean?" she asked.

"The gods exist in a state one might call semicorporeal. They do not age, nor do they experience the physical sensations living creatures do. They, the Alfar, the Jotunar, and the dwarves live in separate regions we call Shadow-Realms."

Mist settled back into a crouch, too dizzy to trust her balance. "Shadow-Realms," she repeated mechanically. "And all the Aesir live there? Odin, Freya, Heimdall, Frigg, Thor?"

"All but those already in the Underworld."

Baldr, he meant—gentlest and, it was said, wisest of the gods, dead because of a filthy trick that had sown the seeds of Ragnarok.

Dainn scraped dried mud from his chin with the heel of his palm. "Since Ginnungagap was the original source of all magic, the gods have learned to shape that raw magic to recreate something of what they lost during their exile."

"Are you saying they've rebuilt Asgard?"

"Some elements of it, yes, after a fashion. The great halls of the gods, their palaces and lodging places."

"And the rest? The forests and mountains and rivers?"

The pointed look he gave her was answer enough. "They are unable to reach Midgard in corporeal form, and only Freya has been able to communicate across the Void. But that problem the Aesir are also working to solve, and it is only a matter of time before they succeed in shaping true physical bodies of their own."

"The Jotunn looked pretty cursed real to me," she said.

"The frost giants have already accomplished what the Aesir are striving to achieve."

Odin's balls. This was getting worse by the second. "How?" she asked.

"That we do not yet know."

"But I never saw a Jotunn here before today. How long have they been in Midgard?"

"Perhaps as long as two weeks."

"Then they've been keeping a very low profile," she said.

"They would not have wished to attract attention until they had achieved their goal."

"And the Alfar? How did *you* get here?"

Dainn hesitated barely a moment. "I was already here. I have been in Midgard for centuries."

She stared into his indigo eyes. "I don't believe it."

"I have walked this earth as far back as I can remember, Mist of the Valkyrie."

Mist's thoughts went round and round like Jormungandr the World Serpent biting his own tail. Until she'd met Vidarr and Vali, she'd never once been aware that she and her Sisters shared this world with other immortals.

"*Why* were you here?" she asked. "How did you survive Ragnarok?"

"That is the difficulty. I don't remember."

She laughed. She couldn't help herself. But she had an idea that if she let herself go on too long, she'd never stop.

"That's exactly what Vidarr and Vali told me," she said, catching her breath. "It's a bad sign when gods and elves lose their memories."

Dainn cast her a stunned look. "Odin's sons? You know them?"

"For about half a century. They live right here in this City. *You* didn't know?"

He shook his head slowly, and Mist allowed herself a brief, uncharitable moment of satisfaction. "Vid and Val were supposed to survive Ragnarok," she said. "If nothing happened according to Prophecy, didn't the Aesir notice they weren't around?"

His shock gave way to that annoying composure that made her want to give him a good, hard shake. "I am not privy to the gods' thoughts beyond what they convey to me," he said.

And Vidarr and Vali certainly hadn't "conveyed" any knowledge about the Aesir's survival to Mist. She was pretty sure they'd be just as shocked as she was.

"So you've come for the same reason Hrimgrimir did," Mist said. "What exactly did Odin tell you to do?"

"It was not Odin," Dainn said, in a tone that managed to suggest he found her question amusing. "It was Freya."

Freya, the Lady, the beautiful, the goddess of love and desire, of fertility and battle, though most forgot that fiercer aspect. Freya had been born to the Vanir, the most ancient gods, who had been displaced by the warlike Aesir, defeated in battle by Odin's children, and finally accepted among them. Her brother was Freyr, adopted as one of the first lords of the Alfar.

Freya was also the First Valkyrie, the founder of the Choosers of the Slain. It was she who selected women—some the daughters of mortal lords, some from among the lesser goddesses—to ride the battlefields in search of valiant warriors worthy of joining the Aesir until Ragnarok. Half of the Einherjar went to her hall, Folkvangr.

But Mist had ever been Odin's servant, not the Lady's. She'd had no dealings with Freya at all.

"Why not Odin?" Mist asked, struck by a fresh sense of foreboding.

"It is Freya's Seidr that enabled her to breach the barriers of the Aesir's Shadow-Realm with her thoughts."

Seidr, called the Witch-magic. Mist knew very little about it, except that only Freya and Odin were said to possess it.

Dainn answered Mist's unspoken question. "Odin and the other Aesir maintain the Shadow-Realm of Asgard. It is the Lady's task to deal with Midgard."

"And she knew you were already here?"

"Even so. She contacted me six days ago. Since I was on the other side of Midgard, it took me some time to reach this city." He got to his knees, bracing his hands on the ground to either side of his body. "And now there is no more time for discussion."

"Wait a minute. I want to know—"

"What you want is of no consequence. You are a servant, and you must obey."

"Obey *you*? I don't remember signing on to serve a cursed arrogant elf with dirt on his nose."

He cracked open his other eye, and there was something fierce in it, an echo of un-elflike anger that put a chink in his façade of dispassion.

"My appearance is irrelevant," he said, trembling as if he were on the verge of some kind of seizure. "My purpose in coming here was to make sure Gungnir was safe and prepare you and the other Valkyrie for what is to come."

All at once Hrimgrimir's words came back to her again. *"A pity that you chose* her *side. You might have lived to see the new age."*

And she knew, even before she asked the obvious question, what Dainn was going to tell her.

"Hrimgrimir was only the beginning," Dainn said, the ferocity leaving his eyes. "We do not know how many Jotunar are here with him, and there will be many others to follow. They will all be searching for the same thing."

"The Treasures," Mist said. A wave of fresh dizziness rolled over her, and suddenly she was in Norway again, kneeling over Bryn's body, slipping the Falcon Cloak on its thong over her neck. And afterward, at the site of the massacre, staring at the broken halves of Thor's unbreakable staff. Believing they would never be of use to anyone, ever again.

She grabbed Dainn's arm before he could get to his feet, feeling long muscle that was surprisingly firm in such a tall, slender body. "Why?" she asked, though she already knew the answer to that question, too.

"What has ever been the Jotunar's intent?" he asked, pulling his arm from her grip.

War with the Aesir and their allies. The old hatreds had simmered since the beginning of time itself, coming to a boil as the time of Prophecy drew near. Old grudges were revived, oaths broken, once-strong allegiances abandoned. Aside from a few giants who had in-termarried with the gods and took the side of light, the vast majority had eagerly joined with Loki, himself the son of giants, Odin's blood brother and most deadly enemy.

Suddenly Mist's breath seemed locked in her throat, unable to reach her lungs. "They want another Ragnarok," she said.

"And the victory they believe was stolen from them," Dainn said.

"The Aesir want it, too?"

"No." Dainn met her gaze, his own clear and determined. "It was never the intention of the Aesir to engage in another war. They in-tend to build a new Homeworld, a better one, in place of that which was lost."

"In Midgard."

Mist was well beyond shock by now, but her stomach performed some interesting gymnastics nevertheless. She could feel the looming disaster behind his words, but she could hardly begin to grasp the enormous and frightening consequences of such a plan.

"You're saying they want to take over this world," she said.

"It is complicated."

Right. The old fallback line when someone didn't want to tell someone else the truth. "It isn't complicated at all. The next Ragnarok will be—"

"*Must* be won by the Aesir," Dainn finished. "Or this world will be finished."

"And the Aesir need the Treasures to win." She suppressed a shiver. "Why hasn't Freya contacted me and my Sisters directly?"

"You are only Valkyrie, and do not possess sufficient magic to hear her."

There was nothing in his tone to indicate contempt for her limitations, but that didn't mean it wasn't there. She wasn't even a demi-goddess, like many Valkyrie. She had been born to mortal parents, and her very limited Rune-lore was a pathetic thing compared to that of an elf.

Or should have been. "What about your magic?" she asked. "How did Hrimgrimir manage to grind you into the dirt?"

He looked away. "Explanations later," he said. "If your curiosity has been satisfied—"

"I'm not going into this blind," Mist said. "You said you came to warn me. What is the plan here? Have the Jotunar located any of the Treasures?"

"None, to our knowledge. But you are the first we have contacted. We have been unable to locate the other Valkyrie thus far."

"And you think *I* can tell you where to find them? I haven't been in contact with any of my Sisters for over half a century."

There was just the briefest flicker of uncertainty in Dainn's dark blue eyes, as if she had hit on a problem he hadn't anticipated. A problem that scared him.

"How did you find *me*?" she asked, taking advantage of his lapse. "Why did you and Hrimgrimir show up here first at the same time?"

"Enough," he said abruptly. He stood, wobbling only a little as he found his feet. "Take me to the Spear."

Mist hesitated. She couldn't get past the instinctive sense that something about all this wasn't right. It wasn't just the shock, the bizarre improbability of it all. It was something about Dainn him-self. Something that made her reluctant to trust him.

And yet . . .

"Please," Dainn said, inclining his head.

Mist found herself playing the word back in her mind to make sure she'd heard right. It wasn't humility, not quite, but it was in the general neighborhood of the ballpark. She found it deeply disturbing that he could make her want to punch him in the jaw one second and then turn her feelings upside-down again in a heartbeat, all after she'd only known him for all of fifteen minutes.

"All right," she said. "But keep your mouth shut and your hair over your ears when we get to my loft. My friend Eric may be there, and I'm going to have to come up with some kind of explanation for bringing an apparently indigent man in off the street in the wee hours of the morning."

"Eric?" he echoed, giving her a long look.

"Just let me do the talking. And you're going to have to answer a lot more questions on the way there."

He nodded, and Mist headed for the Volvo. By the time he caught up with her, his filthy, ill-fitting rags flapping around him like the ratty feathers of a molting seagull, she was already unlocking the doors. She waited impatiently for Dainn to climb into the passenger seat.

He stood on the curb, frowning at the car as if he'd never seen one before. "This is your vehicle?"

"She doesn't look like much," Mist said, walking around to the driver's side, "but she gets the job done."

He regarded her with that flat expression she'd decided meant he didn't want her to guess what he was thinking.

"I always shoot the Norns a little prayer when I get in," she added dryly.

If he got the joke, he didn't show it. Gingerly he grasped the door handle, opened the door, and climbed in.

"Buckle up," she said. "I don't know where you've been living, but we have seat belt laws in California."

With only the slightest hesitation he did as she asked. She wrinkled her nose at the elf's rank odor, cracked open the window in spite of the chill, and released the brake. The heater rattled and coughed as she turned it on. Dainn braced one hand on the dashboard and the other on the armrest.

It was still too early for commuter traffic, though the buses were already trundling along Lincoln Way. Once she was on Nineteenth Avenue heading south, she took a deep breath and starting talking.

"Next question," she said. "How did the Jotunar figure out how to make themselves physical when the gods couldn't do it? How did the Aesir learn what the giants are up to if the races are separated? Are the Realms interconnected somehow?"

"I thought I made it clear that Freya has not seen the need to reveal all her knowledge to me," Dainn said shortly, his fingers tightening on the armrest.

Resisting the urge to lean on the gas pedal just enough to rattle him, she cast Dainn a quick glance. Was that a hint of resentment in his voice? The Alfar had always been considered more or less the equals of the Aesir; in fact, some believed they were directly related to the Vanir. Maybe Dainn didn't like the idea of playing servant to the Aesir simply because he was convenient to their needs.

But he'd want what they wanted, wouldn't he?

Mist adjusted her grip on the steering wheel, aware that she had left her gloves in the park and her palms had begun to sweat. "Why was I the first?" she asked.

"Of the Valkyrie to be found?" he asked, clutching at the front edge of his seat with both hands as if he thought it might come flying off the chassis. "Gungnir itself led us here. As Odin's weapon, it contains more power than any of the others, and Freya detected that power in this region of Midgard."

That was the first time Mist had heard that Gungnir was more powerful than the other Treasures—it didn't make a whole lot of sense, in fact, since anyone would think Thor's Hammer or the

Apples of Idunn would be more important—but it wasn't as if she'd ever been the All-father's particular confidante.

He'd certainly never been clear about why he'd sent the Treasures to Midgard when nobody would be left to use them. Maybe he'd *known* Ragnarok would never happen.

Oh, Hel.

"Okay," she said, forcibly steering her thoughts back to the subject at hand, "the Rainbow Bridge was destroyed along with the other Homeworlds, right?"

"Bifrost is no more."

"Then how are the Jotunar getting here?"

"There are other passages."

"What kind of passages?"

"In some ways they are not unlike Bifrost itself, but linking Ginnungagap to Midgard."

"I assume they don't look like rainbows." She glanced through the windshield at the blue-black, starless sky, half expecting a hole to open up above her and drop another Jotunn on top of the car. "How do they work?"

"The Aesir have but recently discovered their existence, and that the Jotunar have been using them," Dainn said, his voice a little steadier now that he had apparently become more accustomed to the peculiarities of her mechanical mount. "They can transport physical objects and beings, but they themselves seem to have no distinct physical form. We do not know if these bridges formed naturally or were created by some force beyond our knowledge."

Like whatever had put an end to Ragnarok, Mist thought. "So they're like wormholes," she said.

Dainn didn't answer. Mist forged ahead.

"How did the Jotunar find them before the Aesir?" she asked.

"That we do not yet know. The Lady has been making a study of them, as much as she is able to from the Aesir's Shadow-Realm."

"Then the Aesir don't have access to them."

"Clearly not," Dainn said dryly, "or Freya would not find my assistance necessary."

Or mine, Mist thought. "So where do these bridges lead to? It wasn't a coincidence that Hrimgrimir showed up here."

"No."

"So maybe these bridges can be controlled somehow, put wherever the Jotunar want them, like a *Star Trek* transporter. 'Beam me up, Hrimgrimir.'"

Apparently Dainn missed the reference. "We do not believe they have complete control over them," he said. "There are indications that several such bridges lead to this city. In fact, all those Freya has located seem to do so."

Mist laughed, taking humor where she could find it. "It's an odd thing," she said, quoting Oscar Wilde, "but anyone who disappears is said to be seen in San Francisco."

"Unfortunately," Dainn said, "they are appearing, not disappearing."

His straight-man response almost made her laugh again, but she didn't really feel like joking.

"So why this city?" she asked. "Does it have something to do with Gungnir? Maybe, if it's so powerful, it sort of anchored these bridges somehow?"

She wasn't really being serious, but Dainn gave her an odd sideways look, as if he found merit in her speculation. "You may be right," he said.

"Mighty big of you to admit it," she said. She hesitated, hating to admit her blatant failure to recognize that she was walking into a trap. "I felt a compulsion to go to the park a couple of hours ago, and I knew there was something strange going on almost as soon as I set foot on the grounds. Do you think Hrimgrimir used some kind of summoning spell on me?"

"It would seem likely. Clearly Hrimgrimir wished to confront you at a time and in a location least conducive to mortal interference."

"I thought he might be following you, but *you* were following *him*."

Dainn stared out the window as they passed Sigmund Stern Grove, thick with eucalyptus trees whose leaves had been badly scorched by the unusual cold. "I felt the presence of a Jotunn when I reached this city, and I followed him to the park," he said.

Mist slowed as she turned southeast onto Ocean Avenue. "You didn't know he'd summoned me?"

"No. I thought it best to conceal myself and observe him until he took some definitive action."

"He took action, all right," she said, glancing at his battered face, which was already beginning to heal. "He beat you within an inch of your life. You shouldn't have had any trouble defeating him."

Dainn was quiet all the way to the Southern Freeway ramp. "I preferred him to believe that I was no threat to him or his allies," he said at last.

"You mean you weren't unconscious when I found you? You just let me walk right into a trap?"

The muscles in his jaw worked. "No. I was unable to aid you."

Unable to use his magic? Something didn't add up—again—but Mist let it pass. "Inconvenient, since you need me to get Gungnir."

"I was instructed to warn the guardians, not take the Treasures from them."

"Then why do you need to come with me? You've warned me, and now you can run out and find the others, since I can't help you with that. Though even if you find the rest, the Jotunar might follow you right to them."

"We will make every attempt to keep that from occurring."

"Who? You and Freya?" She leaned on the gas pedal, and the

Volvo shot forward with a grunt of protest. "As you pointed out, Lord Elf, we're only Valkyrie. Our magic is limited. It was never part of our job description to hold off a swarm of frost giants."

"I do not believe the situation will become so dire."

"Well, that changes everything. We're safe."

He was silent, but she couldn't tell if it was because he was insulted or simply couldn't provide a satisfactory response. She relaxed her grip on the wheel and pressed lightly on the brake.

"I still don't understand why the Jotunar got here first," she said, as much to herself as to the elf. "The only advantage the frost giants ever had over the Aesir was their sheer numbers. The reason they were such a threat during Ragnarok was because—"

Mist broke off, drawing in a sharp breath. Because they had a leader who would stop at nothing, not even the darkest and most deadly magic, to attain his ends.

The realization hit her like a Jotunn's fist, so terrible that she almost slammed on the brakes in the middle of the freeway. Her guts twisted in panic, and the tattoo began to burn again. She couldn't believe she hadn't already thought of it, that Dainn hadn't mentioned even so much as the possibility.

Because he'd deliberately hidden it from her.

"Where is Loki?" she asked.

Dainn seemed unmoved by her alarm. "That is the other task Freya has set me. She suspects he may be here with the Jotunar."

"And you didn't bother telling me this rather obvious suspicion before?"

"It was clearly not obvious to you."

The elf's complete lack of concern made Mist want to knock his head against the dashboard. "Of course the Jotunar couldn't create or open these gates or bridges or whatever they are by themselves," she said, feeling like an idiot. "Not if the Aesir couldn't."

Her hands began to tremble on the wheel. She remembered

what she'd told Dainn not long ago: that only a minor god could break the wards she'd set over Gungnir.

And for all intents and purposes, a minor god was exactly what Loki was. Minor, but in name only. If he had sent Hrimgrimir with just the right spells . . .

She pressed the Volvo to its limits, reaching eighty as the car crossed over Highway 101. She flew along the Embarcadero Freeway and raced down the Twentieth Street exit ramp. She screeched right on Twentieth, crossed Third on a yellow light, and made a hard right on Illinois.

The Volvo was sputtering when she pulled into the driveway. She set the brake, practically tore the belt buckle apart, and jumped out. Dainn was right behind her as she unlocked the front door.

She knew immediately that Eric wasn't home. A dozen strides along the main hallway and a sharp right at the kitchen carried her to the door of the ward room.

Only it wasn't warded any longer. The Rune-staves painted on the wall above the door had broken to pieces, reduced to a chaotic series of black slashes like smears of rotted blood.

Mist plunged through the door. The case was open.

Gungnir was gone.

3

Mist spun to the nearest wall and slammed it with her fist. Paint fell in flakes at her feet. Dainn ran into the room.

"Loki's piss!" she swore, lapsing briefly into the Old Tongue, which was made for insults, even against oneself. "Short-wit, incompetent . . ."

Dainn stopped before the open case, his gaze locked on the empty space where Gungnir had been hanging before she'd left around midnight. All the other weapons were untouched: two dozen swords, axes, daggers, and knives, each lovingly forged by her own hand, displayed in oak and glass cases built into the walls. The opened case had held knives of all shapes and sizes, eight weapons with hand-carved grips and edges sharp enough to rend flesh like tissue. Each knife was unique, but no one of them appeared substantially different from any other except in subtle elements of design and embellishment.

Whoever had taken it had recognized it for what it was with no trouble at all. The simple Rune-spells that had been meant to hide its true shape had been snapped apart like the thinnest of threads.

"It will do no good to curse yourself now," Dainn said with an almost unnatural calm. "Hrimgrimir has deceived us both."

"I'm not stupid," she snapped. But she *had* been. Very, very stupid to keep Dainn in the park answering questions, believing all the while she'd actually defeated Hrimgrimir, while the frost giant made a run for Dogpatch to steal the Spear.

Dainn paced slowly around the room, touching this case and that as if he could draw vital information out of the wood and glass and steel. Returning to the door, he ducked his head outside and stared up at the fractured Runes.

"I smell nothing of Hrimgrimir here," he said.

Mist slowed her breathing and closed her eyes. He was right. There was a certain stench about Jotunar, whether fire or frost, that had nothing to do with cleanliness or grooming habits. She'd smelled it in Golden Gate Park just before Hrimgrimir had attacked.

"According to what you told me, Hrimgrimir wasn't the only Jotunn who came to Midgard," she said. "Maybe one of the others . . ."

He stared at the wood-paneled floor under his oversized sneakers. "I fear not," he said.

A surge of adrenaline sent currents of fire racing through Mist's veins. Without pausing to question the impulse, she ran into the kitchen, calling for Lee and Kirby, her Norwegian forest cats. They weren't exactly watchdogs, but they were far from ordinary. Maybe Dainn, with his elvish connection to nature and animals, might be able to see something through their eyes.

But the cats, usually afraid of nothing but the rare California thunderstorm, refused to put in an appearance. On the edge of panic, Mist blundered unseeing right into the kitchen table. On the table lay a folded scrap of paper.

Eric. The frantic energy drained from her body, leaving her legs shaking and her heart struggling to work its way out of her stomach. He had been taking a shower when she'd left; he must have gone out and left a her note of explanation.

Her relief lasted all of five seconds. Eric could be foolishly impulsive at times, was generally fearless and always up for a little risky adventure. What if he had glimpsed someone stealing something from the house, naturally assumed the thief was human, and gone after him?

Mist reached for the paper and unfolded the note with shaking hands. The Runic script seemed to pulse on the page like entrails spilling hot from a dying warrior's belly.

My apologies, sweetheart, the note said. *I had hoped to enjoy you one last time, but it was not to be. I will cherish your gift. You may be sure I will use it well.*

The final symbol was the figure of a coiling snake. It came alive as she watched, hissing and seeming to laugh with its gaping, serrated jaws. Then it was still again, and Mist dropped the paper onto the table. It burst into flame and disintegrated into black ash.

"Eric," she whispered.

"Loki was here," Dainn said. He stalked up behind her, breathing in deeply like a wolf scenting the air. She spun to face him.

"If you'd told me as soon as I found you—"

He backed away, watching her face as if he expected her to attack him with her bare hands. "I made a mistake," he said.

But so had she. She'd been so much worse than the short-wit and incompetent she had called herself before. Eric was no devoted lover prepared to spend the rest of his mortal life with her. He had deceived her from the moment they'd met.

Of course, she'd had no reason to think he could be anything but what he claimed. He had been affectionate, affable—the very opposite of Loki Laufeyson. But even if she'd suspected the gods were alive, she would never have looked beyond Eric's smiling blue eyes, his big-hearted nature, his easy confidence.

Hrimgrimir had been no more than a distraction. It had always been Eric. Eric Larsson, also known as Loki Laufeyson.

"How did this happen?" Dainn asked.

Mist stared at the pile of ash, flinching at the question as if the elf had bellowed the words in her ear.

"Why didn't Freya *know* Loki was already in Midgard?" she retorted. "Why did she only suspect?"

"So much is . . . still unclear to us."

"But Eric—" She broke off, unable to find the words.

Dainn ran his fingers through the black powder. "He was your lover."

"No! It was . . ." She swallowed, remembering all the good times. Every one false, Loki's joke on one he might have vanquished with a snap of his fingers. Just the previous morning, in the gym, she'd told him he was getting to be almost as good with the sword as she was. And when they'd made love . . .

"I knew him as . . . Eric Larsson," she said.

"How long was he with you?" Dainn asked.

Mist's throat tightened until she could hardly breathe. "Six months."

Dainn frowned, obviously asking himself the same questions she was. If Loki had been in Midgard for months, he had deceived the Aesir more thoroughly than he had ever done in a long life of deception.

Loki Laufeyson. Scar-lip, Slanderer, godling, trickster, purveyor of chaos and conflict, shape-shifter, foremost of Jotunar, father of monsters, mother of Sleipnir, once ally of the gods and now their greatest enemy. Myth called him evil, but he was so much more than any mere word could define. The codes of morality, Aesir and mortal, were not his to live by.

The destruction of the other Homeworlds wouldn't have quenched his need for revenge—for the slaughter of his son Narfi in punishment for the gentle god Baldr's death; the binding of his other son, the great Wolf Fenrisulfr; the torment he himself had endured when the Aesir had bound him under the serpent that perpetually dropped venom into his eyes.

He was the one who wanted to use the Treasures against the

Aesir. *He* wanted a second chance at Ragnarok. And he had come to Mist to . . .

That was pretty cursed obvious now. Loki must have known all along that she'd had Gungnir in her possession. That was clearly the reason he had come to her in the first place, introducing himself as someone she could learn to love. In all the time they'd had been "together"—and there was no way of knowing if he'd been in Midgard even longer than the months she had known him—she had been absolutely convinced his feelings for her were real.

I had hoped to enjoy you one last time. Loki had always been notorious for having insatiable sexual appetites, and with Eric—*oh, Eric*—the sex had always been fantastic. Eric had made her feel comfortable because he wasn't threatened by her strength and had never considered himself her superior, but she seriously doubted that her sexual skills were enough to make Loki delay his plans.

Why had he waited so long to take Gungnir?

"I didn't know," she stammered.

Dainn rubbed the ashes of the note between his thumb and forefinger. After a few moments of reflective silence he glanced around the kitchen, his gaze passing over the stove, the old-style TV, and the cartoon Thor bobblehead until he found something that seized all his attention.

Mist followed his gaze. The little framed photo of her and Eric in Strybing Arboretum—both of them smiling, for all the world looking like the perfect couple—lay on the ugly linoleum Mist had never bothered to replace when she'd bought the loft, the glass cracked into three pieces.

Dainn bent to pick it up. He studied the picture for nearly a minute and then set the frame facedown on the top of the TV.

"He always chooses a fair disguise," he said, his manner as calm as ever. "You could not have been expected to know who he was."

And, just like that, Dainn absolved her of any wrongdoing and forgave her rank stupidity. But she couldn't forgive herself. Or Freya, for not knowing what she was up against.

Dainn's hand on her arm jerked her out of her bleakest memories. "Do you pity yourself?" he demanded. "Do you think your burdens are greater than those of every man or god who has made mistakes before you?"

She met his gaze, ready with a furious reply, but he cast her a look so dark and savage that she was stunned into speechlessness. For a dozen charged seconds they gazed at one another, and Mist felt her muscles knot as if she were in the presence of Fenrisulfr himself.

And yet Dainn's long fingers felt warm and strong and almost familiar, like a caress in a dream of dulcet melodies and soft spring breezes and all the good things that never quite materialized in the mortal world.

Abruptly she pulled free, and Dainn let her go. His eyes cleared, and suddenly the darkness, the breezes—and Mist's contradictory joy—were gone.

"I can understand why Loki wanted to make an issue of fooling me," she said bitterly. "He's always enjoyed his nasty little games. But why did he choose today to abandon his disguise? He knows the Aesir can't get to Midgard, right? Did he know that someone from the other side had shown up to find the Spear?" She swallowed a laugh. "Hrimgrimir obviously wasn't worried about you, so why would *he* be?"

She could see she'd gotten to him, but he only stared down at the table. "Some Alfar could cause him considerable inconvenience if they wished to."

"But not you. No, either he thinks the Aesir will be on his tail any moment, or—" She inhaled sharply, remembering again that dark, smoldering, almost violent look in Dainn's eyes. "Maybe you're a lot more dangerous than you look."

He shot her a hard glance that almost—*almost*—convinced her she was right. Then his face turned blank again, as if she'd asked him about the weather in Ginnungagap.

Mist paced around the table and came to a stop in front of the calendar of Norwegian landscapes hung on the wall opposite the stove. "So now what?" she asked. "Loki made a body for himself, which even Freya can't do, and helped the Jotunar get to Midgard. What does that say for the gods' chances of winning a war with him?"

"It is only the beginning."

"A very bad beginning." She turned to face him, fists clenched. "Did it ever occur to you that I might not *want* to get involved in another Ragnarok?"

The corner of his mouth twitched. "You would not abandon your duty now."

"But I did," she said. "I kept Gungnir, but I gave up the old life because I wanted a normal one, with normal relationships and normal concerns."

"But now that you have lost the thing that was most dear to you?"

"If not for the Spear, I'd never have met Eric. There wouldn't have been anything to lose." She bent her head, refusing to let the tears escape. "If I still had Gungnir, I'd give it to you right now. If Loki hadn't betrayed me personally, I'd turn my back on the whole thing and wish you luck." She choked on a laugh. "But he *did* betray me. And I'm not letting him get away with it."

"Will you attempt to kill him?"

Mist had no good comeback to his mockery. She had no idea what she would do.

"You should not pursue him," Dainn said. "It is unlikely that he can do much damage with only the Spear before Freya and the others arrive."

His 180-degree change in attitude convinced Mist that one of them was going insane. "After all you've told me, you want Loki to keep a weapon he could use against the Aesir?"

"Pursuing a frost giant is one thing, confronting Loki quite another." He almost smiled. "'We're only Valkyrie,'" he quoted. "'It was never part of our job description to hold off a swarm of frost giants.'"

Her own words hit her one at a time, like bullets meant to cripple instead of kill. "Apparently it isn't yours, either," she retorted. "You only seem to be willing to use your magic for seeking spells. Can you fight at all?"

"How many times have you met Loki?" he asked, evading her question. "You have no conception—"

"I've heard every story ever told about him, and I've already had personal experience of his treachery. I know what I'm up against."

"No. You do not."

"But Freya does. If we can't protect our Treasures from Loki, what was the point of your coming here at all?" She shook her head sharply. "You decide what you're willing to do to fulfill your mission. And for Baldr's sake, wipe that blood off your face."

Striding back to the ward room, she crouched before the chest of drawers against the real wall and opened the bottom drawer. Kettlingr, in its plain knife shape, lay in an unadorned wooden box where she'd tucked it away when she'd bought the loft three years ago.

Mist unlocked the box, lifted the lid, and took the knife from the padded interior. It felt solid and familiar in her hand, though she hadn't worn the sword in over fifty years.

Once, it had been the one friend she could rely on. But a sword was the last thing she needed in her "mortal" life. Only her long connection to the blade had convinced her to keep it at all.

She pulled the blade free of its engraved metal sheath and chanted the spell she'd almost forgotten. The hilt thickened to fill her hand. The knife began to stretch, to broaden, to become what it was meant to be. Not so much as a trace of tarnish sullied the Rune-kissed blade.

All too easily it seemed to become part of her again, and that scared her almost as much as anything else that had happened in the past couple of hours. She chanted it small, set the knife on the chest, and retrieved the sheath from the back of the closet, where the sword's own magic had kept the leather glossy and the metal bright. She looked for the belt, one that could accommodate either an unprepossessing knife or a spatha with equal facility, and found it in a heap on the floor. She picked it up, put it on, and attached the knife's sheath at her left hip.

Dainn glanced up as she returned to the kitchen, the photo of Mist and Eric in his hand. He'd managed to clean the blood from his face and the swelling in his nose was going down, but he was still a mess.

His gaze focused immediately on the knife. "It may already be too late to catch him," he said.

She snatched the picture out of his hands and threw it across the room. The glass seemed to shriek as it cracked in a dozen new pieces.

"I'm going to find him," she said, "with or without your help."

"He may have succeeded in reaching one of the bridges and returned to the Jotunar's Shadow-Realm."

"And you said there are several bridges in this city." She gripped the edge of the table, working to control her immediate impulse to run blindly out of the house. "Could Loki have gone out the way Hrimgrimir came in?"

"It is possible."

"Then *help* me. If you won't use your magic for fighting, maybe you can distract Loki so I can get Gungnir away from him without either of us getting killed. Isn't that to your advantage, elf?"

Suddenly he was very grave, his brows drawing down, his jaw tensing until she could see the muscles clench under his skin. "Not to mine," he said. "To Midgard's."

"Then will you help me find him?"

"Yes. But it would still be better if you remained behind."

"You mean now you want to go alone?"

His expression tightened again. "You have no chance against him."

"That's why we need to work together."

He gave a heavy sigh. "Very well," he said.

And just like that, he acquiesced. She didn't understand him at all.

"So how do we find him?" she asked.

"All the bridges Freya has located seem to appear in the vicinity of physical features that link one place with another."

Okay, Mist thought. Golden Gate Park was, in a way, a link between the city and the ocean, stretching from Ocean Beach to Stanyan Street, even farther if you counted the Panhandle.

But there were a hundred other potential connections. Overpasses? Street corners? Where were they to start?

"Do you have any idea about how to pin it down?" she asked.

"You were close to Loki. Your . . . relationship may have left a residue of connection between you, mental or physical, that will make it easier to find him. If we can isolate this connection—"

Mist's instincts rebelled before she understood why. She could feel Dainn assessing her, probing, teasing out the source of her unspoken resistance like a woodpecker plucking an insect from the bark of a tree.

"You will need little skill," he said. "You are not *entirely* ignorant of Rune-lore."

Her bad feelings about all this were growing progressively worse. "What do you want me to do?" she asked.

"We will temporarily join our thoughts, so I can search for such a residue. When I find it—"

"Wait a minute. You mean you're going to get inside my head?"

"It is how Freya spoke to me."

"Alfar have this ability, too?"

"To some extent, yes. It is why most work closely together when we practice magic on a large scale."

The idea sickened her. No one, not even Odin, had ever done such a thing to Mist, and she realized now just how much she would have hated Freya contacting her instead of Dainn. Her mind had always been her own. Always.

"There is no reason to fear," Dainn said, as if he were already reading her mind. "I can only touch the surface of your thoughts."

"I can't do it."

He took a step toward her, enveloping her in the warmth radiating from his body. "I know you are no coward, Valkyrie."

Pride made her want to lash out at him, but she knew the impulse was only a cover for shame. She *was* afraid—not of Loki, but of letting Dainn see her failure, her stupidity, her weakness.

Gods help her.

Dainn returned to the table, dipped his fingers into the ashes, and lifted them to his forehead. With quick, sure strokes he sketched a Bind-Rune above his dark brows. The ashes caught fire, and Dainn grimaced in pain.

Without another word he turned, walked back into the ward room, and sat cross-legged on the floor. Reluctantly Mist followed him.

"Sit," he said, "and try to relax."

Mist sat facing him. "You may have noticed that I've got this little problem with going blind into a situation I don't understand. What exactly are you going to do?"

He stared into her eyes, and she observed again how dark his were, so different from that of most Alfar . . . the deep blue that came at the end of twilight, when the brightest stars had only just begun to appear. Fathomless.

But no longer unreadable. There was a sorrow that caught her off guard, just as his brief moments of anger had done.

"You will draw the Runes-staves in your mind," he said.

Mist had drawn or carved the staves on wood, on walls, even occasionally on paper and other surfaces, especially those that could be burned. She knew how to chant them. But drawing them "in her mind" was something she'd never even considered. Runes had always been physical things, not constructs of mere thought.

She shifted uneasily. "How?" she asked.

"You must concentrate on the shapes, holding an image of Eric in your thoughts."

"That easy, huh?"

He inclined his head. "Ordinarily I would ask you to clear your mind of all emotion, but in this case it may aid you to allow your feelings to strengthen your will."

But only, Mist thought, if she could control them. "What Runes do you want me to concentrate on?" she asked.

"All of them."

Oh no, not difficult at all. Bracing herself, Mist closed her eyes, called up Eric's face, and imagined the Runes, each of the two dozen of the Elder Futhark in turn, mentally drawing the simple lines that added up to so much more than the sum of their parts. She assembled each Rune-stave carefully, as if she were rendering it in charcoal on precious handmade paper that could never be replaced.

It didn't come naturally. Far from it. Her emotion kept getting in the way, and the staves rippled like heat waves on pavement. But after a while she began to get the hang of it, fixing each stave in place while she constructed the next, and the next. She was vaguely aware of time passing without having any idea just how long it took, so intent on the images that she barely noticed when Dainn began to sing.

He started very softly, barely more than a murmur. Slowly his voice rose, and Mist had to struggle to hold onto the shapes in her mind.

She had always been immune to the heroic poetry and song of the skalds of Asgard. Even Bragi, bard of the Aesir, had hardly been capable of moving her. No elf's song had ever come close.

That was why she didn't understand her reaction now. It was impossible for any of the Alfar to sing badly, but Dainn's voice was extraordinary. It moved through the air in eddies and swirls like water in a stream, ever so gently threatening to carry away whatever it touched. There could be no doubt of the power of its magic.

A prickle of bone-deep awareness washed through Mist as Dainn's mind brushed hers. Her tattoo flared to the point of agony, and the shock almost made her cry out. When she tried to withdraw, she found that she was caught as surely as Fenrisulfr in the magic rope Gleipnir, lost in the intricate, labyrinthine melody of the song.

Yet nearly as soon as she felt Dainn's intrusion, he touched the Rune-staves in her mind, plucking them like strings on a harp, gathering them into a sphere of ethereal light. She "saw" him working as if through foggy glass, deftly manipulating five of the staves and weaving them like the channels of a braided river, giving the Runes power they didn't possess as individual symbols.

And beneath it all, far under the surface, Mist felt *him*. His essence bled through the mental link between them—vivid, saturated colors that resolved into emotion: Anger. Shame. And that sorrow, profound and unmistakable.

Sorrow for the years of isolation, apart from his own people? Alfar were seldom seen alone. Until she had made the decision to give up the old duties and embrace a "normal" life, the centuries of isolation had gotten to her, too. For an elf it must have been infinitely worse. Dainn might as well be sentenced to solitary confinement in a Third World prison, deprived of light and air and the comfort of even a single elven voice.

That might account for the anger and sorrow, since he didn't even remember how he had come to Midgard. But the shame . . . was that because of his failure with Hrimgrimir?

Without understanding what drove her, Mist let herself fall deeper into his emotions. In an instant she passed from a fog of tangled sensations into a clamoring jungle of twisted vines, thorny bushes, and broad, waxy leaves in every conceivable color of green, the kind of forest that had never existed in Asgard.

And hiding in the shadows was a thing. It moved within a cage woven of thorny vines—a hideous creature, as mindlessly vicious as the wolves that would swallow the sun at the end of the world. As she swept through the canopy toward the cage, the thing took shape and form, materializing in front of her, a hulking beast with black pits for eyes and razor teeth.

Hatred, living and breathing and ready to devour anything that crossed its path.

Mist didn't wait to get a better look. She clawed her way out of the vision, leaving the darkness behind her, and found herself alone again in her own mind. One by one the staves dissolved, leaving a stark afterimage like the neon tracings of over-bright lights inside her eyelids.

Shielding her face, Mist jumped to her feet. She staggered toward the door, desperate to shake off Dainn's mental touch and the thing she had sensed inside him.

Or *thought* she had sensed. How could one of the Alfar—or any being allied with the Aesir—harbor such a monster in his soul? Or had she created it herself, out of her fear of the profound contact between them, of her own irresistible compulsion to uncover the secrets she sensed he was keeping from her? Had she shaped that fear into a creature she had some hope of fighting with the skills she knew she possessed?

Stumbling into the kitchen, she leaned heavily on the table. Yes. That was all it was. Her imagination. And fear she could learn to overcome . . . *if* she ever let this kind of thing happen again.

And she didn't plan on it. Next time Dainn needed this kind of "help" . . .

She heard his nearly silent footsteps on the linoleum and stiffened. He came to a stop a few feet behind her.

"Are you well?" he asked.

She couldn't miss the note of concern in his question, and she didn't really understand it. She'd walked out on him without a word, probably messing up all his careful work.

Had he sensed how deeply she'd delved into *his* mind?

Turning slowly, she looked at his face. There was no anger in it, only the same worry she'd heard in his voice. Worry and exhaustion, as if the magic had drained what strength he had left after Hrimgrimir's attack.

Maybe that had been his problem all along. He couldn't use magic without weakening himself to the point of—what? Burning himself out somehow?

Mist was just becoming aware of how tired *she* felt.

"I'm all right," she said. "You?"

"It doesn't matter." Dainn touched the ash-Runes on his forehead. "I think I know where Loki has gone."

"Where?"

"'Gullin' is its name," he said.

Golden. As in Golden Gate Park.

"Then he did go back to the Park," she said, starting into the hall.

"There is another place by that name, is there not?"

Gods. How stupid could she be? A golden passage. A bridge be-tween worlds.

The Golden Gate Bridge was nearly eight miles northwest of Dogpatch as the crow flies, farther on surface streets. Dawn was just breaking; traffic would be picking up, but that was the least of her worries. She had to hope the Volvo had one more gallop in her.

"I know where it is," she said. "Can you tell if Loki has left Midgard?"

"No."

"I guess we'll find out when we get there. I think it would be a good idea for you to have a weapon, just in case. I don't have any firearms, but—"

"No weapons."

"This isn't the time to be stubborn," she said. "If a frost giant could get the better of you, Loki could do a Hel of a lot worse."

"I will not let Loki harm you."

"That's funny," she said. "I'm more worried that I may not be able to protect *you*."

"You will not be required to."

Further argument was a waste of time. Mist knew she was about to find out the hard way just how magically proficient Dainn really was.

"All right," she said. "Let's go."

4

Mist dashed out the front door, barely pausing to lock it with a brief spell before continuing on to the driveway. She already had the Volvo in gear and was pulling out by the time Dainn had jumped into the passenger seat.

"If you have any spells that can work on an engine," she said, "you'd better use them."

"You know Alfar magic is not of a mechanical nature," he said dryly.

She was almost relieved he was back to sarcasm. Of course, he was right. Elf magic was of nature and growing things—or, apparently, in at least one case, digging into someone else's thoughts. But even that had used imagery of nature.

The Volvo coughed as she backed into Illinois Street. Dainn buckled in and braced himself on the dashboard and armrest as he had before. Mist kept her foot on the accelerator as they drove north on Highway 101, merged onto the Central Freeway, and continued north on Van Ness. The traffic was still light, but it took far too long to reach the Presidio and the bridge.

"Can you feel anything?" she asked Dainn.

He touched his forehead, still streaked with ash and sweat. "Somewhere over the water," he said.

"No," she muttered sarcastically. But they were faced with a very real problem. Even though there was a pedestrian walkway across the bridge, there wasn't any way to access it from the San Francisco side without attracting unwelcome attention. She sure as Hel didn't want any mortals involved.

"We'll have to drive across," she said. "You tell me where to stop."

She gunned the engine and sped for the toll plaza, slowing only to pay the toll and pretend she had no intention of breaking every speed law on the books. The moment she was on the bridge she ground her foot down on the gas pedal as if she were in a race against Odin's mighty six-legged stallion Sleipnir himself.

"Here," Dainn said when they were half a mile across. Mist pulled up in the right lane and jumped out of the car.

There was nothing to show that this span of the bridge was different from any other. Dainn vaulted over the railing that separated the pedestrian walkway from traffic. Mist followed him to the suicide barrier. Blue-gray water seethed far beneath them, choppy with a rising wind driving west from the bay. Icy rain blew into Mist's face.

Almost at once she felt the strangeness, a sense of an opening she hadn't recognized when she'd faced Hrimgrimir. Her wrist began to ache again.

"I feel it," she whispered.

"The water is disturbed," Dainn said, leaning far over the railing. He closed his eyes. The air around him shimmered, and the cement under Mist's feet vibrated with barely leashed energy.

And there was more. She could also sense Eric's presence, a shadow of his being altered and twisted into a form almost unrecognizable. She drew her knife.

"Where is he?"

Dainn spread his hands in front of him as if he were reaching for something solid. "He was here," he said, frowning. "But he did not pass over."

Mist peered in every direction. "Are you sure?"

"The location of the bridge is very clear to me, and it is obvious that Loki expended a great deal of effort here. But it appears that something blocked his way."

"Something? Like what?"

"It is as if someone had bricked over a doorway, but I detect no magical signature to indicate that it was done deliberately."

"You mean by Freya or one of the other Aesir?"

He shrugged, which meant he didn't know, and she didn't want to waste any time trying to figure it out now. "If this one doesn't work," she said, "he'll probably look for another."

"I still see 'Golden,'" Dainn said.

"Then we need to get to the park." Mist jumped back over the barrier and returned to the Volvo. A red Jaguar streaked past, blaring its horn. Dainn got in, and Mist made a sharp and very illegal U-turn, heading back toward the city.

It was a straight shot south on Highway 1 to the park, but the minutes were ticking by, and Mist's hopes of catching Loki dwindled a little more with every mile. When they got as close as they could to the area where Hrimgrimir had appeared, Mist swerved toward the nearest curb.

She and Dainn jumped out of the Volvo and ran across frost-brittle grass toward the spot they had left just a few hours ago. Dainn slowed and stopped a good ten yards short of their destination.

Mist turned around and strode back to him. "What is it?"

He looked straight through her, his face taut with concentration. "The bridge is gone."

"What do you mean, gone?"

"Loki was here, and the residue of magic suggests he made a powerful effort, but again he was unable to enter. This one is not only closed, but absent." He met Mist's gaze. "The passage on the bridge was blocked, and this one has disappeared. This may work to our advantage."

"How?"

"Loki may be trapped in Midgard."

"*May* be? You think the other bridges Freya saw are blocked, too?"

"I told you that little is known about how the bridges function. If he cannot leave Midgard—"

"But you don't *know* he can't. Maybe you've heard that California is called the *Golden* State?"

"I have said that all the bridges we have identified are in this city."

"What if you're wrong, and there are bridges to Ginnungagap all over the country, or even the planet?"

"Freya is not wrong in this," Dainn said.

"Okay. But Loki . . . Eric claimed he was a security consultant doing work for the government and frequently traveled around the world. Do you think he, personally, is stuck in San Francisco?"

"If the bridges are here, he would wish to stay where he could easily summon more Jotunar."

"So why hasn't he? Why doesn't he have an army covering every square inch of this city?"

"He cannot have enough Jotunar here yet to constitute an army. If he desired to avoid Freya's notice, and we can assume that was always his purpose, he would not have risked using too much magic or disrupting the daily business of this world. To do so would send echoes across Ginnungagap that Freya would surely have heard."

"But he could have been looking for the Treasures every time he was away. Are you *sure* he doesn't have any of the others?"

Dainn's composure remained impregnable. "As certain as we can be. Again, his obtaining any of the Treasures would have made it very difficult to hide his presence in Midgard and transport more Jotunar over the bridges." He paused. "It is also very likely that making use of the bridges is a heavy drain on his magical energy, and searching for the other Valkyrie, even with the Jotunar to aid him, would be too dangerous."

"You mean even Loki has his limits," she said, catching a little glimpse of hope.

"There is always a price for magic, especially of such a sustained and complex nature."

She wondered again if that was Dainn's problem. "Even if the bridges are closed to him now," she said, "and he's stuck in Midgard, he wouldn't have any trouble hiding Gungnir and getting through airport security if he wanted to leave the country."

"I do not believe he would attempt it."

"He'd have plenty of money to do it. I know Eric—" She broke off and exhaled sharply. "*Loki* wasn't hurting for money, and he wouldn't have to work very hard to get it. He could just conjure it up if he wanted to."

"Again, such conjuring would have been ill-advised for many reasons. And Loki has always found it more satisfying to use trickery to get what he wants. He has undoubtedly found very mundane methods of acquiring large sums of currency to finance his efforts, and he would do so without arousing the suspicions of mortal authorities and law enforcement."

"So he's ahead of us there, too."

"Perhaps it would be best if we return to your home and wait to see what he will do next."

Dainn shifted gears so fast that Mist felt like a commuter watching a BART train shoot past without realizing it had ever reached the station. "I'll put both my hands between Fenrisulfr's jaws and ask him to bite them off before I'll let Loki win without a fight."

He stared at her with such intensity that she found herself instinctively reaching for Kettlingr's hilt. But the moment passed, and Dainn looked away as if nothing had happened.

"You know him better than I do," he said. "Where would he go?"

"We're talking about a city that covers almost forty-seven square miles and has a population of nearly 800,000. He could be anywhere."

"How much did you know of the background he created for himself? Were there any locations he frequented, places he preferred to all others?"

As much as she hated being reminded of her own gullibility, Mist recognized what Dainn was getting at. "He needs more than just Jotunar to help him conquer Midgard," she said. "So he'll have been looking for mortal allies wherever he can find them." She dragged her hand across her face, which felt about as rough as corrugated cardboard. "He could have been building a whole underground empire, and I wouldn't have known it."

"As I said before, he will not have wished to disrupt mortal society in any way that would alert Freya to his presence here. But he almost certainly has been laying the groundwork, and he will no longer have any reason to delay finding such allies."

Mist flipped her braid behind her shoulders again, searching her mind for anything that would help them. "Loki had a computer at the loft, but even if he'd kept his contacts on it he wouldn't have been stupid enough to leave the information for me to find."

"There is another possible source of information in this city which you yourself mentioned," Dainn said.

Mist snapped her fingers. "Vidarr and Vali," she said. An ugly thought settled in the pit of her belly. What if Odin's sons had known all along that the Aesir were still alive? What if they'd known about Loki, and hadn't warned her?

The idea was flatly ridiculous, as ridiculous as the idea that Odin had known there would be no Ragnarok. Vidarr and Vali would never go over to the enemy.

"Loki can't have gone anywhere near them before," she said

aloud, "or they would have recognized him. They'll probably be just as shocked by all this as I was."

And Vidarr wouldn't like it. Not one bit. Though he'd said he didn't remember how he and Vali had come to Midgard, Mist had always had her doubts. He had certainly rejected most of his divine heritage years before Mist had made the decision to leave the past behind. Knowing he'd have to become involved all over again . . .

No, it wasn't going to be easy to tell him. Vidarr hadn't been able to accept that Mist had radically changed from the willing servant she'd been in Asgard, even if *he* was different himself. He'd resented that mere Valkyrie had been entrusted with the Treasures.

But there was no question that he'd take a stand against Loki once he understood what was going on, even if didn't want any part of this new Ragnarok. This was *his* city.

"We'll go to Asbrew," Mist said.

Dainn shot her an inquiring look. "The Rainbow Bridge? I told you it had been destroyed along with Asgard."

It was a natural mistake on his part, since Asbru was another name for Bifrost. "*A-s-b-r-e-w*," she spelled out. "God's brew. It's a pun. I don't suppose you know what that means."

"I am aware of puns," he said. "I have been on this world a very long time." He arched a dark brow. "I believe the English writer Samuel Johnson referred to them as the lowest form of humor."

Dainn's reference to Johnson made her wonder what he'd been do-ing in Midgard over the centuries. She knew that he, like she, would have had to keep moving or change his identity every few decades to avoid calling attention to his extremely slow aging.

Even the Aesir eventually aged without the divine Apples of Idunn, and that had been one of the Treasures Odin had sent to Midgard. But Dainn had indicated that the gods weren't aging in

Ginnungagap, and Mist had changed hardly at all since the Last Battle.

As much as she wanted to hear about Dainn's past, she knew her curiosity would have to wait a little longer. Assuming she and Dainn were still alive when she had the chance to ask.

Without another word between them, she and Dainn ran back to the Volvo, which looked to Mist as it were on the verge of literal collapse.

"Hang in there, girl," she whispered, patting the dashboard. Dainn stared resolutely out the window as they set off again.

Vidarr's bar was in the Tenderloin, once known as the "soft underbelly" of San Francisco for its history of crime and vice, a tradition that hadn't completely been eradicated by the gradual gentrification of the area. Tucked between the wealth of Nob Hill and the busy downtown of Civic Center, the district was a seedy patch in an otherwise respectable neighborhood.

In spite of the dubious location, Asbrew was popular with artists, musicians, and the more affluent youth from the best addresses in the city. Mist hadn't been inside for a decade, but she assumed that things hadn't changed much since Pink and Avril Lavigne were basking in the Top Ten.

The Volvo, having been pressed far beyond its capacity, decided to give up the ghost at the corner of Van Ness, a little over a mile short of their goal. Mist eased the failing vehicle to the curb and set it in park.

"We'll have to hoof it," she said.

Dainn was out of the car a second after she was. She set off north on busy Van Ness, fiercely grateful for the chance to move her body again. She might not trust her own feeble magic, but legs and arms, muscle and bone were tools she had honed to obey her will without thought or hesitation. Dainn kept pace, lithe as a cheetah in spite of his rags, his long legs covering the ground with ease.

At McAllister Mist turned east, leading Dainn past City Hall, and then jogged north on Hyde to Eddy. Suddenly they were in the midst of Southeast Asian restaurants, fleabag hotels, and boarded-up mom-and-pop markets, running past indigents with overflowing shopping carts and more than one dealer on the prowl for addicts looking to score. Panhandlers and drunks stared after her and Dainn with dull astonishment, but they were only a blur in Mist's eyes.

Though it was barely seven o'clock in the morning, Mist knew that Asbrew would already be jumping. It never actually stopped. No cops would come knocking for the simple reason that Vidarr had set Rune-wards to repel them; she could feel their potency as she reached the scarred and graffitied doorway squashed between a rundown residential hotel and a pawn shop. Vidarr might have rejected his heritage, but he could still call upon it when it suited him.

Mist opened the door and walked in. Vidarr employed a doorman to keep out any "undesirables" who might slip past the wards, but she didn't recognize the bruiser with the underbite standing just inside. He did a double take when Dainn came up behind her.

"Where's Vid?" Mist asked the doorman.

He folded his massive arms across his chest. "He ain't available."

"My name is Mist Bjorgsen. He'll see *me*."

"We don't allow no bums in here," the man said, jerking his thumb at Dainn. "And he stinks."

Dainn showed no reaction to the insult. He began to hum under his breath. The doorman was oblivious, but Mist felt the stirring of magic—simple magic, to be sure, but potent enough to repel a mortal, no matter how big and menacing he was.

The last thing Mist could afford was to provoke Vidarr by causing a disturbance. She took Dainn's arm, shoved the doorman out of the way and started toward the back of the bar.

"Hey, bitch!" The doorman clamped one beefy hand over her shoulder. "You ain't—"

Mist spun around and punched him in the stomach. He let her go with a woof of astonished pain. She nodded to Dainn, who offered no comment, and they continued into the dark, smoky pit of the bar. There were three rooms stretching along Asbrew's narrow length, one after another like those of a railroad flat. It was the third one she wanted.

A dozen sets of eyes assessed them from the shadows as they passed through the public room. The radio blasted Norwegian death metal from huge speakers hung on the walls. Sullen kids with multiple piercings huddled over tables strung against the wall opposite the bar, and aging hipsters, ignoring the citywide smoking ban, argued over espresso and cigarettes.

They were of no interest to Mist. She didn't bother to ask the bartender where she could find Vidarr but kept moving through a tightly packed crowd of sleepy-eyed slackers and entered the door behind them.

The clientele in the second room was of a caliber far different from the kids in the public area. The dozen men and women were all mature, attractive, and reeking of wealth . . . the kind who dined every other night at French Laundry, had their clothes tailor-made in Paris, and lived in apartments and penthouses worth more than all Freya's gold.

But there was something off about them, a strangeness that went beyond the fact that they didn't belong in a place like this, especially early on a weekday morning. They stared at her as if she had crashed an exclusive wedding wearing nothing but her sword.

As if she was an enemy.

"Leave," Dainn whispered at her back. "Leave now."

Mist barely heard him. "Who are you?" she asked, looking at each hostile face in turn.

Glances were exchanged, but no one answered. Dainn gripped her arm. "There are too many," he said.

And suddenly she knew. "Where is he?" she demanded of the crowd in the Old Tongue, loosening her knife. "Where is your master?"

Hard eyes fixed on hers. Several of the men began moving toward her, getting taller by the second. Faces blurred, becoming coarse and ugly with hate. Fists lifted. An unmistakable chill rose in the room.

Hrimgrimir emerged from the crowd, grinning with hideous delight. "So we meet again, halfling. Or should I call you cousin?" His pointed teeth were red in the dim light, as if they were already stained with blood. "You must be eager for death. We will be happy to oblige you."

For a moment Mist couldn't process his words. Halfling? *Cousin?* It made no sense. None of it did. Why were the Jotunar in Asbrew? Where in Hel was Vid?

Pulling her knife free, Mist chanted the Rune-spell of change. Dim light raced along Kettlingr's blade. She felt Dainn's touch on her shoulder.

"If you must fight," he said, as if from very far away, "know that you have far more strength than you realize. Feel it, warrior. Let it come."

She didn't understand what in Baldr's name he was talking about, but suddenly he was gone, and Hrimgrimir and his kin were upon her.

Kettlingr flew up to meet the attack. The blade skittered against a wall of ice that dissolved as soon as the sword completed its arc. She swung again, narrowly missing a giant's arm.

Dainn had been right. There were too many, and she didn't have the time or means to draw the physical symbols, the staves, that anchored her rudimentary magic and gave the Runes their power.

You can build them in your mind, she thought. She'd never even considered the possibility before this morning, but somehow she and Dainn had made it work.

Unfortunately, Dainn wasn't here. She danced out of the way of a blow that would have flattened an elephant and tried to shape a repelling Bind-Rune out of her frantic thoughts.

The giantess who had swung at her gave a yelp of surprise and fell back. In the clear for a few precious seconds, Mist shaped a second Bind-Rune for strength and speed.

Suddenly a song rose in her chest—not merely a chant or a simple tune, but a robust, unfamiliar melody that throbbed with unexpected power. Strength greater than that of mortal or Valkyrie pulsed in her blood and blossomed in bone. Battle staves flared before her eyes. Driven by a compulsion she didn't understand, she released the Runes from the pit of her belly like an opera bass reaching for his deepest note.

The giants retreated with cries of rage and dismay. She advanced, slashing at any flesh within reach. Dark blue blood sprayed walls and spattered the floor. For a moment it seemed that she might even win.

But the new power didn't last. It drained out of her all at once, and she felt herself falter under the weight of uncertainty and sudden weakness. Hrimgrimir roared and struck with his enormous fist, knocking her against the wall.

Somehow she kept her grip on Kettlingr, but the strike had paralyzed her arm. She knew then that she was going to die, and she, unlike the giants and elves and gods who had survived Ragnarok, would not be returning. What became of the Aesir and their Treasures would be beyond her concern.

Sliding up the wall on rubbery legs, she grinned into the Jotunn's face and prepared herself for the final, crushing blow. Hrimgrimir bellowed and raised his hand again. Then the door to the bar swung open, and a thickset blond man staggered into the room, his head swinging right and left in confusion.

"Wa's goin' on here?" he drawled, leaning heavily against the doorframe. "Can' a man get any sleep?"

Hrimgrimir and the other giants turned to face the man. "Get out!" Hrimgrimir snarled.

"Mist?" The man took another step into the room, eyes widening. "Issat you?"

She caught her breath and worked her shoulder, feeling it come back to life again. Vali was a hard drinker and usually under the thumb of his elder half-brother, but he wasn't as stupid as he sounded. He hadn't just been wakened out of some drunken stupor. One look at his face told her that he knew what was happening. And he was trying to help her.

With a hoot of laughter, Vali stumbled past the Jotunar blocking the doorway. "So . . . gla' to see you," he said, his full weight crashing into Mist. "Missed you."

Smothered in his bearish embrace, Mist felt the pressure of his body pushing her away from the wall. He was moving her toward the door, inch by subtle inch.

"Get out of here," he hissed, his mouth pressed to her ear.

"Where is Vidarr?" she whispered.

"You can't see him." They reached the door, and Mist heard the hinges creak. "Save yourself."

"Where is he?" she demanded. "Is he in trouble?"

"I said, you can't—"

Without warning Mist shoved Vali aside, swinging Kettlingr before her, and ran for the back door. Hrimgrimir swiped at her and missed. The rest were too startled to intercept her before she got to the back door and flung it open.

Vidarr sat in a battered chair in the room that served as his office, his face blank as uncarved stone. His eyes barely flickered as Mist burst through the door. She slammed it behind her and scanned the room. Gungnir lay in plain sight on the wide, battered desk behind Vidarr's chair.

"Your manners disappoint me, my dear Mist," a voice said from the shadows behind the desk. "And so does your judgment. I had hoped you would take warning and flee. After all the pleasure you've given me, I had intended to spare you."

Eric. But it wasn't Eric's voice. And the figure that emerged from the shadows was not tall and broad-shouldered, but as lean and wiry as a stoat. He was dressed in black from neck to toe, modified biker's leathers adorned with flashy metal trimmings and emblazoned with a stylized flame. His eyes were brilliant green, the irises rimmed with orange. His red hair was artfully styled, and his long, handsome face was smiling.

He looked nothing at all like the man she'd come to love. But her heart lurched under her ribs as she realized who she was seeing. Loki, the great Trickster, once beloved of Odin. The child of powerful giants, Loki was one of the few divine beings—not quite a god—who could change his shape completely without relying on illusion or possessing the body of an animal or man. At times he had saved the Aesir, at other times opposed them. His constant scheming had been overlooked until he had killed Baldr, the blind god, with malice and treachery.

The punishment they had set for him had planted the seeds of the Last Battle.

But he had many flaws besides a propensity for duplicity, not least of which was overweening pride and belief in his own ultimate superiority.

And that meant he could be beaten. Not now, not by her, but by those who were coming.

Swallowing her instinctive fear, she faced him squarely. "I've come for Gungnir, Slanderer," she said.

"How charming." Loki walked past Vidarr without a glance in his direction and stood before her, hands on hips. "You always were impulsive, darling. That was what made you so entertaining in bed,

even if your other skills were not"—he looked her up and down—
"quite as well developed as I might have preferred."

Mist swung Kettlingr at his head. Loki sent the sword spinning
to the floor with three short words and a wave of his hand, violently
twisting Mist's fingers.

"It's no use," Vidarr said, his voice thick with despair. "You can't
beat him."

"Listen to the Silent One, *villkatt*," Loki said. "Like you, Odin's
son has been corrupted by his long residence in Midgard. He let his
magic fade over the years. He proved remarkably ineffective in his
attempts to resist." Loki reached for the glass of red wine that stood
on the nearby desk and sniffed it critically. "I confess I am a little
surprised that you found me so quickly."

Mist made a show of nursing her twisted fingers. They hurt like
the devil, so it wasn't really a show at all. "You didn't make much of
an effort to hide your trail," she said.

"Your magic never amounted to much, nor did I have anything
to fear from you should you find me . . . as our meeting here has
proven." He took a very small sip of the wine and held it on his
tongue. "Amusing, isn't it, that you thought 'Eric' might not be able
to handle the truth about *you*?"

"The Eric I knew was a good man," she said, edging toward Kettlingr. "Who would have thought you'd have it in you to play someone so completely the opposite of what you are?"

"I *was* rather good, wasn't I?" he said. His brow wrinkled in per-
plexity that was almost convincing. "But how do you know how
different I am? I don't believe we ever met in Asgard."

Mist gauged the distance to her sword out of the corner of her
eye. "Your reputation precedes you," she said. "No one in any of the
Homeworlds was spared the tales of your 'exploits.' Especially since
you wouldn't let anyone forget them."

Loki put on an expression of patently false hurt feelings. "I'm not surprised you think so ill of me, but you haven't given me much of a chance."

"I gave you six months, Laufeyson," she said. "But you knew if you ever let me see your true nature, the game would be up."

"Game? That implies some measure of equality between the two parties playing it. I could have taken Gungnir any time."

"But something stopped you." She was only a couple of feet from Kettlingr now. "If I'm as weak as you say, how did I get through your cohorts outside?"

"Ah, Mist," he said, grinning again. "Do you actually believe I didn't instruct them to let you through?"

"I think you forgot to tell Hrimgrimir that."

"He can be . . . shall we say, a little overenthusiastic."

"You might have trouble with him later if you don't keep him in line."

"Your concern for me is touching. However, since you have come here alone with no hope of prevailing, I think it is *your* well-being we must consider."

Mist weighed Loki's words. He spoke as if he believed she'd come alone, so either he didn't know the Aesir's messenger was with her in Asbrew or he simply didn't care. That put paid to the theory that Dainn's arrival, anonymous or otherwise, had convinced Loki to move when he did. Or perhaps Hrimgrimir had simply reported that the elf he had met in the park was no threat to him, and a rank coward to boot.

So, for that matter, was Vidarr, if he had let Loki take him. She moved another few inches sideways and looked at Odin's son, barely able to conceal her contempt.

"How long has this been going on?" she asked. "Did you know Loki was in Midgard?"

"Let us give him some credit, my dear," Loki said with a faint smile in Vid's direction. "He was as fully blind as you were until I opened his eyes. Odin's son saw the wisdom in reaching a certain understanding with me."

"What understanding?"

"Why, to keep his interfering nose out of my affairs."

"And your 'affairs' are the Treasures."

Loki's eyes narrowed. "Ah," he said. "The elf told you, did he? Hrimgrimir was quite certain he had killed the Alfr, but I gather he managed to survive after all." He glanced toward the door. "Where is he now, I wonder?"

"I don't need him."

"That useful, was he?"

"Do you know who he is?" Mist asked.

"Should I?" Loki said, taking another sip of the wine. "Is he significant in some way?"

"*I've* never seen him before," Mist said, quite truthfully.

"And now he has abandoned you." Loki clucked his tongue. "What can Freya have been thinking when she sent an elf to do a god's work? Only more proof of how weak she is. Of course, it's clear none of the Aesir knew I was here at all."

His dismissive attitude was just what Mist wanted to encourage. She knew she had a small window of opportunity to make use of Loki's legendary ego.

"You do seem to have all the advantages," she said, adjusting her position against the wall so that she could grab Kettlingr the moment Loki was distracted. "How did you hide yourself so well?"

He touched the side of his long, rather elegant nose. "A magician never reveals his secrets, and I am somewhat more than a magician. Let us say that the gods make a habit of underestimating me, to their lasting regret."

"Maybe that's because you're not really quite a god yourself."

Green eyes narrowed, flaring around the edges with the dancing light of flame that was barely metaphorical. "I am *more* than a god."

"In that case," she said, "why did you stay with me so long, when, as you said, you could have taken Gungnir any time? Was it because you couldn't find the other Treasures on your own? Did you think I could help you?"

She could see that she'd hit the target by the way Loki tried to hide his scowl. "You overestimate your value to me."

"Overestimate, underestimate. Confusing, isn't it?" She slid down into a crouch. "You're not going to be able to hide yourself now. I wouldn't want to be in your flying shoes when she comes after you."

Loki's fingers tightened on the stem of the glass. "What good is the Sow without her body?"

Mist had heard all the stories about Loki's unrequited lust for the Goddess of Love. Loki wasn't nearly as sanguine about Freya as he wanted Mist to believe. And the Lady had far more magic available to her than the seductive, irresistible curves of her voluptuous body.

"In all the stories I've heard about you," Mist said, "you always make the same mistake. *You* assume your enemies are too stupid to keep up with you."

Abruptly Loki seemed to relax. He laughed the way Eric used to, with sunny good nature and easy confidence.

"Do you think I'm so eager to destroy them that I will make such mistakes?" he asked. He set his glass on the desk and stroked the front of his jacket like a peacock preening its breast feathers. "Asgard is no more. The time of the Aesir is over. Midgard survives, but it is in dire need of change. The mortals have yet to learn the meaning of true freedom." He grinned. "Fortunately, they now have me."

5

———

"What change?" Mist asked, sweat trickling from under her hairline and rolling down her temple.

"Oh," Loki said, arching a brow. "Can it be the elf didn't explain the situation after all?"

"I got the idea that you wanted to take over the world," Mist said, slowly reaching toward Kettlingr.

"You do me a disservice," Loki said. He yawned behind his hand. "I fear the elf may have been withholding certain information from you in an effort to win your cooperation. But perhaps it doesn't concern you that soon this world will become a battlefield, winner take all."

"I know." Her fingers closed around the hilt. Still Loki didn't seem to notice.

"I wonder if you can envision how it will happen," Loki said. "Do you believe the Aesir will tread lightly on this earth, benevolently sparing the creatures here any inconvenience? Do you think they will be better than I?"

"When have *you* ever cared about the well-being of men?" she asked.

"When it serves me."

"How does it serve you now? You never took any interest in

mortals. They were always beneath your notice. Now here you are, lording it over a bar in an unsavory neighborhood." She smiled mockingly. "'How are you fallen from heaven, O star of the morning, son of the dawn!'"

Loki returned her smile, but it was more than a little pinched. "Do not mistake me for the Christians' Satan. This is no tale of good versus evil, where the heroes wear white robes and the villains gleaming black armor."

"Prophecy foretold that Ragnarok would be a wash, with just about everyone dying—including you," she said, ignoring his comment. "I don't see why it would be any different this time around."

"Prophecy was wrong."

"I know you think you'll have the Treasures to give you the advantage, but you aren't just going to walk up to my Sisters and take them."

"Do you think any mere Valkyrie can stand against me?"

Mist jumped up, Kettlingr firmly in her grip, and lunged for Loki. He stepped back, his face registering shock. It only lasted a fraction of a second, but his response wasn't fast enough. Mist landed a good blow and cut deeply into his right deltoid. He jumped back, instinctively slapping his hand over the wound.

Godlings bled as much as mortals when they were wounded, though they healed far more quickly, as nearly all from the lost Homeworlds did. Mist charged again, aiming for his belly.

But by then Loki had recovered from the surprise of her attack and had a sword in his hand—a black one, blazing red Runes inscribed in its blade. It was serrated like a Jotunn's teeth, and Loki didn't have to use magic to meet her fiercest assault.

It was nothing like her bouts with Eric. Loki's wound dripped blood on the stained cement floor, but he ignored it and counterattacked with the full weight of his fury. Mist had to give ground, deflecting his steel with her own, feeling his sword's teeth biting into her own blade and catching, twisting, threatening to wrench Kettlingr out of her hand.

What amazed her, when she had a second to be amazed, was that other than conjuring the sword, Loki used no magic on her. Had he done so, the battle would have been over in seconds. As it was, he seemed to take some pleasure in the duel once he let go of his initial anger.

She didn't expect that to last. She was the better swordsman—at least, she had been so with Eric—and Loki wouldn't stand for being second best. Especially not to *her*.

Metal clanged like bells tolling in a graveyard, and they disengaged again. "You think my Sisters are helpless?" she asked, catching her breath.

Loki laughed, his own breath coming short. "You really have no idea what you're up against, do you?"

"A bunch of Jotunar who let themselves get their asses kicked by a single Valkyrie?"

"If you think the frost giants are my only allies, you are very much mistaken."

She didn't have to ask what he meant. He was talking about his evil children: Hel, who ruled the dead; Fenrisulfr, also called Fenrir, the enormous wolf who was foretold by prophecy to kill Odin; and Jormungandr, the World Serpent.

"Your children are alive, too, are they?" Mist said, throwing off her horror with another feint. "Well, it won't be quite as easy for them to have their way in this modern world."

"And how, pray tell, did you come to that conclusion?" Loki asked, batting her blade aside and closing with her so that their faces were mere inches apart.

"Disaster strikes on a global scale these days," Mist said, barely holding him at bay. "Humanity has dealt with far worse monsters than Fenrir and Jormungandr, and emerged victorious."

"*Human* monsters," Loki said, grinning into her face.

"Fenrir didn't manage to kill Odin, did he? And what about Hel? What are you going to do with your daughter now that she doesn't have the dead to rule anymore?"

"What makes you think she doesn't?"

"Mortals aren't as simple as they used to be," Mist said. "They're not going to go willingly into some dark, gloomy afterlife."

"They will have no choice in the matter."

"You'd be surprised," she said, pushing him back a few steps. "Outside threats tend to unite the people of Midgard."

"Mortals are sheep, incapable of making their own decisions on any matter of importance," Loki said, looking pointedly at her parted lips. "They will always squabble and slaughter each other with the slightest provocation."

"Look who's talking." With a final effort, she threw him off. "All mortals aren't the same, and there are millions more of them than there are Jotunar, or any of your allies."

Loki rolled his eyes. "Oh, *skatten min.* Always the sentimentalist." He lowered his sword and placed his hand over his heart. "Let me assure you that your mortals will be happier under my guidance than they have ever been in all their brief history."

Mist wondered if Loki actually believed what he said.

Of course he did.

"So you're going to set up some kind of throne in the Capitol building and have every government in the world pay obeisance?" she asked, preparing for another attack.

"Perhaps," Loki said. "But I am not interested in ruling in the conventional way, my dear. All I want is for an end to laws that curtail the freedom of the people of this world to act entirely as they wish. Have you any idea how many mortals I will win to my side with simply the promise of such a paradise?"

No law, he meant. No restrictions on what one man or woman

could do to another, one race or culture to another, one country to another. It would bring anarchy, unimaginable cruelty and suffering. Until the world fell apart.

And Loki would watch it all with delight.

"Now you understand," he said, a good approximation of pity in his voice. "Ruling mortal kind takes little effort on my part . . . unless they are as worthy as you say and can constrain their bestial natures. I will only enforce the law that there is to *be* no law. And if they still survive . . ."

"Why such hatred of the people of Midgard?"

"I don't hate them," Loki said, his narrow jaw hardening. "But I know what Freya and Odin will do to your adopted world. The battle they bring here will cause untold suffering and a billion deaths. That is why I will stop them. And when the old civilization is fallen, I will rebuild from the ashes. Then it may be worth ruling."

There was nothing left for Mist to say. Arguing with Loki was like asking a starving tiger to pass by a sleeping child lying in its path.

She looked past him at Gungnir. "If you're so confident that neither I nor the mortals can stand against you," she said, "why did you try to leave Midgard once you had the Spear?"

"I have no idea what you're talking about."

"You tried to escape by one of the bridges." She flicked another glance at Vidarr, who maintained a rigid silence.

"You are mistaken," Loki said. "I was not leaving Midgard."

"You were running. What scared you, Laufeyson?"

He chuckled, though the sound rang more than a little hollow. "Your attempts to provoke me into rash action are futile, my dear."

But there had to be something she could use to make him reveal more information. She was just beginning to form another plan when she heard a faint sound from the room outside. Loki glanced toward the door.

Mist charged him again. She managed to back him up against

the wall before he let his sword fall. She laid Kettlingr's edge against his throat.

"Maybe you can satisfy my curiosity on another point," she said. "If you managed to open these bridges to Midgard before the Aesir did, you must be clever enough to have found out who or what sent all of you into Ginnungagap before Ragnarok had barely begun. What force could be powerful enough to forestall Prophecy and subvert the will of the gods?"

Loki's bicolored eyes showed no alarm at his disadvantaged position. "Whoever or whatever was responsible," he said, "it was unable to prevent me from reaching Midgard or setting my plans into motion. I will discover it, expose it, and destroy it."

"What if this force steps in again when you and the Aesir resume the war?"

Orange flame surged around his irises again. "I will be ready," he said.

"You're certainly going to have your hands full," Mist said. "I look forward to—"

Suddenly Loki wasn't there. She fell forward against the wall, all the air knocked out of her lungs. Kettlingr flew from her hand. A fly buzzed around her head, seeming to laugh in its whining voice.

The fly landed on the wall and rubbed its legs. Loki hadn't had to use force to defeat her. All he had to do was change his shape.

"Better be glad I don't have a flyswatter," Mist gasped.

Loki resumed his own form, leaning against the wall with his thumb hooked under his belt. "What a dreadful image," he said. "I remember the sweet, heartfelt conversations we used to have after our lovemaking. Do you miss them as much as I do, darling?"

Mist had to remind herself again how thoroughly stupid it would be to attack him with her bare hands. "Please, just kill me," she said. "Listening to you talk is worse than spending an eternity in the Christian Hell."

Loki didn't rise to her bait. He plucked at his slashed sleeve with a frown. The bleeding had stopped, and the flesh beneath was already knitting.

"You ruined my new jacket," he said plaintively.

"You can conjure up another one," Mist said. "It *was* conjured, wasn't it?"

"Did you think I was idle all the time I was with you? I have a considerable fortune, Mist. I intend to put it to very good use." He met her gaze. "It need not be this way, you know. Why should we speak as enemies when we could so easily be allies?"

"You're crazy," she said.

Loki drew a small dagger from a sheath inside his jacket and slid the needle tip under one beautifully manicured nail. "You gave up your duty to Odin long ago. You owe nothing to Freya. Is it really concern for this world that makes you turn against me? Or guilt, perhaps, now that you know the Aesir are still alive?"

"I'm not looking for redemption. Only for a way to kill you."

"I see that you are still as intractable as ever," he said.

Mist folded her arms across her chest. "Let's just say I decided to take your offer. What good could I possibly be to you?"

"You have managed to intrigue me all over again, darling. And you will never find a better fuck than me, I assure you."

Mist sighed. "Psychiatrists call your particular condition narcissistic personality disorder. They might have created the category just for you."

In a blur of motion Loki was directly in front of her, the blade of his dagger at her throat. "Even I have my limits," he said. His lips peeled back from slightly pointed teeth. "You're going to tell me where I can find your Sister Valkyrie."

"I have no idea where they are."

"You suffer from the same disease that plagues all those who claim to be honorable. You are a very poor liar."

"The problem with habitual liars like you is that they are seldom capable of recognizing the truth."

"I can make your death very unpleasant."

She shrugged, though the movement pushed her throat into the dagger's edge. Blood trickled under her collar. "I didn't expect anything less."

"Perhaps you think that Vidarr or his drunk of a brother will find the courage to assist you? Or that the elf might return?"

Mist had pretty much given up on the idea that she'd get any assistance from Vidarr. In fact, she'd almost completely forgotten he was in the room at all.

As for poor Vali . . . she could only hope that the Jotunar outside didn't consider him a threat and that he'd had the sense to get out of their way. And Dainn . . .

"I don't need help to die," she said.

Abruptly Loki withdrew the dagger, wiped it fastidiously on her jacket, and sheathed it. "I don't want you dead, *skatten min*," he said. "Look at me. Eric is still here, and he can be very generous to his inferiors."

Mist eyed Kettlingr. "I'm no good to you, Slanderer."

Loki picked Kettlingr up and examined the sword intently. "What is your price? Wealth? Power? To stand by my side as the consort of Midgard's master?"

"By the side of a creature who mated with a stallion and gave birth to a serpent?"

With a grunt of rage Loki flipped his hand in the direction of the desk, raising the wine glass into the air and sending it flying against the nearest wall. It shattered, silver particles rising in a cloud and hovering in midair like powdered ice.

"I am weary of this sparring," he snapped. "One final chance, Mist."

"Nothing has changed," she said, tilting her head back to expose her throat. "Go ahead."

Loki stared at her, the muscles in his jaw clenching and un-clenching. Vidarr moved for the first time since he'd spoken to Mist, turning his head just enough to catch her eye, as if he were trying to tell her something important. Something that might change the game completely.

"Why are you hesitating, Slanderer?" she asked Loki. "You have my sword. If you have any feelings left for me, let me die by her blade."

"No," he said, setting the sword on the desk. "But I wonder . . . shall we test to see if Gungnir is still all it was in Asgard?"

Suddenly the Spear was in Loki's hand, and he was aiming straight at Mist's heart. The Swaying One hummed in his grip as he let fly. Mist desperately chanted Runes of protection in the hope that the strange new power that had come to her when she'd fought the giants would somehow return.

She wasn't fast enough to intercept Gungnir's flight, but no cold metal pierced her chest. The Spear's head penetrated the door just above and behind her shoulder, splitting the wood from top to bot-tom. Mist spun to grab for the shaft, straining to remove it from the door. It wouldn't budge.

"You have worn out my patience, little bitch," Loki said, moving up behind her with a nearly soundless tread.

"And you've tried mine," Mist said, turning to face him. "You were never as good at anything as you thought you were."

"Perhaps I'll take you one last time, and show you just how good I am."

"Try it, and I'll roast your balls like chestnuts."

Loki flinched. It was only a small movement, but it told Mist something she hadn't anticipated.

He's afraid, she thought in wonder. But what was the key to his fear?

"Freya is the key."

Dainn's voice, speaking inside her head. The elf was still here, and in a way she never would have expected.

"Dainn," Loki said. His voice had an odd tone, as if he were truly taken aback. Setting aside her own surprise at his reaction—and his use of Dainn's name—Mist took advantage of his confusion. As she had shaped the Runes in her mind back at the loft, now she did the same with words, projecting them outward in hopes that Dainn would hear.

The elf understood her question before she was finished. *"Loki fears you because he fears the Lady,"* he said. *"He taunted and mocked her and called her whore because he wanted her but could not have her."*

And what in Hel did that have to do with *her*? Mist thought. She tried to ask Dainn again, but Loki was already moving. He caught Mist by the throat, and she felt her breath stop. Within a few seconds her vision began to go dark, and her thoughts were no longer coherent enough to form even the simplest question, let alone project that question into someone else's mind. It was over. She had nothing left with which to fight.

"Halfling," Dainn's silent voice whispered again, beginning to unravel like thread caught in a kitten's claws.

And then she understood.

Loki's piss. *That* was what Hrimgrimir had meant. Why the new song had come to her, briefly making her a match for a dozen angry Jotunar.

They were her kin. The kin she had never known growing up an orphan in Asgard.

"A Jotunn was your father," Dainn said. *"Your mother . . ."*

Dainn's presence faded, but he left in her mind a single image. An image of a face she recognized, a beauty beyond compare.

Mist bit back her disbelief. She had nothing to lose. Her vision cleared and she met Loki's gaze, letting him feel every last particle of her contempt.

"Is that why you lied your way into my bed?" she croaked. "If you couldn't have the mother, you'd take the daughter by trickery?"

Loki's fingers loosened again. "She's a whore," he hissed, his voice not quite steady. "She lay with every elf and god in Asgard, every Jotunn and Dvergar in Jotunheim and Nidavallir."

"Everyone but you."

He tightened his grip, but he never finished. The magic came from nowhere, settling over Mist without any effort on her part, a radiant warmth that filled her with a peace she had never known. The scent of primroses filled the air.

Loki's face blanched. He let her go and stumbled away.

"Freya," he moaned.

Mist raised her hand, and Kettlingr flew into it like a tame sparrow. "It is you who have the choice, Laufeyson," she said in a voice she barely recognized as her own. "Come back to us." She moved toward Loki, one hand beckoning while the other hand held the sword. "Let me show you what might have been," she said. "What might still be."

Suddenly Loki was right in front of her, and she was embracing him, smothering him against her chest, murmuring words of love in his ear. His face slackened like that of a satyr drunk on wine and sex. She felt his lips on her neck, heard his heartbeat rise to a speed no mortal could survive.

She was killing him with love.

Mist pulled back, leaving Loki to stagger as she withdrew her support. He straightened, and his expression cleared.

"You," he croaked. "You are—"

Vidarr slammed into him from behind, and Loki staggered again. He smacked Vidarr aside, leaped up on the desk, and crouched there, hatred in every line of his body. He flung a full-blown blizzard at Mist's face, and she deflected it with a wave of her hand. It spent its fury against the wall, and the air filled with countless drops of water and chips of ice.

But it had not completely failed in its purpose. Mist swayed, no longer able to tell floor from ceiling. All she could see were Loki's eyes, staring at her with cold calculation.

"You haven't won, bitch," he said. "This is far from over."

He snapped his fingers, and a flame burst to life in his hand. He tossed it onto a pile of old newspapers stacked up beside the desk and looked straight at Mist.

"Don't trust her," he said. "And don't trust *him*."

The flames blazed up, obscuring Loki in smoke. Then he was gone, vanished into the shadows, the stench of his rage dispersing like a frenzy of roaches exposed to the light. Vidarr scrambled up from the floor and traced a Rune over the burning papers. The flame winked out.

Mist closed her eyes. The warmth and joy and power she had felt only seconds ago was already abandoning her, leaving her an empty sack of skin and bone. She had no clear idea of what had just happened, but for a moment she had spoken with someone else's voice, succumbed to someone else's will.

She had *become* Freya. Freya, her mother.

Shaking uncontrollably, she set Kettlingr down and turned back to the door.

Gungnir was gone. Loki had taken it.

She leaned against the ruined door and wiped her mouth. Once again Loki had slipped out of her grasp, and so had Gungnir.

But where were the giants? Even if Loki had told them to stay out, they must surely have sensed the powerful magic when Freya had made her unexpected "appearance." Why had they remained outside when their master was threatened by something even he couldn't fight?

Before she could finish pulling the broken door open, Dainn climbed through it, his face as pale as a fish's belly. "Are you well?" he asked.

She turned on him. "Coward!" she said, shock exploding into anger. "You had words in plenty, but where were *you*?"

Dainn said nothing. He simply walked out of the room again. Vidarr got to his feet, popping his shoulder back into its socket.

"Mist," he said. "You have to believe I never—"

Vali burst into the office, looking anxiously from Mist to Vidarr and back again. "You guys okay?" he asked. "The elf said Loki's gone."

"He's gone, all right," Mist said.

"You got Gungnir?"

Mist shook her head, too ashamed to meet his gaze, and pointed at the door. "He did *that* just before he left. What about the Jotunar?"

"They won't be any more trouble."

Mist realized she'd severely underestimated Vali's skill and determination. "They didn't hurt you?" she asked, carefully looking him over.

"Didn't get the chance."

Mist blew out her breath, her anger seeping away. "Thanks for what you tried to do in there, Val. Sorry I couldn't take advantage of it. I had to find out what was going on in here."

Vali's ruddy skin went ruddier still. "I guess it's a good thing you did. You freed Vidarr."

Mist glanced in Vid's direction. He had turned his back to them, clearly in no mood to finish whatever he'd been about to tell her.

Had he been a prisoner, or had Loki been telling the truth about their reaching some kind of agreement?

Mist couldn't bring herself to believe it. Gods knew that Loki would be happy to lie if it meant turning potential allies against each other. And Vid had helped in the end, even if that help had come late. There was a lot more going on here than met the eye.

Even within herself.

Vali pushed his big hands in his jeans pockets. "I can't believe the Aesir are still alive," he said. "Damn. Might take a while to get used to the idea."

"Loki told you?"

Vali nodded. "This is all pretty strange."

That was an understatement. "How did Loki get the drop on Vidarr?"

"I wasn't there when it happened. When I figured out what was going on, Loki just told me to stay out of the way. He didn't think I was much of a threat, so I bided my time until I thought I could be of some use."

"Did anyone in the bar hear what was going on?"

"Loki soundproofed the back rooms when he showed up, and then Dainn—"

"Just what was *he* doing while Loki was trying to kill me?"

"Come with me."

Vali led her through the door into the other room. Mist stopped so suddenly that she almost tripped over her own feet.

The Jotunar were piled in a heap in the middle of the room, most unconscious and the rest groaning in pain. Hrimgrimir was not among them.

"The elf did that," Vali said.

6

Mist stared at Vali. "Did you just say—"

"*He* did it," Vali said, pointing his chin toward the corner of the room. Dainn stood there very quietly, his face as expressionless as ever but haggard and shadowed with exhaustion.

"How?" she asked.

"Magic," Vali said. "Not sure exactly what . . . like a combination of Galdr and elf-magic. Pretty impressive, too. Got them all fighting each other and hardly had to lift a finger."

Impressive was scarcely the word for it. Mist had barely managed to hold off a dozen Jotunar out for blood, and then only for a few minutes when she'd tried shaping the Battle-Runes in her mind. Even Vidarr might have found himself hard-pressed to fight them all at once. But Dainn—

"I think he was trying to get through to you when the Jotunar attacked him," Vali said, "but they were Hel-bent on killing him."

Mist felt her face go hot. She'd branded Dainn a coward without bothering to learn the whole truth.

But he'd lied to her and withheld a couple of pretty vital facts that changed the meaning of everything he'd ever told her. He'd walked into her mind and said that Freya was her mother, right in the middle of a battle for her life.

She still couldn't believe it. During her earliest childhood years in Asgard, believing that her late father was a prince of Midgard, she'd had only the vaguest memories of the woman who had given her birth. Memories that had quickly faded once her destiny had been made clear to her. She had stopped wondering about her parents long before she had been given the gift of immortality and made a Chooser of the Slain.

A Valkyrie who had never really been mortal at all. Half-goddess, half-Jotunn. Dainn had said he'd come to San Francisco because Freya had sensed Gungnir. Mist no longer believed that was the whole story. For a few moments, she had felt Freya, and Freya's power, as if she had become the goddess herself.

Had she? Had Freya somehow entered her mind the way Dainn had done? How had the Lady come to her from the Aesir's Shadow-Realm now, when, according to Dainn, Mist wasn't capable of hearing her?

Because that was also a lie. Mist had been played like a puppet by three immortals in less than half a day, and she didn't like it. Not one little bit.

She walked slowly over to Dainn. "Why?" she asked. "Why did you keep it from me?"

He wouldn't meet her eyes. "I did not think it would be advisable to tell you so soon. Not until you were prepared to trust me."

"Trust? That's a good one." She pulled her hand over her hair. "Loki seems to be the only one who knows anything around here. He knew about *you*, or at least that the Aesir had sent an elf to cause trouble for him, but until we showed up in Asbrew he thought Hrimgrimir had killed the gods' agent. He didn't seem too concerned that the 'elf' was still alive, since you'd apparently abandoned me."

Dainn flicked a glance at her face. "He did not know my name?"

"Not until you . . . did whatever you did in my mind. I think he heard you then." She brushed her temple with her fingertips, still feeling Dainn's voice echoing inside her skull. "How did you do it? You said you could only touch the surface."

"It did not involve anything more than that," he said. "I was not certain I would succeed, but it had to be attempted."

"It didn't exactly succeed. I'm alive, but he took Gungnir." She tried to shake off a sudden wave of despair. "Why did you ask if Loki knew your name?"

He looked away again. "We met in Asgard," he said.

"When?"

"It is scarcely uncommon for elves and Aesir to meet there, and Loki always made free of Valhalla."

"Did you have some kind of quarrel?"

"As a rule, Alfar prefer to avoid quarrels."

You've got to be kidding, she thought. She and Dainn had been at daggers drawn ever since they'd met.

"He was more than just surprised when he found out you were here," she said. She jerked her head toward the pile of Jotunar. "I wondered before if you're a lot more dangerous than you look. Loki seemed to think so, too."

Dainn's expression shifted, twisting out of its usual handsome lines. There was no mistaking the hatred in it. "What I can do is nothing to *his* magic," he said.

"Well, I think it's pretty clear that whatever happened between the two of you, it ended badly," she said, watching him carefully. "And no matter what you elves claim, you can still feel anger and hatred. I've seen it in your eyes before. You're no different from the rest of us."

"I am different," he said, looking away, "but not in the manner you suppose. Once I could have done him harm. I am no longer capable of it."

"Apparently *he* doesn't know that." Mist narrowed her eyes. "By the way, where were you when I was fighting the Jotunar? I went into this blind because you didn't get around to telling me something that could have made all the difference."

"I was attempting to contact Freya," he said.

"Did you succeed? Did she find a way to act in this world after all?"

"I don't understand what you—"

"Was that *me* in there fighting Loki, or was it my mother?"

Genuine shock froze his face. "What are you saying?"

She rapped her knuckles against her skull. "Didn't you stick around to see how things were going to come out after you shared the big secret? Didn't you hear Loki call Freya's name at the end? Who was he talking to?"

"I was not able to reach Freya. You were there. She was not."

"'Loki fears you because he fears the Lady,'" she said, quoting him. "'Freya is the key.' And then I wasn't myself anymore."

"You are more yourself now than you have ever been."

"Do you think this is funny?" she demanded. "First I find out a goddess who never so much as spoke to me in Asgard is my mother, you tell me I can't talk to her myself, and then suddenly I've got some kind of connection with her I can't control." She felt her chest tighten and took in a quick, sharp breath. "What did you do?"

"I did nothing. You drew upon the power that was already hidden within you."

"By fighting Loki in a way I never even would have considered before?" *Killing him with love*, she thought, with a shudder of disgust. "You saw it, didn't you? Why did just knowing who I was change me so much?"

"Your instinct for survival is powerful," he said, still looking more than a little shaken. "You found a part of Freya within yourself and made it real."

"Completely unconscious of what I was doing?"

"Were you ever truly unconscious?"

Once again he was evading her real question, but since she hardly knew how to ask it, she couldn't blame anyone but herself.

"You're a real bastard, you know that?"

"Is it another apology you seek?"

"I don't want your apology. I want you to stop lying to me."

His gaze, deeply shadowed, met hers again. "Since you don't trust me, how can you be sure I will tell you the truth now?"

Mist grabbed the front of Dainn's barely recognizable shirt and pulled it close around his neck.

"I'll *know*," she said.

She was bluffing, but she sensed that Dainn took her threat seriously. Maybe he believed her relationship with Freya, whatever the Hel it was, gave her the ability to sift truth from deception. Maybe it was even true.

"What do you wish to know?" he asked softly.

She let him go. "The giants knew I was half Jotunn, and Hrimgrimir called me 'Sow's bitch,' even though I served Odin. Loki must have known I was Freya's daughter all this time, just like you did."

"He clearly had no idea of your abilities."

"Obviously, since he didn't seem to worry about my finding out who he was when he lived with me. But why should he wait until we were facing each other here in Asbrew before he tried to get me on his side? If he believed I knew where the Treasures were all along, why didn't he try to force me to tell him before he ran off with Gungnir?"

"I have no answer," Dainn said.

Of course he doesn't, Mist thought sourly. "Loki did believe I *was* Freya in there, didn't he?"

"His behavior indicates he was fully convinced."

"And he was scared. He didn't expect any of it. When I . . . did what I did, he didn't know how to fight back." She struggled to find the right words. "I know he never stopped trying to get Freya in the sack. I can see why he'd hate her, but why the fear? He's the one with all the advantages now. He deceived the Aesir, he took Gungnir, but for a few seconds it was as if he couldn't fight at all."

Dainn's hesitation was so brief she almost missed it. "Their relationship was far more complicated than it appeared to others in Asgard."

"How?"

Dainn tugged at his collar, smoothing it as if it belonged to an expensive suit rather than a set of rags held together by dirt and blood. "It is something Freya did not consider necessary to tell me."

"Need-to-know basis again, huh?" She snorted. "That's convenient."

"I am sorry—"

"Skip it. Let's go back to what happened before he thought I turned into Freya. He still wanted me on his side even after I said I couldn't tell him where my Sisters are. Even after he was ready to kill me. Why?"

Brushing black hair away from his face, Dainn studied Mist as if he were deciding whether or not to trust *her*.

"He must have realized you would soon discover who you were and finally come into your power. He would have known that it was not only Gungnir the Lady sought when she sent her agent to find you."

"Then I was right," Mist said, her heart like an iron billet pressing against her ribs. "Freya never gave a damn about me in Asgard. But now I'm useful to her somehow, aren't I?"

"You are her daughter, but you are also Odin's servant. Before the Last Battle, she was unable to—"

"Bullshit." Mist turned sharply away, took a few steps, and swung toward Dainn again. "Why would the First Valkyrie let her own daughter serve another god if she cared about her? She hasn't suddenly developed some powerful maternal instinct for me. She has a use for me now that this war's about to begin, and I know what it is." She pushed her face close to Dainn's. "I'm not completely blind, Dainn. She needs a physical shape in Midgard, and I'm some kind of conduit for her power."

He didn't even blink. "You are mistaken," he said. "She could not simply force her way into your mind, even if she were inclined to do so."

"She's a goddess."

"And so will you be."

"I'm a warrior, not an Asynja."

"A warrior knows she must use every advantage in a fight. You have inborn abilities you have scarcely begun to explore. It is your magic, not your skill with a sword, that will help us in this battle."

Mist searched his eyes, torn between a desperate need to believe him and the fear that he was still lying to her, that he would never stop lying no matter how many times she threatened him.

It didn't help that she saw genuine concern in his eyes. Regret, sorrow, compassion for what she was going through. Almost as if he'd been in the same situation himself.

"Freya regrets that she never acknowledged you in Asgard," Dainn said quietly.

"That's supposed to make me feel better?" She backed away, putting a little more space between them. "Who was my father?"

"Freya did not—"

"Tell you," Mist finished for him. Norns knew it could have been one of a hundred Jotunar Freya had lain with. Not all of them were ugly, barbaric monsters. Some had magic well beyond that of an ordinary giant.

In any case, *this* time she believed that Dainn really didn't know. "If Freya isn't just using me as . . . some kind of anchor in Midgard, what does she want from me? Aside from my apparent ability to scare the shit out of Loki without knowing how I did it."

"Nothing has changed except your knowledge of your heritage. We must keep Loki from turning the Treasures against the gods."

"Gungnir didn't work for Loki."

"He knows his possession of them is the key to ultimate victory. That is why we must and will stop him."

Mist shivered. What if she really did have magic she could use against Loki to get Gungnir back, find her Sisters, and warn them before Loki got to them? Was it really that simple?

No, not simple. She'd have to acknowledge what she was, that she was capable of what she'd done in Vidarr's office. More than that— she'd have to accept it completely and make it a part of herself. Become a creature of magic. The prospect was . . .

Terrifying. But she knew something about unpleasant truths: if you didn't find a way to deal with them, you'd never be able to live with yourself.

And as long as it was *her* choice, she could decide what to do with it. She could find a way to turn the ugly tactics she'd used against Loki into something she could live with. A warrior's way.

"I don't want this," she began, steeling herself for the inevitable. "But if it has to be done, then I'll—"

She broke off. Dainn's expression had changed again, his face growing more gaunt, his eyes haunted, his gaze burning and bitter. It was as if something ferocious, unpredictable, and utterly unelflike had awakened within him, shredding his usual nearly emotionless demeanor like tissue in a typhoon.

She had seen that expression twice before, once when they had first met and again in the loft. She hadn't understood it then, and she didn't now.

"You need do nothing," he said. "Walk away, Valkyrie."

Mist laughed to cover her bewilderment. "Walk away? What kind of crap is this? You just finished doing everything you could to *get* me involved."

"Yes."

His irises were nearly black, and his upper lip twitched like an angry dog's. But there were other emotions in his face—that concern she'd seen before, worry, and fear. But not for himself.

"I give you this chance," he said. "Take it."

"That almost sounds like a threat."

"It is a warning, and the last I will offer."

"It isn't your choice to make, is it? Don't you take your orders from Freya?"

"She and I are not in constant contact, nor can she read my mind. By the time we speak again, I will have found a way to deal with her."

He was deadly serious. But he wasn't making any sense. She'd bluffed about being able to tell whether or not Dainn was lying, but the only thing she *was* sure about was that Dainn was trying to give her a way out of a responsibility she wanted no part of.

Before she could speak again, Dainn spun on his heel and began to walk away.

"Dainn!" she called after him.

He stopped without turning around.

"I don't know what secrets you're keeping," she said, coming up behind him, "but I know you're being more honest now than you've been since we've met. If I supposedly have so much 'power,' why are you afraid for me?"

"For *you*? Perhaps I am the coward you named me."

Mist reached for his arm and grasped it lightly, feeling his pulse throbbing through rags and flesh alike.

"Whatever you are," she said, "I know you tried to help when you kept the Jotunar occupied. You gave me a way to fight back when Loki almost had me. And you know I can't let Loki have Midgard. The Aesir have to win."

"Will they be so much better than the Slanderer?" he asked.

His words sparked the memory of Loki speaking nearly the

same words to her. *"Do you believe the Aesir will tread lightly on this earth, benevolently sparing the creatures here any inconvenience?"* he'd said. *"Do you think they will be better than I?"*

When Dainn had told her how the Aesir planned to build a new Homeworld in Midgard, she'd only briefly considered the consequence, having been focused on more urgent concerns. Like staying alive.

But she'd never doubted the Aesir would be better. It would be impossible for a battle between Loki and the Aesir to occur without collateral damage. Certainly the Aesir, who had once frequently interacted and even intermarried with mortals, would take some care to minimize such damage.

Would they conduct the war in some barren waste, where few mortals could be harmed? The Sahara desert, perhaps, or the Australian Outback? Or would Loki force the Aesir into a position of killing innocent bystanders?

Mist knew that if she could make only the smallest difference, she had to try. Not because she owed Freya a bloody thing, but for the sake of her adopted world. And for all those who had fought so valiantly against tyranny.

Like Bryn. And Geir.

"You don't believe that, Dainn," she said. "I don't know why you've suddenly decided to convince me otherwise, but I'm involved in this up to the wingtips of my bloody golden helmet. I'm not backing out now."

Dainn's shoulders stiffened. "You will help? Willingly?"

"You wouldn't get me any other way." She paused, surprised at the clarity of her thoughts. "Look. For a long time I made myself believe I couldn't have any place in Midgard. That changed when I realized this was the only life I was going to have. Now this world is my home, and I have to defend it."

"You are fortunate," Dainn said, refusing to let her see his face.

She understood exactly what he was trying to say. "This isn't your home, is it?" she asked softly. "Even after centuries of living among mortals, you still don't belong."

"No," he said. "I have no home."

For a moment she was tempted to sympathize with him, even to pity him. She could almost feel his sorrow as if it were her own, feel his loneliness.

Curse it, she wasn't going to let sentiment cloud her thoughts now. Especially not sentiment about *him*.

"Maybe you don't have any personal stake in Midgard the way I do," she said. "But you do have a mission. I can't say I'm ready to trust you completely, but neither one of us is going to get very far if we don't work together."

Dainn half turned his head, once again displaying his handsome, haggard profile. "You asked about my magic," he said.

The non sequitur caught Mist completely off-guard. "You mean about the fact that you use it under some circumstances and ignore it in others, even when the situations may be equally deadly?"

Dainn lifted his hand, and Mist saw how violently it trembled. "As I told you before," he said, "magic exacts a price. I . . . have not . . . had reason to make use of mine in many years. You may think ill of me for my reluctance to act, and for many other failings. But I had no choice but to preserve my strength until it was truly needed."

"So you had to have my help to find Loki," she said.

"Yes. And now . . ." He let his hand fall back to his side. "I cannot be certain how long it will take me to recover. I will continue to require your help."

Mist had a bad feeling she knew exactly what he was trying to say. "You mean you'll be crawling around inside my head again, the way you did at the loft?" she asked.

"Yes." He turned to face her, his eyes still as black as the bottom of the sea. "Choose carefully, Lady. If you ask it, I will leave here now and trouble you no further."

"I've made my decision," she said.

All at once that strange, almost violent intensity was gone from his face, and he was as composed as if the most taxing thing he'd done all morning was brush his long black hair.

Which, like the rest of him, badly needed a good washing.

But that could wait a little longer. "The first thing we need to do," she said, "is get Gungnir back."

"Not the first," Dainn said. "We must dispose of *this*." He gestured toward the pile of Jotunar, several of whom were beginning to stir.

Mist couldn't believe she'd been yammering on with a dozen Jotunar still in the room. "This is Vidarr's problem," she said harshly. "He needs to tell me what the Hel is going on around here. Unless he really did strike a bargain with Loki, he'll be pissed and likely to want revenge."

"Do you trust him?"

That nasty little word again. Had Vid feigned submitting to Loki? It wouldn't be much like him to use subtlety and deception where more direct action would do—in that, he wasn't unlike Thor, another of his half-brothers—but she didn't see any other explanation for his behavior. Including the fact that he hadn't tried to help her until it was safe for him to do it.

"Yes," she said slowly. "I trust him."

She glanced around the room. Vidarr and Vali were either still in the office, or they'd sneaked past her and Dainn without their noticing. They probably had enough functional magic left to do that, but it would look very, very bad.

She was just starting for the shattered office door when the half-brothers emerged. Vali went straight to one of the tables near the wall, bearing a bottle of Scotch and a shot glass. Vidarr leaned against the doorjamb, his expression locked as tight as a frightened virgin's thighs on her wedding night.

Mist walked briskly across the room, skirting the Jotunar—none of whom had yet managed to lift themselves off the floor—and came to stand before Vidarr. He didn't seem to be aware of Dainn at all.

"What happened, Vid?" she asked.

The muscles in his jaw worked as he glared at the opposite wall.

"He . . . don' wan' to talk about it," Vali said from the table, his words slurring as if he'd been drinking hard since he'd last spoken to Mist.

Vidarr turned his hot stare on his half-brother. "Shut up, Val." He met Mist's gaze, head lowered and shoulders hunched like an angry bull, which he somewhat resembled even on his best days. "What do you *think* happened?" he asked. "I invited him in for tea?"

"No," she said, reminding herself that she had long ago stopped letting herself be intimidated by his bluster, Odin's son or not. "He obviously breached your wards and caught you by surprise."

"Tha's right," Vali said.

"Shut up," Vidarr repeated, though he continued to stare at Mist. "If you've got something to say to me, spit it out."

"You started to tell me something just after Loki disappeared, something you wanted me to believe."

"I don't give a damn what you believe." Vidarr smiled unpleasantly. "You think I'm supposed to be impressed that you're Freya's daughter and spoke with her voice for a few seconds? Did you cry for Mommy to rescue you?"

Mist ignored the jibe. "Did *you* know who I was before?"

"No. And it wouldn't have made any difference if I had."

"For the gods' sake, we don't have time for this. I just want to understand what happened."

"Then you'll just have to live with your ignorance."

Mist realized that he wasn't going to be reasonable at the moment, and there wasn't much point in pushing him now. She gestured behind her at the Jotunar. "This is your place. What do you want to do with them?"

"Kill them."

That was the obvious solution. It certainly had the advantage of removing a few of Loki's servants from the field, and it could be done with only a minimal use of magic.

But Mist knew why she was resisting the idea. She couldn't forget she was half-Jotunn. Vidarr *knew* who his giantess mother was, and she had been an ally of the Aesir. Any of the giants here might be Mist's kin. A cousin. A brother. Even a father.

She wouldn't believe that. A father wouldn't try to kill his own daughter. No one had ever claimed that the worst Jotunar didn't love their own. It was everyone else they hated.

"There must be another way," she said.

"What other way?" Vidarr growled, pushing away from the wall. "Throw them out in the middle of Market Street and hope they all get hit by a bus?"

"*I* don't slaughter things that can't fight back."

Vidarr snorted. "You were always so proud that you taught yourself to fight after all those centuries playing dress-up like a little girl wearing her Mommy's pretty dress. You said you fought the Nazis, but—"

"I prefer to avoid unnecessary bloodshed."

"Just like Freya. All peace and love, all the time."

"I'm not Freya."

"No? Then why don't we wake the giants up and offer to challenge them one-on-one? I'm sure Hrimgrimir would like another shot at you."

Mist had had enough. "I can understand why you're feeling so bloodthirsty, Vid," she said. "Your ego has always been a little on the tender side."

Vidarr started toward her, fists clenched, his shoulders straining the seams of his shirt. Mist tensed. In spite of their contentious history, she'd never have believed that Vidarr would actively try to hurt her.

She didn't get a chance to find out if he'd reached his breaking point. Dainn stepped smoothly between them.

"Are you both such fools?" he asked. "This is exactly what Loki desires."

Mist and Vidarr turned to stare at the elf. She had been so intent on Vid that she'd almost forgotten about him, and Vidarr was reacting as if a cockroach had gotten up on its hind legs and started reciting the kennings of the All-father.

Vidarr lifted his hand to strike. Dainn made no move to avoid the blow.

"Stop it!" Mist shouted. "Vid, he's on our side!"

Vidarr lowered his arm, but his body was trembling with rage. "Our side?" he repeated. "The cursed Alfr who betrayed the Aesir?"

"What? Vid—"

"You didn't recognize him? The traitor who should have been dead by Thor's hand?"

Comprehension blinded Mist, leaving her groping for something to hang on to while the ground crumbled beneath her feet.

"Oh, this is rich," Vidarr said. "Freya didn't tell her darling daughter the kind of scum she was dragging around?" He laughed viciously. "He didn't even bother to change his name. Dainn Faithbreaker, the elf who started Ragnarok."

7

Mist's vision began to clear. Dainn's face resolved from a blur to crystal clarity. There was no denial in his expression, no protest. Vidarr might as well have stated that the elf had black hair and deep blue eyes.

She should have known, just as she should have known that Eric was Loki. She had thought of the two most famous Dainns when she'd first found him but had never seriously considered that he might be one of them.

Dainn Faith-breaker. The only one of his people who had not fought with the Aesir in the Last Battle, because Thor had supposedly killed him for his defection to the enemy. Mist knew few details but those she'd heard in the rumors that circulated in Asgard after the Aesir and Alfar had sat in judgment over Dainn and condemned him to death; some had whispered that it was his last-minute warning that had prevented Loki's forces from taking the Aesir completely unaware. Some said it was weakness, not malice, which had led him to join Loki, that Laufeyson had deceived him with claims of a desire for peace.

But neither good intentions nor weakness were excuses for the damage Dainn had done in giving, or allowing, Loki to obtain vital information that had weakened the allies. Though neither side had won the battle, what Dainn had done was unforgivable.

Now Mist understood why Loki had reacted so strongly to learning that Dainn was the elf who had met with Mist. He, like she and Vid, must have believed his former ally was dead.

How had Dainn evaded execution? Perhaps Freya had helped him. She should have despised him as much as anyone who had ever walked in Asgard, but now she had set him a task that would require absolute trust in his loyalty.

"*You*," Mist said to Dainn, unable to find words scathing enough to express her horror and disgust.

"Yes," he said. "I have made many mistakes. I have been foolish beyond any expectation of atonement. But I did not start Ragnarok. I tried—"

"Scum," Vidarr snarled. "Filth. How do we know you aren't serving Loki now? And you—" He turned on Mist, pinching his nostrils as if he'd smelled something even worse than Dainn's rags. "You're no better than *him*. Loki wouldn't have Gungnir if you hadn't let him fuck you for six months."

"Don't go there, Vid," Mist warned. "I didn't—"

"Do you really want to take Gungnir back, or are you just pissed at him for making you his whore?"

Mist lunged at Vidarr. Dainn stepped between them again. Vidarr struck the elf in the temple with a bunched fist, and Dainn staggered. He righted himself quickly, showing no sign that he had been hurt at all.

Vidarr was going after Dainn again when Mist got in his way, steeling herself for a blow. Vidarr stopped just as his fist was about to connect with her head.

"I'm going to kill him," he rasped. "Get out of my way."

"I can't let you, Vid. He may deserve to die for what he did, but now Freya has intervened, and she wouldn't have done that without the agreement of the other Aesir. It's not our decision to make."

She could barely believe the words coming out of her own mouth, and Vidarr certainly didn't.

"You're defending him?" he asked incredulously. "Has *he* been fucking you, too?"

Clenching her jaw, Mist tried to let his sordid accusation pass through her. She turned back to Dainn. "How long did you think you could get away with this little charade?" she asked.

"If I had told you," Dainn said, "you would have left me in the park, or perhaps even killed me."

"You don't claim to be innocent of the crimes you're accused of?"

"I am far from innocent."

"He admits it," Vidarr said. "Move, Mist. Don't make me hurt you."

"He helped save both of us," she said. "Isn't that worth something?"

"He may have saved *you*, but I never needed his help."

"Dainn took care of Loki's Jotunar so they couldn't come charging in to attack us from the rear."

"He was responsible for the destruction of Asgard." Vidarr drew a knife from a sheath at his back. "I will finish what my brother Thor failed to do."

Mist held her ground. "Why so much hatred, Vid? You may be the god of vengeance, but this isn't just about his betraying the Aesir. It's personal."

Vidarr's stare was like Gungnir itself, piercing through Mist's body and burying its point right between Dainn's eyes. "I'm warning you one last time," he said. "Don't interfere."

"You know the old cliché. If you want to kill him, you'll have to walk through me first."

For a breathless moment she believed that Vidarr was going to call her bluff. But he lowered his knife and strode to the door to the bar, walked through it, and slammed it shut.

Mist glanced at Vali. He sank deeper into his chair.

"Let him go," Dainn said.

She faced him, loosing the anger she'd been trying to keep in check. "He was right. Why shouldn't I kill you?" She slipped Kettlingr from its sheath. "You've never stopped lying to me. For all I know, you led me right into a trap." Her hand trembled on the sword's hilt. "Why did you go over to Loki?"

"He deceived me, as he did you," Dainn said, holding her gaze as if he hadn't noticed the sword at all. "I believed I could help broker a peace between his forces and the Aesir's."

"Broker a peace? You mean attempt something not even Odin believed was possible?"

"I had been away from my people a long time, even then. No one remembered me, and so I believed I had a chance not open to those directly involved."

"But you joined Loki in the end."

"When I recognized my mistake in trusting him, I attempted to warn the Aesir. I was too late."

Mist didn't want to hear any more excuses. She raised Kettlingr and set the blade's tip against Dainn's chest. "Where were you, when you were 'away' from your people?" she asked.

"My memory of those times is incomplete."

"You like that excuse, don't you?"

"You said you could tell if I was lying. Am I lying now?"

"Did Freya save you from Thor?"

"The Lady believed I had tried to warn the Aesir. She spoke for me when I stood before the gods and elves."

"And she sent you here to protect me."

He sighed. "Yes. I deceived you on that point. But until a week ago, I had no idea what had happened to the Homeworlds just as the Last Battle began."

"So you never suffered any punishment at all."

"My own people repudiated me," he said softly. "Perhaps you will understand how I felt when Freya contacted me, and I learned the Aesir and my people lived. I could no more have rejected the service the Lady asked of me than could you."

Too little, too late, Mist thought, her anger and disgust far from assuaged. She looked across the room at Vali, who was so lost in his drink that she doubted he'd heard or seen a single thing that had happened since Vidarr had stomped out.

"I'm not buying that that's all there is to it," she said. "But I can't believe Freya would send an unregenerate traitor to find her daughter and locate the Treasures." She lowered the sword. "Are you sticking with your story that it was *my* magical ability at work against Loki, not Freya's?"

"Look inside yourself, and you will see."

Mist didn't want to. She was still afraid of what she would find. But she looked anyway. The Freya part of her was still present, light and gentle as a dusting of pollen on a honeybee's back. It wasn't obtrusive or threatening, as it had seemed when it had led her to attack Loki with the smothering power of seduction. It was just *there*, like a dormant memory waiting to be called up again.

"I still can't talk to Freya directly?" she asked.

"When you are ready."

She sang Kettlingr small and sheathed her. "Let's get a few things straight. I'm no one's unquestioning servant. Unless I get orders from Odin himself, I'm going to use my own judgment. And you're going to do what *I* tell you. No one is going to move me around like a defender on a *hnefatafl* board."

"And Vidarr?"

Mist glanced at Vali again. "I'm not going to let him kill you, if that's what you mean. I've known Vid a long time, and he *is* one of the Aesir. Maybe he doesn't care much about mortals, but he knows we can't be fighting each other when Ragnarok is about to happen all over again. And for real this time."

One of the Jotunar groaned loudly behind Mist, and she realized how completely she'd forgotten about the frost giants. Again. There was a scuffling as one of the creatures began to sit up.

"Odin's hairy balls," she said. "We still have to figure out what to do with them."

"If you do not wish to kill them—"

She flashed him an irritated glance. "You were the one who dealt with them in the first place. What would *you* do?"

"I would send them to a place where they will be of no further trouble for some time to come."

Dainn had made it clear before that he was going to need time to recover, but he looked ten times worse than he had before Vidarr had exposed him. "Are you up to it?" she asked.

"With your help."

"I was afraid of that. I assume it's the same as before? I think of the Runes, and you—"

"No," he said, very quietly. "You must let go of your will and let me guide you."

Her mouth filled with the acrid taste of fear. "You want to control me? I just told you—"

"Not control you," Dainn said. "Guide only."

Again and again, it all came down to how much she believed him, and she had even less reason to trust him than she had ten minutes ago. If she agreed, she would literally be putting her life—her being—in his hands. Her part in all this could end today if Dainn had some ulterior motive.

She turned to him again and stood in front of him, toe to toe. "If I find out you've meddled with my mind again while you're in it," she said, "I'll—"

"Kill me." He smiled, flashing perfect white teeth. "Fair enough, Freya's daughter."

It was the first time he'd really smiled, and it was a revelation. She could count on one hand the times she'd seen an elf smile in Valhalla. Dainn's expression turned the dim, dingy room into a candlelit palace. His rags became velvet, his hair as glossy as Sleipnir's silken mane.

The illusion didn't last, and when it ended, the room, and Dainn, seemed even shabbier than before.

"I may kill you anyway if you don't change your clothes," she said, sharp with annoyance at her lapse. "Did you think you were making yourself inconspicuous when you put those on?"

"I had hoped—"

"It didn't work. Do you think you can manage to keep the Jotunar quiet for a few more minutes? I'm going to see if Vidarr has any spare clothes in his office. Better that you flap around in his stuff than in those rags, and I'm not going to be able to concentrate with that stink in the air."

Dainn sank to the floor, settling himself into a meditative position. As Mist started for the back room, he began to sing.

Dainn's Rune-song died as Mist left the room. The ruined door was propped open, and he knew he would have little time to regain his equilibrium before she returned.

He would need every second. All the peace he had believed he'd found after centuries of searching—the peace not even Freya's sudden appearance was able to destroy—had been severely shaken the moment he had met Mist of the Valkyrie.

Closing his eyes, Dainn steadied his breathing and reconsidered everything that had happened in the past ten hours. That moment of meeting had been indelibly imprinted in his memory. Though he had never met Freya's unacknowledged daughter in Asgard, he had been in no doubt that the Lady's offspring would be possessed of a certain native allure and a striking presence that would affect anyone who saw her.

And she was beautiful, in spite of her obvious unawareness of her beauty. Her appearance was that of a twenty-eight-year-old woman; her candid eyes were gray with highlights of green, her cheekbones high, her lips full and firm, and her hair, fixed in a long braid at her back, was the gold of sun-kissed wheat.

But she was nothing like her mother. She regarded herself as a warrior, blunt of speech and manner. When she had first addressed him, he had actually wondered if she would be suitable for what Freya had in mind.

Mist had proven him wrong. The first time he had touched her flesh, seeking the confirmation of her identity in the tattoo around her wrist, he had already begun to feel it. And when he touched her mind, he had confirmed his impression that she was no mere Valkyrie. She was strong and courageous, to be sure, but Dainn had never had any use for warriors.

It was her inner core of strength, her determination to accept the impossible, that had shattered his preconceptions. She faced every difficulty with her eyes wide open and her mind ready for battle, physical or otherwise.

And that wasn't all. Very far from it.

Dainn filled his lungs on a slow count and absorbed the oxygen into every cell, feeding his weary body as well as his mind. In readying Mist for her ultimate destiny, he had thought at most he would be dealing with mere traces of Jotunar magic along with a little of her mother's instincts, and then only for a brief time.

His mistake had been costly. He had truly been unprepared to learn that the Slanderer had not only found Gungnir, but had also been living with Freya's daughter. The fact that Loki knew so much—and had so flagrantly broken the rules of the game—had been a considerable shock.

Dainn had intended to protect Mist, prepare her and hold her in ignorance of her ultimate fate, as he had been instructed to do. He had deliberately concealed her true heritage. But it had been impossible to keep Mist from following Laufeyson, impossible to prevent her from confronting him. To do so by any means other than physical force might have weakened his control and put her at even greater risk.

So she had come to Asbrew, and it was here that he had experienced an even more profound understanding of her soul than he had ever wished or intended. He had seen under that bold façade. Beneath her confidence lay uncertainty and deeply buried fears, dissonant notes of doubt in her own competence and worthiness to exist. Doubts she revealed to him only in her fear that it was Freya's power, not her own, that had sent Loki into flight.

Ordinarily Dainn could have played upon those doubts. He had failed, and he had no one to blame but himself.

He shifted position, unable to settle into that calm state of dispassion that had saved him so often over the long years. Freya had swept into Mist's mind without warning, without informing Dainn of her intentions, before either he or Mist was ready. She had behaved rashly, determined to make her presence known to Loki without regard for the consequences. Now Loki believed she could act in this world through Mist, and he would be ready the next time.

Dainn would not. Because when Mist had fallen under the mantle of Freya's power, he had seen just what would be destroyed when the Lady came to fulfill her purpose.

And that was when *his* doubts had begun to take hold. Dangerous, gnawing doubts about his mission, about what he had agreed to do to rid himself of his curse. And he had fallen—fallen so far that he had offered Mist a way out.

"You need do nothing. Walk away, Valkyrie," he had said, knowing all the while that her acceptance of his offer would mean the end of his hope for salvation.

But he had been saved from his own folly. His warning had fallen on deaf ears. Mist had defended him from Vidarr. She had chosen to continue working with him even though she knew what he had done. Even though she had seen his anger, the seething rage that he should never have allowed her to witness.

As long as all she saw was his anger, he was safe. If she had found the beast . . .

He shook his head, though there was no one to witness his denial save for the man at the table, insensible with drink. She hadn't found it—or if she had, she'd obviously doubted the validity of her own observation. But she would see it again if he did not take extreme care.

Now that he had a chance to recover what he had almost thrown away, he had to know what the Lady had seen for herself.

He looked toward Vali. Odin's less volatile son still seemed to be in a stupor, but Dainn couldn't afford to take the chance. He sang a sleeping spell, woven from the scent of flowers that had grown only in Alfheim, and waited until he heard a loud snore erupt from Vali's slack lips.

Settling down again, Dainn opened his mind. He sang a new song, a song of primroses, of love long lost, of yearning, of hope beyond hope.

"Dainn."

He bowed his head, the Lady's power pressing down on him like the weight of thousands upon thousands of fragrant blossoms, and for a moment he was unable to feel anything but the white heat of her love.

"I hear," he whispered.

"Where is my child, my Mist?"

"She is well, Lady," he said.

"And Loki?"

"He escaped with Gungnir."

Freya's disembodied voice caressed him. *"Gungnir is of no importance at the moment. I am more concerned with how the Slanderer managed to escape my notice until now. His behavior flies in the face of the rules, and he knows that I am no longer ignorant of it."* Dainn felt her smile. *"It's most fortunate that I sensed what was happening before he harmed her."*

Dainn shivered. He had taken precautions to make sure that the Lady could not read more than his surface thoughts, but even that could be dangerous. It was far better for him to give her as much information as was necessary to allay any concerns on her part. He could not afford to have her angry with him.

"I could not reach you," he said. "I am grateful your wisdom is so much greater than my own."

She was much too vain to grasp his sarcasm. *"How did she respond after I left?"*

"Your daughter believes it was her own magic that drove Loki away."

The Lady's sigh was the caress of a butterfly's wing against his cheek. *"You did right to tell her who she is and make her believe she alone won the skirmish. If she becomes suspicious, this will be much more difficult."*

"You overcame her will, Lady," he said.

"At some risk," she chided. *"I knew she would possess natural talent, but I underestimated the extent of it."*

"As did I," Dainn said.

"Which is why you must discover the scope of her abilities and make certain she has the necessary instruction to accept me. I cannot waste my magic on fighting my daughter's mind and spirit when the time comes."

"I will do my best."

Her response was almost playful. *"Such humility,"* she said. *"You were not always so."* The lightness left her voice. *"I took a great chance in helping you now. I will need all my resources to send my allies to Midgard. I rely on you to see that Mist is not put in jeopardy again."*

Dainn envisioned his mind contracting until there was no possibility that Freya would feel his true emotions. Lie upon lie he had told Freya's daughter, like many seasons' worth of autumn leaves piled one layer upon another, awaiting a spark to set them aflame.

"Forgive me, Lady," he said, bowing his head lower still.

"It is forgotten," Freya said, so gently that Dainn's empty stomach heaved with the knowledge of what lay behind that gentleness. *"I will not be so generous with my enemy."* She sighed, sending delicate zephyrs wafting around Dainn's head. *"Loki must always have known that Mist was my daughter, even in Asgard. It is unfortunate that he has discovered the strength of the connection between us, but at least he now realizes that he underestimated me, and so long as he believes I can appear in my daughter's stead whenever I choose, he will not so brazenly attack her again."*

"Even that belief will not stop him forever."

"He is and has always been a coward. He attempted to escape Midgard with Gungnir, did he not?"

"And found the bridge inaccessible," Dainn said. "Mist and I also discovered that the one Hrimgrimir used has vanished as well. Did you find a way to close them?"

"Why would I do so when I intend to use them myself?" she asked, the faint scent of primroses turning sour.

"Yet now they are being uncreated," Dainn said. "Coward or not, Loki still has all the advantages. The plans we made may no longer be effective."

"Do you still fear him so much, my Dainn?"

Such a tender punishment, Freya's mockery. She knew what he most feared.

"You have no concern that the bridges may no longer function?" he asked.

"It has always been clear to me that Loki does not have as much control over them as he would wish. I am not Loki."

Yet they had been one and the same once, Dainn thought. To him. "What of Vidarr?" he asked.

"It is a pity we did not know Odin's sons were in this city, but he and his brother were never reckoned as players in the game. Do you believe he will interfere?"

"He has no respect for the Lady Mist, and no reason to obey you."

"He, like Loki, is arrogant. But unless you have reason to think otherwise, I cannot see why he would stand in my way. I come closer to achieving our goals every day, every hour. Your only concern now is Mist herself." The scent of ripe blossoms changed to one of cloying sweetness, filling Dainn's lungs and draining the remaining strength from his body. *"I have the utmost confidence in you, my Dainn."*

Dainn gasped, struggling for a single lungful of untainted air. "You know . . . that the more I use my magic, the weaker the cage becomes."

"And you know you must keep control."

As if to emphasize her words, she pierced Dainn's heart with her sensuous power, slicing through the twisted, thorny bars of his inner cage as if they were constructed of paper straws. Her magnificent body appeared in his mind, lushly rounded, full-breasted, and blatantly erotic in its nakedness. Golden hair, bright as the Brisingamen itself, drifted around her shoulders as if it had a life of its own.

She could make him desire her. She could drive him mad with lust. She could do anything she chose to him, and his belief that he could resist her charms was no more than a pathetic attempt to maintain some shreds of what dignity remained to him.

"My poor Dainn," she said, reaching inside the cage. The beast

stirred and stalked toward her, the burning crimson of its gaze fixed on her face. *"There, there,"* she said, stroking the dense black fur. *"Would it be so terrible to love me?"*

Dainn squeezed his eyes closed, though what he observed could not be shut out even with blindness. "That was not our bargain," he said.

She fondled the beast's long, tufted ears. *"There is always a chance that you might choose to act against my will."*

"I would never act against your will," Dainn said, grinding his teeth together to distract himself from the ecstasy of her touch.

The beast vanished, and Dainn felt Freya's incorporeal hand stroke his cheek and move down his chest, penetrating both clothing and resistance, coming to rest on his painful erection. Her red lips brushed his. The kiss brought him to the edge of release, but she drew back abruptly, leaving him in unrelieved agony.

"I will come to you again when I have further instructions," she whispered as she left him. *"Do not disappoint me. You know that if you fail, I can take from you all of Dainn Faith-breaker that remains."*

8

Dainn fell forward over his knees, barely catching himself with his hands before he collapsed onto the floor. His blood roared in his ears and pulsed in his cock, erasing all rational thought.

But his mind was still capable of forming one clear image. Not of Freya, who had so casually tormented him, but of Mist . . . Mist, with her firm and womanly body, her golden hair, her strong and beautiful face. In his imagination that face wasn't frowning at him, full of suspicion and contempt. It was smiling, and her bare arms were stretched toward him, welcoming him as she lay naked on a bed of furs. She parted her thighs, ready for him, but he wasn't interested in her readiness. He fell on her like a brute savage and—

Dainn slammed his head against the floor. Red sparks exploded inside his skull. He rolled onto his side and lay still until the stabbing pain became a dull ache. Slowly he rose to his knees and brushed his hand through his hair, feeling it sticky with blood.

The injury would fade. Shame would ebb. Animal lust would subside, and he would once again become as sober and sexless as one of the ancient monks of the White Christ.

But none of his problems had been solved. Freya would have no patience with any hesitation or weakness on his part, and his only advantage was that she still faced certain limitations to her own powers, those posed by the rules of the game and her disembodied state. She would not be able to observe Dainn's every action or oversee his day-to-day decisions.

Still, there could be no more mistakes. It was not only *his* future that hung in the balance. If the Lady won the game, the Aesir would be safe. His own people would live and thrive again. Midgard—the Midgard Mist wanted so much to protect—would have its chance at becoming the new world the Prophecies had foretold.

At the cost of one woman's life. The life of one too honest, too forthright, too honorable to recognize the true extent of the web of lies he had woven around her.

And every time he touched Mist's mind . . .

He had told her his telepathic ability was a particular talent of his, and among all the other lies that one seemed very small. He had not been certain it would work until he "spoke" to her when she fought Loki.

There had been only one other with whom he'd had such contact, aside from Freya herself. And that had come to a violent end long ago.

Sickened and weary both physically and mentally, Dainn pulled himself together enough to make certain that both the Jotunar and Vali were still asleep. He had *not* lied when he'd told Mist that he was near the end of his strength. Freya had weakened his resistance when she had tampered with the cage he had built with such care. The more he used his magic, the closer he came to—

"Dainn?"

Mist's voice warned him just in time. He got to his feet and watched her approach with folded jeans, a plaid cotton shirt, and a pair of well-worn work boots in her arms.

"A *penningr* for your thoughts," she said, circling around the quiescent Jotunar with hardly a glance. She came to a dead stop when she saw the blood in Dainn's hair.

"What happened to you?" she asked.

"I fell."

"You *fell*?" Her brow creased. "Are you sure you're all right?"

Her seemingly genuine concern was so much at odds with her previous behavior that Dainn was momentarily shocked into silence.

"A moment of dizziness, no more," he said.

"Left over from working your magic?"

"Yes."

She continued to frown at him as she dropped the boots at her feet and brought him the bundle of clothes.

"I think these should be all right for you," she said. "You're about as tall as Vidarr, even if he's twice as wide as you are. Let's just hope he doesn't find out you're wearing his clothes."

Dainn turned the bundle in his hands. "I will do my best to stay out of his way," he said.

She leaned closer and peered at his head. "That's quite a goose egg you've got under there. I'll go get something to wash the blood off."

"It is not necessary. Is there a place I can bathe?"

"There's a bathroom in the bar, and Vid and Vali have rooms upstairs in the back, but obviously that's not an option. Vid has a sink in his office. You can use that to wash up when we've finished here."

"I am grateful."

"Believe me, I'm doing this more for myself than for you."

It was an attempt at humor, if a grudging one. Dainn gave her a brief nod, set down the clothes and began to shed his rags. Mist reddened and abruptly turned her back.

Curious. He had not expected such prudery from a Valkyrie, who saw bodies of every shape and state on the battlefield when she rode out to collect "heroes" to serve Odin in Valhalla. According to custom, the Choosers of the Slain were supposed to be virgins, but

Dainn knew that custom had been more honored in the breach than in the observance. Some of the Valkyrie had even married.

Mist herself had kept a lover, unaware though she had been of his true identity. Doubtless she had had others before Loki.

The image of bodies entwined filled Dainn's imagination, reminding him how close to the brink he stood. He steadied himself and deliberately released the tension from his body. The best defense against such emotions was not to pretend they didn't exist but to rob them of their power.

"I was not aware that Valkyrie were so modest," he said to Mist's back, examining the gaping waist of the jeans in his hands.

Her shoulders stiffened, and she turned around. "I thought you might like a little privacy," she said. "But since you don't—" She looked him up and down boldly. "Not bad for an elf."

"You have seen many Alfar unclothed?"

"Wouldn't touch one with a ten-foot staff."

Dainn tugged the jeans on with some force. "And Loki? Did *his* body please you?"

"His body wasn't—" She took a deep breath. "Loki's body isn't Eric's."

"Loki clearly found yours more than acceptable."

The remark was stupid, childish, and entirely born of the very emotions Dainn was attempting to disarm, but Mist didn't rise to the bait.

"Loki finds just about anyone pleasing," she said with bitter self-mockery, "or any*thing*."

She had no idea, of course, how effectively she struck at Dainn's own shame. Finding his balance again, he shrugged into the shirt. It was a size too big in breadth, but Mist had provided a belt to cinch the pants at the waist. The length of both was nearly perfect. He let the shirttail hang loose to cover the flaws in fit.

Mist looked him up and down again. "Acceptable," she said, "if a little working-class for an elf." She nudged the boots toward him with her toe. "Try these."

He knelt to put on the work boots. They, too, were a size too big, but they were better than the scraps he had worn on his feet for the past two days.

"Good," Mist said. "Now all we have to do is cut your hair."

Dainn winced. Little as she knew of elves, Mist had to be aware how much the Alfar valued their hair. His had been the only vanity he had permitted himself over the years, and he had stubbornly kept it long even when it made him more conspicuous, as it had in various places and times in the centuries following the Last Battle.

"I believe hair of this length is acceptable in the current decade," he said, getting to his feet.

She looked very much as if she wanted to argue, but she knew he was right. Long hair hid the particular feature that marked the Alfar apart from mortals, even if it also tended to attract attention.

"You can keep it," she conceded, "but don't let it get in the way." She glanced around the room, her gaze briefly settling on Vali. Odin's son had barely moved, his arms hanging loose at his side and his stubbled cheek resting flat on the tabletop.

"You put him to sleep?" she asked.

"It seemed prudent under the circumstances."

"Then I guess we'd better get these Jotunar out of here." She licked her lips, briefly revealing her unease. "What am I supposed to do?"

"Only let me guide you."

"Only," she muttered.

Dainn sat, and Mist followed suit. She faced him with legs crossed and hands resting on her knees. Dainn gave himself up to one of the many rituals he had developed to quiet his mind.

What he was about to do would require greater discipline than he had ever asked of himself—not because he might not reach deep enough into Mist's mind, but because he might reach too far and enable her to understand, beyond any doubt, what he truly was and why he was here.

"We will begin as we did before," he said. "But as you form the Runes in your mind, let your other thoughts drift like leaves on the wind."

"Skip the poetry," Mist said. "You want me to let my mind go blank, is that it?"

"As the Eastern masters do it."

"Should I meditate on clapping with one hand?"

"Think only of the Runes. But do not concentrate too hard on the process, or you will fail."

"Thanks for the vote of confidence," she said. She inhaled, slowly expelled the air, and closed her eyes. Dainn felt her agitation like a false note in a spell-song as she fought down her lingering suspicion and fear.

He touched her mind gently. She flinched. He reassured her by remaining on the surface, making no attempt to push, watching and waiting. Only when she had finally relaxed did he begin cautiously probing under the skin of the thoughts she could not quite suppress.

"Breathe deeply," he said. "When you are ready, shape the Runes as you did before."

She didn't respond, but soon enough the staves began to appear, each one flaring bright—far brighter than before—as if it were constructed of Thor's lightning, dazzling fire as quick as Mist's temper. Dainn reached for the Runes, touching one after another, and Mist began to tremble.

"Be easy," he said silently. *"There is no danger here."*

Mist could not yet make her thoughts coherent as words, but Dainn sensed the substance of her answer. *Get on with it.*

He slid a little further in, probing under the Runes and touching what lay beneath.

It was as if he had set a lit match to brittle grass in a drought-parched meadow. Mist's unconscious will to protect her mind—which he had felt only briefly before, when she had abruptly broken their joining at the loft—burst into a conflagration, a searing barrier that stopped him in his tracks. A violent wind hurled him back, and a great wall of seamless, ice-rimed metal thrust up through the seething flames.

Stunned by the attack, Dainn began to grasp what Mist had done. All unaware, and after only two encounters with his mind, she had learned how to create mental wards stronger than Dainn had believed possible for one without experience or training.

But there was far more to this than the building of mental defenses. Mist had created hers from a perfect joining of the elements. Some of the Aesir, like Thor, could control aspects of Air. The Muspellsmegir, the giants of Muspelheim, could wield fire and never be burned. The frost giants, like Hrimgrimir, commanded the forces of snow and ice. The Alfar and Vanir were the tamers of growing things, and the Dvergar masters of metal and earth. None, save the All-father himself, laid claim to power over all, and even he could join the elements only at great cost to himself.

The cost Mist might pay was as yet unknown, but Dainn knew he might not survive to find out. He fought to hold his ground and threw up a shield against the whirlwind, singing it into retreat with melodies of the hush of dawn and still summer days. But he could do nothing about the ice and flame and metal cutting him off from light, from air, from life itself.

He changed tactics, seeking under the wood and cement beneath him for uncontaminated earth, creating from Rune and elf-song a gauntlet of densely woven vines under a skin of air only thick enough to keep it alive. He eased his spectral hand through the maelstrom, barely brushing Mist's barriers with gentle fingertips, searching for even the smallest gap. He sang again, as all Alfar did when they made use of the Galdr.

Perthro, of Heimdall's Aett: the mystery of hidden things, initiation, destiny. Tiwaz, of Tyr's Aett: willingness to self-sacrifice. Kenaz, from Freya's Aett: the torch, symbol of revelation, transformation, opening to new strength and power. Uruz, the wild ox, the Rune of transformation, the shaping of power, the discovery of the self.

But the final Rune didn't obey his will. Mist took hold of the stave and turned it against him. Its angular, simple strokes quivered and rotated counterclockwise, Uruz reversed: lust, brutality, violence. Then the stave straightened, forming a single line with a needle point, and plunged through Dainn's magic-born gauntlet.

Unerringly it found its mark, passing through his heart and into the battered door within its once-impenetrable forest of poison and thorn, the prison Dainn had kept intact so long. The beast awakened and began to stir, swinging its vast head from side to side in search of the one who had disturbed its sleep.

Dainn gasped, undone by the ferocity of the attack and of the primal force that boiled unrealized beneath Mist's flesh, the unbridled strength of her unknown father and her mother's irresistible powers of seduction and desire. She taunted the beast, tossing Dainn's centuries of discipline aside like chaff before the wind. The creature extended its claws and raked at the wall of thorns, tearing the flesh from its massive paws. The intertwined branches began to shriek like souls lost to the Christian Hell.

In a moment the beast would be loose.

Somehow Dainn resisted, though the energy he was forced to expend seemed to feed off his bones and muscles and organs, eating him away from within. Struggling every step of the way, he drove the beast back into its prison and wove the waist-thick branches anew. With the last of his strength he regained mastery of his physical being, singing it down from the rage of its lust.

He came back to himself drenched in perspiration, every muscle quivering, Thor's Hammer beating on the inside of his skull. His stomach cramped, and he lurched up in search of a corner where he could empty it of its scanty contents.

When he was done, he wiped his mouth and leaned against the wall until he could breathe without gasping. Mist, only semiconscious, had barely moved from her original position.

She had no idea what had happened, no notion of what she was truly capable of. This was what he had just begun to sense when he had first touched her mind. What Mist had unwittingly shown him had not come only from Freya's influence or presence within her.

What he had felt was more ancient still—ability gleaned from Freya's Vanir blood, yes—but with elemental aspects that went beyond the magic wielded by most of the Aesir and their allies. Beyond any magic even the most powerful of the Alfar possessed, more than the Seidr that had existed even before the Runes had come to Odin. It was if she had reached back into the time before time and drawn upon the very force of life itself.

Carefully Dainn made his way to a section of the room well apart from both Mist and Vali. He eased himself to the floor, crossed his legs, and breathed rhythmically until he had shaken off all traces of sickness and fear. Sense returned, and with it the sure knowledge that he could no longer expect to complete his task by creeping about inside Mist's brain like a thief casing a house and slipping out again unseen. He had no idea when she might become aware of his attempt to identify and eventually neutralize her native magic.

"You must discover the extent of her abilities and make certain she has the necessary instruction to accept me," Freya had said. *"You must be sure that there will be no resistance."*

Dainn laughed deep in his throat, though the attempt left it raw and burning. Mist's unconscious reaction went well beyond mere "resistance." He must not only keep her from inadvertently killing him, but also find a way to breach her defenses. As long as Mist's power was uncontrolled, Freya's plan would fail.

But the more he pushed, the more magic he used, the closer the beast came to escape.

For now, there was still one task Dainn had to complete. He trained his fragile focus on the Jotunar across the room and called up the Rune Raiho, the chariot—safe enough—along with the image of a vast sirocco blowing the defeated giants into the middle of a bleak desert halfway around the world. A gust of searing wind knocked him sideways. He braced his hands on the floor and pushed himself back to his knees.

When he looked up again, Mist was staring at him, as wide-eyed as a child she most assuredly was not.

"What happened?" she asked. "Are you all right?"

Dainn rose carefully. "I am very well."

"That must be why you look like a snowflake could knock you over." She stretched her arms above her head and frowned. "I don't remember a thing. Are we finished?"

The Fates, Dainn thought, had done him some small kindness in the midst of their punishment. "See for yourself," he said.

She turned her head toward the place where the Jotunar had lain. Only a few dark blue bloodstains marked the spot.

"Where did you send them?" she asked, pushing loose tendrils of damp hair away from her forehead.

"*We* sent them to a place largely uninhabited by mortals," he said. "They will be bound to that place for at least a few days."

"Good," she murmured. But her expression was troubled, and Dainn wondered if she remembered more than she let on. "Did you keep your promise not to meddle in my head?"

"Does it feel otherwise?" Dainn asked cautiously.

She lifted her shoulders and let them fall again. "I don't know *what* I feel, but it's different from last time. How am I supposed to know what's normal?"

"The sensations are unique to each practitioner of magic. In time, you will become accustomed to your own reactions."

"In time," she echoed, meeting his gaze. "Look. I understand what you said about needing someone to help you and teaching me how to use whatever I have, but you can't expect—"

"I expect you to become what you were meant to be, Mist Freya's-daughter. You must learn to wield and control your magic, just as you wield your sword."

She stood up, facing him with legs apart and hands on hips, looking for all the world as if she intended to turn an entire blizzard against him. "I assume we're not only supposed to find the Treasures, but also keep Loki occupied until the Aesir show up, whenever that is. Not to mention finding out what's happened to the bridges Loki and Hrimgrimir used."

"Keeping Loki occupied is not your primary task."

"But getting Gungnir back *is*. Did you get in touch with Freya while I was in the other room?"

Dainn started. Had she heard or felt him speaking with the Lady? He had been too distracted at the time to set up proper wards, and if she had any idea what they had discussed . . .

"I did contact her," Dainn admitted, matching her offhand manner. "I made her aware of the situation. She believes the problems Loki had with the bridges are an anomaly."

"What does that mean?"

"That it may be Loki's problem alone."

"I hope that's true, since otherwise he could bring more Jotunar through anytime, right?"

"Now that the Lady knows that Loki is here and what he attempted in contacting you, she will better be able to counter his actions."

"How? Loki said she can't do much without her body, and she's still working on getting our allies to Midgard."

"She will send them soon," Dainn said, feigning certainty he was far from feeling.

"You never told me how many Jotunar Loki actually has here," Mist said, brushing aside his reassurances.

Dainn knew he still couldn't afford to tell Mist about the game or its rules—especially since Loki had already broken several of them—but she had given him another opportunity to dissuade her from taking unnecessary risks.

"Perhaps two dozen," he said, "perhaps as many as fifty. But he will move cautiously, since he obviously believes that Freya was acting through you and is capable of fighting him on his own terms."

Tugging her braid forward over her shoulder, Mist began to unwind the heavy blond plaits. "Loki may move more cautiously," she said, "but since what he believes isn't true—"

"What matters is that he *does* believe," Dainn said. "He is blinded by his feelings for Freya, both love and hate. He will continue to be deceived if you keep your distance from him as long as possible."

Mist gripped her half-undone braid tightly between her hands. "How are we going to stay away from him when we're both looking for the same things?"

"Loki will sacrifice any number of Midgardians in reckless or even hopeless ventures and use them to distract us and aid him in his search. Now we, too, must find mortals to fight on the Aesir's behalf."

"You mean put ordinary people in danger."

"Even with full access to your magic, you will not be omnipotent, and I certainly am not. It will be necessary for mortals to take their part in saving their world."

Suddenly all Mist's vulnerability and uncertainty were plain in her eyes, striking Dainn more surely than any magic she could throw at him. Fear, not of being hurt or dying, but of failure.

"Okay," she said, her eyes reflecting a painful memory of the necessities of war. "How do we go about finding these allies?"

Dainn permitted himself a moment of relief. "Loki will naturally seek the corrupt and greedy," he said. "We will find those dedicated to the good."

"Oh, of course." Mist finished unbraiding her hair and combed it through with her strong, slender fingers. "The 'corrupt and greedy.' Gangsters? Politicians? Terrorists? Serial killers?"

"I can only guess at Loki's choices, but he will use anyone who can serve his purpose."

"So you're talking about criminals and murderers and amoral public figures, some of whom have whole arsenals of guns and bombs and gods know what else? And you expect decent people to face that?"

"Conventional Midgardian firearms and similar weapons will not be effective in this war."

She stared at him. "Why not?"

Because, Dainn thought, it was another one of the "rules" of the game. "Freya has told me such weapons are *nidingsverk* to the Aesir—dishonorable, the tools of cowards who are unwilling to face their enemies in personal combat. No Alfr, Jotunn, or member of any other race involved will be permitted to use them."

"Why should Loki care about honor?"

"There are certain actions even he will not take if it will bring him bad luck, and his *gaefa* will surely vanish if he casts aside every law of the gods."

"So everyone will be fighting with swords, knives, and axes?

That should work well." She snorted. "You do realize that the people of Midgard haven't believed in us for hundreds of years? We can't just stick an advertisement on Craigslist: 'Wanted: fighters for the Aesir, must believe in giants and be skilled with the sword. Oh, by the way, you're probably going to get yourself killed. Want to join up?'"

"You are forgetting that there are some mortals who possess a limited degree of magical ability. Some will surely become aware of what has come into their world."

"The kind of mortals you're talking about are as rare as—" She grimaced. "Snowstorms in San Francisco. Sure, there are a few who claim to have mastered the Galdr, but most of them are quacks. Even if a few do sense that something is going on, what makes you think they'll find us, or even want to help?"

"Call it a feeling."

"You can't be serious."

"I seldom jest."

"You don't say." She flipped her hair back behind her shoulders in a thick, golden wave. "I hope you're not thinking of using some kind of summoning spell?"

"I do not believe it will be necessary."

"I don't like any of this. And I'm not satisfied with what little you've told me. But we can only do one thing at a time, and I'm most concerned about finding my Sisters. I don't know how far off the grid the other Valkyrie have been living, and obviously magic won't be enough to locate them." She frowned, lost in her own thoughts for a good minute. "We'll need access to every kind of data that might reveal their whereabouts. Computers, and people who know how to access records all over the world. Loki will be on it himself if he hasn't started already."

"I bow to your superior knowledge of Midgardian technology," Dainn said.

"Where *have* you been living, under a rock?"

There were times that he had been doing almost exactly that, entirely by choice. "I have often traveled where there are few such means of communication," he said. "But if you believe I must master these machines, I will do so."

"Do you even have a cell phone?"

Dainn spread his arms to indicate that all he possessed was fully visible to her. Mist rolled her eyes.

"Let's stick with the experts," she said. "Vali used to be good with computers. In fact, if I remember right, he was one of the earliest hackers, the ones who helped expose just how vulnerable electronic data could be." She looked toward the table, where Vali was lifting his head to display slack features and bloodshot eyes. "But he only did it for kicks, and he gave it up some time ago."

"Will he assist us?"

"We always got along pretty well, and he did help me today." She frowned, a distracted look in her eyes. "I have to admit I didn't think he was capable of doing what he did. Vid's always dominated him. Maybe Vali's finally ready to stand on his own two feet again . . . if he can stay sober."

"Do you think he will be prepared to tolerate my presence?"

"He's much more the forgiving type than his brother." Her gaze sharpened again. "What about the bridges? What if Freya's wrong about Loki's access to them?"

"She will monitor the situation and contact me if it becomes necessary."

Mist threw him a wary glance and nodded slowly. "It would probably be a good idea to put a warding spell around my loft in case Loki works himself up into a fighting mood again."

And helping Mist create such a spell, Dainn thought, would give him another chance to probe her mind again. Very carefully.

"I doubt Loki would dare attack your home," he said, "but it would be a wise precaution. Surely he will have Jotunar watching you at all times."

"Right. And once that's taken care of, I'm going after Gungnir."

"You must learn to control your magic if you are to be effective against him."

"But he thinks it was Freya who faced him at the end of the fight. Now is the best time to act, when he's still worried about her returning."

Dainn laughed silently at his assumption that he could prevent Mist from taking risks. "Where do you expect to find him?" he asked.

"Mist?" Vali croaked. With considerable effort, Odin's son levered his head and shoulders off the table. "Wa's happenin'? Where's Vid?" His bleary gaze slid to the center of the room. "Where's th' Jot'nar?"

Mist went to join him. "They've been taken care of," she said.

Vali sighed and slumped over the table again. "'S bad, isn' it?"

"Very bad." She sat in the chair opposite his, her legs straddling the seat. "But you can help do something about it."

"Me?"

"You were very brave today, and I'm going to rely on that courage a lot more from now on."

He blinked. "You wan' . . . *my* help?"

She reached across the table to lay her hand on his arm. "You're Odin's son, Vali. Baldr's avenger. I haven't forgotten, even if you have."

"I . . . don' wanna remember," Vali said, resting his cheek on the worn wood of the table top.

She squeezed his arm. "You need to get sober, Vali. I know how smart you are when you want to be. If we're to have any hope of finding my Sisters before Loki does, your skill with computers will be essential. You can help save this world."

A tear rolled over Vali's ruddy cheek. "I . . ." He looked up at Mist. "Okay." He tried to stand up, staggered, and righted himself again. "Wha' d'ya wan' me to do?"

"Dainn and I have to make some plans, so we'll go home for a while. I want you to come to my place when you're steady enough to drive, but I need it to be soon. Can you do that?"

"Sure." He grinned. "I'm glad you . . . beat Loki."

"I couldn't have done it without you."

"'N' him," Vali said, waving in Dainn's general direction.

Mist rose. "If you get a chance to talk to Vid, maybe you can get him to speak with me again."

"Doubt it," Vali muttered. "Once he's made up 'is mind . . .'"

"Try. He should know better than anyone what's at stake."

Vali nodded, threw back his broad shoulders, and wove his way toward the bar door. Mist returned to Dainn.

"I guess you don't have any money," she said.

He shook his head.

"No wallet? No ID?"

"I seem to have misplaced it."

"Anything socked away in Switzerland or the Cayman Islands?"

"I have a little, but I have not touched it in years."

"Then you'd better think about accessing it. I have a feeling we may need it." She patted the rear pocket of her jeans. "I have more than enough to pay for a hotel room for you until we can arrange something else."

Apprehension tightened Dainn's throat. In spite of her earlier cooperation, Mist didn't want him in her home.

"I do not think it wise that I have separate lodgings, now or in the future," he said. "You have no need to fear that I will invade your privacy except at your invitation."

"My invitation?" Her eyes hardened to opaque chips of ice. "What is *that* supposed to mean?"

"I will need to be on hand not only to teach you, but to aid you if Loki returns before we are prepared."

It seemed they were to engage in a silent duel of wills, a duel Dainn could ill afford to lose. But suddenly Mist dropped her gaze and gave a small, rueful shrug.

"You're right," she said. "I have a couple of extra rooms. If you keep out of my way when we're not actually working together, I may let you stay."

"As you say, Lady."

"I'm not your 'Lady.'"

"What name would you prefer?"

"I guess it'll have to be Mist."

As small a concession as it was, Dainn knew how much it had cost her. She didn't yet like him, but she had chosen to accept his help, if only provisionally.

That she did not like him should not matter to him. In fact, it would be far better if she maintained her physical distance, and he did the same.

Better for both of them.

"Let's go," she said.

Without another word, Mist started for the bar door. Dainn followed her into the front room.

It was soon apparent from the patrons' behavior that none of them suspected what had been going on out of their sight. Loki had warded the back rooms well, and Vidarr would undoubtedly erase any evidence that there had been unusual activity anywhere in the establishment. No one so much as glanced at Dainn as he walked toward the front door.

The brawny doorman was gone, but another man stepped out in front of Dainn as he reached the entrance. Vidarr grabbed his arm and pushed his face close to Dainn's.

"I don't know what you're really doing here," he said in a low voice, "but you're a traitor, and you won't stop being one just because you're working for Freya."

Dainn stood very still, aware that the beast had been drawn to the surface too many times in the past few hours to tempt again now. "I work for all the Aesir, for my own people, for their allies," he said.

"Even if I believed you, I'd know you're hiding something." Vidarr bared his teeth. "Freya is as much a schemer as Loki, isn't she? I know why she didn't contact me or Vali. She has no connection with us. But I expect to hear from my father any time now, and if I find out you've been lying—"

"You may be a god, Vidarr Odin's-son," Dainn said, "but you have no understanding of what has happened. The All-father has his own concerns, and Freya has been charged with protecting the Treasures. Either you assist us, or you are a liability."

"Is that some kind of warning?" Vidarr asked with an incredulous laugh.

"I give no warnings," Dainn said. "I only emphasize the nature of the threat that faces all of us."

"I think you're part of the threat, elf. Sooner or later you'll make a mistake." Spinning on his heel, Vidarr hurled Dainn at the door. "And when you do," he said, "I *will* kill you."

9

Vidarr stalked away without a backward glance. Dainn straightened and rubbed at his arm. There was a part of him, a very lethal part, that was eager to take up Vidarr's challenge.

But he still had enough sense to resist the impulse. And to ignore what both Vidarr had implied about his relationship with Mist. He went out the door, moving stiffly, and joined Mist on the sidewalk.

"Took you long enough," Mist said, subjecting him to a brief but searching glance. "Let's go."

She set off at a fast pace, returning the way they had come. The early morning sun had come out from behind the canopy of gray clouds that painted the sky from one horizon to the other, but Dainn knew the brief respite wouldn't last. He had seen the vast changes in weather all over the world, and snow in San Francisco was hardly the worst of it. It constantly amazed him how mortals could engage in such furious denial of obvious fact.

The fact that Fimbulvetr—the Great Winter—was already here.

He and Mist walked back to her automobile, which sported a parking ticket under the windshield wipers. Mist snatched it free and read it with a muttered curse.

"Just what I need," she said. She unlocked the door and slid behind the wheel. Her efforts to start the engine were unsuccessful.

"It's dead," she said. "Should have gotten it replaced a year ago, but I was sort of fond—" She glanced at Dainn and pulled a cell phone from an inner pocket of her jacket.

After she had made arrangements for the car to be towed to a local repair shop, she scratched out several Rune-staves on a sheet from a small pad of paper tucked inside the glove compartment, tore it out, and placed it under the wipers where the ticket had been.

"Should keep the cops away until the truck gets here," she said. "We'll take Muni."

Dainn followed Mist to the streetcar stop, grateful for her continued silence. He had much thinking to do. He was still troubled by the closures of the bridges on the Golden Gate and in the park. Freya's assurances had eased some of his concern, but he knew he would have to confirm her belief that the other bridges would still serve to transport their allies. He sincerely hoped the Lady would not have a rude awakening when she attempted to send the Alfar across.

"It's here," Mist said beside him, and Dainn returned to the present in time to board the streetcar. He kept his senses alert, both physical and magical, as he and Mist rode toward the neighborhood incongruously named Dogpatch.

He became aware that someone was following them well before the streetcar reached the Twentieth Street station. Mist seemed oblivious, as intent on navigating the maze of her own troubled thoughts as he had been earlier, but he knew that one among the other passengers was a little too interested in their movements.

He observed carefully as he and Mist left the streetcar. None of the passengers who got off at the same stop seemed to be traveling in their direction. Dainn dropped behind Mist as she walked to Twentieth Street. They passed a small ice cream shop, a coffee bar, and a store featuring eclectic apparel, but Dainn caught no glimpse of any follower or sensed the presence of a potential enemy.

It was impossible not to notice, however, how many lingering glances Mist attracted. He had been too preoccupied to pay attention before they'd boarded the streetcar, but it was now apparent that other mortals, males in particular, seemed to find her fascinating enough to compel protracted stares as she passed by.

She was striking, yes, but this was more than a matter of mere beauty or the graceful, almost sinuous motions of a well-formed woman trained to fight. Mist was Freya's daughter, newly awakened to her power. If once she had been able to move unnoticed and unremarked, it was unlikely she would ever be able to do so again.

And that was more than ample explanation for his sense of pursuit. The Norns alone knew how many pairs of eyes had been fixed on her during the ride.

When they arrived at Mist's loft a few minutes later, she paused as if listening for a voice she would never hear again. Her shoulders slumped as she unlocked the door, releasing wards no longer effective against anyone but mortal thieves.

Unwillingly aware of Mist's pain, Dainn followed her into the entrance hall. She turned right almost immediately into a side hallway that ran parallel to the street, facing a large paned window, and led Dainn to the second door.

"You can sleep here," she said, her voice strained with suppressed emotion. "I'd give you a room upstairs, but it's pretty messy up there. I really only use the ground floor. I bought the warehouse so I could set up a gym with plenty of room."

She opened the door to a plain, sparsely furnished room with a narrow bed, a chest of drawers, and a chair painted to suggest a weathered effect.

"I'll show you the bathroom," she said. "And I guess you're probably hungry. I don't have much in the house right now. Can you make a sandwich?"

The question was absurd, but Dainn wasn't inclined to quibble. "Yes," he said. "I would be grateful for the opportunity."

She led him back the way they had come and along the main

hallway leading to the kitchen at the rear of the ground floor. The ashes of Loki's note were still smeared across the tabletop.

Mist went directly to the sink, dampened a dish towel, and wiped up the ashes with hard, fast strokes. She threw the dish towel into a trash can and slapped her palms against each other as if to remove any traces of ash. And Loki.

A pair of large, thick-coated cats—one gray and white, one red—emerged from a small room adjoining the kitchen. The heavy fur along their spines was slightly raised, and they moved cautiously, nostrils flaring, tails low and large eyes watchful as they approached Mist.

Knowing that Mist was observing him with great interest, Dainn knelt to offer his hand to the cats and spoke softly in the Old Tongue. The larger of the animals, the gray and white, chirruped an inquiry but did not come closer. The red and white cat hung well back, refusing Dainn's overtures.

"I wondered how they'd feel about elves," Mist said, leaning against the counter. "Everyone knows the Alfar are better with animals than any other immortal, and cats are sacred to Freya. Interesting that Lee is so standoffish."

Dainn rose. "We understand that the nature of cats is unlike that of any other beast," he said, knowing it could have been much worse. The cats might have rejected him completely, sensing what he could become.

Mist took a pair of small bowls from a cupboard and filled them with kibble out of a bag kept under the sink. She carried the bowls into the adjoining room. The cats trotted at her heels, glancing back at Dainn from the doorway before seeking their meals.

"All I've got is sliced turkey and some Jarlsberg," Mist said, washing her hands and opening the refrigerator door. "A couple of tomatoes, and lettuce, wilted. Mayo and mustard. Sprite. And some—"

She stopped, and Dainn heard her catch her breath. "Diet Coke," she finished, very quietly.

Dainn assumed that must have been Eric's beverage of choice, though he had a difficult time imagining Loki with a soda can in his hand. "Water will be sufficient," he said.

"Good," she said. "Then I can get rid of these." She withdrew four cans from the refrigerator, set them on the counter, and then tossed two thin packages on the table. "Bread's over by the stove," she said, popping the tabs on the four cans one by one.

Dainn found the bread and plates in the cupboard, sat at the table, and watched Mist out of the corner of his eye as she unceremoniously poured the contents of the cans into the sink and tossed the empty containers into a plastic bin. She gazed into the bin for a moment, then returned to the refrigerator and removed a bottle of amber liquid Dainn recognized as beer. As Dainn finished making the sandwiches, she twisted off the cap and took a long drink.

Dainn pushed one of the plates toward her. She set the bottle down and stared at the sandwich uncomprehendingly.

"I'm not hungry," she said.

"Alcoholic beverages will not enhance your mental faculties, or your strength."

She leaned over the table, her stance belligerent. "Do you even drink?"

"On occasion. This does not seem to be one of them."

Abruptly she grabbed the plate and pulled it toward her across the table. Dainn took a measured bite of his sandwich. Mist filled a glass of water from the tap and set it down next to his plate. He nodded thanks, she took the nearest chair, and they ate in silence until the sandwiches, and Mist's beverage, were gone.

"You *can* make a sandwich," she said with a huff of strained laughter. "Can you cook, too?"

Dainn permitted himself a small smile. "I have been known to make meals out of ingredients of dubious provenance and questionable edibility."

"And that's supposed to be an endorsement? Excuse me if I don't ask you to help out in the kitchen." She sobered quickly. "I never thought I'd be sharing a meal with one of the Alfar at my own kitchen table. Where in Midgard *have* you been all this time?"

"There are few places I have not been," he said. "Most recently in the Himalayas, where I was studying with a lama in Tibet."

"Oh, boy. If anyone else had told me that, I—"

Her sentence ended abruptly as she turned to stare in the direction of the front door.

"Someone's outside," she said.

Dainn heard it as well, a faint brush of cautious footsteps on cement.

"It's probably a package delivery," Mist said, starting down the hall. "No Jotunn would make so much noise."

"We were followed on the streetcar," Dainn said.

She stopped. "And you didn't tell me?"

"I determined there was no threat to us."

She cast him a scathing look and went to the door. "There's someone there, all right," she said. "And they aren't ringing the doorbell."

"Your visitor is a mortal," Dainn said, casting his senses wide. "And female."

"Then I'll just find out what she wants."

She flung open the door. There was no one there, nor anywhere within sight. Muddy mid-morning sunlight crowded the shadows crouched at the foot of the wall.

"She's gone now," Mist said. "Do you think Loki's already recruited mortal spies?"

"Perhaps." He hesitated, considering whether or not he should tell her that she would have to become accustomed to being pursued by total strangers. "I sensed nothing unusual about her."

She closed the door almost reluctantly, as if she regretted the necessity of sealing herself in with Dainn. "We should have set fresh wards as soon as we got here," she said. "Are you up for it?"

Dainn's body ached, and there was a hovering blackness behind his eyes he couldn't dispel. "We will not be able to stop Loki," he said, "but we will be warned if any Jotunn approaches."

"That'll have to be good enough for now. Same as before?"

He couldn't risk joining their minds and magic again so soon. He was in no condition to prevent her from unconsciously attacking him as she had before, or keep her from inadvertently provoking the beast.

And this time she might remember.

"*I* will do it," he said.

"I don't think—"

"An alarm ward requires relatively little effort."

The hollows under her eyes suggested that she was too weary to argue for the privilege. She turned and walked toward the kitchen. Dainn followed. The cats had vanished, though Dainn smelled their presence nearby, just as he smelled once-green grass somewhere behind the loft.

He continued through the adjoining laundry room, out the back door to a tiny yard and sat cross-legged on the brown, weedy patch of lawn. After he had called up the Rune-wards, he paced out the perimeter of the entire building and set them in place, tracing intricate, intertwining variations on the walls with his finger and reinforcing them at the laundry room door, the front door, and a door opening onto to the driveway that ran alongside the loft. After he was done, he did the same to the windows, giving special attention to those facing the crumbling factories along the waterfront. Of the intruder there was no further sign.

When he was finished, he returned to the loft, almost tripping over the threshold. Mist was waiting there and caught him by the arm.

"I assume even Alfar have to sleep," she said, quickly releasing him. "You'd better get some rest."

Exhaustion and exasperation battered at Dainn like Jotunar fists. "You still intend to go after Gungnir," he said.

"I intend to find out what Loki's up to."

"You must not." He sighed. "Not without me."

Her mouth set in stubborn line. "You aren't in any state to help me."

It wasn't his intention to touch her, but an impulse beyond rational thought made him seize her arm in an iron grip. "We already discussed the inadvisability of your getting too close to him, and you certainly cannot risk a confrontation."

She stared down at his hand on her arm as if it were a loathsome insect. "I never said I'd hide from him, did I?"

"Your magic is in its infancy. Loki will not long be deceived by any attempt you make to imitate your mother's power."

"I'll be careful," she said, snatching her hand out of his.

"You neither know nor understand what he is capable of."

"And you *do*, because you helped him."

Dainn's hand trembled as he fought off the urge to take hold of her again. "Loki may have been set at a small disadvantage by his confrontation with you, but he cannot have sent all his Jotunar away, and Hrimgrimir escaped. You have some Jotunar magic, some small knowledge of Galdr, and a brief acquaintance with your mother's skills. But even if you had the smallest chance of defeating them with the little knowledge you have now, you must still find them first." He made no attempt to hide his mockery, which effectively concealed his desperation. "Undoubtedly you can locate lost car keys or a misplaced cell phone, but could you have found Loki the first time without my direct help?"

"Loki will leave a trail of magic a mile wide."

"One *I* might follow. You are not ready."

Yanking her loose hair behind her head, she began to braid it again with ungentle fingers. "I'm going to try."

"Then promise me that if you find a trail of any kind, you will wait for me. I will find you."

"Maybe you've forgotten what I told you. No one, least of all you, is giving me orders."

"It is a request," he said.

Leaving her thick hair only half braided, Mist reached inside her inner jacket pocket and pulled out several small squares of wood. The fact that Mist knew she needed them for carving the staves was proof enough that she had no confidence in her ability to use the mental Runes he had begun to teach her.

She tucked the pieces of wood back into her pocket and drew the knife from her belt. She weighed it in her hand and turned it over to display the Runes etched into its silver blade. "Don't come after me," she said, sheathing the weapon again.

"Mist—"

But she was already striding toward the front door. He took a few steps after her and staggered, beaten down by exhaustion. Exhaustion that held him back from pressing his magic too hard, weakening his hold on his other self. He could not help Mist in this state.

He went to his room, took off his boots and lay on the narrow bed. It was far more comfortable than anything he had slept on in many months.

Sleep, however, was not on his agenda. He lay awake, monitoring his strength, waiting for the moment when he could safely follow Mist. The sounds of human activity thumped and rattled and hummed outside, automobile engines and streetcars and raised voices from busy Third Street with its peculiar mixture of small stores, warehouses, and residences.

When the soft footsteps came, Dainn rose, left his room and went barefoot to the front door. He lunged outside, grabbing for the slight figure who was already turning to run. He glimpsed a thin, brown, defiant face before the girl squirmed around to attack him, scratching with fingers bent like claws and kicking frantically at his legs. She was all wiry muscle and very little spare flesh, remarkably strong for her size and weight.

Dainn held her away from him and kept his grip as she cursed and struggled and screamed at him in Spanish. He knew almost at once that his first assessment of the mortal at Mist's door had not been correct.

This one was no ordinary girl. She was either Loki's spy, or the first of the Mist's Midgardian allies.

It was too easy.

When Mist returned to stand outside Asbrew, she smelled traces of Loki in the air, as if he had left the residue of his evil wherever he walked, like a snail laying down a trail of slime.

Of course he hadn't *walked* out of Asbrew. He'd made a dramatic exit, disappearing into thin air. But he couldn't fly unless he turned himself into an eagle, as he'd done more than once in Asgard, or made use of his flying shoes. Mist was pretty sure he didn't have those with him.

No, he'd have found a taxi. It was even possible that he'd had transportation waiting for him somewhere out of sight when she and Dainn had arrived at Asbrew.

And that was the problem. If she could sense Loki with so little difficulty, Dainn was probably right. Loki might very well have laid a trap for her, and only the Norns knew what was lurking in it.

Still, she went around the corner and into the narrow street between Asbrew's block and the block on the opposite side. The lingering traces of magic were stronger here. She knelt to touch the cracked pavement where a large vehicle had left black skid marks on the road.

Loki's escape car. Not big enough to hold a dozen giants, so he obviously hadn't intended them to ride with him when he left Asbrew. Assuming, of course, that he'd expected them to leave with him at all. Mist wondered if he knew where she and Dainn had sent the Jotunar and if—when—Loki would succeed in getting them back.

But that worry was for another time. She pulled a piece of wood from her pocket, laid it flat on top of the tire marks, drew the knife, and carved three Runes deeply into the surface. She nicked her finger and squeezed the blood into the staves. When they were filled, she removed her lighter and put the small flame to the corner of the wood.

It was consumed in a few seconds. Remembering what Dainn had done at the loft, she dipped her slightly bleeding finger into the ash and drew the same Runes on her forehead. A young woman walking a dog paused at the entrance to the street and stared at Mist while her terrier barked frantically.

Mist looked up, and the woman beat a hasty retreat. But Mist wasn't worried about observers. She had focused all her concentration on the Runes sketched across her forehead, imagining them burning into her brain.

Suddenly she could feel something—a sense of direction, of movement continuing north on the street. She got up slowly and followed her hunch.

It didn't take long before she found evidence that the vehicle had pulled into a side alley, made a sharp Y-turn, and reversed direction.

She was about to return the way she had come when she heard the choked cries coming from the alley. Without hesitation, she ran into the dim corridor, racing past colorful graffiti with fat letters the height and width of a man and skirting malodorous garbage blown in by the winter wind.

Two Jotunar in reasonably human shape were crouched in the alley where a battered chain-link fence blocked pedestrian traffic. They weren't the biggest Mist had seen, but they were considerably larger than the figure lying on the dirty cement between them.

A boy. Or, more accurately, a young man, flat on his back and jerking wildly as if he was in the midst of a seizure. Mist launched herself straight at the Jotunn on the left, drawing Kettlingr as she attacked and chanting it to its full and lethal size.

The first giant wasn't prepared. He fell backward as Mist slashed down, belatedly raising an arm the width of a small tree trunk to fend off the blow. Kettlingr bit deep, and the giant roared in pain.

By then the other Jotunn was on Mist's back. He drove her down with the weight of his body, and only her quick reflexes saved her from being reduced to a red splotch on the pavement. She rolled out of his way, gasping as a cracked rib grated in her chest but somehow managing to maintain her grip on her sword. The second giant began a chant as harsh and booming as a wrecking ball slamming into a decrepit apartment building. Mist's breath turned to fog, denser than any ordinary cold could produce. She knew then that they didn't intend to kill her. The first giant, still grunting with pain, had joined the second in creating the spell, and Mist felt her jacket begin to crackle with a heavy layer of frost. It penetrated her jeans and crunched inside her boots, cracked her lips and rimed each hair of her eyebrows. They would encase her in layer after layer of frost, transforming her into a sculpture of living ice.

But they had forgotten about the boy. He was no longer shaking but had rolled onto his side, grasping a length of rebar in his slender hand. He swung it at the first Jotunn's legs with surprising force.

The giant staggered and lost his balance. As he turned on the young man, fist raised, the boy jumped up and ran between the Jotunar like a mouse scurrying under the legs of a hungry cat. The first Jotunn, the wound in his arm still bleeding freely, set out after him.

But the spell was broken, and the ice slicking Mist's clothes and body began to melt immediately. As soon as she could move, she raised Kettlingr and ran after them. She found them just outside the mouth of the alley, the boy hanging between them as if he weighed no more than a handful of snowflakes.

Mist yelled and swung Kettlingr at the Jotunn she had already wounded. The blade seemed to catch fire, blazing as if it had drawn the weak rays of the sun and multiplied their light a hundredfold. The moment it hit the Jotunn, he screamed with real terror and let the boy drop. The second Jotunn backed away in confusion, his gaze fixed on the burning steel.

All at once the giants gave up, spun around and ran, the injured giant clasping his smoking side. Mist followed them a short distance, heard the screeching of tires on Eddy, and stopped. She stared down at the sword in her hand. It was normal again, Rune-etched metal a dull gray as the sky clouded over.

"Are you okay?"

She turned to face the boy. He was Caucasian, about seventeen, maybe eighteen . . . lanky, boyishly good-looking and clearly scared out of his wits. He had a small cut on his chin, and Mist was sure he'd have a whopper of a black eye in a few hours. She suspected there were more injuries she couldn't see. It was more than a little ludicrous that he'd asked if *she* was okay, especially since she was holding a sword in her hand.

"I'm fine," she said, ignoring her cracked rib. "Are you hurt?"

The young man shook his head. "A little roughed up," he said, his voice still hoarse with fear. "But I'm used to that."

Mist didn't ask what he meant. She had a pretty good idea. "Why were they after you?" she asked.

"Those . . . men?" he asked, shivering hard. "I don't know." He looked down at Kettlingr. "That's real, isn't it?"

No matter what she did now, Mist knew the kid had probably seen things more disturbing than the sight of her sword turning back into a knife. She whispered the spell and put the weapon away. The young man didn't make a sound.

"Can you tell me what happened?" she asked.

"I was waiting out here," he said, "and these things attacked me. I think they wanted me for something, but they didn't say what."

"Why do you call them 'things?'"

"Because I know they weren't . . . I mean, they weren't just addicts looking for drug money or anything." He wet his lips. "You fought them. They weren't really men at all. You *know*."

And so, obviously, did he, Mist thought. "I'm sorry you had to go through this," she said.

He brushed a shock of ragged blond hair out of his eyes. "What were they?" he asked.

Mist knew she could stop it right there, give the boy a little money, send him off to urgent care. But over the past twenty-four hours she'd learned not to ignore her instincts. It wasn't a coincidence that the Jotunar had been here, right in the same place where Loki's getaway car had been waiting. It couldn't be just chance that they'd attacked this particular kid.

"I don't think you'll believe me," she said.

He smiled, an expression that was as real as it was unexpected. "I think I will. It's not like I have anything to lose, right?"

Mist hesitated, wondering how to begin. "What's your name?" she asked.

"Ryan," he said. "Ryan Star—" He shivered violently. "Starling."

"You're freezing," Mist said. She shrugged out of her jacket and handed it to him. "Take this."

"Don't you need it?"

"I don't get cold easily," she said, trying to be as gentle as she could. Not that she'd ever had much to do with kids his age—or any age, for that matter.

"My name is Mist Bjorgsen," she said. "We should find somewhere to talk where you can sit down."

"No." Ryan pulled the jacket around his shoulders. "I want to know what's happening to me." His eyes pleaded with her. "I need to know."

And his life might depend on that knowledge, Mist thought. "Do you know anything about Norse mythology?" she asked.

Ryan's gaunt face went blank. "Uh . . . is it like *Lord of the Rings*?"

"Not exactly. The author borrowed from it, though. Elves, dwarves, trolls. Quite a few other things. But it started long before he wrote the book."

"I didn't read it," Ryan said, thoroughly dazed. "I snuck into the movie, when I—" His eyes cleared. "The war," he said. "The bad guy with the burning eye, and the Orcs. And the elves were on the good side."

"In Norse mythology, it wasn't Orcs who worked for the bad guy," Mist said, carefully watching his face. "It was giants. Jotunar."

"Oh, God." The boy dragged his hand across his mouth. "Is *that* what they were?"

"I wouldn't blame you if you didn't—"

"I believe you," he said slowly. "Your sword . . . is it magic, like the one in the movie?"

"Not quite the same," Mist said. "But it's real."

"I saw the fire," Ryan said, dazed again. "It *is* magic."

Mist wondered how she was going to be able to hide her abilities with the Jotunar going around beating up mortals right in front of her. "Do you believe in magic, Ryan?" she asked.

"Yeah. I think . . . ever since I was a little kid. I just didn't know I did. I didn't know what it all meant." He shivered again. "That mythology stuff . . . it isn't just fairy tales, is it?"

"No." She sighed. "I don't know how to make this any easier for you, Ryan. You said you didn't know why the giants were after you, right?"

"I didn't even see them. One second I was alone, and then they were there. They dragged me into the alley. They were too strong for me to fight."

"They're too strong for almost any mortal to fight," Mist said.

"Mortal?"

Too much, too soon. Mist knew she'd have to be a little more careful. "Let's worry about that later. You must have had something they wanted. You can't think what that might be?"

"I think . . . I think they wanted *me*," he said.

"Why, Ryan? Why would they want to kidnap you?"

"I don't know." He looked at her again as if he were seeing her for the first time. "I came here because I was looking for something. Some*one*, I mean."

"Who?"

"I think it must have been you."

Mist stiffened. "What do you mean?"

"I recognize you now. You were always there, in the middle."

"In the middle of what?"

"The war."

10

————

It took Mist a moment to grasp what he was saying. "What war?" she asked, her hand slipping to the sheath of her knife.

Ryan didn't seem to notice her tension. "Winter that never ends. Fire and ice. Things rising up." His voice turned pensive. "I didn't understand until now. I must have known you would be here."

"*How* did you know?" Mist asked, her muscles tensing to ward off an attack.

"In the dreams," he said. "Gabi told me to wait, but I had to find you." He stared around him at the old buildings and pockmarked street. "I didn't think it would happen this way."

Half of what he was saying made no sense. Some of it made all too much. This could have been a trap all along. Jotunar attacking an innocent mortal for no apparent reason. Loki knowing she wouldn't walk away from someone in trouble.

Was it possible that she was facing Loki himself?

Wouldn't I know?, she thought. The Jotunar hadn't been faking their treatment of the kid.

Still, she kept her distance until the boy began to sway on his feet. She caught his arm, and he flinched as if he expected to be hit. Mist concentrated, hoping she'd recognize the taint of Loki's influence if she found it.

Nothing. But she did feel a wisp of emotion like a cirrus cloud quickly stretched and dispersed by the wind, an echo of what she had felt when she and Dainn had linked minds to search for Loki. Even the feelings were much the same: fear, shame, anger. Mostly at himself.

Mist let him go and weighed her options. If he'd been part of a trap, it surely would have been sprung by now. Still, the safest thing would be to leave him here. From the looks of him, he'd been in pretty bad shape even before she'd found him—a street kid, most likely, trying to survive in any way he could. At least she could give him a little money for clothes and food.

But if there was a reason the Jotunar had wanted him . . .

"Dreams," he'd said. Dreams of war and winter and "things rising up." They almost sounded like visions.

"You were having a seizure back there, weren't you?" she asked.

He nodded, as if the question made perfect sense after her long silence. "It happens sometimes. When I have the dreams."

Curse it, Mist thought. The last thing she wanted to do was take the kid home, a total stranger who could be anybody, anything at all.

She looked him up and down, from ragged sneakers to jeans riddled with holes and a long-sleeved T-shirt that had seen much better days. "How long has it been since you've eaten?"

"I don't know. A couple days, maybe." He stared at the ground. "Look," he said. "I know I sound crazy, but I can help."

"Help with what?" Mist asked cautiously.

"I can—" Without warning he fell onto his back, cracking his head on the pavement as he began to convulse. His eyes rolled back in his head again, and his feet drummed on the ground in a violent, uneven rhythm.

Mist dropped down beside him and turned him on his side. She retrieved her fallen jacket, bunched it up, and touched him just long enough lift his head and lay it on the jacket.

An ambulance, she thought, reaching for her cell phone.

But she stopped before she could punch in the first digit. Ryan had suddenly gone still, his body still jerking a little but no longer in the throes of the seizure. He grabbed her wrist and hung on as if she were his last hope of salvation. He coughed and rolled his head toward her. There were tears in his eyes.

"Don't call them," he whispered. "There's nothing they can do."

"Ryan—"

"I have to go with you," he said. "I think you need me. And Gabi."

Whoever *she* was. Mist lifted Ryan's head from the jacket and cradled it in her hand.

"Do you always dream like this, Ryan?" she asked.

"Long as I can remember."

"Can you get up?"

"Yeah." He bit his lip and tried to sit. Mist helped him, and when he was ready she supported him and helped him stand. His skin twitched like that of a horse shaking off flies.

"I'm taking you with me," she said when he was steady on his feet. "You can tell me everything you know. But you'll have to trust me completely."

He nodded slowly. "I get it." He smiled, the corners of his lips trembling. "I won't freak out, I promise."

Realizing she might be making a very bad mistake, Mist helped him to Eddy Street. She phoned for a taxi, and in less than fifteen minutes one pulled up to the curb. The cabbie glanced at Mist with interest, staring just a little too long, but she stared back until he found it prudent to look away and do his job.

The cabbie let them off in front of the loft, and she threw the money down on the passenger seat as she walked with Ryan to the front door, ready to catch him if he started to fall.

Dainn was waiting at the door. He glanced at Ryan with a frown.

"It seems we are to have another visitor," he said.

Mist stopped, holding Ryan by the arm. "Another?"

Dainn stepped back to let her in. Ryan sucked in a sharp breath and turned his head to look at Dainn as he and Mist went by.

"What's going on?" Mist asked as soon as Dainn closed the door.

"Come and see for yourself," he said, gesturing in the direction of the kitchen.

Mist practically dragged Ryan with her and stopped in the kitchen doorway. A Latina of about sixteen sat at the kitchen table devouring a sandwich, a glass of Sprite beside her place. She looked up as Mist approached, almost bolting from her seat.

"Gabi!" Ryan said.

She shoved her chair back and rushed to Ryan, wrapping her thin brown arms around his waist. He returned her hug and pulled away.

"Estupido!" she exclaimed. *"Idioto!* I told you to wait until I made sure it was safe!"

"I couldn't," Ryan said in a soft, apologetic voice. "I had to find her." He smiled at Mist over his shoulder. "She saved me."

Gabi stared at Mist. *"He* said you were coming," she said, jerking her head toward Dainn, who watched the entire exchange with a perfectly bland expression.

But Mist saw the aftermath of worry written in the lines between his brows and around his mouth, and she suffered a brief moment of guilt knowing she'd caused it.

Very brief.

"This is the one we heard lurking outside the door," Dainn said. "Gabriella Torres, she calls herself."

"You let her in without knowing anything about her?"

"I would not have, if I'd thought she had any connection to Loki," he said, unruffled. "Nevertheless, she was behaving in a clandestine manner. I thought it best to detain her until you returned."

Mist turned to catch Ryan's gaze. "Since you seem to know this girl, you can start by telling me why she was spying on my house."

"Ryan said we had to come," Gabi said, her arms folded tightly across her chest.

Mist sighed again. This was going to be as difficult an interrogation as anything she'd gone through with Dainn. "Shouldn't you be in school?" she asked.

Ryan, sitting next to Dainn across the table, swallowed his last bite of sandwich. "We don't go to school," he said, gazing at the tabletop.

The girl scraped back her chair. "If you're going to report us—"

"I'm not." Mist gestured for Gabi to sit down again. "No one asked you to watch me?"

"Ryan *told* you," Gabi said, flashing Mist an exasperated glance.

"Gabi said she wanted to check things out before we just showed up," Ryan said, his head still bowed and his cheeks flushed. "She told me to wait until she thought it was safe. But I saw . . . I felt something I had to follow. I left, and *he*—" Ryan flashed a sideways glance at Dainn. "Well, you know the rest."

The young man's apparent interest in the elf intrigued Mist. There didn't seem to be anything suspicious about it, but he'd barely met Dainn, whom Mist had introduced as her "cousin."

Had he seen Dainn in one of his "dreams," too?

If he had, that would come to light eventually. "Okay," she said. "You said you were looking for me. You saw me in one of your dreams."

Ryan dragged his lank blond hair back from his forehead in a gesture of frustration. "I know we're supposed to be here. With you."

She looked at Gabi. "What were you planning to do when you came to my door?"

Shoving her plate aside, Gabi took a long drink from her glass of Sprite. "*I* don't know," she said. "It was all Ry's idea."

Ryan gnawed his lower lip, already chapped and ragged from previous abuse. "Gabi always thought I was crazy. I knew I had to show her."

"I still haven't seen anything," Gabi said, "except this *cabrón* with the funny ears."

"Ears?" Mist asked Dainn with a frown.

"During our . . . struggle," Dainn said in a tone that made Mist believe he wasn't too worried about it. And considering what Ryan had already seen, maybe he didn't have much cause to.

"He didn't hurt you, did he?" Mist asked Gabi.

Dainn gave her an almost offended glance. Gabi mumbled an answer as she took another sip, finishing off the drink.

"I merely brought her inside," Dainn said.

"Yeah," Gabi said sarcastically. "That's all."

Mist quickly realized it was going to be much easier to talk to Ryan. "Where do you live?" she asked, addressing the top of his wheat-colored head.

"We don't live anywhere," Gabi snapped.

"Where are your families?"

"Don't got any."

Mist doubted that, but she'd already guessed they were on their own. They were both too thin, their clothes soiled and torn, and Gabi's suspicion suggested she'd had a few less-than-pleasant experiences with people in general. They were two of the many teens to be found in any city, runaways fleeing abuse or neglect, addicts living hand to mouth, children rejected by their parents.

"Do you want more to eat?" Mist asked.

Unexpected hope lit the girl's eyes. "Maybe another soda?" she said.

Mist got up, took another diet Sierra Mist from the very back of the fridge where several inoffensive cans had managed to escape the Great Soda Purge and set it down on the table. Gabi popped the tab without waiting to pour it in the glass. As Mist resumed her seat, she glanced toward the open laundry room door. The sun was going down fast, and the air held the tang of snow. It was going to be another bitter night.

"Are you willing to trust your friend?" she asked Gabi.

"You mean about coming here?"

It was the first time she had spoken in a relatively calm voice. Mist nodded.

"I have a lot more questions for both of you," Mist said. "If it turns out that Ryan was . . . mistaken in his reasons for finding me—"

"I'm not," Ryan said. "You don't have to let us stay here. We can find somewhere else."

Under a piece of cardboard in some doorway, Mist thought, or maybe even in the park where she'd found Dainn.

"You can stay here tonight," Mist said, "and we'll talk more about this later." Which meant she'd have to give up on the idea of looking for Loki a little while longer. She got up from the table again, already thinking about where she could put the kids.

Lee strolled out of the laundry room on his big, silent paws, a bit of fluff clinging to one of his long whiskers.

"*Un gatito!*" Gabi exclaimed. She slid from her chair and extended her hand.

"Gabi—" Mist began, intending to warn her that Lee didn't care for most strangers. But the cat surprised her by running straight to the girl and touching his nose to her fingertips. A moment later

Kirby, not to be deprived of his rightful share of affection, trotted out and butted his broad head against Gabi's leg.

It meant something that the cats liked her. It meant they, at least, found Gabi trustworthy. Mist had never found any reason to doubt their judgment, though their attitude toward Dainn had been cautious. That was good sense, too.

Gabi gathered Lee under his front legs, lifted him and kissed his nose. He didn't so much as bare a claw. Kirby meowed piteously.

Mist knew the cats could keep this up for hours if Gabi let them. "Ryan," she said, "If you and Gabi will come with me, I'll show you where you can sleep."

"But it's still so early!" Gabi protested.

"No arguments," Mist said.

With a final stroke of gray, white, and red fur, Gabi got to her feet and waited for Ryan to join her. They stood back to let Mist precede them into the hall. Ryan glanced over his shoulder at Dainn and followed with obvious reluctance.

The stairway was on the other side of the hall from the living room, a very short distance from the kitchen door. Mist started up the stairs and took an immediate right at the top, where a couple of half-finished rooms looked out onto a large open area scattered with the kind of dubiously useful junk you'd find in many long-forgotten attics.

"There're beds in both rooms," Mist said. She pointed to the first door. "You can have that one, Gabi. Ryan, the other room isn't completely furnished and the mattress is pretty near shot, but I've got a sleeping bag somewhere. I'll get you extra blankets and a pillow."

Ryan stared at her as if she'd offered him Donald Trump's Florida mansion. "I don't need anything," he said.

"I'm staying with Ry," Gabi said. "We always stay together, and I have to be with him if he gets sick again."

That was true. Someone had to be available, and Mist didn't feel comfortable watching him. The kid probably wouldn't feel too comfortable either, even if he had come here of his own free will.

"He can have the bed in the first room, and I'll take the sleeping bag," Gabi said.

"Gab—" Ryan began.

"You sort it out between yourselves," Mist said, remembering why she'd never considered having kids, even if she hadn't had to worry about their inevitable mortality. "I think I have a spare tooth-brush or two, and when you're ready I'll show you the bathroom."

Mist left Ryan and Gabi staring at each other, Ryan still vaguely apologetic and Gabi belligerent. Mist was slightly amazed that they could be friends, and so obviously loyal to each other.

She returned to the kitchen, where Dainn was standing just in-side the doorway to the laundry room. Kirby was winding around his feet, tail straight up and purring like a well-tuned engine.

"Dainn," she said.

He bent to scratch Kirby's head, turned and followed Mist into the hall. Mist strode past the stairs and the ward room, where the Rune-wards still streaked the wall above like black paint applied by a toddler's messy fingers, and went into the gym.

The largest room in the loft was a vast, silent space in the dark-ness, but when Mist closed her eyes she could hear her last duel with Eric, the sound of his laughing voice, the caressing touch of his fingers.

She flicked on the light. "Did you see this when you were here alone?" she asked.

Dainn walked into the center of the gym. "No," he said. He cir-cled the room, taking in the weights and equipment before stop-ping at the barrel of staffs and the rack of swords and axes standing against the far wall. Four of the swords were made of wood in vari-ous shapes and weights. There were also eight functional swords, including a katana, two rapiers, a broadsword, a pair of Viking spathas, and a two-handed claymore. Mist and Eric had sparred with the wooden swords until very recently, when they'd switched to the spathas. Hardly more than twelve hours ago Mist had told Eric that he had become almost as skilled as she was.

Another joke on her.

"An impressive collection," Dainn said, leaning closer to the rack.

Mist came up behind him. "I make them," she said.

Carefully Dainn lifted one of the spathas from the rack and examined it with interest and something very like admiration. Alfar were not known to wield weapons even in battle, preferring the less "messy" method of fighting with magic. But Dainn held the sword expertly, as if he had fought with such weapons all his long life.

"You know how to use that?" Mist asked.

Dainn quickly replaced the sword and dragged his hand along the thigh of his jeans as if he'd been touching something filthy. He backed away and leaned against the nearest wall.

"What are we to do with these children?" he asked.

She told him what had happened with the Jotunar. He listened intently, thoughts racing behind his dark blue eyes.

"Visions?" he asked. "Are you suggesting he may be a *spamadr*?"

"A seer?" She paced in front of him, scarcely aware of her own movements. "I don't know. There have always been mortals with that skill. Some say they were the children of the Norns. Most were killed as witches centuries ago, but some had to have survived to pass the trait on to descendents. It's not like Galdr, or even the simpler forms of Seidr. It can't be taught."

"He claimed to have seen a winter that never ends," Dainn said. "'War and fire and things rising up.' The winters have been harsh in many places, and there are always wars in Midgard."

"I know," Mist said, coming to a halt. "But you did say that mortals with magical abilities might show up."

Dainn stared down at his folded arms. "It seems too convenient."

"Do you really think he could be working for Loki?"

"No. One of us would surely have sensed it." He sighed. "It's possible, even likely, that Loki will use improbable agents to put us off our guard, but I think my wards would have detected something amiss when they entered the house."

"And those giants hurt Ryan," she said. "That would be taking authenticity a little too far, don't you think? Loki wanted him for something. And he knew where Ryan was, or at least he had Jotunar following him." She blew out her breath. "The question is, how did Loki know about Ryan? We've known all along that Laufeyson will have someone watching the loft, even if they can't get in. If Gabi had been casing the loft when Ryan supposedly came after me, did the Jotunar follow him from here?"

"I have no answer."

"That's the problem, isn't it? The girl doesn't seem to have any significance except as Ryan's friend and protector, but a *spamadr* would be extremely useful to us, just as he would to Loki." She gazed unseeing at the sword rack. "By now, Loki must know I took him. I think we should hold off any decision until we get more information, especially about these visions."

"They may steal your valuables and run off before you can question them again," Dainn said.

"Somehow I doubt that's going to be a problem."

"As you wish."

Dainn didn't sound terribly enthusiastic, but then he seldom did.

"I'll finish up with the kids," she said. "You check the wards again, just to be on the safe side."

She turned to leave. Dainn was right behind her before she'd gone three steps toward the door.

"I am glad you didn't find Loki," he said.

His voice was gruff, more like a Jotunn's than an elf's, and she could hear the suppressed emotion in it. Emotion she certainly didn't want directed at *her*.

"You couldn't have been too worried," she said lightly, turning to face him again, "or you would have come running after me."

"I am sorry," he said, dropping his gaze. "I was not sufficiently recovered to be of any use to you."

"I *told* you not to come, anyway."

"Do you think that alone would have stopped me?"

They stared at each other in charged silence, and Mist knew then he hadn't been worried about her just because of Freya. It had been *personal* for him."

That scared her. "I won't be treated like some swooning Victorian maiden in need of a big strong man to protect her," she said coldly.

"I am not a man," Dainn said. "And I have done a very poor job of protecting you. But I will continue to keep your warnings in mind."

He'd gone back to his dry, almost remote tone, and she was relieved. "We'll have this out later," she said. "You obviously need more rest, and so do I."

"You rest first," he said. "It will be necessary to begin our lessons later tonight."

Magic lessons, he meant. She knew she needed them, badly, in spite of her idiotic insistence on going after Gungnir by herself. But the mere idea made her wish she could sleep for a century or so and wake up to find this was all a bad dream.

She had a feeling bad dreams were only the beginning.

"Okay," she said, turning her face away so he couldn't see her fear. "I'll rest for a while. Just don't let me sleep too long."

Before he could answer she was striding across the gym and into the hall. She found her sleeping bag rolled up in a storage closet, picked up a few blankets and a pair of pillows, and went upstairs.

Though it was only midafternoon, Ryan was already sprawled on the bed in the nearly finished room, snoring lightly. Gabi was sitting half asleep on the bare floor next to him, all thick black hair and oversized hoodie. Her eyes flew open when Mist came in.

"Don't wake him up," she whispered. "I'll take care of that stuff."

Mist set the blankets and pillows down on the single chair. "Do you want to see the bathroom?" she asked.

"*Sí.*" Gabi hesitated. "*Gracias.* Thank you for letting us stay here." She cast a worried glance at Ryan. "It's been a long time since he's slept on anything but the ground."

"But you look after him."

"He needs it." She frowned at Mist. "I don't trust you, but Ry does. He says you're okay. Maybe you can help him, so he don't get sick no more."

"From the dreams?"

"All they do is hurt him, and I can't make him better." She hugged herself, pulling the hoodie tight to her chest. "Can we go now?"

Mist showed her the bathroom, clean towels, and a spare, unused toothbrush. She needed a shower herself. Suddenly the prospect of lying down on a soft bed seemed more important than saving the world.

"There are a couple of frozen dinners in the freezer," she said as she left the bathroom. "You can borrow some of my clothes, and Ryan can have—"

Eric's, she thought. She hadn't had a chance to get rid of his stuff, but now his clothes would do more good covering the kid than providing fuel for the small bonfire she'd had in mind.

"I'll leave some clean clothes outside the door," she said. "Throw the ones you have on into the washer."

Gabi nodded and retreated into the bathroom. Once in her own room, Mist pulled a shirt out of her closet, found some new underwear and fairly new socks in a drawer, and picked out a pair of jeans for Gabi. The girl was considerably shorter than Mist, but at least the clothes would be clean.

Eric's clothes still hung in the other half of the closet, as if he planned to return any moment to put them on again. Four business suits, neatly pressed polo shirts, pants carefully arranged on glossy wood hangers. Eric had almost never worn jeans. He'd always been . . .

Stop it, Mist told herself. She snatched a pair of khakis, sending the hanger clattering to the floor, and threw one of the polo shirts on the bed. She rummaged for a pair of socks in Eric's drawer and gathered them up, holding them away from her chest as if they were soaked in venom.

She left both sets of clothes on the floor outside the bathroom and returned to the bedroom, too exhausted to dwell on the ugly fact that she and a man who hadn't really existed had slept together in this room only yesterday morning. She removed her belt and knife, flipped back the blankets, and toppled onto the bed.

A faint, rhythmic noise woke her a little while later. She stared blearily at the alarm clock and sat up, trying to figure out where the sound was coming from.

It was a voice. An elf's voice, singing spells of protection outside her door.

Curse him. He should be . . .

She never reached the end of the thought.

11

"Senator Briggs?"

The young woman rushed up to the portly politician, breathless and tottering on her spike-heeled pumps. Briggs, disturbed in his conversation with an important local businessman, cast her a forbidding glance. His expression changed almost immediately as he took in the woman's short, tight-fitting skirt, long, elegant legs, and the cleavage that showed at the neckline of her mauve silk blouse, winningly emphasized by the shadows cast under streetlights flickering on with the coming of night.

He muttered a word of apology to his companion and turned to the woman. "Yes?" he asked with a patently false smile. "May I help you?"

"Oh, Senator. I'm sorry to disturb you, it's just that I . . ." She halted in mid-gush, flustered, then resumed in more measured tones.

"Senator Briggs, I heard you speak today on the evils of a secular society." She filled her lungs, the better to show off her succulent breasts. "I just wanted to tell you how *very* impressed I was. I agreed with everything you said, and I'm sure the American people will listen and applaud when you do your television interview."

The senator, visibly pleased, pretended to focus on her face, which the woman knew was as seductively beautiful as her body. "Why, Miss . . ."

"Lori. Lori Larsen." She batted her eyelashes. "I've been following you ever since you won the election. I can't believe I'm finally meeting you!"

"Well, Miss Larsen, the pleasure is all mine." He turned back to the businessman, spoke a few soft words, and shook the man's hand. The man glanced once at Miss Larsen and reluctantly walked back into the hotel. "Now, what about my speech did you like most?" he asked.

Lori smiled, showing off pearly white teeth. "It's so hard to choose. I think it was when you talked about the dogma of Darwinism. It's so awful what they're doing in schools these days!"

Senator Briggs nodded solemnly. "So true. We're doing our best to put our own people on the school boards, but the forces of Satan are powerful." His assessing gaze slewed down to her legs and crawled back up to her bustline. "Are you enjoying the conference so far?"

"Oh, yes! But it wouldn't have been nearly so enjoyable if *you* hadn't come."

Puffing out his chest, the senator offered his arm. "Perhaps you'd like to discuss this over a drink," he said. "The hotel has an excellent bar. That is, of course, if you indulge."

She met his eyes. "The Bible says, 'He makes grass grow for the cattle, and plants for man to cultivate—bringing forth food from the earth: wine that gladdens the heart of man, oil to make his face shine, and bread that sustains his heart.'"

"You know your Bible! I congratulate you." Briggs's brown eyes assumed a libidinous gleam. "Shall we?"

Lori took his arm and, giggling with excitement, accompanied the senator to the bar.

She was very good at having her way. It didn't take much encouragement to press the congressman to drink much more than he ordinarily would or to shield him from awareness of the effects of imbibing to excess. Nor was it difficult to persuade him to let her escort him to his suite, or to sit down beside him on the bed and bathe his forehead. When she complained that the room was too hot and removed her jacket, further exposing her breasts, small waist, and shapely ass, she struck the most provocative poses with beguiling innocence.

In the end, the senator fell. Satan was in his heart, tempting him beyond his meager power to resist. When she helped him out of his suit jacket, he buried his hot, heavy face into her neck. When she unbuttoned his shirt, he insisted on returning the favor. Soon his fat, broad hands were on her breasts, squeezing her nipples, and she knew then he would never turn back. Like all his kind, he was a hypocrite, weak and stupid. Just the kind of mortal she needed.

She didn't resist when he bore her back on the bed, pushed up her skirt, and revealed her complete absence of undergarments. She moaned in anticipation as he pulled his pants down around his legs and planted his gross, sweaty body between her thighs. She wrapped her legs around his waist and cried out as he thrust inside her.

Lori had always enjoyed sex, and it didn't much matter to her what form it took. As a mare, she had become impregnated by a stallion, and she had made love as woman with man, man with woman, and man with man, dominant and submissive. All of it was good. Briggs was well-endowed, which was almost enough to make up for his pale, ugly body.

So she took what pleasure she could out of the grunting pig inside her, suppressing her climax until the good senator had spent his seed. Then she let go, bucking and gasping just before the mortal collapsed on top of her. She pushed his unresisting body over onto his back. Almost at once he fell into a drink-sodden sleep, his flaccid penis dangling over the open waistband of his trousers.

With a curl of her lip, Lori shed the remainder of her clothes and stepped into the shower, washing his stink away. Then, still naked, she stood in front of the fogged mirror, cleared it with a gesture, and watched herself change.

Loki Laufeyson examined his sleekly muscled body with approval and walked back into the bedroom. He sat on the edge of the bed, chanted a quick spell and watched the senator begin to emerge from his postcoital slumber. Once he was sure Briggs was nearly awake, he went to work.

The senator's eyes snapped open. He didn't see Loki at first; he was too busy enjoying Loki's expert ministrations. It was only when he reached out and tangled his fingers in Loki's hair that he began to realize that something was amiss.

"Lori?" he croaked. "What—"

Raising his head, Loki grinned. "What is it, my darling? More teeth, perhaps?"

The senator's eyes nearly popped out of his head. He reared up, mouth working in soundless protest, and tried to push Loki away. Loki wrapped his fingers around Brigg's flagging member and held on.

"Calm yourself, Senator," he said gently. "I wouldn't want you to be injured."

Staring into Loki's eyes, Briggs began to tremble. "Who are you?" he whispered. "Where is Lori?"

"Lori's here, my love," Loki said in her voice. He touched his own chest. "Didn't you enjoy fucking her? Or was it *him*?"

"Oh, my God." Tears leaked from the corners of Briggs's eyes. "Oh, my God. What have you done?"

"Your god has nothing to do with it," Loki said. He released the senator and got up from the bed. "I believe the sin was all yours, Senator."

Briggs went as limp as a flag on a windless day. "You . . . *you* are Lori?"

Primping his hair, Loki gave the senator a good look at his body. "I have been many things. At the moment . . ." He snapped his fingers, and a large photograph appeared in his right hand. "At the moment, dear Senator, I am your blackmailer."

Briggs was still weeping when Loki left him. The senator had tried every trick in the book: pleas, bribes of insultingly miniscule proportions, and finally threats of impressive magnitude. The congressman, as Loki well knew, had a vast web of connections that extended throughout the city, state, and beyond, many of them illegal. Hypocrites were surprisingly good at justifying their lapses in the name of ultimately serving their god, or because they were merely feigning devout belief, all the better to fleece their flocks.

The senator fell into the latter category, and he knew being caught in bed with a man would ruin him, as it had so many others of his ilk. When he realized that Loki could neither be bought for a few thousand dollars nor threatened with a beating or worse, he began to see reason. The bargain Loki struck made him very unhappy, but not as unhappy as the prospect of losing a very promising, and profitable, career.

By the time it was over, Briggs had the original memory card, convinced it was the only one and that no copies had been downloaded elsewhere. That was actually the truth. Of course, Loki could conjure up as many photographs as he needed at any time. But he only had to exert a little will to persuade the senator that he was sincere, and a few hours later, during the tail end of the evening commute rush—and after adorning himself with a very expensive-looking suit and shoes—Loki walked out of the hotel a member of the senator's personal team.

Oh, this was just the beginning, of course. It would only be a matter of time before he rose higher still to a much more vital position, and with only a minimal exertion on his part. He would have "real" money rather than the false currency he conjured up at some cost to his magical energy, which must be preserved for much more vital purposes. And since Freya knew he had been in Midgard in defiance of the rules . . .

His good mood evaporating, Loki scowled at an elderly man walking a ridiculously tiny dog. Both dog and man shied and retreated to the very edge of the sidewalk, where the dog promptly evacuated its bowels.

Loki swung his ivory-headed cane with the ruby insets, feeling the Spear humming with life under his hand. At least he had Gungnir. It had failed him once, to be sure, but even if it did him little good by itself, it was excellent bait for Mist.

Mist. Heat surged into Loki's face. She'd always been a wild card in the game; he'd known Freya would use her eventually, just as he would use his own children. He had stayed with Mist to learn her value to her bitch mother and because he had hoped to deceive her into revealing the locations of the other Treasures.

He had underestimated her, and her mother. He couldn't forget the moment when Freya had looked at him through Mist's familiar eyes. He had been completely unprepared for that appearance.

He had made an utter fool of himself.

The tip of the cane struck sparks against the cement as Loki slammed it down in front of him. He *should* have been prepared. When he'd found the bridges, he had chosen to break the rules in the belief that he could establish a strong base of operations that would more than compensate for the price demanded for his transgression. He had believed that his own watchers would detect the arrival of Freya's agents from the Aesir's Shadow-Realm in Ginnungagap.

But even Hrimgrimir had failed to identify the elf Freya had sent to find her daughter.

Dainn.

One of the doormen rushed ahead of Loki to flag down a taxi, but Loki summoned an empty stretch limousine waiting to pick up a client. He smiled at the driver, who went blank-eyed under his influence and quickly moved to open the rear passenger door. The limo possessed a well-stocked minibar, and Loki poured himself a Scotch and soda as the driver eased into late commute traffic, bound for the Ritz-Carlton.

Dainn.

Loki stared at the back of the driver's head through the glass partition. In all the centuries since the Dispersal, he had been ignorant of Dainn's fate. The catastrophic event had taken place just as he had been violently resisting Dainn's attempt to kill him. Dainn should have been sent to the Shadow-Realm of the Alfar, as each race had joined its own kind in the Void.

But Dainn had been rejected by his own people and the Aesir. Even though Freya had convinced Odin to stop Thor from executing the elf, Loki had very good cause to know that Odin's curse had been in full effect. The pain in his mind had been exquisite as the beast tore through it, raking his thoughts to shreds with invisible claws even as Dainn's strong but ordinary hands were locked around his throat.

That was the last they had seen of each other. And now Loki knew Dainn was alive. Alive and working for Freya. Doubtless waiting for another chance to destroy his most hated enemy.

Rubbing at his throat, Loki closed his eyes. Was the curse still in effect? Dainn had lost so much of his magic when the Eitr had been taken from him, but he had enough to be of use to Freya above all the other Alfar she might have sent to Midgard. He had defeated

Loki's best Jotunar fighters. He had spoken into Mist's mind. He had opened the path for Freya's possession of her daughter's body.

"He fears you because he fears the Lady," Dainn had whispered, his thoughts going wide of their intended mark. But the elf was wrong. Utterly, egregiously wrong.

Loki laughed, causing the driver to look nervously in his rearview mirror. Loki fogged the glass between them. How ironic that Freya had offered him a "choice" to come back to the Aesir. As if Odin and Thor would ever have him. As if he would go crawling to them, begging forgiveness.

They still didn't understand. Without him, all the Homeworlds would have descended into rot and stagnation before the first intelligent mortals walked on Midgard.

If there were choices to be made, others would be making them. He had offered Mist an alliance before Freya's arrival, certain she knew her Sisters' whereabouts and that he could find a way to use her against her mother now that he had been forced to act.

But she had turned him down. *Turned him down.* And then she had lost herself.

For a time. But he had seen Freya leave her, known when Mist had reclaimed her body and struggled to make sense of what had happened to her and what she had done. There had been no direct communication between Freya and her daughter, no willing cooperation—of that, Loki was certain. If his suspicions were correct, Mist wouldn't be permitted to understand. Freya intended to return to that same body whenever she wished to work her will in Midgard.

And how convenient it had all turned out to be for her. Loki glanced at a passing Humvee, considering whether or not it might be pleasurable to blast out all its windows.

He decided against the effort and forced his thoughts back into far less satisfying channels. Of course, neither he nor Freya had known what would happen before Ragnarok. She could not have made such plans in advance, nor had she shown any interest in her daughter in Asgard.

But she knew her daughter had been sent to Midgard before the Dispersal. She knew how much magic it would take to shape herself a new physical body of her own while she struggled to hold the others in their quiescent state; she would have to use her Eitr as Loki had, losing her single advantage and her ability to enforce the rules of their game.

No, Loki could not imagine that she would allow Mist to learn what she really intended for her offspring. Mist might have days left, perhaps weeks, before Freya took full possession. And Mist deserved it, the bitch. Unless she discovered what was happening and fought against it.

Loki stretched, amused by the idea of Freya and her daughter at odds. Of course, there was no doubt which of the two would win. Mist had almost no magic of her own. Freya was going to be a problem much sooner than Loki had anticipated, but he would deal with it. *And* Dainn.

"Sir?" the driver's voice spoke through the intercom. "We're at the Ritz-Carlton."

The limousine pulled up to the curb, and a uniformed bellman was immediately at the passenger door to help Loki out of the vehicle. He seemed confused at first that Loki had no luggage, but Loki's quick smile convinced him that there was nothing unusual about such a well-dressed, attractive man desiring to check in without baggage.

The bellman accompanied him to the front desk, where an efficient, obliging clerk assured him that the guests who had reserved the Presidential Suite would not be at all put out if Loki took the rooms instead. He ordered room service with a bottle of Veuve

Clicquot Cave Privée Rosé, 1978, kicked off his shoes, and lay back on the bed, listening to the rush of traffic far below his window.

There was one thing that still puzzled him. He still didn't understand why Dainn hadn't tried to kill him. He would have defeated Dainn in a head-to-head match, of course, but he knew that the elf was capable of very human emotions, including an irrational and reckless anger that had become all the more deadly under the influence of the beast.

Yet Freya trusted him. She must expect him to protect Mist. Why hadn't he come to Mist's direct aid in Asbrew?

Because he fears me, Loki thought. He closed his eyes as a fresh rush of bubbles slid over his tongue. *He fears me because he once loved me, and he can never forgive himself.*

That was one *very* pleasant thought. So was the memory of how easily he'd gotten the better of Odin's son. No, Vidarr would be no trouble. He, too, was afraid.

Still, as much as it galled him, Loki knew he must be patient a little longer. Considering that he'd found several of the bridges closed since he'd taken Gungnir—closed for no reason he could yet determine—he couldn't be sure how soon he would be able to bring more Jotunar into Midgard.

Once his alliances with Briggs and with mortals of a lower and more violent sort were fully established, he would be able to buy himself more time. Tomorrow his new headquarters would be ready for occupation, the apartment fully furnished to his specifications, the conference room ready for meetings, offices prepared for the employees he was already beginning to accumulate. Freya still had a great deal of catching up to do. And as long as she maintained her own mind, Mist would try to come after him. Dainn would try to stop her. But if he failed . . .

Loki licked his lips. *Then, Lady Sow,* he thought, *we shall see who determines the fate of Midgard.*

❧

Dainn was standing over Mist's bed when she woke.

She nearly jumped out of her skin, snatching for Kettlingr on the bedside table.

"*Skita*," she swore, putting the knife down again. "What do you think you're doing?"

"Vali is at the door," he said, his face expressionless.

"What time is it?" she asked, rubbing her eyes.

"Nearly nine o'clock."

Mist swung her legs over the side of the bed. "I didn't know I'd slept that long."

The elf regarded her out of eyes nested in circles as dark as his hair. He still wore Vid's clothes, which hung on his body like deflated airbags.

"The kids?" she asked.

"Sleeping."

"I'll check on them later. Take a shower while I'm talking to Vali. You need it."

Backing away silently, Dainn left the room. She wondered briefly if she'd offended him and dismissed the thought as irrelevant. Sparing his pride was not high on her list of priorities.

Vali was waiting in the kitchen. The burly blond was sober—a very good sign—but his expression was grave.

"Sorry I couldn't get away earlier," he said. "I didn't want Vidarr to know I had urgent business. He would've been suspicious."

Indeed he would have, Mist thought. The only urgent business Vali ever had was with a bottle. At least, until now.

Mist poured herself a glass of water. "You weren't able to talk to him?"

"Nope. He's avoided me ever since you and the elf left Asbrew. I think you really surprised him, Mist."

"Surprise" wasn't really the way Mist would have described Vid's reaction. "I have a few things to tell you. Can I get you anything to drink?" she asked.

"Same as you're having." He smiled and sat down at the table. "I'm jumping on the wagon."

Mist wanted to hug the old bear. "Good. I'll be needing you to think clearly."

She gave him a brief account of the teenagers' strange arrival and what little she knew of them. Vali made all the appropriate noises of surprise and concern.

"What are you going to do with them?" he asked when she was finished.

"Not sure yet. But there's something more important I need to discuss with you. Remember when I told you I was going to need your help?"

Vali blinked at her. "You really need me?"

"Desperately." She filled a glass from a bottle of spring water in the fridge and set it in front of Vali. "You've always been sharp—smarter than Vidarr in most ways—and you've never gotten the credit for it."

"What exactly do you want me to do?"

"You understand what Loki is planning, Val? What's really at stake?"

"Sure. Loki wants to take over the world."

"And are you okay that Dainn will be working with me? Can you accept someone your brother called a traitor?"

Vali shrugged. "I figure you wouldn't have anything to do with him if he were as bad as they say. Freya trusts him, I guess. Maybe he made mistakes, like he said, but everyone needs a second chance."

Bless you, Mist thought, relieved that she'd judged Vali correctly. "Thanks," she said. "As for your part in this . . . I remember how good you were with computers. I seem to recall that you did a little hacking back in the nineties."

Staring down at his glass, Vali shook his head. "It was just showing off. Mainly practical jokes, nothing really harmful. I wanted to prove I was better at something than Vid was."

"Well, what you'll be doing now—if you agree—is hacking for a vital purpose. We need to find the other Valkyrie and the Treasures before Loki does, and you can help us do that."

Vali looked up, surprise and speculation in his eyes. "You really don't know where they are?"

"No. They could be anywhere. We'll need access to databases in every part of the world—and not just the publicly accessible ones—so we can look for clues that might lead us to them."

Rising abruptly, Vali floundered about the kitchen like a boar in a birdcage. "Odin's bloody eye," he swore. "You're talking about stuff like banking accounts, personnel files, phone records—"

"And a lot more, including national and international security organizations, if we have to go that far. I hope we won't. Wherever they are, my Sisters have been living in Midgard as long as I have. They've adapted, as I have. They all have lives that can be traced."

"Do you have any idea what that would involve?" Vali asked. "They've probably moved around, just like you did before you came here. Maybe *you* kept your real name, but do you think the others have? Especially after dozens of mortal lifetimes?"

"We'll work out some parameters for the search, like references to names or objects associated with what mortals regard as Norse mythology."

"Do you think the other Valkyrie would have used their Treasures?"

"I don't know." She watched Vali pace from one end of the

kitchen to the other. "Look, Val, I know it's not going to be easy, and it may take time, maybe even months—"

"Months?" Vali laughed. "More like centuries."

"Maybe not. When you used to hack, did you ever use magic?"

Flushing, Vali thumped against the counter like a pinball finally coming to rest. "Sometimes," he stammered. "I figured out a few tricks. But I always thought it was cheating, so—"

"It won't be cheating now. You can be sure Loki won't leave anything to chance. He'll be hiring his own experts. Every resource is crucial. *You're* crucial, Val."

Odin's son returned to the table and fell into the chair again, setting the wood to groaning under his weight. "I don't know," he said. "I can't guarantee I'll be able to do even half of what you're asking. The Internet can only take you so far. Even private government databases aren't likely to have records on more than a fraction of their citizens. And there are dozens of countries that barely have any kind of computer records."

"All I ask is that you try. Use any magic you think will help."

Vali released a gusty sigh, for once clean of the scent of hard liquor. "I'll give it my best shot." His eyes brightened. "Maybe it will even be fun."

Mist squeezed his shoulder. "I believe in you."

He didn't seem to hear her. "I'm going to need my own data center to do this. Lots of hardware and questionably legal software I can adapt."

"I have quite a bit of money saved," Mist said. "I'll make sure you have everything you need. And while you're handling that, Dainn is going to be teaching me a little more about magic."

"A little?" Vali rose again, hitching up his belt. "Vid isn't going to be happy if he finds out. You caught him with his pants down, and he doesn't like being mocked."

"I don't much care what he likes."

Rebellion flared in Vali's mild blue eyes. "Neither do I. I'll think up some excuse to stay away from Asbrew. He probably won't even notice I'm gone."

"You can always tell him you've joined AA."

It wasn't funny, but Vali smiled anyway. "This ought to be just as good. And if he gives me a hard time, I'll spit in his eye."

"I hope that won't be necessary." She glanced at the clock on the wall. "It's getting late. You won't be able to do anything tonight, but I can show you where you can set up."

Vali followed her along the hall to Eric's home office. There had been no time to get rid of his furniture and belongings, though Mist had checked to confirm her assumption that Loki had taken his computer when he left.

"When you get the equipment you need, we can always expand," she said. "There are two unfinished bedrooms on the second floor, and a whole lot of empty space. You can arrange your stuff any way you like."

"What about the elf?" Vali asked suddenly, eying her sideways. "Will he be staying here?"

Mist stiffened. "For the time being. If it wasn't that I need him to teach me . . ."

"Sure. I understand." He flushed again. "Do you think you can go to the bank tomorrow and get me some of that money you mentioned?"

Mist thought about Loki and Gungnir and magic lessons and the kids and all the things she still had to do, every one of them urgent. "I think so," said. "Is twenty thousand enough to start with?"

"More than enough, until I see what's what." He grinned and slapped Mist on the back, nearly knocking the air out of her lungs. "It'll almost be like old times."

Maybe he really believed that. Vali had always been a bit of a dreamer—too much so for his own good. But Mist well knew they could never go back.

Vali left a few minutes later. Mist checked in on the kids, who were so deeply asleep that they wouldn't have heard a mob of Jotunar barreling straight through the loft. Too restless to sit still, Mist went outside and scanned the street. It all looked completely normal, as if Jotunar and magic weapons and evil gods didn't exist. No one knew the actors had assembled on stage, and the curtain was about to go up.

There was no question now of returning to bed. Mist went to the gym and began her workout, starting with stretches and continuing with a series of judo and karate stances before moving on to practice with the various swords and ending with weights. She stripped off her sweaty clothes in the bedroom and was headed for the shower when she met Dainn in the hallway, bare-chested and lithe with his black hair flowing around his shoulders. He came to an abrupt halt.

"Have you—" he began.

"Are you—" she said at the same time.

He looked a little too long at her body, scantily covered as it was with a short terrycloth robe and nothing underneath. The robe was securely cinched around her waist with the belt, but she pulled the neckline closer around her upper chest.

"Forgive me," Dainn stammered, and fled back the way he'd come. Mist was left shaken and appalled by the gooseflesh on her arms and the heat in her groin.

Fenrir's teeth. She'd seen him naked before, in Asbrew. He'd made a mockery of her embarrassment, though he had been right: there was no such thing as a modest Valkyrie where bodies in their various living and dead states were concerned.

Dainn had proven to be more solid than she'd imagined when she'd first seen him in his indigent's rags. He had the look of a man who had done plenty of physical labor, with sleek, defined muscles and broad shoulders. No bodybuilder, the elf, but probably ten times as strong as one. Not an ounce of fat on his body, and . . .

Stop, Mist told herself.

She managed to shut off her highly inappropriate thoughts and rushed into the bathroom. She locked the door from inside and leaned against it as if Dainn might try to break in.

And do what? She took off her robe and stepped into the shower, turning the water all the way to cold. The discomfort brought her back to her senses, and she returned to her room in a much calmer state. She braided her hair, dressed as if she were going outside, complete with boots, jacket, and Kettlingr, and went to find Dainn.

12

The elf was sitting cross-legged on the area rug in the middle of the small living room, facing the black rectangle of the flat-screen TV as if it were the doorway to some uncharted dimension. His feet were bare, and he was wearing a pair of Eric's sweatpants and a deep purple T-shirt—also Eric's—which Mist realized had been left in the laundry basket after the last wash.

It was a shock to see him in Eric's things—things Loki had worn—but she couldn't fault Dainn for his practicality. Without interrupting his meditation, she took a seat on the leather couch Eric had bought a few months ago. She had to get rid of that, too. Curse him, she'd nearly have to strip the loft bare to get rid of every reminder.

She cleared her throat, a sudden tide of heat surging into her face. "Dainn?"

He turned around and looked up at her, as remote as Lee on one of his more standoffish days. "I have been considering explanations for the sudden closure of the bridges."

Thank the Norns Dainn was going to pretend their awkward meeting in the hall hadn't happened. But the way he'd looked at her . . .

"What did you decide?" she asked quickly.

"As you said regarding the young mortals, we must have more information. We must find other bridges and test them as well."

"Just put it on the list," Mist said, biting off the words.

Dainn cocked his head. "Loki will be doing the same."

She clasped her hands between her knees. "Okay, *you* tell *me*. What should I do first, now that I've got Vali working on helping us find my Sisters? I thought getting Gungnir back should be at the top, but I admit that was . . . probably not the greatest idea I've ever had."

She hadn't meant to sound so vulnerable, so uncertain, but Dainn didn't seem to notice. "Without the understanding and control of your magic," he said, "anything else you attempt against Loki will ultimately be futile."

"My, but we're Mr. Sunshine tonight, aren't we?"

"The sun seldom shines at night," he said. "And there may soon be no sun at all if we fail."

"Gods." She spiked her hands through her hair, pulling more strands free of the messy braid. "Have you got anything *useful* to say?"

"I doubt you'll like it."

"I'm sure I won't. Go ahead."

"I don't believe it is a coincidence that the boy found you today."

"According to him, it wasn't. And I thought you said Loki didn't send him."

"Yes. But did you consider that it might be more than his visions that brought him to you?"

"What do you mean?"

"Even if Ryan is a seer, he doesn't seem to have any other magical skill. He has never seen you before. It is unlikely that he could have found you with only the help of the images he has described." Dainn tensed and inhaled deeply, like a high diver about to plunge into icy water. "You may have summoned him here yourself."

"What?"

"When you confronted Loki in Asbrew with your mother's power," he said, "you used a certain type of magic against him."

Mist suddenly realized she had forgotten to turn on the heater. The house was freezing. "Do you think I've forgotten that?" she said. "I don't care what Freya does. That kind of . . ." She shuddered. "I won't use those tricks on anyone again."

"They were not tricks, Mist. They will be among Freya's primary weapons when she is ready to confront Loki directly."

"And that's why we're here?" Mist said, beginning to rise. "I'm supposed to learn more of that kind of magic?"

"No," Dainn said steadily, holding her gaze. "Not today."

"Not ever."

"Listen to me. The Lady possesses a glamour that can have a profound effect on anyone who sees her, god or mortal. She can induce feelings of lust, love, and devotion with only the slightest effort and draw all attention to her with no more than a glance. As Freya's daughter—"

"Forget it."

"It is not a feature you can remove as you would your shirt."

Heat flared in Mist's face again. "I'm *not Freya*."

Dainn dropped his eyes. Mist stared at the top of Dainn's head and turned the dial up to heavy sarcasm.

"Look at me," she said. "Do my eyes sparkle like the dew? Am I shaped like Raquel Welch rising out of the ocean on a clamshell? Is mine the face that launched a thousand ships?" She laughed. "Loki wasn't seeing *me* in there. Maybe if I hadn't created some kind of illusion . . ."

Dainn declined her invitation to gaze upon her glorious perfection. "It is not only a matter of beauty," he said quietly, "but in the very nature of the goddess. Your nature."

Mist shivered, getting colder by the second. "So what exactly are you trying to say? That this nature of mine made Ryan look for me?"

"Or simply find you, since he already had some idea of who he was looking for."

"But you were talking about drawing attention with a glance, making someone fall in love . . . I never met Ryan before in my life!"

"Your innermost self—what Freud called the unconscious mind—knows what you, what Midgard, must have to survive. Just as it did in Asbrew. Perhaps Ryan heard you call in his dreams."

"That's unbelievable. I wasn't even thinking—"

"You do not have to *think*," Dainn said, his voice suddenly harsh with anger.

Mist flinched. "So you're saying I'm . . . some kind of living, breathing homing signal?"

"In a manner of speaking."

"That's why you were so sure all along that we'd find mortal allies?"

"Yes."

"So they show up here, and then they fall in love with me? But Ryan certainly doesn't have any interest, and Gabi—"

"They will recognize the need to follow you, regardless of gender."

"Then I'll send them away."

"You will be denying them what they most desire, which is to save their world. You will merely make them aware of why they must fight."

"Like I said before, it isn't going to happen. People being drawn to us by some general magical knowledge or feeling I can understand, but I won't accept this kind of responsibility."

"And as *I* said," Dainn said, meeting her gaze again, "you cannot simply choose to rid yourself of it. Your inherent abilities were already at work before Ryan and Gabi arrived to declare their allegiance."

"You mean in the fight with Loki?"

Dainn didn't answer, but Mist heard him anyway. He wasn't talking about Loki now.

He was speaking of himself. This was why he'd stared at her in the hall. Not because he decided she was "hot" in her bathrobe, but because she'd somehow made him . . .

Loki's piss. No wonder he couldn't stand to look at her half the time.

"You should leave," she said, hopping off the couch. "Go back to Freya. Tell her . . . tell her . . ."

"You know that is impossible."

Mist felt her guts twist as if they were about to burst out of her stomach like some alien parasite. "If I can't turn this off myself, you'll have to teach me."

"There are more important skills you must learn."

"Then you can do it, if you want to."

"Not without great risk."

"To who? Me?" She stood over him, clenching her fists. "I'm not giving you any choice. I'm ordering you to help me."

"Freya will never permit it."

"You said she can't read your mind. She doesn't have to find out until it's done." Mist crouched before him, very careful not to get too close. "At least teach me to control it, like the other magic. Let me have some choice."

"I cannot," Dainn said, turning his face away.

"So you'll let yourself suffer from some artificial emotion every second you're around me? How effective can you be as a teacher then?"

Dainn didn't move a muscle. He hardly even seemed to be breathing. "I am not suffering," he said.

Mist rubbed her tattoo over and over again. "Did *she* make you love her?"

"She has never deprived me of my will," Dainn said, his gaze fixed in a two-thousand-yard stare.

"Did you love her? Do you still?"

Dainn unfolded his body and rose, moving aimlessly around the room. "No," he said.

She closed her eyes. "I'm sorry. But this is wrong, Dainn. You know who else does this kind of thing? Loki. I'll slit my own throat before I play his kind of game."

"Mist. Look at me."

Even before she met his gaze she could *feel* him—the inner agitation and desire he didn't want her to see, the worry, the anger. All aimed inward, not at her.

"Loki uses his magic to manipulate others," he said. "You will never do so. It is not in your character. Eventually you will learn to govern this ability like all the others. *After* you know how to help defend Midgard, and yourself."

Mist swore, carefully backing away as she got to her feet. "I wish I could find out who or what prevented Ragnarok so I could squeeze the life out of it."

"Then this world as you know it would no longer exist."

War. Starvation. Disease. Constant misery for so many of Midgard's inhabitants. She had seen the slaughter of innocents by evil men who considered those different from themselves of less worth than cattle. How could the loss of such suffering be a bad thing? Midgard would have become a paradise, as the Prophecy foretold.

But then there would have been no Aristotle, no Leonardo da Vinci, no Einstein, no Gandhi. No Geir and no Rebekka.

"I guess I really don't have any choice, do I?" she asked bitterly.

There was such real sorrow in Dainn's expression that she had to look away again. "There is another benefit to this ability you may not have considered," he said. "You may attract one or more of your Sisters."

Would that make it worthwhile? Mist thought. She didn't know. There was always a price. Always.

"We should waste no time in commencing your instruction," Dainn said briskly, almost as if the whole painful conversation had never taken place. "If you are ready, we will begin."

"Now?"

"The young mortals are asleep, are they not?"

She got up again. "I need a little time to . . . make sense of all this in my mind. Can you give me another hour?"

"Of course. I, too, will prepare."

"Are you sure you're up to this?" she asked.

"Much will be demanded of both of us. But we will survive."

Somehow that didn't make Mist feel a whole lot better. She grabbed an energy bar from a cupboard in the kitchen and went outside. A light sleet glossed the pavement. The lots across the street, occupied only by rusting warehouses and long-abandoned factories, were still and silent, even during the day, and only the occasional patrol car, making a desultory sweep of the area, ever came close to interrupting Mist's work. She'd set up her workshop in one of the least decayed buildings, where the noise and smells of hot slag wouldn't disturb the neighbors or raise unwanted questions about zoning laws.

Once in the workshop, she fired up the forge and set about tempering the blade of the custom gladius she had been making for one of San Francisco's more influential citizens, an overbearing politician who had never fought a real battle in his life. After she'd heated the blade to the proper temperature and quenched it, she put the sword on the cooling rack and stared into the low-burning flames of the forge. Making a sword properly was a kind of magic. She would have been happy if it were the only kind she'd ever have to perform, but that decision had been taken out of her hands.

She would dearly have liked to pick up one of her billets and pound the living daylights out of it with her hammer. But that wasn't going to change a thing.

And, truth to tell, she'd rather pound on Loki instead.

She cleaned up, took off her gloves and returned to the loft, turning her face up to the delicate kiss of the snow.

"Why didn't you tell me this before?" Loki demanded.

Hrimgrimir shook his massive shoulders and stared down at Loki with an insolent sneer. Dim moonlight, filtered through a heavy mat of clouds and the panoramic window overlooking the sleeping Financial District, silhouetted the giant in a way that made him seem half again as large as the thuggish shape he had chosen.

"You wouldn't want me to bother you with something like this until I was sure," the Jotunn said, his colloquial English thick with mockery. "Sometimes I think you don't trust me."

"Don't push it," Loki said irritably. "Just because you worked for my daughter doesn't give you leave to forget your place." He jerked the sash of his silk Derek Rose dressing gown tight around his waist. "I gave you a chance to take the initiative, and you failed."

"*You* didn't find the kid," Hrimgrimir said. "We did."

"And you lost him."

Hrimgrimir cracked his knuckles, the sound loud enough to rattle the windows. "The bitch had a bit of luck. It won't last."

"Luck? She and Dainn tossed the rest of your crew halfway around the world, and now I have to waste precious time and resources getting them back."

"You could have stopped it, if you hadn't—"

"Silence," Loki snapped. "The fact is that you discovered the presence of a mortal who could have been useful to us, and you let him slip through your fingers."

"We'll get him back," Hrimgrimir said with a toothy grin. "Then maybe you'll realize you can't treat us like a bunch of disposable leg-breakers. We're all you've got."

Loki clung to his temper by the merest thread, reminding himself that tolerating the frost giants' generally bad dispositions was a small enough price to pay for their obedience. Such as it was. It had been obvious from the beginning that Hrimgrimir was going to be trouble, but the others respected Loki. And Loki was smart enough to know what open rebellion would mean.

He didn't have the magic to defeat Freya, not even with all the frost giants behind him. And they wanted their share of the prize when Midgard was taken.

"Not even *you* are indispensable," Loki said, striding back to the bathroom, which—like the rest of the Ritz-Carlton's Presidential Suite—was *almost* fit for a god. "And I forbid you to attack Freya's daughter merely to retrieve a mortal who may or may not be what you seem to believe. I will not waste the opportunity for surprise when it arises."

"That's your plan? Waiting for an opportunity to arise?"

"Patience has never been a virtue of your kind," Loki said, "but—"

Hrimgrimir cut him off with a nasty laugh. "*You're* our kind," he said. "You're the son of two frost giants, even if you did hang around with the Aesir. Do you think they ever counted you their equal?"

Hearing Hrimgrimir state the obvious was almost more than Loki could tolerate. "Hold your tongue," he said, "or I may let the maid have it in place of toilet paper."

Hrimgrimir grumbled ominously as Loki stopped before the vast marble sink. He looked into the mirror, ran his hand through his wet hair to dry it, and met Hrimgrimir's reflected stare. It was time to change tactics.

"I'll have plenty to keep you busy soon enough, in any case," he said in his most soothing voice. "You won't be idle, I assure you."

The Jotunn's densely muscled body overfilled the door frame behind him. "You're going to break the rules again?"

"Oh, not openly. To act precipitously now would force Freya to take the very actions she threatened when we struck our bargain. And we must continue to look for functioning bridges if we are to bring more of your brothers to Midgard."

"And the humans? Did you find what you were looking for?"

"Naturally." Loki smiled at himself, admiring his perfect white teeth. "An excellent addition to my growing stable of corrupt mortals, and just as easily manipulated. The effects will not be immediate, but they will be too subtle for Freya to detect until I am well established."

"What did you do to get to this guy?" Hrimgrimir asked with leering curiosity.

"A method *you* could certainly never employ."

Suddenly the Jotunn began to shrink in on himself, his body seeming to grow leaner and shorter until he resembled a flawed copy of Loki.

"Are you so sure, Scar-lip?"

Loki spun lightly around and struck Hrimgrimir hard across the face. No magic, only a Jotunn's power and the element of surprise. Hrimgrimir lost his hold on his new shape, staggered back, and crashed into a delicate chair, shattering it as if it had been built of toothpicks and spit.

"Don't ever call me that again," Loki said pleasantly, leaning against the doorjamb.

Hrimgrimir groaned and sat up, rubbing at his bloody lip. "One of these days, Laufeyson," he snarled, "you'll go too far."

"Unless you get there first." Loki sighed and extended his hand. "Come, kinsman. Let us quarrel no more."

Ignoring Loki's offer of assistance, Hrimgrimir heaved himself to his feet and shook himself like a woolly mammoth in molt. He opened his broad mouth, closed it again, and dropped his head between his shoulders.

"What do you want us to do now?" he asked sullenly.

"I'll be meeting with a few of my shady characters tomorrow," he said. "They don't know just how much their petty lives are about to change."

"When we take over," Hrimgrimir said.

"It will not be done in a day. We must move slowly and with subtlety."

"You mean you don't want us to have any fun."

The other Jotunn, silent until that moment, muttered and shifted restlessly. Loki gave them a quelling glance.

"I do not know how to make it any clearer," he said. "You will have your 'fun' when matters are arranged to my satisfaction, and no sooner. When that happens, however . . ." He strode to the window and flung his arms wide. "This city shall quite literally be your stomping ground." He turned around again. "In the meantime, continue what you've been doing—without the failure, of course. Keep watch on the loft and on the streets. Report anything of interest to me before you act." He dropped his arms. "Now, go. And go quietly. I don't want to find myself in the position of covering up any clumsy mistakes."

Hrimgrimir looked into Loki's eyes for a measure of a dozen heartbeats and then lowered his head. "We will make no mistakes," he said. "But will you, Laufeyson? What about *him*?"

"Your concern is touching," Loki said in a dangerously soft voice, "but he cannot take me off guard again. I fully intend to draw him away from Freya's daughter. Now get out."

Hrimgrimir thumped out the door of the suite, his lieutenants at his heels, all taking on more ordinary forms as they left.

Loki stared at the door, lost in thought. On the city streets far below he could hear the wail of a siren, approaching and then fading away.

There were likely to be plenty more where that came from if the Jotunar broke too soon. But he didn't think they would. He was no fool, and they knew it.

He was certainly not fool enough to tell them what he had discovered about Freya's plans for Mist.

Returning to the bathroom, Loki untied the robe and let it fall to his feet. He conjured up a conservative, rather ordinary-looking business suit and critically studied the effect. He'd already made arrangements to have representatives from Saks, Wilkes Bashford, Armani, and Bottega Veneta come to his room at eight in the morning with their best selection of fine ready-made menswear.

But nothing could match the hedonistic pleasure of having a $10,000 handmade suit cut from the finest fabrics mortal money could buy, even if he could only wear it in private for the time being.

When he was satisfied with his appearance, he placed a call to Fredkin and Associates and made an appointment for the next morning. After making clear to the tailor that he would be giving them regular business and was more than willing to pay for a rush order over the Yule holidays, he grabbed his cane and went downstairs to the magnificent dining room. He was shown to the best table in the place and ordered a Blood and Sand.

He sipped the drink, his mind busy with strategic calculations. Sometime over the next few days, while he handled any number of other problems and concerns, he would be meeting Briggs for a long and very private discussion about his vital role in shaping the senator's very promising future. And then there was the matter of the criminal element, who would soon learn that this city was theirs no longer.

And once he had opened the bridges again, he wouldn't only bring more Jotunar into Midgard.

Fenrisulfr, Loki thought, would be first. They had not always been on good terms, but the boy knew that his failure to kill Odin was a nearly unforgivable black mark against him and would therefore be unquestioningly obedient and enthusiastic in his work.

The crisply dressed server, a young man with bedroom eyes and very kissable lips, expertly delivered a second cocktail, smiling with more-than-professional enthusiasm. A female server had stopped a few feet behind him, a water tray balance on one hand, and was staring at Loki with a rapt expression. She licked her lips.

Midgard, Loki thought, was a world of endless opportunities.

He sipped his drink again and crooked a finger.

13

Ryan and Gabi huddled together in the darkness, sitting on the sleeping bag Mist had dug up for Gabi. The house had grown quiet, which meant Mist and Dainn had probably gone to bed . . .

Together? Ryan wondered. "Cousin," Mist had said, but Ryan didn't believe it. There had definitely been something going on between those two.

That was one reason he couldn't seem to sleep.

"*Caramba,*" Gabi said, her voice thick with drowsiness. "I don't remember when I had so much to eat."

Ryan couldn't, either. He knew it was right to be here. He'd known it since Mist came to his rescue. It was already more than he'd ever expected.

And he was scared shitless.

"Hey," Gabi said, punching him gently in the shoulder. "What's wrong? You change your mind or something?"

"No."

"I know you're not *loco*, Ry, but everything else about this is crazy. Magic swords and giants and all that shit . . ."

Ryan drew his legs up to his chest. It amazed him that his only friend in the world had trusted him enough to accept the things he'd told her and hadn't just decided he wasn't worth bothering with anymore.

"And elves," he said, "and dwarves."

"Oh, yeah. Almost forgot about those. And what about *her*?" She pointed toward the door as if Mist were standing right outside it. "Who is she, anyway? Sure, she looks tough, and she's supposed to be some kind of warrior. But she don't look so important to me. Shouldn't she live in a castle or something?"

"This isn't a fairy tale, Gab," Ryan said, resting his chin on his knees. "It's real. There're going to be more of those giants, and a war that could destroy the whole world."

"Yeah. I seen that movie, too."

"Bad stuff is coming. We have to be ready."

"Then we should get out of here."

"You know I can't leave." He touched the center of his chest. "It isn't just the dreams. It's knowing I'm supposed to be here. You, too."

"Me?" Gabi laughed. "I'm only here because of you."

"So you'd go back to the streets if you could?"

"What makes you think we'll still be here tomorrow? *She* didn't say nothing about us staying after tonight."

"No," Ryan said, closing his eyes. "But we will."

"It's not like you've ever been wrong before, Ry, but I'm the one who keeps us alive."

"I haven't really been alive in a long time," Ryan said. "Neither have you. We both have a new chance now."

She snorted. "To get killed."

"He won't let that happen."

"He?" Gabi looked at him out of the corner of her eye. "The elf guy? If it wasn't for the pointed ears, I'd never believe it. Everyone knows elves are those little things with wings."

"That's fairies," Ryan said, flushing.

"Elves, fairies, whatever." She lowered her voice. "You *like* him, don't you?"

"I don't know what you're talking about," Ryan said, his own ears beginning to burn. "I barely even talked to him."

"Lot of people would say he's pretty hot. All that long black hair."

"He didn't even look at me. And even if I was interested, which I'm not, it's obvious he and Mist . . ." He trailed off, unable to meet Gabi's worried gaze.

"Maybe not so obvious to *them*," Gabi said.

"As soon as I met Dainn, I knew he was important, like Mist. I mean, to save the world from the giants and the Sauron guy. Loki, I mean."

"Loki. Sounds like some kid's toy or something."

"That's not what Mist told me." He turned to face Gabi, willing her to understand. "I know we can help them. And they'll protect us from the giants and everything else."

"I always protected you, Ry," she said, sadness in her eyes.

He clasped her hand. "I know. But it's not just you and me anymore. It's everyone."

Gabi's jaw set. "If you say so. But the second something looks funny, I'm outta here. You can come with me or not."

Ryan knew better than to keep arguing with her. He always ended up giving in, and he couldn't do that this time. "If you have to go," he said softly, "I'll understand."

"Shit," Gabi snapped. She laid a small, warm hand on his shoulder. "Sorry, Ry," she said. "I know this is important to you."

"We should get some sleep," Ryan said. "I think Mist is going to be asking a lot more questions tomorrow."

"Yeah." Gabi got up. "You're still taking the bed."

"Okay." Ryan tugged at his oversized pants, not minding at all that they didn't fit. He had a bandage on his chin where the giants had cut it. He was clean. He wasn't hungry. And he didn't have to walk the streets, hoping he'd earn enough to get him and Gabi through one more day.

"G'night," Gabi said, stretching out on the sleeping bag. "And try not to dream, Ry."

He shivered and pulled the blanket all the way up to his chin.

"Are you ready?" Dainn asked.

He sat across from Mist on the living room rug, gazing steadily into her eyes. She was still tense, and all too aware of Dainn's natural elvish scent, clean and brisk as a cool wind over the mountains of Alfheim.

She averted her gaze from the swallowing darkness of his gaze, focusing on the next thing she saw. Unfortunately, that was still Dainn: his long, elegant hand resting palm-up on his knee. It was the kind of hand that could bring pleasure with the lightest touch of a fingertip.

And she'd asked Dainn if she was a problem for *him*. Did this glamour thing work both ways?

Curse it.

"Is your rib troubling you?" Dainn asked, a muscle twitching almost imperceptibly at the corner of his mouth.

"It's nearly healed," she said. Which it almost was, given her capacity for fast healing, though she hadn't helped it by working in the forge and it still hurt like Hel.

"I'm ready," she said.

"Very well." He hesitated, as if even he didn't quite know where to start. "There are several kinds of magic among the peoples of the Eight Homeworlds."

"I know," she said, ticking off her fingers as if repeating a rote lesson. "Elf, growing things; Dwarf, earth and stone; Jotunn—two kinds, fire and ice; Galdr, the Rune-magic, ranging from the most powerful kind Odin uses to what any Valkyrie can do. And Seidr, Freya's magic."

"Known to only a few of the Aesir," Dainn said. "It was once the sole province of the Vanir, but Freya taught it to Odin. And there is a magic more ancient still, also of the Vanir but long forgotten." He glanced toward the door to the hall as if he had heard something outside it, then turned back to Mist. "Your Jotunn abilities will come more naturally in time. I do not know the Seidr or the ancient magic, and you would not benefit from elven magic now, which only very few non-Alfar can master. We will concentrate on the Galdr."

"Fine by me."

"First I will teach you to breathe. It is the foundation for everything that follows."

"I *know* how to breathe," Mist said. "That's one of the first preparations any fighter makes before practice."

"This is different," Dainn said. "It is the awakening of the mind to accept what as yet lies beyond your reach."

"Take the pebble from my hand, Grasshopper," she quoted.

"I beg your pardon?"

"I don't suppose you ever watched television back in the seventies."

"Is there some significance to the reference?"

"Never mind." Mist sighed, aware that she was only putting off the inevitable. "You said you studied with a lama in Tibet. I should warn you that I'm no more a New Age groupie than a sorceress."

"I do have some difficulty imagining you at the feet of an ancient wise man in a mountain cave, sitting absolutely still for days at a time."

Only the slightly wry tone of his voice told Mist that he was teasing her. "I hope you're not suggesting that's what I'm going to be doing," she said.

"I am only moderately wise, and I anticipate hours, not days. We both have bodily needs."

Bodily needs. She could no longer tell if he was joking.

"Go to it," she said, swallowing hard.

Dainn cleared his throat. "Given your own long time in Midgard, you may not be surprised to learn that there are many diverse disciplines that can enhance the shaping and controlling magic. In India . . ."

Mist did her best to listen attentively, but when Dainn began to speak of chakras and how they corresponded to the Runes, her eyes nearly glazed over. Once the actual breathing exercises began, however, she saw the value in his seemingly pointless instruction. They dulled her awareness of his physical body, and her own.

Dainn seemed pleased with her progress. Like Mist, he had gradually become more relaxed, his shoulders slightly dropped and his eyes half closed.

"Very good," he said. "We will always begin every lesson in the same way."

At that rate, they'd never actually begin the lessons. Mist almost wished she could encourage more procrastination.

"You sure you haven't taught magic before?" she asked dryly.

"Not during my time in Midgard."

"You could have fooled me."

He tilted his head, his gaze turning inward. "It is late. Do you wish to continue?"

"Do you?"

"I am not tired."

"Neither am I."

"Remember that I will need to touch the surface of your thoughts. Until you can hold the Runes in your mind and fully utilize their power, I will have to guide you."

Her muscles began to tense up again. "I can handle it," she said.

"Then let us work through the Rune-staves one by one. First is Fehu, of Freya's Aett. It is the Rune of abundance and plenty, success and happiness."

"I know what it means," Mist said, too sharply.

"You know the surface meaning," he said, "but that is only of use in the rudimentary magic you required as a Valkyrie. When you aided me before, you simply held the shapes in your mind. Now you will learn every major and minor aspect of each stave in the Runic Alphabet so that every Bind-Rune and charm you choose to employ will create the precise result you intend. Each of the Runes must become a part of your very being, summoned with the merest thought."

"And what is the price?" she asked.

"The price?"

"Just fighting the Jotunar took nearly all of your strength. Loki was weakened by trying to leave Midgard. What's going to happen to me?"

"You are already paying a price in losing the life you knew and taking on the grave responsibilities your mother has bequeathed you," he said.

"That's not what I meant, and you know it," she said. "If I'm going to have to hoard my magic to keep from burning out—"

He gathered himself to rise. "If you are not prepared to continue—"

"Sit down, Dainn. Fehu, right?"

Dainn resumed his position, his body stiff and his expression guarded. "Fehu," he said, as if he were reciting from a book. "The Rune can bring great good fortune to those who master it. Fehu reversed is failure, discord, bondage. Like all the Runes, it can be used for good or evil. And there is a fine balance between the two aspects. It requires great skill to keep that balance and not fall into that place where the Merkstave, the Reversal, takes precedence."

"You sound as if you think I'll be tempted to use it."

"You must walk both paths before you can control either aspect. It is the darker way in which you will need the greatest guidance. If you surrender to hubris, the magic will fail you when you most need it."

Was Dainn speaking from experience? Had he walked that same path and gone astray when his own magic had flowed freely?

She knew better than to ask.

"Are you ready to open your mind?" Dainn asked.

Mist nodded and closed her eyes, bracing herself as if for attack. She could never forget what it had been like when they'd touched minds the first time—the way his emotions came to her so clearly, the anger and the shame and the sorrow. She didn't want to feel that again.

But her personal fears didn't matter now. She tried to relax, and after awhile she began to sense Dainn's mental presence, resting feather-light on the surface of her thoughts.

"Let go," he said. "Release your barriers."

"What barriers?" she whispered, as if a louder voice might jar their fragile connection.

"There are doors in your mind. Let them open."

Mist tried to envision such doors, but they didn't seem to exist. "I'm not trying to keep you out," she said. "If there's something in the way, I can't feel it."

"It is there, I assure you."

"Then show it to me!"

After a long silence, Mist opened her eyes. Dainn was staring at her, his eyes black and cold.

"Very well," he said.

Dainn attacked.

He threw everything he had into the assault, every Merkstave he had avoided so assiduously, every particle of anger and hatred he had nurtured since the fall of Asgard. He remembered the laughter in Loki's eyes when he had revealed his hideous deception . . . remembered each humiliation, each betrayal, the contempt on the faces of the Aesir and Alfar as they pronounced his punishment.

With rage and black Galdr he constructed a Rune-etched blade sharper than anything made by god or man, swinging it mercilessly at the wards Mist denied, aiming for the very heart of her being.

Still she resisted him, utterly oblivious to her own power, shattering the blade and casting him off as easily as a hound sheds water from its coat. The fierce icefire gale she had thrown at him so unwittingly in Asbrew—the terrible weapon that could have destroyed him had its owner understood what she possessed—remained quiescent behind the gates.

This was the trial Dainn knew would come when his mind touched Mist's again. She hadn't known what she'd done in Asbrew; she couldn't drop her instinctive barriers unless she accepted that they were there. He would have to rouse those frigid fires once more, hoping that Mist could control them when she understood that they, and the wards that bound them, were equally a part of her nature.

One more weapon remained to him. He would never have considered it if he believed Mist was incapable of protecting herself. If Mist had failed to recognize the true nature of the beast before, now she would see it for what it was. She would *know*. And there would be nothing he could do to call that knowledge back.

Nor could he be sure he could ever again defeat the thing he had fought so long. The cage had already been weakened by his use of magic, by Freya, by Mist herself. If he was lucky, he would keep enough control to avoid causing damage. He would have to.

Pushing himself beyond the restraints of rational thought, Dainn unleashed the beast. The creature, fed by his rage, was as strong as it had ever been. It slammed its bulk against the bars and burst through, roaring in triumph, slashing through Dainn's defenses as if they were built of ancient, crumbling parchment. Dainn had just enough will left to send it outward, leaping for the enemy walls.

Mist screamed.

Dainn had no time to brace himself. Mist's counterattack came hard and fast, slamming against the beast, driving it back with ice and flame and air and stone. It scrambled for purchase on formless ground, snarling and slavering and howling defiance.

Wracked by indescribable pain, Dainn tried to call it back. He had achieved what he had intended. Mist had broken through her own wards, her resistance purged like pus from a festering wound. He could not enter her mind yet; that would be impossible until Mist ceased her furious assault. But as long as the beast resisted . . .

Come back, he sang in a language he had not heard spoken by anyone else in centuries. *You will have what you desire. We will be one.*

The creature was far from stupid. It knew Dainn might deceive it for his own protection. But the temptation was great, and Mist's unrelenting onslaught was telling on its strength, burning the black fur from its massive body, blinding it with slivers of ice and rock.

In the end it had no choice. It began to retreat, edging back toward the relative safety of Dainn's mind. Dainn felt it come and cried out in agony, his own breached defenses attempting to rise against it, instinctive rejection he could not afford to permit.

So he embraced it, endured the searing pain of its invasion as he had done so long ago. When it was safely within him again, he soothed it with promises until, exhausted, it fell into a momentary stupor.

But Mist was not finished. She drove after it, sweeping through the raw wound it had left in its wake, carving out a void in Dainn's mind and controlling his body with all the ease of a mortal child manipulating a puppet. Runes and Merkstaves, their true shapes barely distinguishable—scythe-wheeled chariot, driving hail, seething flood, needles of yew—plunged like flame-tipped arrows into his heart, his belly, every vulnerable part of his body. The icy-hot wind picked him up and flung him across the room while her will stabbed at every nerve, flaying him alive. His throat was too raw for screams, even as every bone shattered when he hit the floor.

He had failed. In the fury of her attack, Mist had lost herself.

An ebony veil fell over Dainn's eyes, and he began to let himself go. He had feared death, and longed for it; so many times he had tried to take his own life and had been prevented by the instincts of the beast. But if he had driven Mist mad by forcing her to confront her own vast power, his existence was meaningless.

And the beast would die with him. He would never have to pay Freya's price for its destruction, abandoning the last traces of decency he had clung to since his fall.

Mist would never know how he had planned to betray her.

He closed his eyes and released his life.

"Dainn!"

At first all he knew was that the pain was gone. Hands fluttered over him, strong, long-fingered woman's hands, touching him here and there as if their owner could not keep them still.

"Dainn! Can you hear me?"

Mist's voice. A little rough, and urgent with fear. He felt Mist's hands cup his face, Mist's breath on his lips. She pulled his mouth open and covered it with hers, blew air into his lungs, turned her head away for a count of two and shared her breath again.

It was sweet, this revival, and it almost made him forget the agony of living. He opened his eyes. Mist pulled back, whispering a prayer even the White Christ might have approved.

"You're alive," she said. "I thought—" She bent her face to his chest. "I'm sorry. I'm sorry."

Dainn was incapable of responding, though he knew he had

suffered no lasting harm. He didn't feel broken anymore. His lungs functioned. His heart beat as it should.

Had it all been illusion, then, the shattering of bones and the tearing of flesh?

Perhaps that part had been. But not her magic. Yew needles were scattered on the carpet around him, and melting water soaked his clothing. Lingering manifestations that accompanied only the most powerful magic.

"Do you think you can drink?" Mist asked. She left him for a moment and returned with a glass of water. "Tell me if anything hurts." She positioned herself behind his head and lifted it with utmost care, wedging her knees under his shoulders.

"There," she murmured, helping him take a swallow of the water. "You'll be all right. You'll be all right."

Dainn closed his eyes again, relishing the feel of her strong thighs supporting him, her loose hair caressing his face as she leaned over him.

She was sane again. But she was not blind. She knew that something incredible had happened and that she was responsible for it. Perhaps he had not failed after all.

But neither had the beast. It had not been badly damaged by the assault, only driven back for a time. He felt it sleeping the sleep of utter exhaustion, but it was far from sated. When it woke it would remember his promise. A promise he must continue to resist as he resisted the emotional weakness that threatened to consume him all over again.

"Mist," he croaked.

"Don't try to talk," she said.

"Are you . . . well?"

"Me?" She hissed through her teeth. "Everyone keeps asking me that when I'm the healthiest one around. Aside from wondering what in Hel just happened, I'm fine."

"What . . . do you remember?"

"Rest now. We'll talk la—"

"What do you remember?" he repeated more urgently.

"Power," she said. "Inside me. Something . . . breaking through, wanting to hurt. Fighting . . . fighting you."

He gathered up the tattered rags of his courage. "Do you under-stand . . . what I did?" he asked.

The bewilderment in her eyes cleared. "You attacked me."

Now. Now it would come.

He tried to sit up, and this time she didn't prevent him. He braced himself on his elbows. "You asked that I . . . show you the barriers you have created within your mind. The only way to make you aware of them, and what lay behind them, was to force you to defend yourself."

"But I . . ." She moved from behind him and knelt facing him, her expression tight with worry. "There was fire, and ice, and . . . such anger—" She shook her head. "I think I wanted to kill you. I remember thinking of the Runes, the way you showed me. But the rest of it . . . it wasn't from Freya. It couldn't have been. And it wasn't the Jotunn magic I used in Asbrew, either. I never felt anything like this before." She glanced at the carpet, at the yew needles, at the melting hail on his shoulders. "You said you expected me to become what I was meant to be. What *am* I?"

"You are remarkable," he whispered.

She rejected his answer with a jerk of her head. "Maybe you should start by telling me exactly what *you* did."

A painful shiver wracked Dainn's body. Was it possible that Mist had been too absorbed in her counterstrike to understand what she was fighting, the terrible truth of his dual nature?

"That is not important," he said. "What matters is what *you* did. I recognized at Asbrew that you had great potential. Now I believe you may have . . . talents even your mother does not possess."

Mist looked at him as if he were mad. "How can I be more pow-erful than a goddess?"

Dainn knew it would be better to say nothing at all. This was far beyond his skill.

But she needed—deserved—to understand.

"Do you remember when I spoke of an ancient, almost forgotten magic?" he asked.

"Are you saying that's what I was doing?"

"You may be drawing on abilities that reach back to the very source of Vanir power."

She ran her fingers through her loose hair. "But the way you talked about it—"

The way he had talked of it had suggested that no living being could wield that magic. Freya had not suspected, or she surely would have prepared him to anticipate greater obstacles. She had admitted that Mist was more than she expected, but could she ever have imag-ined this?

"I have no explanation," he said. "Yet the facts are clear. You were capable of driving me out of your mind, and you used both the power of thought and Runic elements to do it, imagery that came as in-stinctively as the glamour. Even at my full strength, you would have overcome my defenses."

Mist stood, backing away until the couch prevented her from moving any farther. "And these are the 'talents' you expect me to develop?"

"Freya expects me to help you use all your abilities."

"The glamour is bad enough. I'm not going to do anything that can destroy someone the way I almost destroyed you."

"As you see, I am not damaged."

"Don't give me that, Dainn. I threw you against that wall. With my mind. And water, and pine needles, and spears of flame. Loki's piss, I could have *killed* you." She raised her hands, turning them forward and back. "Fighting with these, or a sword, is one thing. Even getting rid of Jotunar with magic is acceptable, because sometimes there's no other choice. But there's evil in this other way, just like there is in making people come to me. Even if I don't know I'm doing it."

"It is like any other tool, like the Runes. It is even more essential that you understand how to use it."

"And how do you know I'll choose the right path?" She stared down at him, fists clenched and jaw set. "You talked about the danger of misusing the Runes. They shape the magic, right? Did I use Merkstaves against you, Dainn?"

He couldn't deny it, and Mist clearly saw the answer in his face. "If I'm so cursed powerful, what makes you so sure I won't use this . . . force inside me to attack anyone who threatens me?"

"There is no wickedness in you, Lady," he said, meaning it with all his heart.

"But there *is* something dark, isn't there? Just like there is in you."

Dainn laughed silently at his own naïveté. He hadn't escaped after all.

"When you attacked me," Mist said, "something came after me. This isn't the first time I've seen it, either. When you helped me shape the Rune-staves the first time, it was there in the shadows." She crouched where she was and stared at him, grim and implacable. "At first I thought it was just something my thoughts invented, some kind of image I made up because I was scared and needed something solid to be afraid of. I didn't want to believe it was really part of you.

"But it is. And it hates me, Dainn. It hates the whole world."

14

─────

Dainn pulled himself to his feet and leaned heavily on the wall. "Yes," he said. "It hates. It hates everything that lives or ever lived."

"And you sent it into my mind."

"I would not have done so if I believed there was a chance you couldn't overcome it."

She folded her arms and glared at the carpet. "Where did it come from? Did you . . . create it?"

The idea sickened him. "It was not of my making, but it feeds . . ." He had to swallow several times before he was sure of his voice. "When we met, you believed that Dainn Faith-breaker had died at Thor's hand before the Last Battle began. That was the story put out by the Aesir. But I clearly did not die. I was cursed."

Mist sat down on the couch hard enough to make it squeak in protest. "Cursed? By whom?"

"Odin, with the approval of the Aesir and my own people. Only Freya spoke for me. And she could not save me."

"Then you were lying when you said you didn't remember how you got to Midgard," she said. "You were *sent* here, with this curse on you."

Dainn bowed his head. "Before the Last Battle had fully begun."

"But what *is* it?"

Dainn put his back to the wall and let it take his weight as he sang the increasingly ineffective Rune-spell that had once allowed him to detach himself from all emotion. Mist heard nothing of it; a year of continuous meditation and practice had made the use of his voice unnecessary.

It was not entirely effective, and he had not expected it would be. The spell only muted the memories and allowed him to speak without weeping.

"It is a beast of thought," he said, "but it has no real intelligence of its own. Only the will to hate. And to seek freedom from the restraints that prevent it from attacking others as it attacked you."

"In the mind?"

So many things he could have told her then, if he'd had the courage. If the beast itself hadn't reminded him why he could not.

"It has the potential to destroy what mortal psychologists have called the 'psyche' of other intelligent beings. It claws its way through any resistance and devours what it finds."

Mist's face revealed every emotion as she absorbed his meaning, puzzlement to comprehension to horror. "You mean it makes people crazy?" she said.

"No. It obliterates their minds."

"Gods," she said, her eyes flaring with revulsion. "You talk as if you're not even connected to this thing. I've almost gotten used to hearing you speak like someone who doesn't understand normal emotions, but how can you be so cool about *this*?"

Cool. She had seen so deeply into him and still believed he felt nothing. His spell had succeeded beyond his wildest dreams.

"Emotion is one of the things that feeds the beast," he said.

"*Your* emotion?"

"Dark emotion."

"Like anger. Anger over what the Aesir did to you? At Loki? Over everything you lost?"

Those were questions he could not answer. Would not. "I have had to learn how to dampen the beast's power," he said.

"The bars," she said. "The cage."

"The work of many centuries," he said.

Mist drew her knees to her chest and wrapped her arms around them. "What's the other thing that feeds it?" she asked quietly.

"Magic."

It was as if the proverbial lightbulb had winked on over her head. "Of course," she said. "It wasn't just that you were out of practice that you held back."

"I couldn't tell you then. You would not have understood."

"I still don't." She rubbed at the wrist that bore the wolf and serpent tattoo. "Did Freya know about this thing when she sent you to find me?"

"She did not believe the beast would be an . . . impediment."

"Not very good judgment, if you ask me," she said with heavy sarcasm. "You said she couldn't save you when you were cursed. Doesn't she have any way of helping you get rid of it now?"

So close, so very close to the truth. "She cannot," he said.

Mist clamped her lips together, clearly not satisfied by the answer. "I think I know now why Loki was so afraid of you."

Dainn looked away, unwilling to lie to her face yet again. "He was not involved in the curse."

"You said your parting didn't end on a 'cordial note,'" Mist said. "You said that once you could have done him harm, but you couldn't do it anymore. That was a lie all along, wasn't it?"

"We met once after Odin laid the curse on me, before I came to Midgard."

"Finally, a little honesty," she said. "But I won't ask you for the details now. You said you had it under control. That has obviously changed." She lifted her head. "Maybe you've kept the thing inside you from being a threat to others, but what about to you? You're an elf. Elves are aesthetes, civilized, peaceful, even though they think they're better than everyone else. They don't use weapons, and they only fight with magic when they have no other choice." She searched his eyes. "It tears you apart, doesn't it?"

"I have learned to accept it," he said.

"And what happens if the beast escapes again?"

"I found a way to contain its power before. I will do so again."

"That isn't good enough, Dainn. I want to help make sure it *can't* happen again."

Brave Mist. Stubborn, impulsive, headstrong Mist.

"No," he said.

She swung her legs to the floor. "You said I could be more powerful than Freya. You want me to understand my own abilities. What good is any power if I can't help my friends?"

Friends. She didn't know what she was saying.

"You have no grasp of your magic," he said. "You are incapable of what you suggest."

"I can obviously do things with *my* mind that only gods can. I was able to stop the beast. If I can help you rebuild that cage . . ."

"If you reach too far, you could destroy yourself."

"That's *my* risk."

Holding his arm out in case he should fall, Dainn went to the door. "Come with me," he said. "There is something I must show you."

She glanced at the clock on the mantelpiece and yawned. "It's already seven in the morning," she said, "and the kids'll be up soon if they aren't already. Where are we going?"

"It would be better to do this in a larger space, where there is no chance that others might hear."

His words must have sounded ominous indeed, but Mist got up and followed him into the hall. Almost at the same moment, Ryan came pelting down the stairs in his bare feet, oversized pajamas flapping around his spare frame. He came to a sudden stop halfway down when he saw Mist and Dainn.

"Shit!" he said. "I thought something was wrong!"

Dainn stared at the boy, whose pupils were so dilated that the light brown of his irises was barely visible. Mist went to him immediately.

"You'd better sit," she said, pushing him down onto the stair. "Are you having another seizure?"

Ryan shook his head. "I thought it was already here," he said.

"*What* was already here?" Dainn asked, moving closer to the boy.

"I don't know," Ryan said, his voice rising. "I thought—"

Suddenly the cats streaked out of the kitchen, tails puffed up to twice their normal sizes, ears flat. They stopped just past the stairway, hissing and arching their backs.

They were facing the door to the gym.

Dainn felt it a moment later. "Go upstairs, Ryan," he said.

"But—"

"Go!" Mist shouted, helping him up and turning him around. "Stay with Gabi!"

Once Ryan was at the top of the stairs and out of sight, she looked at Dainn. "What?" she asked.

He breathed in deeply. The cats, having done their duty, turned and ran back to the relative safety of the kitchen.

"Jotunar," he said.

"We meet again, Sow's daughter," Hrimgrimir said.

She came to a stop just inside the gym door, Dainn a step behind her. The giant, about seven feet tall and 350 pounds of solid muscle, stood in the center of the gym, hands on hips, grinning with all the evil relish of a nineteenth-century melodrama villain. The only thing that ruined the effect was his too-tight jeans, bulging at the thighs, and the loose plaid shirt.

He and the two Jotunar with him had not been among those she and Dainn had—hopefully—sent to a desert half a world away. Loki's forces might have been reduced, but they were by no means eliminated. And Hrimgrimir was among the strongest of them. And the worst.

"Where's the forest?" Mist asked, feeling for Kettlingr at her hip.

Hrimgrimir lost his grin, his face creasing in confusion. "Say what you mean, bitch," he said.

"You look like a lumberjack. Shouldn't you be out somewhere cutting down trees?"

It was a consummately ridiculous thing to say, but Mist wasn't interested in trying to be clever. Her only goal was to get Hrimgrimir angry enough to make stupid mistakes. Making him angry wasn't very hard to do.

But Hrimgrimir didn't take the bait. He looked at Dainn, who had moved to stand beside Mist, and chuckled.

"I've never felt such pathetic wards," the Jotunn said. "Was that really the best you could do, Faith-breaker?"

Mist closed the door behind her, refusing to reveal her emotions. Dainn's wards *had* failed. He had seemed confident enough when he'd set them, but the presence of Hrimgrimir and his two friends— one in biker's leathers and the other wearing an incongruous red silk shirt and striped trousers—proved that he'd screwed up somewhere. Perhaps fatally.

She could tell by Dainn's rigid stance that he fully understood his responsibility for the current situation. But she didn't have time to ask him what might have happened.

"What's wrong?" Hrimgrimir taunted. "Fenrir got your tongue?"

Dainn stepped in front of Mist. "You should not have come here," he said.

"The threat of a weakling and coward," Hrimgrimir jeered, rumbling laughter.

"I am not alone," Dainn said. "Or perhaps you have forgotten what happened in Vidarr's establishment."

"You had the element of surprise on your side." The Jotunn stared at Mist. "You won't have it again."

Mist shoved ahead of Dainn. "But Loki made the mistake, didn't he?" she asked. "He knew I was Freya's daughter, but he didn't think I'd be able to fight him." She smiled. "Did he actually tell you to let me through to him?"

For a moment Hrimgrimir seemed at a loss. "Do you think you'd ever have made it past us if he didn't?"

"Actually, I do."

"Only because Freya was there. Loki told us. You couldn't have done jack shit without the Vanir bitch. Where is she now?"

Good, Mist thought. Loki still credited her abilities to Freya's presence within her, just as Dainn had said. And that assumption would hurt him, and his allies, as long as he held it.

"Waiting for you to do something stupid," she said. "What should worry you now is that Loki didn't know that Dainn was around, or how much damage *he* could do. And your boss ran off without checking on his Jotunar minions. That's why about a dozen of your comrades are halfway across the world." She clucked her tongue in sympathy. "Doesn't that piss you off just a little bit?"

Hrimgrimir cracked his knuckles. "Loki didn't send us here," he said. "We've come to get the kid."

"What kid?" Mist asked, raising her brows.

"You took him away from my men."

"Because they were beating him up. What's so special about him?"

"You think we're that dumb? We're taking him back. And if we happen to kill you on the way—" He exposed his sharp, yellow teeth in another grin. "Well, that'll be the icing on the cake."

"Good luck with that," Mist said. She flicked a sideways glance at Dainn. His expression was rigid, but she could feel the tension in his muscles, the anger building up inside him.

The beast. The beast of thought, driven by dark emotion and the implacable will to hate, to destroy. A devourer of the mind.

Mist had no reason to doubt that it could also devour Jotunar minds. But Hrimgrimir apparently knew nothing about it. Dainn had kept it hidden, under control. Until tonight.

Magic fed it, too. But magic was the only way Dainn could fight the Jotunar.

Unless she sent him away.

"Go, Dainn," she whispered. "If you stay—"

"I know," Dainn said, very softly. "But I will not leave you to face them alone."

"Freya can't help us at all?"

"Even if she could, I have no time to reach her."

"Then I can handle it. You just finished saying how powerful I—"

"Why the whispers?" Hrimgrimir asked. "Trying to figure out how you're going to get out of this alive? Give us the kid, and maybe we'll spare one of you." He met Mist's gaze. "You, since Loki still has some use for you."

"And you always give Loki what he wants," Mist said.

"Only as long as he gives us what *we* want," Hrimgrimir said.

"To grab whatever you can of this world when Loki unleashes chaos," she said. "Better hope he leaves enough of Midgard for you when he's finished."

"He needs us," Hrimgrimir growled.

"For now." She deliberately bumped Dainn's shoulder with her own. "Get out of here," she hissed.

He didn't budge. Hrimgrimir was cracking his knuckles again, opening and closing his fists.

"Enough talk," the Jotunn said. "Give us the elf, and we'll take you and the kid alive."

Dainn moved so close to Mist that his chest was pressing against her back. "I can hold them off," he said, "while you get Ryan and the girl to safety."

"You notice that you're the one they want to kill?" she asked. "You have to go."

"Listen to me," Dainn said. "When they attack, try to remember what you did when I sent the beast to confront you. Use that power. We must hope that you can control it well enough to—"

Hrimgrimir charged, his flunkies behind him, their booted feet clumping on the rubber tiles. Mist drew her knife and chanted it to full size, desperately trying to remember what she'd done to Dainn out of the pure, instinctive need to defend herself.

Darting sideways, Dainn yelled out a foul insult Mist would never have believed she'd hear from an elf's lips. Hrimgrimir didn't break stride, but the gangster Jotunn in the silk shirt split off from the others and headed straight for Dainn. By the time Hrimgrimir reached her, Mist had Kettlingr out and ready.

To her amazement, Hrimgrimir stopped. "You think *that* can save you?" he asked.

Suddenly Mist knew why he hesitated, in spite of all his bluster. "Freya will save me," she said. She envisioned how she had felt in Asbrew when she'd faced Loki. "My mother is here."

Alarm crossed Hrimgrimir's face, but she wasn't quite convincing enough. He swept his arm at her, aiming to knock the sword out of her hand and send her flying across the room.

Mist ducked, stabbing upward. But Hrimgrimir was already out of her path and preparing another strike, while the biker Jotunn behind him was circling around to approach her from the rear. All the warmth was leached from the room as the air crackled with newly formed ice, Jotunn magic meant to freeze her, immobilize her, make her helpless.

Curse it, Mist thought, addressing that part of herself she was so far from understanding. *What did you do to Dainn?*

Fire and ice and anger. Water and wind and stone. Vanir magic, Dainn had said. Not *of* the Runes, but able to shape their inherent power outside the boundaries of logic.

Mist closed her eyes and spun, swinging the sword with her body, feeling the Runes dance in the air like snowflakes caught in a whirlwind. Runes of protection. Runes of strength. Uruz the Ox danced on the edge of Kettlingr's silver blade, thrashing the air with his horns. Kenaz the Beacon burning behind her eyes, aflame with the power of transformation. Hagalaz, Hail, the uncontrolled forces of nature, lifting her hair with the crackle of electricity and bathing her skin in cool moisture.

Hrimgrimir came at her from the front, the other Jotunn from the back. Uruz bellowed and, cloaked in the whirlwind, impaled Hrimgrimir's arm on one deadly horn.

The Jotunn yelled and retreated. The giant behind Mist bounced off the wall of water her spinning had formed around her.

Mist snatched a very brief moment to look for Dainn. He was halfway across the gym facing the third Jotunn, who was buffeting him with sprays of ice needles. As she watched, Dainn staggered back, one arm raised to protect his face.

He wasn't defending himself. Only his elven nimbleness had kept him out of the Jotunn's reach so far, but the giant was obviously wearing him down. He would let himself be killed rather than use his own magic.

As if he'd heard her soundless shout of fear, he leaped back and began to sing. Vast roots burst through the floor, nearly transparent at first, becoming more and more solid as shoots sprang up and wove themselves into a dense and impenetrable shield. Dainn lifted his arm, and the shield broke off and flew into his hand. The roots vanished.

That was the last Mist saw of Dainn or the shield. She had lost both her concentration and her momentum, leaving her vulnerable to attack. Hrimgrimir slammed into her, knocking her off her feet. She managed to take a swing at the second Jotunn before he could pile on. The blow connected, snapping bone.

Using his good arm, Hrimgrimir yanked Kettlingr from her hand and wrapped his sausage-sized fingers around her neck, freezing her skin from the crown of her head to the tips of her toes. His companion screamed in rage. Mist turned her head in the direction she'd last seen Dainn, struggling to break through the darkness clouding her vision.

Dainn was also on the ground, pushing against the Jotunn on top of him with the oak-root shield. The giant grabbed his hair and slammed his head against the matting. He lay there, his chest heaving, as the Jotunn lifted his fist.

Fight, Mist urged Dainn silently, praying she could reach his mind. *It doesn't matter what else happens. Fight!*

Dainn's shield unraveled, the shoots separating and reaching toward the giant, sinuous as serpents. One caught his raised fist and wrapped around it. The other shot toward his mouth and darted inside. The Jotunn's face went red as he began to choke. He fell back, struggling with his free hand to dislodge the shoot in his throat.

Rolling out from under him, Dainn scrambled to his feet and ran toward Mist. The giant Mist had injured swung to face him, all teeth and muscle. Dainn looked like a stoat facing down an elephant.

But he didn't fight. He dodged around the Jotunn and hurled himself at Hrimgrimir's back, locking his arm around the giant's neck. Hrimgrimir lost his grip on Mist and reared to fling Dainn off, while his crony kicked the elf repeatedly in the back with his heavy boot.

Her vision clearing, Mist pushed against Hrimgrimir's chest and punched him in the jaw as soon as she had enough room to move. It was like hitting one of the faces on Mount Rushmore. Hrimgrimir bellowed and flung Dainn off. Mist squirmed out from under him and got to her knees, sucking in as much air as her lungs could hold, her fist a lump of pain. Desperately she scanned the floor for Kettlingr's familiar shape.

The biker Jotunn had Dainn pinned to the ground with his good arm as Hrimgrimir rose to his feet. The gangster giant Dainn had attacked with the roots had finally escaped them, leaving blackened, twisted ropes of withered vegetation in his wake as he thundered across the gym to join his comrades. He stopped next to Hrimgrimir.

"Let me have him, boss," the gangster said, rubbing his throat.

"Here!" Mist shouted. "Are you blind? I'm over here! Or would you rather beat up on a half-dead elf than face me again?"

Hrimgrimir bared his teeth at her. "There's no rush. Whatever you did, you've lost it. Freya isn't here. You're just as helpless as the dirt-sniffer." He glanced at the biker, who was holding his injured arm against his chest. "Dofr, you go find the kid. I promise I'll let you have a turn at the bitch, as long as you don't kill her."

Dofr was about to protest when the gym door opened a few inches and Ryan's head popped through the gap.

"Ryan!" Mist shouted. "Go back! Run!"

The young man's face went pale, but he didn't follow her orders. He stepped into the room, still barefoot and completely defenseless.

Mist knew it was her fault. She should have found a way to make Dainn leave with the kids. Now it was too damned late. She couldn't protect Ryan and save Dainn at the same time, if she could manage either one.

Through a gap between the giants' legs, Mist could see Dainn's head on the matting, battered and bloody. He turned his face toward her, unbearable sadness in his eyes.

"Dainn!" she shouted. "Let it go!"

Dainn had nothing left. Nothing to save Ryan, nothing to help Mist. Nothing but the one thing he knew could destroy every living creature in the room. It was so strong now, slavering with hunger, eager to obey Mist's reckless command.

But *he* was weak. So weak from holding it back, forced to use magic that made it stronger still.

"Dainn!" Mist cried. "Do it!"

"Dofr!" Hrimgrimir snapped, ignoring Mist completely. "That's the kid. Go get him."

Dainn managed to lift his head. The Jotunn in biker's leathers headed for the door while Ryan, fragile as a porcelain statue, only stared.

Dainn let his head fall back and closed his eyes. There was one chance, and little hope he would succeed. More likely the beast would break loose completely, casting him aside like a half-eaten carcass and consuming his body as well as his mind.

But it was the *only* chance. He met Mist's gaze again.

Get their attention, he thought. *But don't let them catch you.*

The spark in her eyes told him she had heard, or at least enough to figure out what he wanted. She jumped up and broke into a wild, giddy dance, leaping and whirling and throwing every conceivable rude gesture at the Jotunar.

"Nyah, nyah," she jeered like a child on a playground. "Whasa-matter, ya big apes? Still scared of li'l old me?"

Hrimgrimir and his companion turned to stare. "You must've hit her too hard," the silk-shirted Jotunn said.

"Shut her up for me, Bakrauf," Hrimgrimir said. "She's getting on my nerves."

Bakrauf lowered his head between his shoulders and stalked to-ward Mist, his right hand frosting over with a gauntlet of ice.

The Jotunar's brief moment of inattention was all Dainn needed. He opened the cage door and caught at the beast as it emerged, burying his hands in its thick mane, drawing its savage strength into himself as it struggled and clawed and bit.

When he moved, the giants seemed like insects caught in amber, trapped forever in one instant of time. Dainn raced toward Mist's sword rack and snatched at the first weapon he could reach, a heavy Viking spatha. He wrapped his fingers around the grip and charged Hrimgrimir and his companion, who had barely begun to notice his absence.

He swung, feinting high and then swinging low to cut at Hrimgri-mir's legs. The Jotunn, his arm still bleeding freely from Mist's mag-ical attack, leaped back just in time and beat down on the blade with the flat of his other hand, riming it with a crust of frost and tempo-rarily freezing the muscles in Dainn's right arm.

"So," Hrimgrimir said, "the little Alfr thinks he can handle a sword. Out of magic, Dirt-sniffer?"

Dainn let the anger come. "I've forgotten more magic than you will ever possess, Loki's cur," he said, baring his teeth. "Better run home and lick his feet."

"The way I heard it, you licked more than Loki's feet." Hrimgri-mir widened his eyes mockingly. "I have to admit, this is the first time I've seen an elf look as pissed off as you do right now."

"You have no idea," Dainn said.

Bakrauf, halfway to Mist, turned around. "You need help, boss?"

"I don't need your help to flatten this *nidingr* again," Hrimgrimir said. He grinned at Dainn. "I don't expect him to last very long."

Dainn felt the sword become a living thing in his hand, intensely aware of Mist's spirit burning at the heart of its deadly steel. Calculating speed and angle, Dainn swung again and pretended to lose his balance, letting Hrimgrimir strike him on his left arm with just enough force to cause pain without fully connecting.

He fell back with a cry of fury, hoping that the Jotunn would believe he was too angry to act any less recklessly than most of *his* breed would do under the same circumstances. Deep inside him, the beast flexed its claws and howled as it absorbed the pain.

Still Dainn retreated, holding his left arm at his side as if it had been damaged by the Jotunn's blow. He gradually circled toward the hall door and Ryan, letting his arm drop lower and lower.

Hrimgrimir didn't bother to taunt Dainn for his weakness. He followed slowly, obviously enjoying what he must have believed would be an easy victory.

Dainn turned and lifted the sword, feebly swinging at the Jotunn, who conjured a barbed icicle and sent it flying at Dainn's heart. Dainn dropped into a crouch as the weapon flew over him, severing a few loose hairs on the top of his head. Hrimgrimir followed up with a bunched fist in Dainn's stomach. Dainn fell to his knees, gasping for breath, and let the sword slide out of his hand.

"I yield," he whispered. "Spare my life, and I will help you capture the female."

"What makes you think we need your help? Take a look for yourself."

He gestured in Mist's direction. She was on her feet again, pressed against the wall, but she had managed to retrieve Kettlingr and was holding Bakrauf at bay with all her considerable skill. There was no fear in her expression, but Dainn knew the burst of magic he had seen her use earlier had abandoned her.

Hrimgrimir bent over Dainn, grabbed a fistful of his hair, and yanked his head up. "How do you want to die, elf? Since you tried to put up some kind of fight, maybe I'll make it quick."

"Dainn!" Ryan shouted.

Dainn spun around with his right leg extended, kicking Hrimgrimir's left leg out from under him. He grabbed the spatha and swept it downward in one smooth motion. The blade caught Hrimgrimir in the shoulder of his wounded arm. He roared like a foghorn as his arm went limp, nearly sliced free of the joint.

Without waiting to make sure the Jotunn stayed down, Dainn turned and raced toward Dofr and Ryan. The giant was almost on top of the boy, and Ryan wasn't making a single attempt to get away. He reached for Ryan with a casual swipe of his hand.

Gabi lunged through the half-open doorway and stabbed Dofr in the neck with a small knife, sinking it into his flesh up to the hilt. Dainn closed the remaining distance as Gabi grabbed Ryan and pulled him out of the way. Dainn thrust the spatha into the Jotunn's back, instantly severing his spine. Dofr toppled sideways and lay still.

"Watch out!" Gabi shouted. Dainn heard too late. Hrimgrimir came at him with all the blind fury of a bear protecting its young, his injured arm hanging at his side. The full weight of his body slammed into Dainn, throwing him against the wall next to the door and wrenching the sword from his hand. He slid to the floor as the toe of the giant's boot connected full force with his stomach. He curled in on himself, gasping, but the Jotunn was already aiming another kick.

"Run," he gasped, praying the young mortals would hear him. Hrimgrimir kicked him again, and ribs snapped. Dainn knew that when Hrimgrimir was finished with him, every bone in his body would be broken and his internal organs damaged beyond his ability to heal. Still he tried to hold on to the beast with imaginary hands, resisting its ravenous hatred, feeling his grip begin to loosen.

Hrimgrimir's fourth kick turned his vision dark. The fifth caught him in the groin, bringing agony so acute that he lost the last of his control. The beast broke loose, its endless hunger infecting his blood like a deadly sepsis. The strength he had borrowed increased a hundredfold. Every pore in his flesh itched like the bites of a million tiny insects. His senses became keener than any elf's, bringing the stench of Jotunn sweat and mortal terror.

A high-pitched scream cut the air, bringing the giant's leg to a suspended halt before he could complete his next kick. Dainn grabbed Hrimgrimir's boot and wrenched it sideways, snapping all the bones in his ankle and foot. The Jotunn tottered and fell. Dainn swept up the spatha again, stood over Hrimgrimir, and pushed the tip against the giant's throat. For the first time, he saw fear in the Jotunn's eyes.

"What are you?" Hrimgrimir croaked.

15

Dainn held the blade firm against Hrimgrimir's flesh and looked for Mist. She was still holding Bakrauf off and had hit him at least once. Dainn could feel elemental power swirling about her, directionless, lost without her guidance. If she could focus on it again . . .

Lowering the spatha with a flick of his wrist, Dainn ran it through Hrimgrimir's chest. A rush of air and blood burst from the giant's lips as he fell backward. Dainn used the heel of his boot to hold Hrimgrimir's body in place as he pulled the blade free and turned toward Mist again.

During the brief time he'd been occupied with Hrimgrimir, she'd not only managed to keep out of Bakrauf's hands but had retrieved her sword and was edging her way toward the young mortals, who seemed unable or unwilling to move from their places just inside the door. Ryan's face was blank. The girl still clutched the small, bloody knife in her hand.

Dainn understood that Mist planned to get the children away, and she trusted him to deal with the remaining Jotunn. Dainn ran at Bakrauf, ready to hack his legs out from under him.

But this one had taken to heart what Mist and Dainn were capable of. Abruptly he abandoned Mist and loped toward the door that opened onto the driveway. Dainn tossed the spatha into the air, caught the grip from the underside, and hurled it like a spear straight at Bakrauf's back.

The Jotunn fell onto his face halfway to the door. Dainn stood very still, panting hoarsely, holding his muscles rigid against the assault from within. The beast still wanted death, death, and more death, though there were no more enemy lives to take. Its frustrated rage pumped like acid through Dainn's veins, rage that was as much ecstasy as torment. He went for the sword, pulled it free, and scanned the room searching for one more chance to kill.

Not all the enemies were gone. He could smell another. A male. Mortal. *Human.*

The man stood beside Bakrauf's body, staring toward Dainn with a look of astonishment on his face. In an instant, Dainn took him in: of medium height, fit and casually dressed, dark hair a little longer than the current fashion, features unmistakably those of the Japanese islands. The outside door stood open behind him, letting in gusts of cold night air Dainn saw as breath condensing out of a gaping mouth.

Dainn tensed as the man shouted words he couldn't understand and strode toward him. He raised the spatha. The man stopped again, glanced past Dainn's shoulder, and raised his hands. He began to speak softly, soothingly, each word carefully chosen to convey his harmlessness.

There was enough sense left in Dainn's mind to recognize that the mortal was trying to make him drop his guard. The beast snarled. The stranger looked past him again. Dainn could smell that Mist and the mortal children were no longer in the gym. They were safe.

He attacked.

The man dropped his hands, spun around, and raced for the sword rack. He came to a skidding halt before it, grabbed one of the weapons, and slid the long, slightly curved blade from its sheath. He cast the sheath aside and stalked toward Dainn. His mouth formed words, no longer soothing but commanding.

It was all so much noise, meaning no more to Dainn than the buzzing of flies. He stopped just out of the sword's reach. The man's heartbeat was deafening, and the smell of his sweat nauseated Dainn as the scent of blood excited him.

But some remnant of sanity held him from skewering the mortal like a roast on a spit and tearing his body apart. In the midst of that deadly, waiting silence, someone plunged through the open door and ran into the room, shouting as he pushed himself into the narrow space between Dainn and the stranger.

Dainn stared at the boy, seeing only an obstacle that stood between him and his enemy. He raised the sword.

And slowly lowered it again, his arms growing heavy, his vision washed with scarlet. The stranger shouted for the boy to move aside just as another enemy, his biker's vest nearly black with blood, rose from the floor and lunged for the nearest target. The giant knocked Ryan across the room with a massive fist. The boy's back slammed into the wall, his head rebounding from the hard surface with a sickening crack. He slumped to the ground.

Dainn was already swinging at the enemy lunging toward him. He feinted, slicing toward the giant's belly. When the Jotunn bent to protect his already injured torso, Dainn thrust the tip of his sword into the creature's eye with such force that it lodged in the skull beneath. The Jotunn shrieked like a child. A whirlwind of sleet and deadly slivers of ice began to spin around him, ever expanding until it threatened to engulf Dainn and strip his skin from his body.

Dainn jerked the bloody blade free and hacked at the giant's throat. The whirlwind collapsed into colorless debris at the Jotunn's feet. He gurgled, clamping his hand over his neck, and staggered in a circle, his injured eye weeping blood and clear fluid. His legs buckled under him and he fell to his knees.

Casting the sword aside, Dainn leaped on the Jotunn and encircled the giant's neck with his hands. He pressed into the Jotunn's wound with his fingers, widening the gash, and didn't stop until the last breath left the Jotunn's body.

But there was another like him, coming from behind, wheezing like a dying engine. Dainn spun, leaped, and kicked out with both feet, striking the Jotunn in the face with the heels of his boots. He landed on all fours like a cat and lashed out again, crushing the giant's already flattened nose. The Jotunn wheezed one final time and crashed to the floor.

Dainn turned to face the last enemy. Behind the mortal with the sword he could see the boy and the girl huddled against the wall. There was blood splashed on the wall around the boy's head.

And the woman was with them.

He rushed the swordsman, the beast's strength moving his muscles like pistons. The man dodged aside without attempting to strike.

"Dainn!"

He knew the voice, and the sound of it locked his joints and stilled his heart. All at once the beast began to retreat, slinking backward, shaking its head in confusion. Mist stood behind the swordsman, Kettlingr in hand, all pale features and wide gray eyes.

"You *know* this man?" the stranger said over his shoulder, his gaze never leaving Dainn's face.

"Drop that sword," Mist said, "unless you want to die, too."

The man's grip on the weapon didn't waver. "Ma'am," he said, "I came in when I heard someone screaming. I saw this man kill these people, and—"

"Drop it," she said, "or I'll take it from you."

The stranger set the katana carefully on the floor. "Ma'am," he said, a little more steadily, "This man is probably either psychotic or acting under the influence of powerful drugs. Take those kids out of here. I'll call the police and an ambulance."

Dainn tried to speak, but all that came out was a grunt. He had begun to feel every broken bone and the severe pain in his belly that meant internal bleeding.

"He would never harm the kids," Mist said, her voice unsteady.

"Ryan," Dainn croaked, finding his voice. "He . . . the Jotunar—"

"I'll take care of him," Mist said. "I'll take care of everything. You've got to get out of here." She kicked the katana out of the stranger's reach. "Whoever you are, you've interfered enough."

The mortal still didn't move, and neither did Dainn.

"On your knees," Mist said, gesturing with the sword.

"You seem like a decent person," the man said. "If you do this—"

"I'm not going to hurt you," Mist said. She laid Kettlingr aside, undid her belt buckle with one hand and pulled the belt free of her jeans. "You're going to let me tie you up until all this is sorted out."

The stranger raised his hands. "Okay. I'll do what you say."

"Down."

He began to drop to his knees, but he never completed the act. He fell to his side, rolled out of reach of the sword and scrambled to his feet in one smooth motion. A second later, he had a cell phone in his hand.

Dainn was moving before the mortal punched in a single number. The human was fast, but Dainn could have killed him then with as little effort as he would expend on plucking a flower. Instead, he wrenched the phone from the stranger's grasp, threw it to the floor, and ground it under his heel until he felt it give way with a crunch of metal and plastic. He heard Mist moving behind him and waved her back sharply.

"I do not know you, or why you are here," he said to the mortal, "but you are making a mistake. You saw how the boy was hurt. These . . . men attacked with the intent to kill."

"Maybe they did," the stranger said, rubbing his wrist. "If you really don't want to hurt anyone else, you'll let me call the police. They can help you."

Help him. Dainn couldn't even summon up a laugh at the absurdity. He looked over his shoulder at Mist, who was poised and ready to attack.

"I will take him with me," he said. "You see to the young ones."

"You'll kill him," Mist said. "I can't let you do that."

"I will not kill him," Dainn said. "But I will see that he doesn't interfere again."

"I can't trust you not to hurt him, Dainn," Mist said. "Just let me call an ambulance, and I'll take care of him."

Dainn closed his eyes. "Make your call," he said. He heard Mist speak into her cell phone, though he couldn't seem to understand the words. When she was finished, she walked past Dainn to the stranger and pointed Kettlingr toward the floor.

"On your stomach," she said. "And don't try anything again."

The mortal hesitated. Dainn drew back his fist and punched the young man squarely on the jaw. The stranger reeled and fell to his knees, all resistance lost to the blow. Mist put Kettlingr down again and knelt beside the stranger.

"He's okay," she said to Dainn. "Go. Go, and keep going."

Dainn backed away. The pain in his chest and belly was growing worse, and soon the injuries would either kill him or release the beast in another mad frenzy of rage.

He turned and ran toward the hall door. He plunged through it, slammed it behind him, and collapsed.

For a few minutes he lay where he was, coughing as blood began to fill his lungs. Leaving the loft was no longer a possibility. His vision was fading, and the beast was already clawing its way back into his mind.

Pulling himself to his knees, Dainn found his way to the nearest room. He fell against the door, pried it open, and crumpled to the worn carpet. Working the door closed with his foot, he struggled to raise repelling wards to discourage any mortal from looking into the room. He could feel the wards fail almost as soon as he created them.

He crumpled and lay very still, sinking into his body, assessing his wounds, whispering elvish spells to help close the torn blood vessels and mend the injuries to his internal organs.

They, too, failed him. His wounds were beyond mending by any but a true Healer, and they were all trapped in Ginnungagap with the others.

As he forced himself to breathe, his drowning lungs straining against broken ribs, he began to fall again ... down, down into a dream of darkness, remembering the wet sound of his blade piercing Bakrauf's eye, flesh, and muscle, the crunch of Hrimgrimir's nasal bones driving into his brain. He drew his body into a ball, head tucked against his knees, the blood trickling from his mouth sticky under his cheek.

He could let himself die now. Die, and remove the danger he would pose to anyone who came near him. End the tortured existence the beast had never let him abandon.

But it still wouldn't let him go. It roared and claimed him again, its strength flooding his body and wrenching at his gut, its implacable will fighting to do what the elf could not.

Dainn screamed, and the beast granted him mercy.

When Mist returned to the kids, Gabi was on her knees beside Ryan rocking back and forth in distress, the bloody knife just out of her reach. She looked up as Mist knelt beside her.

"It'll be all right," Mist said, carefully touching Gabi's shoulder.

"*No,*" Gabi said. "*No todo es derecho.*"

The knot in Mist's throat expanded to fill her whole body. "The ambulance will be here any minute," she said. "They'll know what to do. He'll be fine."

Skuld will it be so, Mist thought, well knowing Skuld wouldn't change this mortal girl's fate even if the Norn were alive and capable of interfering.

But no one was to blame for this horror except Mist herself. The kids had been hurt because Ryan had trusted her to protect him, because she'd let them stay at the loft. She had never anticipated that they'd interfere with the fight or have the courage to face what they couldn't possibly understand. Especially Ryan, who'd already had a taste of Jotunar violence.

And then there was Dainn.

Oh, he'd tried not to let it out. He'd allowed the giants to beat him down, distracted them, done everything but let loose the thing he had so urgently warned her about.

But she hadn't been able to bear his pain. "*It doesn't matter what else happens,*" she'd told him, urging him to fight for himself.

She hadn't understood. He'd told her the beast would attack the mind, the "psyche," and devour whatever it found. But that hadn't been how it had played out. She could still see him thrusting the spatha into Hrimgrimir's chest, spinning and striking like Jackie Chan without the wires. He had handled the sword as well as she did, as if he'd trained for centuries. He'd deceived Hrimgrimir and allowed himself to be kicked nearly to death, only to gain the upper hand again and impale Hrimgrimir like an insect on a pin.

His savagery had bought her time to get the kids away. But Ryan had slipped out of her hands during a moment of inattention. She and Gabi had followed him right around the front of the loft back to the gym and the door that opened onto the driveway. They'd arrived just in time to find Dainn on the verge of killing someone who definitely wasn't a giant.

Someone who'd been holding her katana and obviously thought he could beat Dainn in a fight. If she and Ryan hadn't interfered, the mortal would be lying dead in a pool of his own blood, not tied up and half unconscious. And now Dainn was gone—far gone, Mist hoped—and fighting to regain his own soul. She would find him when she could, find some way to help him. Or, if he couldn't be helped . . .

Ryan moaned, and she pulled her thoughts away from things she couldn't control. She touched the boy lightly on the shoulder, but he didn't react.

"I should never have let him come downstairs again," Gabi said, hunching over her knees. "He said he had to, that something terrible was happening. If we hadn't tried to help Dainn—"

"It's not your fault," Mist said. "I should have realized he wouldn't stay upstairs." She swallowed. "Ryan warned us that something was going on. It would have been much worse if he hadn't."

"Worse?" Gabi said in a voice far too bitter for one her age. "Dainn tried to send us away, but Ry wouldn't . . . he just wouldn't *listen*."

"I know," Mist said, awkwardly stroking Gabi's rigid arm. She felt helpless to comfort the girl, and she didn't like that feeling. It had become far too common lately, and today she'd had her face rubbed in it.

Just as she had during the war. As Gabi cried, her face buried in her arms, Mist checked the makeshift bandage she'd tied carefully around Ryan's head. Her experience in treating mortal injuries didn't extend to head wounds, and she was no healer.

What in Mimir's name had she really learned? What had she *done*?

She clenched her fists, feeling as if she could become a beast herself with only the slightest effort. It wasn't just what *she* had done. Loki would only have risked a direct attack if he had overcome his fear of Freya and her supposed ability to manifest her power through her daughter.

If his intent in sending the Jotunar had been to kidnap Ryan and create as much chaos as possible in the process, he'd been wildly successful in the second goal. Would he consider that success worth the loss of three of his minions and the questions that might be raised when their bodies were examined by mortal authorities?

Mist laughed. Oh, he'd find a way to deal with it. He wouldn't be constrained by pedestrian mortal ethics or morals. She was. She had known about the Aesir's survival for all of thirty-two hours, and already she'd lost any small advantage she'd ever had, dead Jotunar notwithstanding.

She hadn't thought it was possible to despise Laufeyson more than she did already. She'd hated him for what he'd done in Asgard. For what he'd done to *her*. But now, her hatred was something incandescent, a spark that required only the lightest touch to become a conflagration. He was responsible for what had happened to the kids, to Dainn, even to the stranger.

She glanced across the room at the mystery man, who still wasn't moving beyond a few random twitches. Who in Hel was he? He certainly didn't look like someone who could hold a katana like a fifth-*dan kendoka*. He was wearing casual but well-made khakis and sports jacket, now torn and rumpled, but no overcoat. His build was slim and wiry, and his handsome Asian features were more pleasant than threatening. The lines framing his light brown eyes fanned out from the corners the way they often did in people who loved to laugh.

All in all, he could be any young and successful professional enjoying a day off from work, if being out in this kind of weather was something he found enjoyable. But why would a man like him be walking by on Illinois Street just in time to join a battle?

If she was going to make any attempt to salvage the situation, she had to do something about him, and quickly. He had witnessed a savage fight between one man and three giants, a battle the "man" had won beyond all probability and with stunning skill and brutality. Mist had been deliberately vague with the ambulance service dispatcher about the circumstances surrounding Ryan's injury, but she doubted *this* guy would be so discreet. He looked like the kind who would describe everything in loving detail. He would say that she hadn't only defended Dainn unequivocally but had also encouraged him to leave the scene of a crime.

Once the ambulance showed up and the EMTs called the cops— which she wasn't going to do, since she needed to buy all the time she could—she wouldn't have any chance to turn things around. The police would be after Dainn, and Mist might find herself under arrest.

Not that they could hold her. But Dainn could turn on anyone who threatened him. The cops wouldn't stand a chance. And Loki would win.

Mist scrubbed the sweat away from her forehead with the back of her arm. She might be able to hide the stranger until the cops were gone, but that was hardly a permanent solution. If it came down to his life or the fate of Midgard . . .

The fate of Midgard wasn't in *her* hands, she reminded herself, but Freya's. Freya, who had given her daughter skills she couldn't depend on.

Except one.

The bile rose in Mist's throat. Dainn had told her that her mother had glamour that could "induce feelings of lust, love, and devotion with only the slightest effort," and that mortals would be particularly vulnerable to the effect. Mist had the same ability. An ability she hated with all her heart.

Hel, maybe it wasn't even possible. But it might stave off disaster until she could find a better solution.

"Gabi," she said. "I know this has been very difficult for you, especially when you still don't really understand what's going on."

"I *do* understand," Gabi said, rubbing her hand across her wet face. "Those things are giants. They came to get Ryan. This is all some kind of war."

"Whatever Dainn might have told you isn't enough," Mist said. "But I promise I'll explain as much as I can once Ryan's okay. Right now I need you to listen to me. There are a few important things I have to take care of, and I don't know if I'll be able to speak to you again before the ambulance arrives. The police will be coming, too. Dainn and I could get into bad trouble, and things could get very complicated for you."

Gabi stared at her, defiance on her deceptively innocent face. "If it wasn't for Ryan, I'd just go. But I won't leave him." She glanced at her friend, her lips turning down. "What do you want me to do?"

Mist leaned closer so the stranger couldn't overhear if he came to. "I told the dispatcher that we heard noises in the gym when we were sleeping, and we came down to check it out. There were three men, and one of them hurt Ryan when he tried to stop them. They got away. You don't know anything else. Got it?"

"It would be better if I didn't talk to them at all."

"I need to make sure they don't start looking around the house until I'm finished. Do whatever the paramedics tell you to, and take care of Ryan. I'll come after you as soon as I can."

She shook her head, flinging her dark hair away from her face. "No. Call the ambulance guys and tell them not to come."

"Gabi, you know Ryan might be badly hurt."

"I know." She looked down at her hands. "I can help him."

"Gabi—"

"I know how," she said. "I was just afraid to try it before."

"Try what, Gabi?"

"Do you know about curandismo?"

Mist had heard about it. Curandismo was a kind of folk magic, usually healing, that was practiced by certain men and women in Latin culture. It was strongly based on their Catholic faith. As she and Dainn had discussed earlier, there were mortals who *could* work magic, but they were few and practiced under a shadow of anonymity.

"Are you saying you're a curandera, Gabi?" Mist asked gently.

"You think I'm crazy," Gabi said, "but I know how. *Mi abuela* taught me in Mexico, before my brother and me came here. I can heal him."

Mist could understand why the girl would want to claim a gift to match Ryan's in some way, even if it was all fantasy. "I can see you believe in it, Gabi," she said, "but—"

"Let me try." Her eyes filled with tears. "I don't want the police to come. You have to let me try."

Something in the passion of Gabi's voice struck Mist with doubt. It was remotely possible. Two kids with magic might be drawn together. They might be drawn to Mist.

"*Por favor,*" Gabi said. "You said you had important things to do. Give me your phone. I'll call them and tell them not to come. If I can't help Ryan, I'll call the ambulance guys again. I promise."

Mist looked at Ryan. It wouldn't make much difference now if she could comfort Gabi by letting her try to help her friend. The ambulance was bound to show up any minute.

She looked at the stranger again. He was finally showing signs of waking up. She had to work fast.

"Okay," she said. She pulled out her cell phone and handed it to Gabi, rose, and then started toward the stranger. He was still too dazed to resist when Mist threw him over her shoulder and carried him into the hall. There was no sign of Dainn except a smear of drying blood on the hardwood floor and the wall near the door.

Gritting her teeth, Mist hauled the mortal straight to the kitchen and into the laundry room. Kirby and Lee, crammed in the small space between the washer and dryer, hissed and streaked from the room, glossy coats bristling like a porcupine's quills.

Mist dropped the man to the floor near the door to the tiny yard and removed the belt from his wrists. He opened his eyes and slowly focused on her face.

"Easy," she said when he moved to rise. "I'm not going to hurt you."

"Where are the kids?" he demanded, his baritone voice hard with accusation.

"The ambulance is on its way," Mist said. "They'll be taken care of."

"Where's your *friend*?" he said, biting off the word.

"Gone."

He moved again, and she pushed him back down. His eyes widened as he felt her strength.

But he recovered from his surprise quickly enough. "I don't know how you know that lunatic," he said, "but you helped him and urged him leave. You're an accomplice to murder."

"Murder?" Mist laughed grimly. "You have no idea what you saw."

"Why don't you tell me?"

All at once his voice had gone soft, almost sympathetic, as if he hoped to lull her into some kind of confession. She knew better than to fall into that trap.

"Those men attacked the loft," she said. "They tried to kill us. Dainn protected the kids and defended himself."

"Protected them?" the stranger said, losing his brief calm. "You let him—"

"I tried to get the kids away," Mist interrupted, "but they got back into the gym."

"Are they yours?"

"I don't intend to be interrogated by you or anyone else," she said.

"You do realize that your friend threatened the boy before you interfered?"

"I told you he'd never harm them."

"You made it clear you thought he'd kill *me*."

"I wasn't going to take any chances."

"Then you told him to go, even though you knew he could hurt others."

His accusation was painfully close to the truth. "I couldn't control him," Mist said with complete honesty. "I did calm him down for a little while. But I don't believe he'd hurt innocent people. Just the ones who attack him and his friends." She glanced at his swollen nose. "I'd say you got off easy."

The stranger's hand flew to his face. "You think that's funny?"

"I'm deadly serious." She held his hostile gaze. "Now you can tell me who you are, and what you're doing here."

"Who are *you*?" he demanded.

"This is my house. You're as much an intruder as the men who tried to kill us."

"Koji Tashiro," he said shortly.

"And what are you, Koji Tashiro? A Good Samaritan who just happened to be walking by at eight in the morning?"

He must have heard the sarcasm in her voice, but his demeanor didn't change. "I was here looking for someone," he said. "But that's not the issue now, is it?"

"It is to me." She rose to her feet, taking full advantage of the potential threat her looming height presented.

"I asked you if those kids were yours," he said, staring up at her calmly.

"They're street kids," she said. "They were hungry and scared, and I gave them food and a place to sleep."

"They'd have been safer on the streets," he said.

He was right, and for that she had no excuse. "I didn't expect someone to attack my home."

"But you obviously have some idea who those men were," he said.

"I didn't know them," she said. "As I told you, they were trying to kill us."

"Very few people, even hardened criminals, just burst into a house and start killing. Do you have any enemies?"

Only the worst, Mist thought. "None that I know of," she said.

He weighed her words and frowned. "Then it must be your violent friend. Did he get on the wrong side of some drug lord?" His expression softened to one of earnest concern. "If he's involved in trafficking, he could bring more violence down on you and anyone close to you. Do you really want that?"

"He isn't on drugs," she said.

"Do you know how many people say that about their loved ones?"

Loved one. How wrong he was. "It's my turn," she said. "What did you mean when you said you were looking for someone?"

He seemed to realize he wouldn't get anything more out of her unless he gave her something in return. "I was looking for a boy named Ryan Starling," he said.

16

———

Mist's immediate thought was that he'd been sent by Loki along with the Jotunar to get Ryan. If one method didn't work, try another.

"What do you want with him?" she asked.

"I'm a lawyer representing his aunt's estate. He's the boy in there, isn't he?"

A lawyer. She wasn't sure it could get much worse. If he was telling the truth.

"How is it that you happened to come looking for Ryan just in time to witness all this?" she asked, shrugging out of her torn jacket.

"Are you accusing *me* of something?" Tashiro asked.

"It can work both ways, Mr. Tashiro. I don't know you, and you're making pronouncements on things you know nothing about. Why should I trust anything you tell me?"

He began to stand up again, and this time Mist let him. They stared at each other. She noticed that Tashiro was fidgeting, clenching and unclenching his fingers as if he was aware of some danger he hadn't anticipated. His hand trembled as he lifted it to brush dark, sweaty hair away from his forehead.

It wasn't fear, at least not of violence. She saw it in his eyes: the awakening of desire, the heat, the sudden awareness that she was not only an antagonist.

She hadn't even begun to push her "glamour," but he was beginning to feel it anyway. Even if he was Loki's agent, he was still susceptible to Freya's influence.

And she had to take full advantage of his weakness.

She undid the top two buttons of her shirt. "Did someone send you to look for Ryan?" she asked softly.

He blinked. "I told you. His aunt asked me to find him. She left him substantial assets in her will."

"How *did* you find him?"

"I have contacts all over the city. I asked around." He sucked in a sharp breath. "Why does that matter?"

Mist knew she couldn't put it off any longer. Holding her self-disgust at bay, she remembered again how it had felt to "become" Freya that moment in Asbrew . . . golden honey-mead warmth and the scent of primroses, the peace and love—and naked lust—that had so completely enveloped her and overwhelmed Loki Laufey-son. She began to fashion a new image of herself as she had shaped the Rune-staves in the gym—a figure of surpassing beauty, perfection of skin and hair, full of hip and breast. An illustration drawn solely for the pleasure of men.

She leaned very close and undid the rest of the buttons one by one, pulling the shirt open to reveal the thin T-shirt underneath. "Tell me the truth, Koji."

His eyes focused just where she wanted them to. "I don't . . . know what you're talking about. No one else sent me."

Mist knew he was telling the truth. She heard it in his voice, saw it in his body, felt it in his soul.

"Whatever business you have with Ryan," she said, "you're not going near him until he's safe in the hospital." She moved closer still, her chest almost touching his. "Is there anything else you want to tell me?"

"You . . . have to tell the police everything you know." He hesitated, swallowing several times. "You must see that your friend needs help."

"Is that your judgment as a lawyer, Mr. Tashiro?"

"It's the only choice you have."

"And what do plan to tell the police?"

"Only . . . what I witnessed."

She raised her hand to brush his cheek with her fingertips. "Just facts? No speculation?"

His head jerked. "I—"

"Why don't you remind me exactly what happened?"

Confusion crossed his face. "You *know* what happened," he stammered.

"Do I?" She ran one fingernail along his jaw.

His gaze dropped to her parted lips. "I . . . they—"

"It was self-defense, wasn't it?"

"I . . ." His eyes met hers, and his expression told her he was slipping out of her grasp. "What's your name?" he asked.

"Mist."

"Ms. Mist, I'll only report what I saw. The kids can make their statements when they're able to. There'll be someone there to—"

"Koji," she said, stroking his hair. "You don't have to make this so difficult."

His eyes began to glaze over again. "I know you're hiding something," he said, glancing away.

"Look at me, Koji. What could I be hiding?"

Sweat trickled down his temple. He was still fighting her. "You know . . . who those guys were," he said, "but you're afraid to . . . identify them."

"What would I be afraid of?" Mist purred.

"Like I said," Koji whispered, gulping audibly, "it'll be better if you . . ." He drifted into silence and closed his eyes.

Mist dropped her hand from his face and listened. Still no sirens. Gabi must have called off the ambulance.

Norns will she knows what she's doing, Mist thought. Pushing that worry out of her mind, she leaned so close that her lips nearly touched Tashiro's. "I'm sorry we had to meet under such unfortunate circumstances," she said. "But everything will be all right now, won't it?"

He opened his eyes. "I'm sorry, too, but—"

"Look at me, Koji."

He obeyed her, though his head jerked in a last-ditch attempt to resist. In his brown eyes she saw the reflection of the beast *she* had created. A beast of beauty, as hungry as any wolf.

"What . . . what do you want?" Koji asked, his breath coming faster.

What did she want? Mist thought with amusement. Everything, of course.

"Let's go over what happened one more time," she said, "just so there isn't any misunderstanding. You wouldn't want to get anyone into trouble, would you? That would make me so unhappy."

"Yes," he murmured.

She told him what she wanted to say. His lips parted, revealing even white teeth. "I— Yes. That's how it happened."

"Wonderful." She took his hand in hers. "Now I want you to go into the kitchen and sit quietly for a little while. I promise I'll be back very soon."

"No," he said, clasping her hand more tightly. There was strength in those hands. She liked that. She liked the way he gazed at her like a puppy hoping that a delicious scrap would fall from the table.

Vaguely she remembered there was something else she needed to be doing. Something she should be worried about. But she couldn't quite remember what it was, and it didn't really matter. She won-

dered why she'd bothered to go through this ridiculous business at
all.

She worked her hand free of Koji's and strolled into the kitchen.
What in the world had she been thinking? This was no fit hall for
Freya's daughter. She opened the refrigerator and wrinkled her nose
in disgust. Nothing worth so much as tasting. And her clothes . . .

It would not do. She would go shopping as soon as possible and
find suitable garments to adorn her body.

"Mist?"

She turned to Koji. The skin around his eyes was turning dark
with bruises, and dried blood caked the bottom of his nose. He
smiled, hopeful and pathetic.

"Tell me what I can do for you," he said, pulling a chair out from
the table. "Do you want something to eat?"

She sighed. How could she have thought, even for a moment,
that he was worthy of her interest? He was going to become very
annoying soon. Perhaps if she sent him out for a suitable meal, she
could get rid of him for a while. But that wouldn't take care of him
for good.

There was only one way to make sure he stayed away. She would
have to become plain, ordinary, boring Mist again just long enough
to break the spell.

"Come here, Koji," she said, taking the offered chair.

He knelt before the chair, his eyes fixed on her face. "You're so
beautiful," he murmured.

She wondered vaguely if he would suffer any damage from being
abruptly separated from the object of his affection.

That really wasn't her concern. He was only a mortal. There were
many more where he came from. Perhaps she would let him kiss
her, just once.

Freya's daughter smiled and held out her arms. Koji rose and
leaned over her, bracing one hand on the tabletop. She tilted her

face up, and his lips touched hers. She permitted the slightest pressure and then began to undo the spell, deconstructing the image she had made in her mind, erasing the glamour. Koji put his arms around her, deepening the kiss. She banished the primroses and the honey and the joy that had borne her up since the seduction began.

"Mist," he murmured.

She bounced back, nearly upsetting her chair, and pushed Koji away. Her heart slammed under her ribs, resisting the pull of the vast, black emptiness yawning beneath.

Mist. That was her name. She looked down at her unbuttoned shirt and pulled it closed with a shaking hand.

"Mist?" Koji said, turning his head this way and that as if he couldn't see her. "Where are you?"

She stared at him in horror. He was looking for the other. The one she had become in her need to protect Dainn and the children from the consequences of the Jotunar's attack.

Her spell of seduction had worked perfectly. She had deceived not only Koji, but herself.

What in Odin's name had she done? If she let go now, would Tashiro remember?

Gods curse her, she couldn't let him.

"She's not here," Mist said, easing out of her chair. "But she'll be back soon. She wants you to wait right here until she returns."

His gaze met hers, and there was something like panic in his eyes.

"Are you sure she's coming back?"

"Yes. Very soon."

"Then I'll wait."

"That's right," Mist said. "Don't move until she comes. In fact, maybe you should rest. You've had a rough day."

"Rest," he echoed. He crossed his arms on the table and laid his cheek on his wrists. In a matter of seconds he was asleep.

Mist backed away and stumbled against the stove, jarring her arm. The glamour was still working. Even though she knew who she was now, who she really was, she could still make him do what she wanted.

That was terrifying enough. But now a flood of memory returned, and with it the realization that there were still no sirens, no urgent voices to suggest the EMTs had arrived.

She turned and ran back into the hall. The gym was still empty except for the kids and the Jotunar corpses. Ryan was on his feet, leaning on Gabi's shoulder.

Mist barely hesitated. She ran to join them.

"I did it," Gabi said shakily. "Ryan's okay."

And Ryan did look okay. More than okay. He seemed bewildered, but the blood had been wiped from his face, and Mist knew the wound was gone.

Still, she had to be sure. "Turn around, Ryan."

He obeyed her, with Gabi's support. She parted his matted hair and found the place where the wound had been. It was still a little raised and rough, but it was otherwise completely healed.

"I got hit," Ryan said slowly, turning around again. "Gabi healed me." He raised his fingers to his head, and Gabi slapped his hand away.

"Leave that alone," she said. She met Mist's gaze. "I did it, Mist. I really did."

"That's good, Gabi," Mist said, genuinely impressed. And more than a little worried. "You were right."

Gabi flexed her fingers, and for the first time Mist noticed that they were red, as if she'd been badly burned.

"Are *you* all right?" Mist asked.

Suddenly the girl seemed embarrassed, as if she'd been caught doing something shameful. She touched the silver cross hanging from the chain around her neck.

"*Sí*," she said. "I didn't really know what would happen, but it's okay."

Mist wondered. But Gabi had proven herself beyond any doubt, and she had to be taken at her word.

"You called the ambulance service?" she asked.

"I told them it was all a mistake."

But that, Mist thought, only solved half the problem. The mess left in the wake of the fight was still untouched. She hadn't expected she'd even get the chance to address that situation before the authorities showed up.

Now she had an opportunity, but she might as well try cleaning every street in the city with a paper towel. If she *didn't* find a way to take care of it, the small advantage she'd gained from Gabi's actions would be undone as soon as someone in the neighborhood called the cops to investigate suspicious noises or strangers in the area. The police could still be on their way.

But she had an idea. A crazy one that hadn't a chance of succeeding. She didn't have the control. She hadn't been able to sustain that strange new magic during the fight with the Jotunar or call up any other kind to help Dainn and protect the kids.

But she hadn't been sure about using Freya's glamour, either, and it had been more effective than she could have imagined.

"I want you to go upstairs, and stay there this time," Mist said to the kids. "Both of you need rest, or you're going to keel over any minute. Ryan, you may be healed, but that doesn't mean you're completely well. And I want you to take care of those hands, Gabi. You'll find disinfectants and gauze in the bathroom."

"You got important things to do again?" Gabi asked with a belligerent tilt of her head.

"Look around you. I can't leave things this way. I may be able to do something about it."

"More magic?"

"If I can. But you're not going to be here to see it. I want you out of the way, and safe."

"What if the giants come back?" Gabi asked. "Who's going to protect us?"

Mist shook her head. These crazy kids actually wanted to stay and watch, after everything they'd been through and the horrors they'd witnessed.

"They won't come back," Mist said, "at least, not right away. Go upstairs. If you distract me again, I could fail. And I need to make this work."

Ryan shivered, and Gabi took his hand. "Where's Dainn?" he asked. "Is *he* okay?"

How could Mist answer that? "You saw—" she began.

"Yeah." Ryan swallowed. "He's gone, isn't he?"

"Yes."

"Is he coming back?"

"I don't know," she said.

Ryan closed his eyes. "It was our fault," he moaned.

"Then make up for it by doing what I tell you. Do you want me to walk you up?"

"We're not afraid," Gabi said. She pulled Ryan away from the wall and led him toward the hall door, carefully skirting the bodies without looking at them.

Mist watched them go. She hadn't wanted them here, but it seemed Dainn had been right. They'd come for a reason, and now they were her responsibility. Norns save her.

Grabbing Kettlingr, which she'd laid on the floor near the wall after she'd removed it from her belt, she went straight to the closest Jotunn body. Bakrauf. The blood-filled, empty socket of his right eye stared up at her with seething hatred, even in death.

Willing herself to remember what she'd done before, she raised the sword. There'd been something about the Rune-staves coming alive. Uruz and Kenaz, the Ox and the Beacon. And the elements, the Vanir magic. No logic, no careful spells, just emotion, and need, and power.

But try as she might, she couldn't make that strange new magic return. Maybe she'd exhausted her energy, the way Dainn had said happened to anyone who used their abilities to their full capacity for an extended time. In spite of what he had implied, she must have the same limits he did. Or like Loki or Freya or other gods, for that matter.

Or maybe it was just because she wasn't being directly threatened. Dainn's beast seemed to be provoked by physical or mental threats, and she couldn't forget what she'd done to him in the living room with those same elemental powers.

There had to be another way. She decided to start from the beginning, the very first things Dainn had taught her. She concentrated on what she wanted to accomplish and drew the Rune-staves in her mind. They hovered before her inner eye, deep gray and seemingly solid, until she began to chant the Runes aloud. Then, all at once, they broke apart as if struck by Mjollnir itself, brittle as glass, shattering into a million pieces.

She tried again. This time the Runes held steady halfway through her chant before the centermost, Raiho, snapped in two. The others quickly followed, each portion vanishing in an explosion of miniscule particles like spores from a mushroom.

After two more tries, Mist knew it wasn't going to work. Her Runes were fragile constructs, flawed by her inexperience and not nearly strong enough for what she had to accomplish. Holding them in her mind wasn't enough.

Curse it. It was almost as if her Rune-staves had nothing to cling to, nothing to support them. But she knew instinctively that finding a piece of wood or paper and inscribing the staves wouldn't help in the slightest.

Something to cling to. Something solid, but not physical. Something as real to her as her own body. If she could find that something, she could make it work. Just the way she could make a steel billet into a sword.

Steel. An image sprang into her mind, as natural as sunrise, and she let it take her. She envisioned her workshop, the glowing coals, the rush of hot air, the clang of metal on metal. She imagined herself picking the first Rune-stave up in her tongs and setting it on the anvil, striking it with her hammer, but not merely to reshape or refine it; with every blow it grew thicker and darker, layer upon layer, until it became heavy as the anvil itself, gleaming black and red.

She set down the tongs and gestured upward with one hand. The stave flew back into its place, suspended in midair, still radiating heat Mist could feel through her whole body. She chose the second stave and repeated the process twice more until the Bind-Rune was complete. She began to chant as she spread her hands, palms down, over the body on the floor in front of her.

Nothing happened. But the tattoo around her wrist began to throb, and she remembered the essential step she had forgotten.

Drawing her knife, she sliced her palm. Again, nothing happened . . . until her blood dripped onto Bakrauf's corpse. The Bind-Rune began to glow with its own internal flame, flushing scarlet, blackening around the edges. She "dropped" it onto the Jotunn's chest. One by one the fingers and toes shriveled and burned away to ash. The fire moved rapidly inward, up the legs and arms, down from the head as the hair sizzled and the face melted into slag.

Mist watched intently, tempering relief with caution, half afraid the magic would stop before the work was complete. But in a minute even the ashes had consumed themselves, and nothing was left of Bakrauf. Even the blood surrounding the place where he had lain disintegrated and vanished as if it had never existed.

Without hesitation she moved to the next corpse, Hrimgrimir's, and forged the staves again. The process was slower this time, and Mist began to sweat. Two full minutes passed before the deed was done.

She ran to the third Jotunn, whose head was detached from his body, and started again, stumbling over the words of the chant. She spilled her blood as she had done before, but the body remained unaffected, and Mist's time had nearly run out.

Acting purely on instinct, Mist imagined catching one of the smoking Rune-staves in her bare hands. Into it she poured the heat of her emotions: her concern for the kids, her fear for Dainn, her rage at Loki and her own helplessness. She screamed as the red-hot metal burned the stave's angular shape into her flesh and turned the tattoo around her wrist to a ring of flame.

She chanted through the pain as she dropped the stave onto the body at her feet. It sank through the rough clothing into the lifeless flesh and disappeared. She called up the second and third staves again, letting them sear her palms, charging them with her deepest passions until they, too, fell.

When she looked down, the third corpse was gone, head and all, and so were all traces that it had ever been there. Not so much as a scuff or burn mark streaked the rubber tiles. The burns on her palm were already fading.

But one final task remained. She tried to raise the fire in her mind once more, but it barely sparked before it went out. There had to be some other imagery she could use, something she had *lived*.

The forest on the border of Norway and Sweden. The driving snow, the frigid winds, the weather almost as dangerous as the Nazis themselves.

This wasn't just the elemental magic that still hovered somewhere just out of her reach, or even a Jotunn's inborn control over the very essence of winter. It was built of her own experiences, and when she chose the Runes she created a template constructed of frost and bitter cold, the legacy of that day when she had parted from Rebekka and Geir.

With the images came the rage and guilt she had never been able to root out from the depths of her heart. She envisioned a brutal North Wind, carrying with it tiny slivers of ice that scoured everything they touched. The wind filled her with such a bitter chill that she thought it would congeal the air in her lungs, but she didn't stop until every blood vessel and organ in her body was nearly frozen.

Then, with a low cry, she released the gale. The Rune-staves were torn apart as the blizzard roared through the gym, sweeping over the floor, the walls, every corner of the room. It devoured every particle of dirt, hair, or dried liquid, scrubbing away any biological residue Dainn, the stranger, or the Jotunar might have left behind, all without damaging anything else in the room.

The wind died abruptly, and the air turned still and heavy as stone. Mist collapsed to the floor, holding herself up on her hands and knees.

She'd done it. She'd made it work. She'd controlled her magic.

Mist pushed herself to her feet again, lost her balance, and focused on the simple goal of getting to the hallway door. Koji was no longer at the kitchen table. He wasn't in the kitchen at all.

A card lay face down on the counter. Mist stiffened, remembering the last time someone had left her a note.

The writing was neat and precise. *I have to go,* the note read, *but I'll call you later today. We have a lot to discuss. – K.*

Mist turned the card over to a simple name and address printed in an elegantly minimal typeface. He was who he'd claimed. Koji Tashiro, attorney-at-law.

Had he broken the spell she'd laid on him earlier? And if he had, was he going to the police?

No. He wouldn't have left Ryan or Gabi here if he'd remembered the slaughter in the gym. And he still had business with Ryan.

An aunt with an estate, Mist thought. That suggested some kind of inheritance. Mist knew nothing about Ryan's background, except that it had probably been rough. Where was his family? What of Gabi's?

And how was she going to protect the kids? A Healer and a *spamadr* would be valuable allies until Mist found her Sisters, but they were still only teenagers.

Dainn couldn't help her now. Obviously Freya couldn't, either. If Mist sent the teenagers away from the loft, she couldn't guarantee that Loki wouldn't find them.

But Tashiro . . . maybe he could get them away. Until she knew what he wanted with Ryan, she couldn't be sure if that was even a possibility.

She clenched her fists on the tabletop. There were only two things she wanted now. One was to look for Dainn, and the other was to find Loki and beat him to a pulp.

But she couldn't do what she wanted, even if she'd had the strength to try. She needed to deal with the teenagers, explain what had happened and was likely to happen—in short, all the things she hadn't told Ryan already. She had to call Vali. And she needed to figure out how she was going to carry on this fight alone for as long as she had to.

Forcing herself out of the chair, she started for the stairs.

17

The door rattled. Dainn opened his eyes, blinking into the glare of the alarm clock on the bedside table. The display read 11:00 a.m. Three hours had passed since he'd staggered into the room, and he had no memory of them.

"Is someone in there?" Vali called, shaking the door knob again. A few seconds passed, the smell of minor magic singed the air, and then the door burst open.

"Dainn!" Vali said, stopping abruptly in the doorway. "What are you doing in here?"

Eyes burning, Dainn watched Vali set down an armful of several boxes—a greater and wider load than any mere mortal could manage—on the floor beside the desk and fall with a woof into the office chair.

"What's going on?" Vali repeated, peering at Dainn with open concern. "Why are you on the floor?"

Dainn stared at the big man blankly. He was aware that his body no longer hurt, that he could breathe without pain, that his bones were whole again.

But that did not affect him as much as the fact that Odin's son was here and obviously unaware of the attack. That meant that there wouldn't have been any other assaults during the past several hours.

It also meant that there weren't any police or medical personnel on the premises.

If he hadn't been so close to death and in such fear of harming someone else, he would never have left Mist or the young ones alone. But Vali's ignorance didn't make any sense. Mist hadn't found Dainn, but then he'd expected her to be fully occupied with the trouble he'd left her. She would have assumed he'd left the loft, if she'd thought about him at all.

"I'll take care of everything," Mist had told him just before he'd run. Now it seemed that she had.

"I don't know where she is," he answered Vali. "I've been asleep."

"In the middle of the floor?" Vali peered at Dainn's chest. "You've got blood all over your clothes. What—"

"We were attacked by Jotunar."

Vali jumped up and loomed over Dainn as if he wanted to pull him up off the floor and shake him. "Jotunar? I thought you warded the house. What happened?"

None of it would have happened at all if Dainn's wards had worked and given the alarm before the Jotunar could take them all by surprise.

He told Vali in a level, emotionless voice, provoking growls that nearly shook the walls.

"*You* killed them?" Vali asked. "An elf? With a sword?"

Dainn had no intention of going into details. Vali didn't know about the beast, and he wouldn't hear of it now.

"They are all dead," Dainn said.

Vali ran out the door and down the hall toward the gym. Rising to his feet, Dainn tested his balance, found it acceptable, and started for his room. He knew the house was empty as soon as he walked into the hall. No strangers other than the man from the gym had been in this part of the loft. Even the scent of blood that had saturated the building seemed to have vanished.

Whatever Mist might have done, Dainn knew he had to get out. He reached his room, stripped out of his torn and bloody clothing, and sat naked on the bed, staring at the cell phone Mist had given him soon after he'd first arrived at the loft. He picked it up with numb fingers.

Unless she was in police custody, Mist was likely at the hospital with Ryan. Phoning her would only distract her, and perhaps cause even more trouble.

Heavy footsteps thudded outside his room, and he dropped the phone. Vali burst through the door.

"They're gone!" he said. "No bodies. The gym is empty."

"They would have taken the bodies," Dainn said, still resisting the treachery of hope.

"You don't get it. No police tape, no marks on the floor, no signs of blood. It's like nothing happened." He crouched to face Dainn. "If it wasn't for the way you look right now—"

"It happened," Dainn said. "But I have no explanation for what you saw."

"Shit." Vali rubbed at his short beard. "We need to find Mist."

"She may be at the hospital with Ryan," Dainn said.

Vali glanced at the cell phone Dainn had put down. "I'll call San Francisco General, and if she and the kids aren't there, I'll call the others."

"If you reach Mist, you must not tell her I'm here."

"Why not? She'll want to—"

"Because I must leave."

"You'll probably get just about two steps before you fall again."

"Will you do as I ask?"

Vali hesitated. "Okay. But you stay put until I get back to you."

He jumped to his feet and rushed out of the room the same way he'd come in.

Dainn sank into himself, breathing slowly. Vali was right. He had to know what had happened before he left.

But he could feel the beast, as exhausted as Dainn was, waiting. The cage was shattered, and there was nothing to hold it back the next time something aroused it. Aroused *him*. Even if he found a way to remain with Mist, he couldn't use violence or magic of any kind to help her the next time Loki attacked.

And there would be more such assaults, of course. Until Freya could fully manifest her power in Midgard, Laufeyson would have little to get in his way.

Except Mist herself. But though she had natural skill with both Galdr and the ancient Vanir powers, astonishing in strength and potential, she lacked the inborn understanding of magic possessed by the Jotunar, the Alfar, and the gods. It would take weeks if not months to teach her such understanding. And even if she regained Gungnir and located several of her Sisters with their Treasures, it wouldn't be enough.

But as his thoughts cleared and reason replaced fear and raw instinct, Dainn realized that running away had never been an option, no matter what the risk from the beast, no matter how much he wanted to bury himself where he would never meet god or mortal again. Freya would come to Midgard, and Mist wasn't prepared to serve the purpose for which the Lady intended her. Her barriers had been breached by his first attack on her mind, but they were not yet broken.

Either he could break those barriers utterly, or give Mist the means to resist the destiny that had been intended for her even before her birth.

The Fates had given him a choice, and he was afraid.

Dainn rocked forward and leaned over his knees, fighting nausea and self-contempt. He *knew* Mist now. She had worried over him after he'd challenged her inner barriers, believing she had hurt him. She had offered to help him rebuild his cage when the beast had first escaped within his mind. She had sent him from the gym before he could be taken by the authorities, and he knew it hadn't only been to protect herself and the young ones.

She cared about his fate. She cared about *him*, even if she would never admit it outright. And he more than merely desired her. It didn't matter if that desire was fed by the glamour she had so unwillingly inherited from her mother. He felt emotions he had thought long put behind him. Emotions he must continue to resist every moment they were together.

But not for Midgard. Not for Freya. Not for the Aesir and Alfar and humanity.

Not even for himself. The beast was not deceived. It stirred again to remind him of what he would have sacrificed and faced the worst of his fears to obtain. To remind him that everything he had sworn to fight for could die because of the choice he made now.

He stared down at his bloody hands, retreating into a state of cold calculation. He would not attempt to contact Freya again. Even if he could reach her, which was by no means certain, he couldn't allow her to know what he was about to do. He had to buy time—with deceit, with guile, with magic . . . even with the beast, if there was no other option.

Rising unsteadily, Dainn made his way into the hall. He stumbled to the bathroom and cleaned off the worst of the blood, working it out of his hair with a few handfuls of water from the tap. Then he made his way to Mist's bedroom and opened the closet. He selected a pair of khaki pants and one of many polo shirts from among the leavings of Loki's alter ego and pulled them on. The shoes were a size too big, as Vidarr's had been, but they were good enough. He had no need of a jacket. By the time he left the loft, a dim, fitful light stained the eastern sky.

"Hey, Dainn!" Vali called, catching up with him as he started toward Twentieth Street. "I got through to Mist. They're not at the hospital. The kids are okay. I think they're all at some kind of coffee shop."

Dainn exhaled. "The police?" he asked.

"Come and gone. There won't be any investigation. The way Mist said it, I think she had something to do with getting rid of the bodies before anyone saw them. Some kind Rune-magic, I think. Pretty amazing."

Amazing, indeed. If Mist had done such a thing, Dainn thought, it would have required considerable skill to accomplish before the authorities arrived. It would also have required far more control than Dainn had believed Mist possessed, and she had done it entirely without his help.

Hope was nearly as terrifying as despair.

"Did she speak of the man who witnessed the fight?" he asked.

"Tashiro?" Vali scratched at one bristling cheek. "She said he wasn't going to be a problem, but she didn't go into details."

Tashiro. The name meant nothing to Dainn. But if he "wasn't going to be a problem," something must indeed have changed a great deal since Dainn had left the gym.

"Does she need help?" he asked.

"I don't think so. Those kids must be pretty shaken up, but I'm sure Mist is taking care of them." His brow creased in worry. "You think the Jotunar will come after the kid wherever they are now?"

"Not in a public location," Dainn said.

"Yeah. Right. She'll probably be looking for a safe place to put the kids where Loki can't find them." He sighed. "I guess we should just let Mist do her thing. Sometimes she's really stubborn, but I think she'll ask for help if she needs it." He looked Dainn over carefully. "Are you really leaving? You still look like Hel, and for any elf to do so much killing, especially with a weapon . . . you should take more time to deal with it."

Vali's perception surprised Dainn, but he couldn't let the god's worry stop him. He had to move quickly, while Loki was still likely to be distracted by his Jotunar's failure.

"I'm well enough," Dainn said. "And I must get away from the loft to, as you said, 'deal with it.'"

"What about the wards?"

"As you know, mine failed," Dainn said, not quite able to keep the bitterness from his voice. "Perhaps between you and Mist, you can do better than I did."

"My magic isn't what it used to be, but I'll do whatever I can. Do you have your cell, in case Mist needs to contact you?"

In fact, Dainn had left it behind. He could not be interrupted in what he must do, but he didn't intend to tell Vali.

"I have it," he said.

"Good."

"I would ask you not to speak of this to Mist until I return. She will come after me, and I must be alone now."

"Sure. I understand."

"I am grateful for your assistance."

"Yeah, well . . ." Vali pushed his hands into his pockets and stared at the sidewalk. "Don't stay away too long. I know Mist is going to need you, no matter what happened."

He turned before Dainn could find a reply and walked back into the loft.

It was nearly noon, and a small group of mortals, bundled up in heavy coats like ambulatory sausages, were waiting at the stop at Twentieth and Third. A light snow had begun to fall, dusting the parked cars, streetlamps and roofs.

"Crazy weather," remarked a pleasant-faced, middle-aged businessman as they stood together waiting for the streetcar. He looked Dainn up and down. "You must be freezing."

Dainn sank his chin into his collar. "Thank you for your concern."

The man eyed him as if he wasn't sure whether or not Dainn was mocking him. "You look like you really tied one on last night. Maybe you better go back to bed."

Meeting the mortal's gaze, Dainn smiled. "There will be plenty of time to rest if the world comes to an end."

Backing away, the man stood as far from Dainn as he could until the streetcar arrived, and then he flung himself aboard as if the Christian Devil were on his tail.

He was very nearly right.

"Why couldn't we meet tonight? I have fucking business to take care of this afternoon."

The mortal who spoke was sallow, skinny, and ugly. He wore an Armani suit, and his slight accent revealed his ties to the Russian Mafia, but he hardly looked the part of one of San Francisco's most notorious sex traffickers.

Loki stared at the man until he was forced to drop his nearly colorless blue eyes. Of all the crime lords, street gang bosses, extortionists, drug traffickers, money launderers—as well as those who ran extensive prostitution, credit card fraud, and auto theft rings—Bovarin was the one he despised most. Loki wasn't above coercing sex from time to time, but he preferred seduction. It wasn't as if he had to put much effort into it. Any mortal who had to rely on slaves to provide him with satisfaction was a pathetic creature unworthy of life, but Loki had to take what he could get.

"I called all of you here now," Loki said, sweeping the room with a scathing glance, "because I have no time to waste in carrying out my plan."

"Your *plan*," Chavez said, scorn heavy in his voice. "You offered us some good shit if we just listened to you. We didn't give you no promises."

"You will, when you hear what I have to say," Loki said. He chanted a quick spell under his breath, and Chavez doubled over with a shout of pain. The other men looked from Loki to Chavez with expressions varying from unease to feigned indifference, but Loki didn't think it would take long to convince them not to be so disrespectful in the future.

"If you do as I tell you," Loki said, leaning back in his chair, "you'll all be more wealthy than you've ever dreamed of in your short, miserable lives. If you stand against me, I'll see that your rivals get everything you would have had. And you'll be dead."

The bold captains of crime eyed each other, weighing the possibilities. Most of them would rather slit their own throats than be in the same room with any of the others, but Loki had made each of them believe that they were meeting with him alone. Now they couldn't escape.

Donatello snorted. "Where's your crew, Landvik?" he asked. "Where's your Borgata?"

Loki snapped his fingers. Five of his biggest and most vicious-looking Jotunar stomped into the room behind his chair.

"Will this do?" he asked sweetly. "There are more where these came from."

Mortal eyes looked up. And up.

"Fuck," said Barker, the leader of a prominent outlaw biker gang. "Fuck this shit."

He stood up to leave. Loki lifted his forefinger and slammed the man back into his seat.

"As I said before," Loki said, "you can either cooperate by helping me gain control of this city, or die. If you need further convincing when we're finished with our discussion, it can easily be arranged." He signaled to Forad, who walked around his chair to hover over Del Mar, a forger not far into his twenties who looked as out of place among the others as a reed in a redwood forest.

"Now, gentlemen," Loki said. "Shall we get down to business?"

Ryan gulped down his second soda, wishing it were vodka. Or tequila, the cheap kind you could get in any grocery store. He needed something stronger. A *lot* stronger.

But he knew Mist wouldn't let him. There was something comforting in that, knowing that someone cared about him and Gabi that much. Someone who was actually grateful for what they'd done.

Caring and grateful enough to do him and Gabi more harm than good by sending them away. And Mist was so powerful, according to what she'd told them, that he didn't really know if he was talking to a woman, a warrior, or a goddess.

He studied her covertly. She was really all three, each part somehow out of tune with the others. But every one of those parts was strong and determined and unafraid, the way Ryan could never be. She was the key to everything. He didn't think he'd ever really understand her, no matter what he'd "seen" in his dreams.

The fact that he couldn't figure her out made him half afraid to talk to her, a lot more than he had when they'd first met, even though Gabi didn't seem to have any trouble. Maybe it was because they were both female.

But Dainn . . . it wasn't the same with him. He was powerful in a different way than Mist, almost like some kind of ferocious animal—graceful, fast, deadly. He'd killed the giants without mercy, and

Ryan was pretty sure he would have killed Tashiro, too, if Ryan hadn't stopped him. For a second, he'd even forgotten who Ryan was and thought he was just another enemy.

All that should have made him seem even more scary than Mist. But he didn't, not to Ryan. That was the trouble. It was partly his fault that Dainn was gone. Maybe mostly his fault. He'd made it worse by refusing to stay upstairs and by getting Gabi involved. He should have *seen* what was going to happen—should have seen it earlier, when it could have done some good.

My fault.

Unaware of his thoughts, Gabi stared at the shiny metal napkin dispenser in the middle of the table. "Okay," she said, "I get all that." She jerked a napkin out of the dispenser and crumpled it in her fist. "It's not like we're stupid. But if you think we could help some-how—"

"Your help isn't worth your lives," Mist said in the same firm, confident voice she'd used since she'd begun explaining everything.

No, not everything, Ryan thought. There was still lots of stuff she wasn't telling him and Gabi. Because she didn't trust them.

"It's only a matter of time before Loki comes after you again," she said. "You have to understand—"

"Ryan told you something bad was coming just before the fight," Gabi reminded Mist for the third time, "and I healed him. We may not be like *you,* but—"

"I know nothing of the source of your abilities, Gabi," Mist said, meeting her gaze. "It's a completely different type of magic from the kind I understand. I don't deny it was effective, but you said you'd never really tried it before. How do you know it'll work next time? And you, Ryan—" She focused her unyielding stare on his face. "You don't know when the dreams or visions are going to come, do you? Even if there's a way to teach you to control them consciously, the seizures are too dangerous to provoke."

"I'm not afraid," Ryan said, clenching his teeth.

"I know that. But you don't even know how Loki knew about you or where to find you. Do you want to put Gabi in danger? Loki could use her to get to you. And if he finds out she's a healer, he'll make her serve him, too."

"What if we learn to fight?" Gabi asked suddenly, meeting Mist's gaze. "Maybe not with magic, but you said Loki and the giants couldn't use guns here. You could teach us how to use swords and stuff, and then you wouldn't have to protect us."

"You wouldn't stand a chance," Mist said, "even if I could teach you anything worth knowing in time to make a difference. Until I find my Sisters, I'm going to try to avoid risking mortal lives. The Jotunar aren't the only concern here. Loki is going to build up some kind of army in Midgard, probably out of people who don't much care who they work for."

"But you're going to do the same thing, right?" Gabi asked.

"The more mortals get involved on both sides, the more people are going to get hurt. Once the authorities start noticing that something strange is going on—and they will, no matter how much we try to hide it—it's going to become even more dangerous for anyone working with us."

"But you said you fixed it so the cops couldn't find anything in the gym," Ryan said, barely noticing the neon-lit jukebox against the wall flip to another oldie.

"Look," Mist said, her patience obviously beginning to wear thin, "I was wrong to bring you into this in the first place. If we can keep you safe, we can always call you back once we really need you."

Which, Ryan thought, she never would. Not if she made them leave now.

"I still have to talk to this lawyer dude, right?" Ryan asked, hoping to buy more time.

"That's up to you. You said your aunt was wealthy. She might have left you something valuable, like a house. A real home."

Ryan ducked his head. He'd told Mist some of what he and Gabi had gone through the past year, though he'd kept the ugliest details to himself.

"Yeah, my aunt was rich," he said, pushing his soda aside so hard that the heavy glass almost fell over. "But she never paid any attention to me before. And I don't trust Tashiro. Gabi told me he would have turned Dainn over to the police."

"He did what he thought he had to do," Mist said, though the way she stared out the window told Ryan she agreed with him. "He wanted to protect you and Gabi, too."

"Okay," he said. "Then I guess I'll need to talk to him before we leave. If I get money, I can send it to you, right? To help fight Sauron and the Orcs?"

Mist turned her attention back to him, but she wasn't smiling. "I have money," she said.

"When would we have to leave?" Gabi asked, playing with her paper straw cover.

"I think I've told you everything you need to know for now," Mist said, pushing back her chair. "I'll find somewhere for you to stay until more permanent arrangements can be made."

"And who's going to protect us then?" Ryan asked. "Dainn?"

"You know he can't. You might as well stop worrying about him." Mist reached inside her back pocket for her wallet and slapped a twenty-dollar bill on the table. Men all around the coffee shop gawked at her as she headed for the door at her usual fast pace, pausing outside to make sure Ryan and Gabi were right behind her. She seemed totally oblivious to the men's stares and to the "normal" world around her.

She was so cold about everything, Ryan thought with disgust.

She pretended she wanted to protect him and Gabi, but she didn't give a shit what happened to Dainn. He could die for her, and she wouldn't care.

But when Ryan glanced at Mist's strong-boned, beautiful face, he realized how stupid he'd been. She wasn't calm and confident and fearless now. Her eyes were wet, and her lips were pinched as if she was afraid she might start bawling.

She was thinking of Dainn, just the way *he* was. She wasn't angry at what Dainn had done. She was scared for him.

Like Ryan. It wasn't just because of how he felt about Dainn, which was stupid since he knew Dainn could never feel the same way. But he also knew that Dainn was almost as important as Mist in what was going to happen. And Ryan wasn't afraid of him. Could never be afraid.

Neither could Mist, no matter what he did. But now she and Dainn would never figure out how they felt about each other.

Ryan had something in common with her after all. And knowing that didn't help at all.

It was after 1:00 p.m. when they got back to the loft. Vali was waiting for them outside the door, a deep crease between his pale eyebrows. Snowflakes were melting in his hair.

"Vali?" Mist said. "What's wrong?"

"It's Dainn," he said. "He was still here when I got to the loft around eleven."

Shock froze Mist's face. "And you didn't tell me?"

"He asked me not to."

She swore. "Where did you find him?" she asked.

"In the office. He wasn't himself, but he wouldn't be after he killed three Jotunar with a sword."

Mist's lips tightened. "Is that what he told you?"

"Isn't it true?"

She hesitated for such a short time that Ryan almost didn't catch it. "Yes," she said. "Where is he now?"

Vali glanced at the kids. "Maybe you should send them inside."

"Why?" Ryan asked, moving to stand beside Mist. His "visions" weren't working now, when he most needed them. And he was scared all over again.

"Go inside," Mist said to him.

Ryan didn't move, and neither did Gabi. "We need to know if something's wrong," Gabi said. "We'll find out anyway."

Mist swung around to stare at Gabi the way she always did when she was furious and trying to hide it. "If you swear to me," she said, glancing at Ryan, "if you swear you won't try anything, no matter what you hear, you can stay."

This is bad, Ryan thought. "What do you want us to swear on?" he asked.

"In the old days, we used a sword hilt. But you can swear by whatever's most important to you. Whatever you'd never betray."

Ryan knew what that was for him, but he couldn't say it out loud. "Okay," he said, looking away.

Mist seemed to accept his answer. "Gabi?" she asked.

The girl jerked her head in a sharp nod. *"Mi abuela,"* she said.

"I accept your oaths."

Ryan released his breath, and Gabi kicked at the sidewalk with the toe of one borrowed shoe. After that, neither Mist nor Vali seemed to notice they were there.

"What *exactly* did he tell you?" she asked the big man, watching Vali's face very carefully.

"He was in bad shape when I found him," Vali said. "He—"

"You said he told you he killed three Jotunar with a sword."

"That's right. Looked like they got in some good licks, too. Like I said, he wasn't exactly himself, but he was healing. Once he was walking around again, I told him he should take some time to deal with what happened. He said he had to get away from the loft to do that. When he said it, I figured he was going to take a long walk or something, but—"

"When did he leave?" she asked, her voice clipped and urgent.

"About an hour ago."

"Curse it, Vali!"

Odin's son stared down at his feet. "He could be taking a walk or riding around the city. But—"

"But he's not," Mist said, resting her hand on the hilt of her knife.

"We can't be sure—"

"I know him," Mist said. "It's exactly what he would do."

"Do what?" Ryan asked. "What are you talking about?"

Mist glanced at him blankly, her thoughts obviously so troubled that she had none left to spare for anything or anyone else.

"I'm going after him," she said.

"You can't," Vali said, his eyes widening in distress. "I knew I had to tell you, but you don't even know if you can find Loki."

"If Dainn can find him, I can."

"They were . . . I mean, they knew each other before. He might have a way of finding Loki you don't. And if you get between them—"

"Dainn can't think rationally now, no matter how he behaved with you. You didn't see what he did in the gym. He fought the way he did because he wasn't himself." She lowered her voice, and Ryan could see how much she was trying to keep calm. "If I don't find Dainn, the rage will consume him, and Loki will use that against him. He has no reason to spare Dainn, and every reason to kill him."

"Are you sure?" Vali asked, even more softly. "Isn't it possible they're still . . ."

They stared at each other. Something Ryan didn't understand passed between them, but in the end Mist rejected whatever Vali was trying to suggest.

"I could ask the same of your brother," Mist said, cold as the winter wind. "And I don't think you suspect that, or you wouldn't be here."

"Yeah," Vali said, dropping his gaze again. "But you still can't go, Mist. Whatever happened at Asbrew, you aren't ready to face him. Not alone."

"I won't be alone. Not if I can—" She broke off, and her gaze swept over Ryan and Gabi as if she had just remembered they were there. "I'm holding you to your oaths. You're to do what Vali tells you and not try to interfere."

Ryan shivered. "Is Loki really going to kill him?"

Mist didn't answer. "Take the kids away from here," she told Vali. "Do whatever you can to keep them hidden."

"How are you going to get around?" Vali asked. "I took a taxi, and your car's still in the shop."

"I'll borrow a vehicle. I don't think any mortal who really understands what's at stake would object."

"I'd like to see you try to explain that when you bring it back," Vali said, half joking. His strained smile didn't last a second longer than it took for Mist to meet his eyes. "Listen. As soon as you left Asbrew yesterday, Vidarr called a few people he knows and got them to start looking for Loki. Just legwork, checking out large cash and credit card purchases at luxury stores and car dealerships, going through real estate records. The kind of stuff you want me to look at to find the other Valkyrie, but easier, since Loki's probably still here in the city."

Mist raised her head like a dog smelling steak scraps in a restaurant Dumpster. "Does he know where Loki is?"

"I don't know. But Mist—" He reached toward her and dropped

his hand a second later. "When you talk to him, be careful. He's pissed as Hel."

"He'll talk to me, and I don't plan to be careful."

"Okay." Vali's throat bobbed. "Just one more thing. What if you don't come back?"

She gripped her knife until her knuckles turned white. "I will, and I'll bring Dainn and Gungnir with me."

Without another word, she strode into the loft. Ryan hung back with Gabi.

"Vali," he said, "what if I can find help find Dainn with my dreams? Do you think she'd let us stay then?"

"You heard what Mist said," Gabi said, her dark eyes angry and worried at the same time. "You can't really control them, and you'll just get more seizures if you try to make them come."

"Right now we have to get out of here," Vali said. "If you have any stuff you want to bring, go get it."

Ryan knew there was no point in more arguing. He couldn't help Mist and Dainn now. But whether he was at the loft or somewhere else, he wasn't going to give up.

"Come on, Gabi," he said. "Maybe they don't think they need us yet, but they will. And we're going to be ready."

18

The wind off the bay was so cold that even Dainn, with his ability to withstand Midgardian weather in all its forms, felt it cut through his thin shirt. He sat on a bench near the end of Hyde Street Pier, seagulls circling and crying above him. The snow had gradually grown heavier, melting on the pavement but beginning to gather on the deck of the old sailing ship docked at the side of the pier, deserted and waiting for spring and the flood of tourists who would arrive with better weather.

If spring ever came.

At the moment the Maritime National Historical Park was empty of visitors, and Dainn was free to do what he must without the risk of being seen.

He scrubbed the moisture from his face and stared out at the water. The seeking spell he planned to create was not of the usual kind; he was too drained and weak to hunt Loki down. He would let Laufeyson come to *him*.

The Slanderer had been frightened before, but Dainn didn't believe for a moment that Loki would surrender to such a shameful emotion again. Quite the contrary; he would have been anticipating just such a meeting ever since he had learned that Dainn was Freya's agent in Midgard.

But did he know how badly his attack on the loft had gone

awry? He had clearly decided that Freya was not as great a threat as he had believed when he'd faced Mist in Asbrew, but Dainn had never sensed the presence of any spell to indicate that Laufeyson was observing the assault. Even with the proper vector to carry out the observation, such a spell was fraught with danger for its composer. And there were no Jotunar survivors to report what had happened.

Given their failure to return with their prize, Loki might have realized things hadn't played out exactly as he'd intended. But if he thought his attack had succeeded, he would assume this meeting was in response to it. Either way, he would be prepared to deal with his most intimate enemy.

In every way but one.

Dainn closed his eyes and felt the bay surging beneath the pier. Alfar were not of the sea, and their magical connection to it was minimal. But the ocean was still of the natural world, and so Dainn hoped to coax a little of its restless energy into his service—drawing not upon its vast stores of life and unfathomable potency, but that small part of it that appeared to men, spent but not completely stripped of its power.

Salt spray spattered against the piles as Dainn raised his hands and sang of his need and the grave threat to Midgard and its inhabitants. A wave surged over the end of the pier, slapping him in freezing water.

An appeal to the fate of mortals did not interest even the muted force he summoned. It had never cared for the things of the land, and it had cause to hate the creatures who ruled it. Dainn accepted the rebuke and altered his melody, singing of Njordr, god of the sea and Freya's own father. He sang of his service to Freya and the restoration of the Aesir and spirits of the sea.

Foam swirled up and danced in the air, slowly circling Dainn's head. He opened his hands and let the foam settle in his palms. He wove it between his fingers, shaping the Rune-staves that spelled out Loki's name.

The staves became distorted, resisting his control. He soothed them with another song and they leaped out of his hands like dolphins, hurtling skyward, disappearing among the snowflakes.

Dainn toppled from the bench. For a time he was aware of nothing but a distorted view of the bay, the waves agitated by more than the wind.

"You okay?"

A young woman bundled in a heavy coat leaned toward him from a safe distance, clutching an oversized handbag against her side. Her dark eyes were concerned but uneasy, and Dainn was aware that he must look more than a little mad.

"I saw you fall," she said, backing away as he worked his hands underneath his chest and raised his head from the pavement. "Do you need an ambulance?"

Dainn made no attempt to move any further. He didn't want to frighten a mortal who had been compassionate enough to help, and he wasn't sure he could do so in any case.

"I am not injured," he said, "but I thank you for your concern."

She peered at him a while longer, evidently confused by the contrast between his current position, his clothing, and his voice. He was grateful that he had taken the time to tie back his hair in a way that still covered his ears.

"If you're sure you're okay . . ." the woman said.

"Yes." He winced at a sharp pain in his shoulder. "Thank you."

The young woman accepted the dismissal and quickly retreated. Dainn lay on his stomach, gathering his strength to rise. If even one of the Jotunar was to come after him now with the intent to kill, he would be helpless to defend himself.

But he didn't think Loki wanted him hurt. Not by anyone but himself.

Dainn pulled himself up by clinging to the bench, his breath forming white plumes that streaked away on the wind. His shoulder ached in the joint where he had fallen. He took a few steps toward Hyde Street and the deserted Visitor Center, paused to catch his balance against the wooden railing, and continued along the pier until he reached Jefferson Street. He took the next bus to the Ferry Building, barely earning a glance from fellow passengers who had undoubtedly seen almost every kind of peculiar, bizarre, and deviant human being that could exist in a major city.

Something more like a wheeze than laughter caught in Dainn's throat. The sight of a Jotunn in his true form might shake them out of their complacency. He hoped by then it would not be too late.

The motorcycle Mist "borrowed" was an unprepossessing model of the kind urban motorists purchased to make themselves feel just a little more daring and rebellious when they left their Fiestas, Elantras, and Infiniti crossovers at the curb. It had been years since she'd ridden one, but now it felt as natural as galloping over the battlefields with her Sisters, determining which gallant warriors would live or die.

In so many ways, nothing had changed.

As she sped toward the Tenderloin, weaving among cars and buses struggling to deal with the ice and snow, she wondered if she was on a fool's errand. The last thing she could afford was to waste time with Vidarr, and if he didn't have the information she needed, that was probably what she'd be doing. Vali was right; he wasn't going to start being reasonable just because she needed him to. She had no illusions that her glamour was going to work on him.

But the only viable alternative was trying to formulate a seeking spell, building it piece by piece as she had the ones she'd used in the gym. Maybe it would work, but she had a feeling she was finally paying the price for her previous magic. Her mind felt as empty as a gas tank after the kind of car chase she remembered seeing in a Steve McQueen movie.

She just had to hope that, if it came down to it, she'd still have a few fumes left.

Parking on the narrow side street closest to Asbrew—the same one where'd she found the Jotunar beating upon Ryan—she set the brake and continued to the bar on foot. From the way the passersby, reputable or otherwise, stared after her as she passed, she knew her glamour was at work. A couple of the men drifted along in her wake until she turned and confronted them with a glare that sent them running with their tongues firmly back behind their teeth and their tails between their legs.

At first she thought Vidarr wouldn't see her. The doorman—a new one—was less than encouraging. The bar itself, usually busy at this hour, was nearly empty. That was a bad sign. But Vid finally emerged from the back room and stopped before her with legs braced, meeting her gaze with no hint of welcome.

"Well," he said, "what is it?"

"I need your help."

He stared at her as if she'd spoken in the tongue of the Dok-kalfar, the dark elves who, like most of the Dvergar, had attempted without success to remain neutral during the Last Battle.

"My *help*?" he asked, his mouth twisting with mockery. "I seem to remember you didn't take my advice about the Jotunar who in-vaded my bar."

Curse the arrogant bastard. She didn't have time for this. "We got rid of them, didn't we?"

"'We.'" Vidarr wiped his mouth as if he'd tasted something foul. "You mean that *nidingr* is still with you?"

Nidingr, the foulest insult one of the Norse—or Aesir—could call another, reserved for cowards, oathbreakers, and those without honor.

But Mist didn't try to defend Dainn's reputation. Speaking of him at all would make things worse.

"Look, Vidarr," she said in as humble a voice as she could manage, "Hrimgrimir and a couple other Jotunar attacked the loft very early this morning and almost hurt a couple of kids staying with me."

He didn't look very surprised, and certainly not upset. "Huh. I never knew you liked kids," he said, as if that were the primary subject of her statement. He cocked his head. "Wonder what Scarlip wanted with you so soon? He seemed pretty scared of the bitch-goddess when he left. And he has Gungnir already."

Since Dainn had always been convinced that Freya had come to help Mist in Asbrew, Mist saw no reason to suggest otherwise. And telling him about Ryan was out of the question. "We knew his fear wouldn't last," she said. "Loki reacted a little more quickly than we expected. He was obviously testing to see if we'd be ready for another attack."

"I guess you weren't."

He wasn't giving her any choice but to tell him part of the truth. "Dainn killed all three of the Jotunar."

Vidarr's brows shot up. "Him? How?"

"With one of my swords."

"It seems our little traitor has more secrets than you suspected."

"The point is that he killed them. But I don't want Loki to think he can get away with this again."

"So why are you coming to me? Why not ask Mama to help you out again?"

"She has plenty of other things going on right now. This is something I can take care of myself."

"How?" Vidarr said, idly scratching his jaw. "You going to negotiate with him? Threaten him with Freya's big tits when she's not even around to watch your back?"

"I've got magic of my own, Vid, a lot more than you'd be willing to believe."

"The elf teach you?"

"That's not important now. I'm the one who has to handle Freya's end of the fight until she's able to come herself."

"And the traitor? If he's so good at fighting, why isn't *he* with you now?"

"He has other important things to do."

"I'll bet." Vidarr leaned against the pockmarked wooden counter and folded his arms across his broad chest. "I don't care what magic you think you have, you're committing suicide. You'll never be able to stand against Loki if you challenge him on his own ground."

"Where *is* that ground, Vid?"

"What makes you think *I* know?" He barked a laugh. "Don't tell me. My idiot brother. He thought I wouldn't notice he was sneaking around." Vidarr leaned toward Mist, his eyes almost as chill as Hrimgrimir's. "I don't know what he's doing for you, but he's simple as a child, and he's always been in love with you."

Gods, no, Mist thought. *Not him, too.*

"Vali isn't as simple as you think," she said. "Maybe he has a better idea of what's going to happen if people like you stand on the sidelines."

Vidarr clenched his hammer fists. "You're walking on the edge of a very sharp blade, Mist."

"Look, Vid. You know Loki isn't just planning to bring more Jotunar into Midgard. What'll happen when Fenrisulfr shows up? The monster you were supposed to kill, remember?"

Vid hawked and spat somewhere behind the bar. "*After* he killed Odin. You know cursed well—"

"You can still do it." She took a step toward him, trying again to moderate her tone. "We're facing the possible end of this world as we know it"

"What makes you think I care?"

She could hardly believe she'd heard him correctly. "Come again?"

"Why should I care what happens to this bloody world?"

"You've been living among mortals as long as I have," she said. "Are you telling me you don't give a damn about the people of Midgard?" She stood a little taller so that she could look directly into his eyes. "Why did you let Loki take you prisoner, Vid? To suffer that kind of humiliation—"

Vidarr's face went very still. "Are you calling me a coward?"

"Coward" was, like *nidingr*, a slur worthy of *einvigi*, single combat. But Mist was well beyond caring.

"I'm saying you didn't try to interfere when Loki was trying to kill me."

"I saved your ass," he snarled. "Maybe Loki was confused by the trick you pulled, but he wasn't going to stay that way for long. If it hadn't been for me, you'd be dead, or worse."

And Loki had swept him aside like so much refuse.

Vidarr seemed to sense her thoughts. "I didn't make any deals," he snapped. "Loki threatened to kill everyone in Asbrew. I had to make him believe I was giving in."

Mist let go of the breath she hadn't realized she'd been holding. "Then you do care."

"These people are my customers. While they're in Asbrew, I'm responsible for them."

"But not for all your future customers out there?" she asked, waving her hand toward the door.

The tension in Vidarr's shoulders eased, but there was no lessening of the hostility in his eyes. "You're so gullible, Mist. Look at what Loki was able to do to you for six months."

"That's right. He managed to live in the same city as Odin's son and fly completely under your radar."

"You were *living* with him. He stole Gungnir right out from under your nose." He laughed. "Why Odin would ever trust you with anything bigger than a toothpick I'll never know."

Mist wondered why they'd ever called Vidarr the Silent God.

"Okay," she said. "You win. This is all my fault. But we can't change what's been done. If we don't show some fight at the beginning, we're setting ourselves up for a pounding before we can do anything to counter Loki's forces."

"You think you have the right to give orders?"

"I'm not trying to give orders. I didn't ask to be Freya's daughter. I didn't ask for any of this."

Vidarr cut the air with his hand in a gesture of angry dismissal. "Quit your whining. If you want my help, get rid of the elf."

"You know I can't do that, Vid."

Vidarr turned on his heel and strode for the back room. Mist jogged after him.

"If you can't stand up to your father's greatest enemy," she said, "just say it. You can go back to running this shithole and getting drunk with Vali while Midgard falls. You might not even notice."

He swung around, his heavy blond brows nearly meeting over his eyes.

"The only thing that's stopping me from teaching you a lesson," he said, "is that you're a woman. You and Freya used female tricks to defeat Loki, but they won't work on me. Next time you won't be so lucky."

Mist knew it was much too late to be humble, and her kind of persuasion obviously wasn't working. "At least tell me where he is, Vid," she said. "You don't care what happens to me, so you have no reason to keep it to yourself."

"I told you my price."

"And I won't pay it. What else will you accept?"

She regretted the words as soon as she'd spoken them, but she knew it was too late when Vidarr favored her with the kind of grin some women actually found attractive.

"Gungnir," he said.

"What?"

"You heard me. I want the Spear."

"Odin left it in my care, and he said—"

"You let Loki steal it."

"And *you* let Loki take you prisoner!"

The hostility between them was as thick as Thor's beard. Vid set his jaw in a way that told Mist he wasn't going to back down.

But giving up Gungnir to a man who despised her, wouldn't fight, and had already fallen to Loki once . . .

She reminded herself that the important thing was to find Dainn and worry about the rest later. "All right," she said. "It's a deal. But I have to get it back first, and I don't have time for any more of this crap."

Vidarr stared at her a moment longer and then walked behind the counter. He pulled a folder from a shelf underneath and slapped it on the counter.

"I didn't get very much yet, but the guy I sent to look had some luck and found records of a recent lease of an office building on Battery Street. Found the name of the lessee and where he lives now."

Mist didn't touch the folder. "And?"

"He didn't make much effort to hide himself. Lukas Landvik, esq."

The tone of his voice seemed to suggest he found the name funny, but Mist saw nothing humorous about it. "The address," she said.

Vidarr extended himself so far as to write it down for her, and she headed for the front door.

"Mist!" he called after her.

She kept walking. "What?"

"I'll offer a little advice. Don't think just because Freya and that traitor are behind you that you'll win. You take one wrong step and you'll fall, and take everything else with you."

She paused at the door. "You act as if it all depends on me. It's not my personal war, Vid. I'm only one of the foot soldiers."

"You're an arrogant bitch, Mist," Vidarr said. "That's what's going to get you in the end."

Turning her back on him, Mist flung open the door and strode through the bar. On her way to the motorcycle, she almost ran into an old man with a cane and a jaunty smile. She caught at him to steady him, but he only grinned at her as he slipped from her grasp.

"Good afternoon, young lady," he said. Before Mist could reply, he had walked past her, and when she turned to go after him he was gone.

Jotunn. Mist was certain of it. And she knew the message he was giving her: "We are watching. We know where you go. We will always find you."

Loki would be waiting for her.

Freya, she thought, *if you can hear me, if there's anything you can do, now would be the time.*

Once he was inside the Ferry Building and no longer shivering, Dainn found his way to the back of a small coffee shop, keeping his head down as he gazed into his untouched cup of espresso. At 3:00 p.m., the Ferry Building was only beginning to fill with early commuters bound for the East Bay and Marin. A few minutes after four, a man in a black trench coat arrived, sat next to Dainn at the table, and handed him a small white envelope. He stayed just long enough to watch Dainn begin to open it and then left as quietly as he had come.

Inside was a note card with gilded lettering on snowy, white handmade paper.

You are cordially invited to attend the fitting of
Lukas Landvik, Esq.
at the rooms of Fredkin & Associates
Sutter Street
San Francisco, California
at 5 p.m.

At the bottom of the invitation was scrawled a single handwritten line: *Don't be late. —L.*

Dainn tucked the note back in the envelope and put it in his pants pocket. It was only about a mile to Sutter Street from the Embarcadero. Dainn lingered a few more minutes and then started southwest along Market Street, lost among hundreds of workers and shoppers caught up in the last-minute Yuletide rush.

It was five minutes to five when Dainn walked into the shop. The showroom was elegant in its simplicity, with comfortable chairs placed in convenient locations, a few racks of expensive suits and handmade ties on display, and various other tasteful appointments meant to appeal to the discriminating man of means.

Almost immediately Dainn was approached by an immaculately dressed gentleman with a formal smile and quick, narrow hands. He took Dainn in from his plain loafers to the crown of his head with such subtle disapproval that most mortals would not even have noticed. His smile widened.

"Welcome, sir," he said with the merest trace of a British accent. "My name is Javier. How may we assist you today?"

"I received this," Dainn said, withdrawing the invitation from his pocket.

"Of course, sir," the man said with barely a glance at the card. "You are expected. If you will follow me . . ."

Loki was in one of the fitting rooms in the rear of the establishment, a chamber every bit as impressive as the showroom. He wore unhemmed trousers and a dress shirt open at the neck. A tailor was obsequiously fluttering around him, chattering nervously as he measured Loki's inseam.

He must have done something wrong, because Loki abruptly kicked him away. "If you don't watch your hands," Laufeyson said, very softly, "you may one day find yourself without them."

For a moment the tailor was unable to speak. Javier fled the room.

"I see you haven't lost your natural charm, Laufeyson," Dainn said from the doorway.

Loki turned around. His face broke into a broad, welcoming, and entirely deceptive smile. He glanced once at the tailor, who rapidly followed his fellow employee out the door.

"My dear Dainn," Loki said, coming toward him with outstretched hands. "How very delightful to see you. I am so very pleased that you contacted me. It has been centuries since we last spoke."

Dainn stood unmoving, watching Loki's approach with emotions so violently in conflict that he felt almost nothing at all. *Centuries.* Centuries during which Loki had been utterly unaware that Dainn had been alive in Midgard.

Now he greeted Dainn as if their last encounter had been one of tender feelings and good-natured sparring. Except for his clothing, Loki looked exactly as he had at Asbrew, wearing the shape he preferred: the slightly vulpine, handsome face; thick, wavy ginger hair; and emerald-green eyes with a thin rim of orange-red. There was nothing in his manner to suggest that he had ever been humiliated by his defeat at Asbrew.

Or how shocked he had been to learn Dainn was the elf Hrimgrimir claimed to have killed in Golden Gate Park.

"I confess I have missed you," Loki said, smoothing the front of his half-open shirt. "I had hoped we might have a pleasant chat after my little tête-à-tête with our darling Mist."

"Is that what you call your defeat at her hands, Slanderer?"

Loki dropped his hands. "Now, now," he said, clucking his tongue in indulgent disapproval. "No need for bad manners. Let us be frank with one another, as we once were." He smiled amiably. "I confess I hadn't expected that Freya would use you as her messenger. I was never quite sure where you had gone after the Dispersal."

"To Midgard," Dainn said. "Freya sent me just as I was about to kill you."

Loki gave no visible sign of surprise. "What excellent timing for me," he said, more than a touch of acid in his voice. "She could not have anticipated the Dispersal, so perhaps she thought it best to get you out of Odin's sight before you drew more unwelcome attention to yourself. I presume it was not because she wanted to spare my life."

"It seems unlikely," Dainn said, echoing Loki's tone. "I don't know why Freya chose the moment she did, or why she sent me here, but I was never in Ginnungagap. I was in Midgard long before you were."

"And yet you never knew I had come."

"As you didn't know another former inhabitant of the other Eight Homeworlds had preceded you."

"Ironic, isn't it? You must have felt rather lonely. We could have kept each other such good company these past six months."

It was difficult for Dainn to believe that Loki could behave as if there had been no attack on the loft. Dainn had expected no guilt or shame—Loki was almost impervious to such emotions—but Laufeyson seemed not in the least concerned with the purpose of Dainn's visit, or what he might intend.

"So," Loki said over Dainn's silence, "I presume that once Freya and the Aesir had awakened and rebuilt a poor imitation of Asgard, she remembered where she had put you, located you, and assigned you the duty of fetching her daughter. And of course you would have felt obligated to obey." He began to unbutton his shirt. "You were always rather talented, at least before Odin looked upon you with disfavor. But I didn't realize how much you had retained, since our last meeting was so—" He gave a rueful shrug. "You were quite effective against my poor Jotunar, defeating them single-handedly and tossing them into the Sahara Desert. Oh, yes, I found them, but it was most inconvenient."

"As inconvenient as losing three more of your Jotunar this morning?" Dainn asked.

"My dear Dainn, you seem to have lost track of time. It's hardly any wonder, considering how Freya has you jumping to do her bidding." He gestured to a pair of ornate chairs and small table set against the wall. A gilded tray held the remains of a meal and a half-empty glass of orange juice. "Have you had breakfast?" He shook his head reprovingly. "Don't look at me that way, sweetheart. It doesn't suit your lovely face."

"What game are you playing, Scar-lip?" Dainn asked coldly.

"It's not *I* playing games, at least not at the moment. I presume you contacted me on a matter of business, since I doubt you are here for pleasure. Unfortunately." He picked up the glass and took a sip of the juice with relish. "Did Freya send you to warn me again?"

"I am here of my own accord. The Lady does not observe my every move."

"Perhaps it wasn't wise for you to tell me that."

"Wisdom does not interest me at the moment."

Loki's long lashes dropped over his eyes. "Obviously, or you would have joined my cause already."

"I have made many mistakes," Dainn said, showing his teeth, "But I would sooner go under the serpent myself than join you."

"There," Loki said. "That's better. You never did smile enough." He set down his glass. "May I presume you bring empty threats of your own?"

"I never make empty threats."

"Good." Loki yawned behind his hand. "There are so many more interesting topics of conversation. For instance—what does the Sow really intend for Mist? I confess I didn't anticipate how useful she would be to her mother, channeling Freya's power as she did. Knowing what I do of our little Valkyrie, I would imagine she has found this situation . . . difficult. But of course you haven't told her that she's little more than Freya's puppet, have you? She might actually object."

So, Dainn thought, Loki had indeed drawn the desired conclusion. "She knows enough," he said.

"I wonder."

"You underestimated the Lady when you determined to break the rules."

"I only stretched them, though I admit Freya may see it differently." He flicked a piece of lint from his sleeve. "Surely you know I will not make the same mistake twice."

"Yet you continue to flout those same rules even now."

Loki spread his hands. "What rules have I flouted since I took Gungnir from Freya's daughter?"

"Since you sent Hrimgrimir on a cowardly mission to attack Mist in her own home, I presume that is a rhetorical question."

"What?" Loki asked, lifting his ginger brows. "When?"

"Approximately seven o'clock this morning."

All the sly good humor left Loki's face, and his eyes took on a reddish tint. "*Who* attacked her?"

"Your chief henchman, Hrimgrimir, and two of his followers. Or have you forgotten his name in the past ten hours?"

Loki displayed his slightly pointed teeth in a very convincing approximation of outrage. A neat array of empty hangers suspended from a rod set in an alcove at the side of the room detached themselves and went flying across the room, landing haphazardly, like a child's pick-up sticks.

"Hrimgrimir," Loki spat. "I did not send him, or anyone. He defied my direct orders."

Dainn laughed.

"It is the truth," Loki said, the muscles in his jaw flexing. "I explicitly warned Hrimgrimir not to make any move except on my command."

"Then they disobeyed you, and they paid the price."

"Oh?" Loki seemed to relax all at once, undoing the last button of his shirt and letting the tail hang loose. "Can I expect them to return yelping with their tails between their legs?"

He was doing his best not to show his alarm, but Dainn knew him too well. "You have three fewer servants," he said. "You had better use the rest more wisely."

The hangers flew up again and slammed against the closed door all at once. "I did *not* send them," he repeated. He took a sharp breath. "You must have raised wards against me," he said. "How did Hrimgrimir break them?" He searched Dainn's face. "They didn't hold. How very peculiar."

Devastating was the word Dainn would have chosen, but he reminded himself that Laufeyson was the one at a disadvantage. And must be kept there as long as possible.

"Do you know why Hrimgrimir came after us?" he asked.

Loki shrugged. "Revenge? You humiliated him quite thoroughly."

"Would he take such a risk for something so unimportant?"

"We're talking of Hrimgrimir," Loki said, affable again. "How did they die? Did Freya descend in all her glory to make a puppet of her daughter again and blast them with loving kindness?"

"Freya wasn't there," Dainn said. "*I* killed them."

19

Loki strode toward the door and slammed his palm on the buzzer beside it. Javier opened the door and took a step back when he found himself nose-to-nose with his client.

"Two screwdrivers, Stolichnaya Elit," Loki snapped.

Without a squeak of protest, the mortal bowed and hurried off. Loki pulled the door shut and scowled at it as if he were about to blast it off its hinges.

When he turned to face Dainn again, his mercurial temper had changed once more. "How did you manage it?" he asked in a casual voice. "Did you do to them what you unsuccessfully tried on me all those years ago?"

"I was not entirely unsuccessful, was I?"

Loki knew very well that Dainn was referring to his fear, both in Asgard and Asbrew.

"You failed," Loki said. "I am still here."

"I was unable to control it then," Dainn said. "I can make the creature do what I want, whenever I wish."

It was impossible to tell if his lie had worked, but Loki's body was unusually tense. Dainn moved closer to Loki as if he planned to pin him against the door. Loki edged sideways and walked back to the table.

"You devoured their minds?" he asked, gesturing toward the hangers scattered around the door. They flew back to the alcove, neatly aligning themselves along the rod again.

"Nothing of the creatures is left," Dainn said.

"Have you become a devourer of flesh as well?"

His unease was palpable, but Dainn remained silent. Loki had never been able to leave a silence unfilled.

"You have come to kill me after all?" he asked softly. "Dainn, Dainn. I am prepared for you this time."

"I know," Dainn said.

Clearly biting back questions he was desperate to ask, Loki assumed a pose of indifference that was anything but convincing. "Where was Mist during this epic engagement?" he asked.

"Fighting. As you may remember, she is an excellent swordswoman."

"Ah. Then you cannot claim full glory for your victory, despite her undoubtedly meager contribution."

"The desire for glory is your weakness, Laufeyson, not mine."

"But such desire is also Freya's, and yet you say she wasn't there."

"She had faith in our ability to deal with three Jotunar."

"Then I suppose I should thank you for taking three willful, disobedient, and unpredictable servants off my hands."

"You seem unable to control your so-called servants, Laufeyson."

"A few Jotunar more or less hardly matter to me." He began to remove his shirt. "I am beginning to wonder how much Freya actually values *you* if you have been reduced to a mere guard dog." He strolled toward Dainn with a sympathetic smile. "Whatever you may feel you owe her, you know she is not what mortals have always believed her to be. I understand human nature better than the Sow ever could. As I said to our little Valkyrie, they need me, and when they recognize this simple fact, I will win."

It was all Dainn could do not to slam his fist into Loki's smug face. "Such posturing may persuade some mortals," he said, "but it will be no more effective with me than it was with Mist."

"No? I seem to remember certain postures that worked very well with you." Without warning, Loki grabbed Dainn by the shoulders and kissed him, punishing with sharp teeth that drew blood from Dainn's lips, pushing his tongue inside Dainn's mouth before he could free himself. Dainn shoved Loki away, disgust and hatred threatening to overwhelm him.

"Ah. Sweet as ever," Loki said, licking his lips. "You were always good, darling. One of the best I've ever had."

Dainn dragged his arm across his mouth. He had to be careful. So very careful.

"*You* were not," he said. "But then again, you made sure I didn't notice."

Loki threw his shirt over the nearest chair, flinging pins in every direction and tearing the expensive fabric in several places. "Perhaps I will have to remind you of what you threw away."

"That would be a mistake," Dainn said, holding his gaze.

"A pity," Loki said. He unpinned the fly of his trousers. "You've bet on the losing horse."

"Sleipnir is your son, and yet he, the swiftest of all horses, belongs to Odin."

"But we both know that Odin—" Loki broke off, putting his finger to the side of his nose. "Ah, but we must not speak of that. Perhaps you would prefer a more private setting to continue our conversation. Though if you merely intend to offer more threats . . ."

"I have made no threats, Laufeyson."

Loki let the trousers fall. "Well, then. I've a lovely apartment on—"

"I prefer a more neutral setting."

Loki kicked the trousers out of the way, strolled to the door, and pushed on the buzzer. The door opened again, and the tailor's fearful face appeared.

"May I . . . be of assistance, gentlemen?" he said, his voice quivering.

"I am leaving now," Loki said. "We will resume tomorrow." He stared at the mortal with a look that might literally kill. "I did not receive my drinks. Tell Javier that he had better bring what I request more quickly next time."

"Yes, sir."

"And see that you have better command of your fingers tomorrow."

The tailor bobbed his head as if he were trying to appease a barbarian king and slunk into the room, as near to crawling as a man could do on two legs. Loki jerked his head toward the cast-off shirt and trousers. The tailor left hurriedly with the half-ruined clothing carefully folded over his arm.

Loki stood all but naked in the center of the room, striking a pose reminiscent of a Greek statue.

He was beautiful, Dainn thought—perfect, as the White Christ's great enemy Satan was said to be. That, of course, was Loki's intention.

Dainn turned his back. Loki sighed dramatically, and Dainn heard the rustle of fabric as Loki dressed in his own clothes. When he was finished, he came up beside Dainn, close but not quite touching.

"Shall we go?" he said.

Dainn preceded him out of the shop, leaving the pale and silent tailor bobbing in his wake. Javier was approaching on the sidewalk from the right, a waiter with drinks immediately behind him, as Loki stepped through the door. Loki extended his arm, and both Javier and waiter plunged to the icy sidewalk amid spilled screwdrivers and shattering glass.

Dainn stopped to help the men to their feet. Javier was bleeding from a small cut to his forehead, but the waiter seemed more flustered than harmed.

"Do you need assistance?" Dainn asked.

Javier shook his head, his eyes pleading with Dainn for an explanation. Dainn had none to give him.

The Financial District was clogged with cars, buses, and pedestrians, and Loki wrinkled his nose at the smell of gasoline fumes and the various odors of the mortals hurrying along the street, rushing in and out of shops adorned with red and green streamers, silver wreaths, and elaborate window dressings.

"This will never do," Loki said. He grabbed Dainn's arm, and all at once they were standing inside a spacious, elegantly furnished room with a wall of vast windows framing the darkening sky, the bay, and the hills of Marin County on the other side of the water. A Rodin statue adorned a pedestal between two leather couches, and what Dainn presumed to be a Kandinsky original hung opposite the window.

"Surely you didn't think I would walk into whatever trap you've set up for me?" Loki asked.

Dainn kept his expression neutral so as not to reveal that he'd noticed Loki's quickened breathing and the strain in his face. Teleportation, as mortals called it, required a great deal of magical energy, and Loki had expended it merely for the pleasure of temporarily getting the better of him. The beast stirred, scenting blood.

Not yet, he told it. *Wait.*

"Drink?" Loki offered, strolling toward the bar adjoining the kitchen.

"You always drank too much, Laufeyson," Dainn said.

"You need to drink more." Loki laid his hand over his heart. "But your concern touches me deeply, sweetheart."

"Do you wish to know why I've come?"

Loki turned around, leaning his hip against the marble-topped counter. "Since you apparently don't intend to kill me right away, I'm fascinated."

"I want you to swear that you will not attack Mist or her mortal associates with magic or physical violence until Freya or the Alfar arrive."

Loki crossed his ankles and examined his beautifully manicured fingernails. "You surprise me, *skatten min*. You aren't usually so dull-witted."

"Because you would never make such an oath, no matter what the compensation?"

"You do intrigue me, my Dainn. But I have already acknowledged that I will not risk forfeiting the game by deliberately provoking your Lady further." He reached casually for a crystal shot glass. "I assure you—"

"You will forgive me if I want more than your assurances," Dainn said.

"Ah." Loki selected a bottle of Macallan whisky in an exquisite Lalique decanter. "Why do I feel that this request has a more personal basis than the need to safeguard one of Freya's earthly assets?"

Dainn ignored Loki's innuendo. "Freya has authorized me to use my own judgment in such matters," he said. "I simply wish to prevent future . . . misunderstandings."

"Yet it seems, in spite of your victory, that you are uncertain of your ability to protect our little Valkyrie." He poured the whisky and held the glass close to his nose, closing his eyes in appreciation. "Did Mist send you?"

"Do you believe she would?"

"No. But I don't believe you've been completely forthcoming with me. Or her. Is the Sow's reliability in question, perhaps?"

Dainn held Loki's gaze, careful not to reveal how uncomfortably close he had come to the truth. "I told you we did not require her assistance."

"Then perhaps you are afraid that Mist will act recklessly and attack me without Freya's assistance." He sipped his drink and sighed. "That's a rather significant problem for you, isn't it? Not merely protecting Mist from me, but from herself. And, not incidentally from you."

"Why would I harm Freya's daughter?"

"You misunderstand me. I have never actually seen the two of you together, of course, but your behavior is reminiscent of what I so very intimately observed in Asgard. You helped Mist at Asbrew because you were obligated to do so, but now . . . now that Freya has possessed our Valkyrie, perhaps she has no need of her mother's immediate presence to work the charms she never possessed before."

"If you are suggesting she has used glamour on me . . ."

"Has she?"

"If you believe she would, you never knew her."

"Even your words betray you, my Dainn. I know you too well to believe you feel nothing for her."

"Your belief that you know *me* is badly mistaken."

"How many women have you had since you've been wandering Midgard?" Loki asked. "Before we began our affair, all Asgard thought you celibate and above anything as crude as sex. You quickly proved them wrong . . . with the right encouragement." He lifted his glass in salute. "I have been told more than once that one of my greatest weaknesses is arrogance. Freya's is the belief that some emotional force called 'love' outweighs the necessities of self-interest and true freedom. You believed yourself in love with her. Now you're thrown into the company of a woman who can *become* her mother. You'd like to get her in your bed as much as I'd like to get you back in mine."

"Neither will ever happen," Dainn said, swallowing bile.

"And of course, Freya would strongly object. She trusts you with her most valuable possession, in spite of your feelings. Still, sweetheart, I fear for your state of mind."

"I gladly absolve you of any responsibility for my welfare."

Loki drained his glass and poured another three fingers. "Very well. Let's go back to your proposition. You want me to stay away from Mist and her 'human associates.' Leaving aside the fact that the parameters are too broad to be acceptable"—he held the glass up to the light, admiring its flame-amber color—"What are you prepared to offer me in return?"

The Century Tower, all clean modern lines, glass, and gleaming steel, loomed over the Financial District, fifty-eight stories rooted at the corner of Mission and Beale and thrusting upward like a crystalline spear sheathed in ice.

Mist entered the subterranean parking garage and worked a very simple Rune-spell to get past the guard and barriers. She found an empty parking space and cast another warding spell, preserving her energy by drawing the staves with chalk on the concrete around the bike. If anyone noticed the motorcycle, they would see only the vehicle that belonged in the space. She didn't intend to be around long enough for the spell to become stale.

Either she'd get Dainn back, or she'd be dead.

The lobby was immense, with a fireplace set in a huge marble block, two fountains, a gallery of exclusive art on the high walls, and clusters of luxury armchairs, sofas, and tables scattered throughout. A pair of mortals, male and female, stood behind a reception desk, ostensibly to assist the residents, but Mist knew they were also security personnel who could act decisively in case of emergency.

They might even be Loki's.

Two men sat in chairs on either side of a round table, one with his nose in a tabloid and the other working on a laptop. Neither looked up as Mist walked across the black marble tile floor, but their mortal appearance didn't deceive Mist in the slightest. They were Jotunar.

At least Mist knew she was in the right place.

She paused near a square pillar some distance from the reception desk to assess the situation. She had no sense that Dainn had walked here, no sense of his presence.

He could be dead by now, for all she knew.

No. That she *would* have known.

Her heart pounding more out of fear for him than for herself or the future of Midgard, Mist approached the bank of elevators.

"Pardon me, ma'am," the male receptionist said, coming up behind her. "Will you come to the reception desk?"

There was no way out of it, so Mist followed him. The woman gave her a probing look.

"Have you come to see one of our residents?" the man asked.

"Yes," she said. "Lukas Landvik."

He picked up a clipboard. "Your name, ma'am?"

"Brenda Jones."

"I'm sorry, ma'am. I have no listing by that name."

"There must be some mistake."

"Perhaps you would like me to call Mr. Landvik?"

That was the last thing Mist wanted. She already knew the Jotunar were listening. Her assumed name hadn't deceived them. Her one chance of getting past the receptionist-guards was to use the method she had sworn never to repeat.

But Dainn's life was at stake. This time she had to be in control. She closed her eyes, letting the glamour come. The scent of primroses drifted around her head. The female receptionist sniffed and frowned at Mist.

But it didn't take long before Mist felt her mother's power. *Her* power. Her body relaxed. She smiled and opened her eyes.

"What's your name?" she asked the man, looking into his brown eyes.

His gaze flickered this way and that in confusion, and he blushed. "Shaw," he stammered. "Robert. Bob."

The woman threw him an astonished glance and then began to study Mist with narrow-eyed intensity.

"Well, Bob," Mist said, leaning over the desk, "I really need to see Mr. Landvik. It's *so* important to me, and he's expecting me. I'm sure you wouldn't want to make either one of us angry?"

"Excuse me," the woman said. "I think you should leave, ma'am."

"No," Mist said, meeting her gaze. "I don't think I will."

The woman flinched. Mist hadn't been too sure how the glamour would work on the woman, but it was obviously having some effect.

"Bob," she said, "You can see I won't do any harm. Look at me."

She stepped back, imagining her body seductively curved, her breasts heavy inside her shirt. She didn't even need to show anything, because Bob was transfixed.

"Will you look on the list again?" Mist asked. "I'm sure my name is there."

He looked, running his finger down the page. "Here it is," he said. "I don't know why I didn't see it before."

"Let me see it," the woman said. She scanned the page. "Ms. Jones . . ."

Mist moved along the desk toward her. "Look at me," Mist said. "It's really not a problem to let me go up, is it?"

The woman's lips compressed. She fidgeted, as if she were trying to throw off Mist's influence.

In the end, she gave in, if reluctantly. "You can go up," she said, "but if Mr. Landvik isn't expecting you, we'll have to ask you to leave."

"Of course." Mist started away, stopped, and returned to the desk. "Silly me," she said. "I forgot the floor."

"Top," Bob said. "Fifty-eighth. Penthouse."

"Thank you so much."

The woman shook her head sharply. Mist didn't waste any time. She went straight to the elevator lobby. The elevators required a key card to operate, but Mist got it to work with only a little more effort than she had expended on getting past the guard in the garage, sketching Rune-staves with a number 2 pencil on the steel door where the small marks could hardly be seen. The Galdr was coming to her more easily every time she used it, but she wasn't about to take it for granted.

And it sure as Hel wasn't likely to work against Loki.

She entered the elevator and punched the button for the fifty-eighth floor. Just as the doors were sliding shut, both Jotunar forced their way into the cab. The one who'd been reading the paper slammed his fist on the stop button.

"Going somewhere?" he said.

"Who's asking?" Mist said, backing into the far corner.

"Is Mr. Landvik expecting you?" the laptop Jotunn said.

Oh, so polite. This one, at least, was completely unlike Hrimgrimir and his kind—almost certainly not as powerful, but better adapted to this world. Jotunar like him would be far more dangerous than the oafs and leg-breakers.

But she'd known all along that she wouldn't be able to walk right in without Loki's minions getting in her way.

"You wouldn't be here if he wasn't," she said.

"You stink like the Sow," the first one said, proving that his partner's manners hadn't rubbed off on him. His body expanded, widening and lengthening until his head threatened to bump the elevator's ceiling.

The other one maintained his mortal size. "Please, Egil. I think Mr. Landvik would very much like to see her in one piece." He held out his hand to Mist. "Give me your knife, Ms. Bjorgsen."

Mist calculated how much space she had. The cab was bigger than most, easily able to accommodate twelve people at a time without crowding, but it wasn't exactly the right size for a fight.

And she didn't want Loki to realize she could work her own magic without the Lady's help. Apparently these Jotunar hadn't been affected by her glamour. Better to let them think she was just stupid than that she might actually have some hope of standing up to Loki.

That hope was still slim. She'd left the loft with only a vague idea of how she was going to get Dainn out, and she hadn't come up with any better plan since she'd met with Vidarr.

Out of sheer desperation, she'd tried to call Freya. It was the last thing she'd wanted to do, but it was no longer a question of what she wanted.

But Dainn had been right. She didn't seem to have the skill or strength to cross the Void with her thoughts, and she'd never felt the slightest response.

So now she was on her own. She could forget about using the Galdr, since Loki was a master of it. That left her with the Vanir magic, if she could make it work. If she could surprise Loki without giving herself away too soon.

And she still didn't know if her magical energy would give out right when she needed it most.

"All right," she said, carefully unsheathing Kettlingr and offering it hilt-first to Laptop. "As long as you promise to give it back when Loki and I are finished with our meeting."

"You ain't gonna need it once Loki's finished with you," Egil said.

"Oh? Do you speak for your master?" Mist asked. "Maybe he'd like to know how easily you can predict his actions."

Laptop chuckled. "You have backbone, Ms. Bjorgsen, I'll give you that."

The elevator climbed to the appropriate floor without stopping, probably a bit of light magic on Loki's part for those times when he didn't want to be inconvenienced—in other words, every time he or his servants used it. When it reached the top, the polite giant turned to her with a pleasant smile.

"Here we are," he said. And slugged her across the face.

Dainn was a long time responding. Beads of perspiration stood out on his forehead, and his mouth was tight. His hatred burned as hot as any fire in Muspelheim.

Loki smiled to himself and took another very small sip of whisky. He had always found it amusing how easily he could read Dainn's thoughts with the merest glance at his face, even when everyone else in Asgard had seen only a stoic elf with a mysterious past and little in common with his own kind.

Dainn's power, the extent of which even Odin had never suspected, had acted like an aphrodisiac on Loki from the moment he had met the elf and recognized how utterly different he was. Loki had even felt some regret when he and Freya had stolen the very source and foundation that fed and sustained that power.

Not that Dainn remembered that life-altering event. But even before the betrayal, Dainn's self-control had never been as effective as he wished to believe. That was what had made him such an ideal bedmate, even when he had believed he was fucking Freya and not the Aesir's worst enemy. And Loki still wanted him, as he wanted Freya.

But not in the same way. Yes, he had desired Freya long after she had rejected him. He had come to hate her, but his hatred had not banished his need to possess her lush body.

With Dainn it was different. Loki knew himself incapable of those tender feelings the skalds sang of, but if there had been any such propensity within him . . .

"I will give you the one thing you could not take from me," Dainn said, putting an end to Loki's brooding.

Loki licked his lips. "Do you think I could not take it if I wished?" he asked.

"I am speaking of Alfar magic."

Finishing his drink in one swallow, Loki set the glass down. "Is that all?" he asked. "I was expecting something much more . . . valuable."

"Only two of the Aesir know how to work my people's magic. Odin understands something of it, as he understands all forms of magic, but only Freyr uses it as we do."

"Not even his sister?"

"Not even the Lady."

"Why should I want it?" Loki said in a tone meant to convey utter boredom. "Its limitations are significant. This modern world is full of steel and concrete, crowding out the forests, polluting the streams and poisoning the earth itself. Alfar must draw upon the life of growing things. It's true, I did admit that you were capable of brilliance in the old days. But now . . ." He shook his head gently. "Whatever you accomplished in Asbrew, I think we can find a better arrangement."

Before he could draw another breath, Dainn closed his eyes and began to sing. The syllables were long and sibilant, curling and twisting around each other like vines laden with perfumed blossoms. They reached inside Loki and wrapped around his heart, sending needle-thin tendrils into every bone, every muscle, every nerve.

Loki called up the darkest Merkstaves against the attack, Uruz and Algiz to repel and weaken, sending through his own veins poison that would have killed a lesser being. It touched the tendrils, withering them black and lifeless. Yet Dainn's magic persisted, refusing to be completely dislodged. Loki could feel the tendrils growing again, sucking all the life from his body.

"Dainn," he gasped.

All at once the tendrils snapped back like fingers held too close to a flame. Loki staggered, falling against the shelves behind. Bottles and glasses rattled, and several went crashing to the floor.

"Freya's tits," he gasped, pushing himself upright. He locked his muscles, afraid his trembling would be all too apparent.

Dainn was shaking, and it was evident that he, too, was struggling to stay on his feet. "Do you see the worth of my offer now?" he asked hoarsely.

"Indeed," Loki said, working a quick spell to mask his consternation. "You must have drawn very deep to reach the life beneath this city."

"Yes," Dainn said, panting like a wolf in the sun.

Fear and excitement and lust tangled in Loki's chest. Even though Dainn had forgotten the full extent of the power he had possessed before he'd lost lifeblood of the Eitr, even though he had shown no sign of such extraordinary abilities in the moments just before he and Loki had been violently separated by the upheaval that ended Ragnarok, even after centuries in Midgard, he had not lost himself.

But there was always a price.

"I am impressed," Loki said. "But look at yourself, my Dainn. You're weak as a woman's will." He stepped over broken glass and spilled liquor, approaching Dainn cautiously. "I could kill you now with a single word."

But Dainn was no longer listening. He was gazing into another world, one only he inhabited. It was as if Loki didn't exist.

No one ignored Loki Laufeyson, not even Dainn. Especially not Dainn, even the near stranger who stood before him now.

"Look at me!" Loki commanded.

Dainn did nothing, said nothing. Loki raised his hand and struck Dainn across the face with all his Jotunn strength. Dainn's head snapped to one side, but he didn't react. Loki struck him again, raising blood from his lips.

No effect. But Loki knew of one other way. A way that had worked most effectively on an ascetic elf who had suppressed his physical needs so long that it took only a single spark to ignite a universe of lust.

Loki leaned close to Dainn's face and breathed a Bind-Rune against his lips, seductive and heavy with desire. He knew when Dainn's body began to stir. His own excitement rose as well.

"I don't believe you've fucked anyone in a very long time," he purred. "You know what I can do. I can become what you most desire."

Dainn blinked. "I want no part of you."

"No part at all? Your body says otherwise." Loki grabbed the back of Dainn's neck. "Admit it," he said. "You have never found a lover to compare with me. Take my word for it. Screwing Mist is like making love to the handle of an ax."

Dainn jerked away, but it was clear he was still beyond the ability to resist. "Your tongue is not so agile that it cannot be removed," he whispered.

"That would be a terrible waste," Loki said, "when I can put it to such better use." He flicked his fingers, congealing ice out of the moisture in the air and shaping it into a rope. With it he bound Dainn's legs and sealed his lips. The restraints might not hold the elf long, but Loki didn't need much time. Dainn was caught in Loki's bonds like a fly in amber. Only his eyes expressed his rebellion. And hate.

"Easy," Loki purred. "I promise this won't hurt at all." He wedged his hand under Dainn's shirt. "Your heart is beating fast, Dainn Faith-breaker." He slid his other hand down to cup the bulge pressing against Dainn's trousers. Slowly he unfastened the button and pulled the zipper down. His long fingers probed inside Dainn's fly.

"Lovely," Loki murmured. "I had almost forgotten how very well-endowed you are." He released the object of his desire from its confinement and began to stroke.

Dainn's breath caught in his throat. The ice covering his mouth melted and dripped onto his jacket. "Stop," he whispered. "I don't . . . want . . ."

"You *are* the stubborn one," Loki chided, halting his caresses. "Very well. Perhaps this will suit you better."

And then he changed, his shape melting into something softer, something curved and bountiful in breast and hip, golden-haired and perfect.

Freya. But not Freya, of course. Only the image of her, the illusion Loki had used to seduce and control Dainn, deceive him and blind him and steal his will.

"Better?" Loki asked in the husky voice of a practiced seductress. She knelt at Dainn's feet and went to work.

But somehow Dainn fought him, refusing to give Loki satisfaction no matter how skillfully he practiced his arts. He quickly changed himself again, becoming strong and wiry and firm-jawed, a tawny lioness, a warrior.

This time Dainn reacted. His breath came fast, and his fair skin flushed nearly to his navel.

It would be only a matter of moments now, Loki thought. And then . . .

At first he thought the vibration under his knees was coming from the floor itself, and he pulled away, anticipating an earthquake.

But there was no earthquake. The shaking came not from the earth but from Dainn himself, and when Loki looked up, Dainn had begun to *change*.

20

————

Startled, Loki hopped up and back, pressing himself against the wall behind him. What he saw made it impossible for him to maintain his female shape, and in an instant he was Loki again. Loki, father-mother of monsters, who had never seen such a creature as this before.

You have, he thought. But only in the mind.

That had been dangerous enough. This was far worse. In the Old Tongue of the northern peoples, the thing before him was a *berserkr*: almost impervious to pain, immune to the cut of a blade, indestructible by fire. The body was massive and slightly hunched, the neck set low between the powerful shoulders, the fur black with a rainbow sheen worn by no living animal on Midgard. The face was neither human nor beast, though it, too, bore a sleek covering of fur as smooth as velvet. Ears set halfway between the top and sides of the head lay flat to the broad skull. Its teeth were white and sharp, its claws gleaming at the tips of blunt fingers.

It was not one of the Ulfhednar, the Wolf-skins, or the Bjornhednar, clothed only in bearskins and savagery. It was something even Loki, for all his skill in shifting shape, could never become.

And Dainn had claimed he could control it.

"What are you?" Loki whispered.

The creature glared at Loki through slitted red eyes, the pupils showing only a narrow penumbra of deep blue. He grunted a sound that might have been a word and took a step toward Loki.

Loki glanced past him toward the door of the apartment. "What do you want?" he asked. "Is this supposed to be a challenge? A warning? A threat?"

Dainn growled and lifted a pawlike hand, claws like crescents of silver catching the dim lamplight.

"You won't hurt me," Loki said. "You could have come after me in Asbrew and again in this very apartment, but you didn't. Ask yourself why, my Dainn. Ask yourself why you didn't even make the attempt to kill me."

With a roar Loki felt deep in his bones, Dainn lunged toward him. He swiped his paw at Loki's head. Before Loki could leap aside, Dainn changed his angle of attack and struck the wall, raking parallel grooves in the paneling. Then he froze, staring at his hand in bewilderment.

Sick with fear, Loki retreated to a safe distance. He could escape in an instant if he chose, become a fly and keep out of Dainn's reach as long as necessary. But that would require a great deal of energy after the teleportation, and there were things he wanted very badly to know.

"You see?" he said. "There is too much between us, my Dainn, no matter how vehemently you deny it."

Dainn wrapped his arms around his chest in a pathetically human gesture and closed his eyes.

"There, now," Loki said. "What are we to do next? Will you cast off this shape, or shall I sell you to a circus?"

The beast began to shiver, every coarse hair on its body erect, and a moan of agony burst from its chest. It spoke another almost incomprehensible word.

No.

Loki never saw the transformation. It was nearly instantaneous, as if the whole episode had been no more than an illusion from the beginning.

But it wasn't. For as Dainn opened his eyes, he looked directly at the quintet of deep slashes in the wall. And wept without making a sound.

Loki approached him with great care. "When did this happen, *elskede min*? When did it become flesh and blood? Was it born when you found yourself exiled to this world, stalked by loneliness, raging at your fate?" He traced a grotesque shape in the air between them. "Is this the last thing my Jotunar saw before they died?"

The elf shook his head. "Not this," he said, his voice cracking on the second word.

"Does our little Valkyrie know?" Loki asked. "How can she bear to look at you?" He seized Dainn's jaw in his hand. "You don't want it, do you? You couldn't accept the beast when it was merely a creature of the mind, and this is a thousand times worse. Or better, depending upon your point of view. *Look* at me, Dainn."

The Alfr met his gaze, passive in the grip of his own self-loathing.

"Of course," Loki said. "It all becomes clear. You aren't serving Freya out of some profound loyalty to the Aesir who rejected your attempt at atonement, or to the goddess who spared you. Not even to Mist herself." He laughed. "You surely can't believe even the Lady can cure this malady." He released Dainn's chin and patted him lightly on the cheek. "My poor little elf. You don't control it at all."

Dainn took a step back, lost his balance and righted himself again. "You asked what I am," he said. "The beast is a weapon. I do not want it. But it is not completely outside my control, or you would not still be breathing." His indigo eyes darkened, and his voice grew stronger. "You asked if this was a challenge, a warning, or a threat. It is all of these. You will refrain from attacking Mist and any mortals she takes under her protection until Freya arrives. I will teach you the elf-magic with the understanding that if you should break the oath we make now—"

"Oh, you have made yourself very clear."

Dainn shuddered like a horse shaking off flies. "You must learn not to provoke the beast."

"You have not told me how one provokes it."

"That you will have to discover for yourself."

"Ah. And what about your mistress? You would give me new power, and in doing so betray the Lady."

Dainn jerked up his zipper. "I never promised to explain myself to you, Laufeyson."

"Still, beast or not, you cannot believe I would allow you to break your word to me. You were never—" Loki stopped, caught in the blinding light of comprehension. He whistled softly. "Of course," he said. "I mistook the nature of your feelings. It isn't that you're concerned about protecting Mist from me until Freya comes to Midgard. It isn't that you see the object of your lust in her daughter. You know that once the Sow gets her claws into Mist, our Valkyrie will essentially cease to exist. And that you cannot bear."

The way Dainn flinched told Loki just how right he was. "I do not betray Freya," Dainn said.

"You're no better a liar than your lady-love," Loki said. "You're prepared to sacrifice yourself and Midgard to save *her*."

"You will never have Midgard."

Loki moved closer to Dainn, jealous almost beyond his ability to conceal. "Can you actually be attempting to buy time so that you can convince Freya that there is a desirable alternative to assuming Mist's body?" he asked. "Oh, my Dainn, you will never stop the Sow from fulfilling her scheme. She has far too much invested in it." He brushed Dainn's ear with his lips. "If you give yourself to me, to my cause, there will be no need for this elaborate deception. We, the three of us, can defeat her. She will never be a threat to Mist again."

Dainn planted his hand firmly on Loki's chest and pushed him away. "Never."

"Because you know Mist would never agree. You may have kept her in ignorance of the fate intended for her, but our girl is nothing if not courageous. Wouldn't she gladly sacrifice her body and soul if she believed it could save Midgard? Will she not hate you when she learns what you've done?"

"I do not fear being hated."

"Perhaps it is even the fate you desire," Loki said. He pursed his lips. "Since you refuse to see reason, let us be very clear. You will teach me the magic you displayed before your other self put in its appearance. I agree that neither I nor my Jotunar will attack Mist or her mortal associates while they are within a radius of one mile of the loft. All bets are off when any of them step outside those boundaries. Agreed?"

"No. If they step outside that radius—"

"Then they must take their chances. You cannot expect me to stay my hand everywhere in this city."

It was evident that Dainn was considering refusal. But, in the end, he surrendered.

"Agreed," he said.

"Everything else is fair game," Loki said. "The Treasures belong to those who find them."

"If they *can* find them."

"I have people working on that. And now, what is *my* guarantee that you will teach me as you have promised? How will I know you are not holding back, or deliberately misleading me?"

Dainn turned and walked unsteadily into the spotless kitchen, found the knife block, and withdrew a chef's knife. Loki tensed, but Dainn resumed his place without making a single threatening gesture. He held up his hand and sliced his palm with the edge of the blade. Blood ran down his hand and dripped onto the floor. He offered the knife to Loki.

Startled by the gesture, Loki hesitated. For Dainn to offer the blood-oath to his greatest enemy was almost incomprehensible. In fact, nothing that had happened in the past hour was comprehensible. Dainn was still holding something back.

But he and Loki would be spending some "quality time" together in the very near future. And Loki would learn exactly what that something was.

He took the knife from Dainn's hand and cut his palm, then dropped the knife to the floor. He held up his hand. Dainn mated his palm to Loki's. Their blood mingled, as once Loki's had mingled with Odin's.

Dainn tried to withdraw immediately, but Loki clenched his fingers around Dainn's hand and held on.

"Now," Loki whispered. "Now you can never betray me."

Dainn wrenched free. "We are not blood brothers, Slanderer," he said. "I am still your enemy. I do what I must, and no more."

"Naturally." Loki held his palm to his mouth and sucked on the wound until the bleeding stopped. "When shall we begin?"

"It must be carefully arranged."

"Then arrange it quickly, my Dainn." Loki walked into the kitchen and pulled a snowy white towel out of a drawer. He tossed it at Dainn, who caught it with less than his usual ease. His blood stained the towel crimson, and he dropped it onto the floor beside the knife.

"I quite enjoyed our little discussion," Loki said. "And who knows? You may change your mind about resuming our former relationship."

Dainn smiled, an expression as chilling as the beast itself. The effect was ruined by the darkening shadows around his eyes and the trembling of his legs when he backed away. "I will contact you," he said, turning toward the door.

It opened before he could reach it. Two Jotunar barreled through, dragging a limp form between them.

Mist.

ɕɕ

She regained consciousness lying on a cream-colored leather sofa, her nose clogged with blood and her head pounding.

Loki was standing over her, displaying his full array of very white teeth.

"Well, well," he said. "Speak of the devil. Here is our little Valkyrie, boldly charging to the rescue. Dainn must have done a very poor job of concealing his intentions. But his judgment does seem to be rather flawed these days."

Mist bolted up and tried to stand, but nausea overwhelmed her and she sank back to the couch.

"Mist!"

Dainn's voice. She looked for him and found him standing between the two Jotunar, who stood ready to grab him the second he moved. He had clearly lost the battle. Blood was spattered over the front of his shirt, and his face had that terrible, gaunt look, but he was alive.

"Why did you come?" Dainn asked, anguish in his eyes.

His naked emotion nearly undid her. "Did you really think I wouldn't?" she asked, deliberately injecting hopelessness into her voice. "Did you think I'd let you take him on alone?"

"How poignant," Loki said. "It seems Dainn's feelings are not unrequited. But I thought better of you, Mist. I have you both in my hands now. One might say the game is as good as won already."

Dainn stared fixedly at Loki's back until Laufeyson turned to face him. "This is, after all, nowhere near the loft," he said.

Mist didn't understand him or the look they gave each other, but she was more concerned about how and when to make her move. She'd only get one chance, and she still had no idea if she could make the Vanir magic work.

"I've called Freya," she said. "If you do anything else to me or Dainn, she'll be pretty pissed."

"And pour her power into you, as she did in Asbrew?" he asked. He glanced at Dainn again, smiling slightly.

He doesn't know, Mist reminded herself. Dainn had been right. Loki still believed that power was Freya's alone. What did he think she'd experienced when Freya had apparently "possessed" her?

It hardly mattered, as long as he thought she was incapable of fighting with anything more than her sword. All she had to do now was make him think she was helpless and trying to cover her fear with bravado. Get him off his guard and keep him there until she found just the right moment.

Oh, yes. That was all she had to do.

"She's coming," Mist said. "She could be here any second."

"And you welcome her arrival," he said. "You truly don't know, do you?"

Mist bit back her desire to ask him what he meant. "I know you're not ready to face her again, Slanderer."

"You misjudge me," Loki said, his lips compressing into a hard line. "But then, so did your lover."

"Dainn?" Mist laughed, hiding her shock. "Where did you get that idea? I'm here because he's my mother's ally, and mine."

"A very pitiful company," Loki said.

"Maybe, but you're bleeding allies right and left yourself. I assume Dainn discussed your attack on the loft?"

"Must we go through this again?" Loki asked. "I authorized no attack."

"You're a liar."

"Ask Dainn. He believes me."

She glanced at the elf. Dainn met her gaze without blinking. He *did* believe Loki, crazy as it seemed.

Later she'd get an explanation from him. If they survived.

"Maybe he does," she admitted. "But you're still facing a little problem, aren't you, Slanderer?" Mist said, rubbing the fading bruise on her cheek. "How many Jotunar have you got to spare? The bridges are closed, and you're going to lose a lot more giants before you figure out how to open them again. If you ever do."

Loki leaned over her, bracing his arms to either side of her head. His breath was hot on her face.

"If you know something useful," he said, "I may spare your life."

"You'll kill us anyway, if that's your intention," Mist said. "But you won't stop Freya from fighting you. We're not as irreplaceable as you seem to think."

"I doubt *you* can be replaced," Loki said. "After all, you are her—"

Mist caught a flash of movement behind Loki, and suddenly Dainn was on top of him. It didn't take long for the Jotunar to grab him, peel him off Laufeyson's back, and throw him against the wall. Dainn slid to the ground and lay where he fell, unable to resist the giants when they dragged him to his feet and pinned him against the wall by his collar.

The distraction—if that was Dainn's purpose—worked perfectly. Loki left Mist, strode to Dainn, and struck him hard across the face.

"You never learn, do you?" Loki said. "You have no bargaining chips left, my Dainn. Not even that thing that shares your mind."

Mist shifted very slowly, careful not to let Loki or the Jotunar observe her movement. *That thing that shares your mind,* Loki had said. So Dainn had let it loose in hopes of killing their enemy, just as she'd believed all along.

"I see that you do know about the creature inside him," Loki said to Mist over his shoulder.

"Yes."

"And yet you trust him?"

"It doesn't bother me at all."

She tried to catch Dainn's eye again, but he was staring into Loki's face. "Mist is right," he said. "Freya will not be deterred by our deaths."

Loki pressed so close to Dainn that their lips almost touched. "I may let *you* live, if you agree to serve me. In every way."

"Let her go, and I agree."

"Let her go?" Loki stroked Dainn's cheek where he had struck him. "I think I would be wiser to hold her hostage to ensure Freya's good behavior. And yours. Don't you agree?"

"Yes," Dainn said thickly, as if he could barely force the words from his throat. "Hold her prisoner, but do not harm her."

Loki kissed Dainn gently on the lips. "It will be as if we had never parted."

Mist looked away. She had understood that he and Dainn had worked closely together before Dainn had recognized his error and tried to warn the Aesir. But she had never expected *this.*

They had obviously been far more than partners in a supposed attempt to establish a lasting peace. And though Dainn's hatred of Loki was clear in every line of his body, Laufeyson still wanted him. Dainn would submit to keep her alive.

There was a heaviness in Mist's chest—anger, grief, a profound sense of loss. But with those feelings came that sense of half-familiar power gathering inside her—that same magic she had turned against Dainn in the loft and again, less successfully, in the gym—an instinctive awareness of the elements around her, of ancient forces at work in her body. And slowly, slowly, the tattoo around her wrist began to come alive.

It was like a battery recharging. She still had no idea if she could control the magic, but she knew, even without understanding her certainty, that she couldn't succeed if she didn't give the magic time to build to the highest level her mind could accept.

She had to buy more time. She didn't know if Loki was still susceptible to Freya's presence in spite of his claims to the contrary, but it was worth a try. If it would help her keep him guessing until she was ready . . .

"Are you sure this is what you want, Slanderer?" she asked, gathering Freya's mantle of honey, sex, and primroses about herself.

Loki spun around. Dainn slumped back to the floor as Mist draped her body seductively over the couch and smiled ever so gently.

"Mist," Loki said, his lip curling. "Whatever you're playing at, you can give it up now."

Mist looked around the room. "Mist? I don't see her. Perhaps she's hiding behind the draperies?"

With an angry laugh, Loki strode to the couch. He grabbed the collar of Mist's jacket and hauled her up.

"Do you seriously think I'd believe you're Freya?" he demanded. "Don't you think I can tell the difference?"

She let him hold her up, pliable as a silken ribbon, and linked her arms around his neck. "You are always so sure of yourself, Laufeyson. But sometimes even you are wrong."

Pushing even the thought of revulsion out of her mind, she kissed him. His arms tightened around her, and he thrust his tongue inside her mouth. She responded as ardently as she once had with Eric.

Abruptly Loki let her go and threw her back onto the couch. "Try that again, Mist," he said, "and I'll make both of you suffer."

"Are you sure you can?" Mist asked, stretching her arms above her head. "Why don't you try and find out?"

Something in her act must have worked, because Loki hesitated. And while he did, Dainn spoke in her mind.

Tell him about the time he tried to give you roses in Sessrumnir.

She witnessed the scene in less than a second and reminded Loki of that long-ago encounter. He reared back, his face going red. But he recovered quickly.

"You find this amusing?" he hissed. "I can still kill this body and send you back to the Void. If you were prepared to use the Eitr now, you would have done it already."

Mist had no idea what he was talking about, but she didn't drop the mask. "Perhaps I wanted to toy with you a while, as you have toyed with my servants," she said.

Again Loki seemed uncertain, wavering between belief in Mist's claimed identity and the suspicion that he was being tricked. Mist felt power flow through her as if carried by an invisible network of vessels like chi meridians, pumping magic into every fiber of her being. The tattoo flared, not painful but aflame with energy. She could smell the clouds hanging over the city, heavy with precipitation . . . feel the limestone in the concrete, hear the flame leaping in the fireplace far below in the lobby.

But something blocked the flow. Something inside her still didn't want to let go.

Abruptly Loki spun around again and strode back to Dainn. "How much does *this* servant mean to you, Sow?" he asked. He grabbed Dainn's long, tangled hair and dragged him to his feet again. "You have never cared for anything or anyone you could not use to your benefit or for your pleasure. This creature has failed you. Shall I kill him quickly, or slowly?"

He was calling Mist's bluff, knowing she'd do almost anything to keep Dainn alive. But he didn't think Freya would.

"Do what you like with him," she said.

Loki took Dainn by the throat. He ran his fingertip across the smear of blood at the corner of Dainn's mouth and began to paint Rune-staves on the elf's forehead.

Merkstaves. Runes of death.

Dainn's thoughts touched hers again—wordless but utterly clear. *Save yourself.*

All at once she was back in Asbrew, hearing Dainn's mental voice for the first time. Something released inside her, a dam giving way before a relentless flood, a tree cracking in two as lightning struck to its very heart. Mist clenched her fist, and the Rune-stave Thurisaz, the giant, leaped free of her hand and charged toward the huge window overlooking the Bay. It exploded inward, hurling shards of glass like arrows that narrowly missed Dainn but pierced one of the Jotunar's cheeks. He bellowed and ran at Mist.

She reached through clouds and darkness for the rising moon and tried to catch the reflected light of the sun in her open hands— Sowilo reversed, destruction and retribution. The light was weak, but she shaped what she had caught and hurled it like a burning coal at the Jotunn. He burst into flame if he had been dipped in gasoline.

Loki backed away from Dainn and swung around to face her, his face almost comical in its astonishment. Dainn's knees began to buckle, but he forced himself upright and looked at Mist with hope in his eyes.

"Dainn!" she shouted. "Find Gungnir!"

She didn't have a chance to see if Dainn obeyed. Loki jumped over the Jotunn's writhing, blackened body and came straight at her, his lips moving, the air coalescing into a solid block of ice that threatened to shatter Mist's body on contact.

Instinct alone saved her. She reached skyward again, flowing into the light, becoming a spear flung as high as the highest branch of the World Tree Ygdrassil.

The spear struck the clouds and reflected back on itself as if the sky were a mirror. Lightning laced the gray canopy and plunged earthward, striking the ground between her and Loki, scorching the polished hardwood floor and flinging Loki halfway across the room.

He recovered almost immediately and raced toward her, his face distorted with rage. An instant before he reached her, he changed.

It was only illusion, but it stopped Mist cold. The face and body belonged to Eric—Eric, with his broad, open smile, his good humor, his love of life. And Mist.

"You don't really want to hurt me, do you?" he asked in his deep voice.

Mist recognized the trap too late. Her hands fell, nerveless and limp. Eric's eyes lit with satisfaction.

"It *was* you," he said. "I admit you have astonished me, little Valkyrie. But now I think it is time to—"

Mist heard nothing of what Loki said after that, felt nothing but raw power that wasn't her own, saw nothing but golden light.

A part of her clung to consciousness, and she knew what was happening to her. Freya was with her, inside her, controlling her body as if she were a mere shell of flesh and bone.

Her mother had come at last.

21

Dainn staggered away from the wall, blood filling his mouth, his head still resounding with the violence of Loki's blow. He was incapable of magic, almost incapable of walking. The beast that had been so powerful minutes before had left him as helpless as any mortal.

He couldn't help Mist now, but he could do as she asked and find Gungnir, if it was hidden anywhere inside the penthouse. No one in his right mind would conceal the Spear where it was most likely to be found.

But Loki had never been completely in his right mind. That was one reason why Dainn believed Mist could survive this—this incredibly foolish and desperate attempt to save one who wasn't worth the effort. She had wielded the ancient Vanir magic as if she had used it all her life. She was Loki's match in everything but malice.

Bending low, Dainn crossed the room and ducked into a hallway where he could catch his breath. He closed his eyes and shut out the sounds of battle, striving to find any trace of magic that would allow him to locate the Spear.

At first he felt nothing. Then, like a whisper in the midst of a hurricane, he sensed a locus of power that belonged to no living thing. The cut in his hand, nearly healed, began to throb. He touched his lips to the wound and tasted magic.

Magic that had seeped into the kitchen knife's very substance, penetrating only a few molecules deep into the common steel.

That was all Dainn needed. Still ignoring the violent conflict in the adjoining room, he ducked into the kitchen and searched for the knife block.

The moment he touched the carving knife next to the empty slot, Gungnir's power raised all the hairs on his body and sent spikes of sharp, burning pain racing up his arm. He didn't have the spell to return it to its true form, but his only concern now was to keep it away from Loki until Mist was either victorious or dead.

He knew what Mist would want him to do. He didn't do it. He ran back into the living room, holding the knife behind his back, and took in a scene of utter chaos.

Loki was on his back, throwing handfuls of fire at Mist, who stood over him like an avenging goddess, her blond hair loose and flying about her head in a golden aura. Every blast of flame splashed harmlessly against the watery sphere that surrounded her. She was smiling, and her face . . .

Dainn fell to his knees. It wasn't Mist who had Loki pinned down and fighting for his life. Freya had taken her. She had found a way past her daughter's instinctive defenses.

And she was winning the fight against both her daughter and Loki.

Gungnir throbbed in Dainn's grip, and he remembered again why he had come at Freya's call, why he served her, why he had agreed to let her take Mist's body as her own.

And why he had chosen to prevent that from happening, no matter the damage it might do to Freya's chances of victory.

Now he faced the choice all over again, and it was tearing his soul apart. Laufeyson might have defeated Mist alone. He would have faced an equal in Freya. But now the Slanderer's opponent was more than goddess, more than Valkyrie, more than the sum of both.

Let it happen, Dainn thought, *and Midgard will be saved from chaos. There will be peace, if not freedom. And I will be—*

He struggled to his feet. "Freya!" he shouted.

She glanced at him with all the interest she might afford a speck of dirt forgotten by a housemaid's broom. But in that brief moment when she held Dainn's gaze, he saw the spirit that could not be quenched trapped behind her brilliant blue eyes.

"Mist!"

The goddess smiled at him, striking him to the ground with the full fury of her love, and returned her attention to Loki. He had given up his attack and was scrambling away, frantically chanting spells of defense.

Mist, Dainn thought. *Fight.*

Freya didn't hear him. She pursued Loki across the room, striding like a giant, ever smiling. Dainn got to his feet again and stumbled toward them, knowing that if he intervened he would be struck down.

Before Dainn could lay a hand on Freya's arm, Loki bounced up and struck at him, flinging a rope of flame meant to burn Dainn's fingers and force him to drop Gungnir. Dainn dodged, but not before the fiery rope slashed across his chest and licked at his jaw, searing his flesh almost to the bone.

He clung to Gungnir with the last of his strength. The fire winked out, and every surface in the room grew a slick coating of ice as the lingering traces of warmth left in the apartment flowed into Loki's raised hands.

Freya's eyes lost their gentle rage, and her hair fell back around her shoulders with a hiss and crackle of static electricity. Just before Loki struck, Dainn tossed the knife. She caught it in her right hand, whirled to face Loki again, and chanted the Rune-spell that restored Gungnir to its original form.

The Spear's head caught the brunt of the ice storm Loki hurled at her, and the steel glowed deep red as if it had just emerged from Mist's forge. Radiating heat Dainn could feel from several yards away, it seemed to waver in the frigid air as if it existed in two realities at once and belonged to neither.

Still Mist didn't move. She, too, was frozen between worlds, between minds, between herself and the goddess who wanted her body and the magic that was as much a part of her as her strong sword arm and her selfless courage.

Loki dropped his hands, water dripping from his fingers. Dainn tensed.

"Why did you stop, my Lady?" he asked, breathing hard. "You almost had me."

Mist blinked. She looked at the Spear and tightened her fingers around the shaft. Loki turned his hand palm up and curled his fingers inward, pulling the heat from Gungnir's blade. It engulfed his hand, freezing instantly, and in a second Loki had shaped the ice into a heavily spiked ball like a mace on a medieval flail.

Loki's weapon couldn't kill Freya, who was not yet fully attached to this world, but it could destroy a physical body. Mist would die, and Freya would still be free to seek another shape, even if it took time to find one capable of containing her power.

Dainn began to move. But before he could take more than a step, Loki threw the ball directly at Mist's head. She swung the Spear to intercept it. It bounced against her arm, slicing through her already shredded jacket and shirt and engraving deep slashes across her skin. She dropped Gungnir, and Loki sprang onto the rosewood coffee table, perching there like an eagle ready to swoop down on its prey.

"We could go on, Sow," he said to his enemy, "but where would be the fun in that? Especially when even I can see you're losing your grip on your daughter."

Mist-Freya picked up the Spear with her left hand as blood soaked her right sleeve. "I can still kill you," she said.

"I don't think so." He brushed water from his shoulder. "In truth, you want me humiliated, not dead. I still want a real contest, Lady. And I think you do, too."

They stared at each other, goddess and godling, with hatred and complete understanding.

"We will continue our game," she said, "so I can crush you utterly before you die."

"And the bridges?"

"Do you think I closed them?" she asked. "You shall have to hold yourself in suspense a little while longer. But I still have the Eitr. For the time being, you will pay the penalty by losing ten percent of your Jotunar. You will obtain funds only by conventional mortal means, not through magic. If you flout our bargain again, I will use it." She pointed Gungnir at Loki's chest. "Do you understand me, Slanderer?"

"You couldn't be more plain." Loki glanced at Dainn. "Our witness is hardly neutral, but I will accept his honesty. Shall I see you both to the door?"

Freya hurled the spear at Loki's head. If he hadn't twitched slightly to the left at the last possible moment, it would have pinned his skull to the wall behind him. Instead, it sliced off several inches of his hair on the right side of his head. Loki fell to his knees.

"Take the Spear," Freya told Dainn, dusting her hands on her thighs. "We will go."

She shot Loki a poisonous glance and strode to the door, trailing the benevolent warmth of the sun, golden butterflies, and the scent of primroses. Ignoring Loki, Dainn pulled the spear from the wall and glanced quickly around the room. He saw Mist's knife at the feet of one of the dead giants and paused to retrieve it.

He tucked the sheath in the waistband of his pants and followed Freya, his stomach churning with horror at what he had permitted to happen.

They met five Jotunar as they reached the elevator. The giants comically skidded to a stop when they saw Freya.

"Never fear," she said, her voice all seduction again. "Your master is alive. For the time being. You may choose whether or not to continue to serve him by standing in my way, or die."

The two giants in the lead exchanged glances and moved to the side, leaving the path clear. When she and Dainn reached the lobby, Freya moved to the nearest chair and sank into it. Guests stared at her, but she ignored them.

"Fetch me something to drink, Dainn," she said. "A sweet drink to cool my temper. I do so dislike being angry."

Dainn held the Spear against his body and remained where he was. "*Did* you close the bridges?" he asked.

She glanced up at him. "You had no need to know before. It was only a temporary measure, until I could be sure my allies were ready."

She might be lying, Dainn thought. He could no longer separate truth from falsehood. But she was still as confident as she had ever been.

"I expressly told you not to allow my daughter to come to harm," Freya said with a very small frown, "but I shall forgive you, since the need for such precautions is past. I will soon have other tasks for you."

"Searching for the other Treasures?"

"Among other things."

Dainn shifted his grip on Gungnir's shaft. "How were you able to take Mist so quickly?" he asked. "I thought you needed more time to prepare."

She patted his arm. "These are not your concerns, my Dainn."

My Dainn. Loki called him the same many times, but he belonged to neither one of them. And never would.

"Are your allies ready as well, Lady?"

She laughed, the sound drawing the stare of every male in the room. "Those who fight for me shall be free to come within the next two Midgardian weeks." Freya casually waved her hand. Mist's warm, calloused hand, and the wrist that bore a tattoo no longer red, but black. "In the meantime, now that I am here in body, I can have every man I meet eager to serve me. How many can I gather in a day? A week?" Her fingers drifted along Dainn's thigh. "My daughter has power that enhances my own in ways I could not have anticipated, and it is all open to me. And I *shall* reward you well, my Dainn. Just as I promised."

Dainn looked away, feeling nothing of Freya's caress. If there was anything left of Mist behind Freya's stunning blue eyes, she would soon have no hope of escaping her mother's control. Soon—in minutes, hours, days—she would be completely absorbed into a mind that would use Mist's own power to prevent her resistance until she no longer had the strength to fight.

"Don't look so sad," Freya chided in a voice rich with sympathy. "I can see you developed some fondness for the girl. That can scarcely be a surprise. But now she serves the greater good. Midgard will be saved."

"As you say, Lady."

"Then fetch that drink, and we will begin looking for proper accommodations. Loki's apartments were richly furnished, but very dull. I think—"

Dainn dropped the Spear, leaned over Freya, and caught her mouth with his. She pressed her hands against his chest, and he could feel the power building, power that could turn him into a gibbering drone with a single embrace.

But it wasn't Freya he was kissing. And in that moment when he took Freya off guard, the beast began to stir, roused again from the place inside him where it had hidden since its encounter with Loki, awakening to the sexual heat coursing in Dainn's blood.

The beast began to possess him again, demanding more, drawing blood from Freya's lower lip. She laced her hands in his hair, pulling him down to his knees.

And then she flung him back, her face contorted in fury, her gaze all indignation, all outrage, all chagrin.

All Mist.

She sprang up from the chair, staring at Dainn as if he had suddenly risen out of the tiled marble floor. "What the Hel—"

Quick footsteps approached from the direction of the reception desk. Dainn shuddered, shaking off the beast, and grabbed Gungnir. He thrust Kettlingr into Mist's hand.

"We must go," he said, "or we will be facing more questions than we can answer."

Without debating his suggestion, Mist chanted the spell to reduce Gungnir to knife shape, tucked it inside her jacket, and ran for the door to the street. Dainn hung back long enough to discourage anyone who might choose to follow.

The male receptionist came to a stop, chest heaving. "We've called the police," he said. "Whatever you've done—"

"—may save your world," Dainn said. The beast strained against its new-made chains, and Dainn let it look through his eyes.

The man backed away. The guests huddled in the corner nearest the fireplace, eyes wide, whispering frantically. Forcing himself to draw on the beast's strength, Dainn sang a spell that would strip the minds of every mortal in the room of any memory save that of two vague figures quarreling and kissing in the lobby.

The beast howled, and for a moment Dainn almost lost himself again.

Someone screamed. Dainn turned and ran. Mist was just pulling up to the curb on a small motorcycle.

"Get on!" she shouted as the wail of approaching sirens began to drown out the hum and rumble of evening traffic. Once Dainn had mounted the vehicle behind her, Mist squealed away, cutting between trucks, taxis, and double-parked vehicles with reckless abandon.

They outran the sirens, and when Mist finally pulled over into the deep shadows of an empty warehouse on a pier about a mile north of Dogpatch, she slumped over the handlebars and cursed herself, Dainn, and Loki in rapid and violent succession. Dainn climbed off the motorcycle and crouched a little distance away, shaking with exhaustion and waiting for her to remember.

She lifted her head to meet his gaze. "What did you think you were doing?" she demanded, her words catching as if she were just becoming used to speaking with her own voice again.

"You knew I would be with Loki," he said, pretending not to understand her question.

Groaning, Mist pressed the heels of her palms into her temples. "Did you seriously think I wouldn't figure it out?" she snapped. "When Vali told me you'd been hiding in the house all along and you needed to get away from the loft to 'deal with' what happened . . ." She gasped as her massaging hands found a particularly painful spot. "You thought you didn't have anything else to lose, didn't you?"

"I had already lost."

She dropped her hands and scowled at him. "You've really pissed me off this time, Dainn. I saw you change in the gym, in a way you never warned me about. If I'd known, things would have gone very differently."

Once she found out just how *much* he could change, Dainn thought, she would be more than merely "pissed." "I . . . didn't expect it to escape my control," he said.

"You kept telling me you could keep it in check. But I—" She swallowed. "*I* told you to let it go. I just didn't realize—"

"Yes," Dainn said softly. "It transforms me into a creature capable of physically destroying anything in its path. It feels no pain, no loyalty, no mercy."

She slammed her fist on the bike's handlebar. "I told you I wanted to help!"

"You could not. Whatever your power, this is beyond it."

"No. I won't believe that. You said it feels no loyalty, but you weren't just trying to kill Loki, or those Jotunar in the gym. You were protecting the kids and me. You could have killed Tashiro, even Ryan, but you didn't. How do you account for that?"

He shook his head, unable to answer. "How did you find me?" he asked.

She hissed through her teeth, recognizing his dodge. "I went to Vidarr. He's been keeping tabs on Loki without sharing the information with us, and he was able to find out where Loki has been living when he . . . when he wasn't with me. I saw a Jotunn on the street outside Asbrew, so I knew they'd be waiting for me at the tower. I let them take me to Loki."

The beginnings of dangerous anger gnawed at Dainn's frayed nerves. "They struck you."

She touched her face gingerly. There were no visible injuries, and the cut in her arm had healed. Only the blood on her nose and clothing served as a reminder of the wounds.

"I wanted to make Loki think I was helpless for a while," she said.

"But you had a plan when you arrived."

"I hoped I could use my own magic to get you out of there, and take Gungnir if I could." She smiled grimly. "Don't look at me like that. I didn't think I could work the Rune-magic against him . . . though I've been doing pretty well with that since you left."

"Vali said you disposed of the Jotunar bodies."

"And the evidence of what had happened. But I wasn't kidding myself that I'd be good enough with the Galdr to defeat Loki that way."

"The old Vanir magic," Dainn said.

"I had a feeling it would come to me when I needed it again, and it did. Or at least, it started to. I knew I had to stall Loki until it felt strong enough. Then you stepped in like three kinds of idiot, and Loki—" She met his gaze. "But you know all that."

"Yes."

"Have I ever told you how much I hate it when you answer my questions that way?"

"Was it a question?"

"Curse you, you son of a . . ." She sagged over the handlebars. Dainn studied her face. There was still confusion in her expression, the knowledge that something was amiss. "All the time I was pretending to be Freya," she said, "I could feel the magic building, but it wasn't opening up to me. Loki wasn't convinced I was really the Lady. When I told him I didn't care if he killed you . . ." She trailed off again, flushing to the roots of her fair hair.

"I understand," he said. "You bought your time."

"Yes," she murmured, lifting her head. "And when the magic came, it was like becoming one of the Aesir. More powerful than the Aesir. But then Loki became Eric, and I—"

"Something seemed different to you?"

"I remember telling you to find Gungnir. Then I felt Freya come to help me." Her gaze fixed on something only she could see. "Then . . . Gods, I don't remember. Until you tried to kiss me."

Dainn released his breath slowly. She didn't know everything that had happened. He still had time to prepare her for the full truth.

But not yet. If he told her what Freya had intended and how he had planned to help the Lady, she would turn on him and never trust him again. And she *must* trust him. The Lady would not give up now that she knew what her joining with Mist made her capable of.

"You lost yourself in the magic," he said, "as I lost myself to the beast. You forced Loki to retreat, but you were unprepared to handle the unleashed potency of your abilities."

"Is that what gave me this pounding headache?" she asked, her voice rough with a brave attempt at humor. "Or was it the kiss?"

Dainn could never forget the look on her face and how she had laughed when Loki had called him her lover. "I am sorry," he said, staring at the pavement between his feet. "It was necessary to shake you out of your fugue state."

"I guess it worked." She probed her lower lip with a fingertip. "Did the beast come back then? You said that strong emotions . . . I mean—"

"By then it was under my control again."

"Well, now I know you were lying when you suggested I wouldn't pay a price for magic."

"I had no idea what that price would be," Dainn said.

She looked up at the sun as if it were some foreign object instead of a tool she had used in her battle with Loki. "I guess I'd better keep you around to tell me what I do next time I 'lose myself in the magic.' Just don't try that particular tactic again, okay? It isn't good for either one of us."

"No," Dainn said, closing his eyes.

Mist sighed. "What did happen with Freya? I felt her for a short time, and then she was gone."

"She still lacked the physical presence to fight Loki effectively, regardless of her desire to protect you. He was able to send her away."

"I hope she makes a little more progress soon. I don't think I can keep this up much longer. Dainn, look at me."

He obeyed her, and she gazed out of eyes as bruised as her body had been. "There's one more thing I need to know. Before I stopped Loki, you bargained for my life."

So, Dainn thought, it was to come at last. "Yes," he said.

"You would have traded—" Her throat worked. "The things he said to you—"

"As if we had been lovers."

She pressed her lips together, refusing to continue. Forcing him to tell her.

"We were," he said harshly. "When he convinced me he was Freya in order to use me against the Aesir. He took on her shape. He learned my weaknesses and how to manipulate me. When I discovered his tricks, it was too late."

"Then you *did* love Freya. Who you thought was Freya."

"I believed I did."

"You turned on him, but he . . ." She glanced at Dainn with an almost helpless expression. "He wants you back. He . . . *feels* something for you."

"No. It is only submission he desires. He would have done the same to you if he had taken you."

"And you'd have chosen that for me instead of an honorable death?"

"I had hoped—" He broke off, well knowing he could never tell Mist of his bargain to teach Loki the Alfar magic. He knew it could no longer be considered in effect. "You are too important to this world, Mist. I would go to Laufeyson again if I thought it would save Midgard."

"Forget it." She hopped off the motorcycle and strode to stand over him. "You hate him. You hate what he did to you. I'd never let you make that sacrifice. Not even for Midgard."

"Perhaps it is not your choice."

She turned and marched to the edge of the pier, glaring down into the cold gray water. "The beast is just waiting for another go at

Loki. You *have* to stay away from him. You have to avoid any violence if you want to stay sane and not hurt innocent people. That means leaving the fighting to me, no matter what kind it is."

"Would you not be better off without me?" he asked softly.

"Quit it with the whining," she snapped. "You still have to teach me, remember?" She brushed a tendril of hair away from her lips. "Or is that too dangerous, too?"

Water slapped against the nearest piling, reminding Dainn of the small sea-magic he had used to send Loki his message. She was right. Even that could become deadly now.

"I can only know what is safe through trial and error," he said, staring out at the increasing turbulence of water and sky.

She must have heard the despair in his voice, for she crouched near him again and reached out as if she might touch him. She didn't.

"We'll just have to be very careful," she said.

"And you must set aside the Vanir magic for the time being. Once you have gained complete mastery of the Galdr, you will be ready to try it again."

"But it *worked*, Dainn. I got rid of those Jotunar in the gym. I stopped Loki."

And somehow, Dainn thought, it had given Freya full and apparently permanent access to Mist before Dainn had believed it possible. It had opened Mist's mind, shattering all her unconscious defenses.

As long as Mist avoided such magic, Freya might be held at bay until Mist's defenses were fully restored again. But when next the Lady spoke to him——and she would undoubtedly do so very soon—she would have many questions. *She* was unlikely to have forgotten the kiss, and how it had restored Mist to her body. Unless he could convince Freya he'd had a very good reason . . .

Such worries were pointless now. There was no going back. There hadn't been since he had chosen Mist over her mother.

"Your talent with the Runes can be developed to a level almost as powerful as the elemental magic you used today," he said, "and with far less risk."

"But—"

"Do you wish to lose your mind?"

Her face relaxed, and Dainn knew she was more relieved than she would ever admit. "Then we're pretty much back where we started. Except now Loki *knows* I have power of my own."

"No. I am certain his beliefs in that regard have not changed."

"And Freya? She came when I called her, but I still can't hear her."

"She will contact me again when she is ready."

"What did Loki mean when he said she'd never cared for anything or anyone she couldn't use for her benefit or pleasure?" she asked. "I know she ignored me in Asgard, but—"

"Can you still doubt that Loki would employ any lie to increase his advantage, physical or psychological?" Dainn said. "Would he not try to plant suspicions in your mind at every turn?"

She met his gaze. "Did Freya think the beast would be a weapon for her all along?"

"I cannot believe so."

"And what about this Eitr stuff Loki mentioned?"

Dainn had known he would have to explain about the game sooner or later, but now he could risk only part of the truth. "It is a particular power Freya is holding in reserve," he said, "but she cannot risk spending it until there is no other choice. The price for wielding it could destroy Midgard. We must hope its use never becomes necessary."

They both fell silent, intently studying everything but each other.

A light snow began to fall, settling on Mist's fair hair and lingering there like dew on ripe wheat. "At least we have Gungnir back," she said after a long interval. "Where did you find it?"

"In a knife block."

"And Loki's supposed to be the clever one."

"Cleverness does not preclude stupidity." He shifted his weight, stretching cramped, aching muscles. "There is more to discuss, but perhaps we should be returning to the loft."

She glanced toward the street, clogged with sluggish traffic as commuters struggled to negotiate icy pavement. "You're right," she said, sensible and pragmatic again. "I need to make sure the kids are safe. And Tashiro—"

"Vali said he would be no trouble."

"I don't think he will be. His memory is—" She broke off, flushing again. "He still wants to talk to Ryan, and maybe I can convince him to take Gabi away as well. We need to raise much better wards around the loft. And then we're going to decide how I can help you with the beast without . . . without setting you off."

Dainn held his peace. It would do no good to protest now, and he was too weary to think of an alternative.

"*Skita,*" Mist said suddenly, snapping her fingers. "I forgot that I was supposed to call Vali. The Jotunar took my cell phone."

"It is easily replaceable," Dainn said.

"Unlike a lot of things." She rose and returned to the motorcycle. "Let's go home."

22

They were halfway home when Mist realized they were being followed.

Dainn knew it, too. His arms tightened around her waist, and she could almost feel him pricking his ears as he looked over his shoulder. She wondered if he was using the beast's superior senses or only the extremely good ones any elf was born with.

"See anything?" she said over the roar of the bike and surrounding traffic.

"Nothing," Dainn said. "But I do not believe they are Jotunar."

Maybe human minions, then. She hadn't seen any of Loki's mortal followers yet, but she was sure he'd already recruited a number of them by now.

"I'll take some side roads and try to shake them," she said.

The bike responded to her hand like her old Valkyrie steed. She veered and dodged down narrow streets and between apartment buildings, through the Mission District, Dolores Heights, and back around via Cesar Chavez Street.

"We aren't shaking them, are we?" she asked Dainn.

"They are still following," he said.

"I'm not taking them back to the loft." She looked for a place public enough to discourage their pursuers from direct attack. If they looked as if they were going to try, she'd lead them away.

She'd have to attempt the Galdr again, and she wondered how she was going to find the energy when she could barely keep the bike moving in a straight line.

"Whatever you do," she said to Dainn, pulling over into a rare empty parking space along the curb, "leave any fighting to me."

He didn't answer, and she didn't press him. They remained on the bike, watching and listening, but no one showed up. After about an hour, Mist decided they should try moving again. She pulled out of the parking space and drove as slowly as she could, choosing bigger streets as a test.

"They are gone," Dainn said.

Expelling her breath, Mist turned for home. She stayed on the alert, but she was sure Dainn was right. Either they'd both been paranoid, or their pursuers had given up.

Still, she didn't hurry. When she reached Third, she pulled over again to watch the nearly empty street. After another hour, she finally accepted that they were safe.

She rolled into the loft's side driveway and dismounted. The place seemed quiet, every sound in the neighborhood muffled by the soft, heavy snow.

"Let me go in first," she said.

Dainn gave her a long look, and she shrugged. They went in by the outside door to the gym.

It was empty, as Mist had expected. Dainn's gaze swept over the room. He stood very still, as if the memory of what he had done there had assumed a physical presence that bound him as he had tried to bind the beast.

"You did very well," he said.

She knew she should have been far more angry with him. He had no right to talk to her as if she needed his approval. But his praise felt like a rare and precious thing, a gift she couldn't afford to accept.

It was also comfortingly mundane, as if everything had gone back to normal.

Maybe someday there would be a new kind of "normal." But she wasn't counting on it happening anytime soon.

They continued across the gym toward the door to the hall. Dainn stopped suddenly, tensing like a hound on the scent.

"Someone is in the house," he said.

Mist reached for Kettlingr. "Who?"

"Vali. And the young mortals."

"Nidhogg's teeth! I told Vali to take them away!" She strode through the door and along the hall, narrowly avoiding a pair of very animated cats, and burst into the kitchen without giving the occupants a whisper of warning.

Vali shot out of his chair at the kitchen table, knocking it over. Gabi and Ryan looked up from their plates, Ryan with a sandwich suspended in midair. He dropped it, and his face lit with joy and relief.

"You're back!" he said, rising almost as quickly as Vali had. "Are you okay?"

"It's about time," Gabi said with some asperity. "Did you get Loki?"

"We can discuss that later," Mist said, staring at Vali. "I told you to get them away."

Vali shoved his hands in his pockets like a boy who'd been caught playing with Mama's swords. "I did," he said, "but—"

"He got away from you."

"Uh—"

"He's very good at that."

"The kid did say he had to be here when you came back."

"I knew you would," Ryan said softly. "Come back, I mean."

"Did you have another seizure?" Mist asked him.

"Do you think we'd just be sitting here if he had?" Vali asked indignantly. He took a step toward her as if he would have liked to hug her. "You're . . . you're not hurt?"

"We're here, aren't we?"

"He—" Vali glanced furtively at Dainn, who seemed not to hear them. "He *was* going to kill Loki, wasn't he?"

"That was his plan. It didn't quite work out that way, but we got something out of Loki before we left." She took Gungnir from inside her jacket.

"Hey," Vali said, his open face breaking into a grin. "Good job, Mist. Wish I could have seen Loki's face."

Mist tucked Gungnir away again, remembering her promise to Vidarr. "Nothing's really changed," she said, her legs beginning to shake. "But Loki's going to be just a little more careful from now on, I think."

Vali searched her eyes. "I believe it," he said. "I've never seen you look this way before."

I've never felt this way before, Mist thought. "Magic has a way of changing a Valkyrie," she said. She stared down at her scuffed boots. "I never wanted this, Val."

"I know you didn't," he said, tentatively laying a broad hand on her shoulder. "I'll always be here to help you, Mist. Whatever you need."

"I know." She smiled and covered his hand with hers. "Right now the first thing we have to do is reset the wards. I don't know how much use Dainn'll be to us right now."

"I sort of get that impression," Vali said. "I'm not sure how much good *I'll* be, but I'll do whatever I can."

"That's all I ask." She glanced at Ryan, who stood halfway between a silent Dainn and the table, as if he didn't know where he should be. "Since Tashiro's not going to be a problem—"

"Why not?" Ryan asked. "You never told us."

Mist ignored him. "I'll be calling him first thing tomorrow so he can meet with Ryan. He's a lawyer, so maybe he can figure out a more permanent way to get these kids off the streets and into a decent life."

"You're still going to make us leave?" Gabi asked, starting up from her chair.

"Nothing's changed. I'm doing whatever I have to keep you safe."

Ryan sank back into his chair, and Gabi pouted very effectively for a kid who worked so hard to make herself look and sound tough. Mist noticed that her hands were still red, and there was a swollen, stiff look to her fingers.

She moved to stand over Gabi. "Let me see your hands."

"They're okay."

"Show me."

Reluctantly she let Mist examine them. "They don't hurt as bad as they look," she said.

"We're going to the hospital."

Gabi flinched away. "*Sin médicos!* I can fix myself, I promise!"

Mist hesitated. There was genuine terror in the girl's voice, and considering what she'd been through already, Mist was reluctant to make her face another traumatic situation.

"We'll see what we can do here," she said. "But if it doesn't get better . . ."

"*Sí,*" Gabi said, slumping in relief.

Mist sighed and glanced at the half-eaten sandwich on the girl's plate. Right on cue, her stomach rumbled loudly.

"Funny," she said to no one in particular, "but I feel as if I haven't eaten in weeks."

"Magic," Dainn said, suddenly coming back to life. "You must eat more than you did in the past."

"You'd better follow your own advice," she said. "Sit down. Make yourself a sandwich while Vali and I see about the wards."

It was a measure of Dainn's exhaustion that he obeyed her immediately and took a seat at the table. Ryan edged into the chair beside him. Vali leaned against the counter as Mist opened the fridge. There was still a little sliced turkey and Jarlsberg left.

"We're going to need groceries," she said, amazed that she could discuss such banal matters without breaking into gales of incredulous laughter. "Dainn, make me a sandwich, too, will you?"

He stared at her blankly. He was a long way from returning from that dark place he'd barely escaped such a short time ago, but she didn't intend to let him wallow. She had to pull him back from the brink.

"As I remember," she said, "you *can* make a sandwich." She set the makings on the table in front of him. "Go to it."

Mist found Dainn's wards shattered in every place he'd set them. Once they had been a series of carefully drawn Runes made of scrolled staves interlocked with intricate vines so complex in design that it was difficult to make out where one ended and the other began. Now they were torn apart as if someone had stampeded through a pristine forest with a blowtorch.

Not much could be done to salvage them now. Vali and Mist began to set their own, Vali struggling to call up abilities he had put aside years ago, Mist trying to find appropriate imagery to help her engrave new Runes into the brick and cement.

After a while she settled on drawing every fighting weapon she had in the gym and painstakingly reproduced them with a black permanent pen, interspersed with appropriate Runes, along every wall of the loft. She drew the weapons pointing up, so that their protection would be extended to the second floor, and then smeared her blood across every image.

Vali went over them again, drawing the name of Odin between the figures of every sword, spear, and ax. He added his blood to hers, wincing a little as he drew the blade of his Swiss Army knife across his palm.

"I think we done good," he said, stepping back to examine the product of their efforts. "If these don't hold for a while, I don't know what will."

"We need more than wards," Mist said. "We need better defenses, better ways of telling when Loki might plan to attack."

"To get Ryan back, or to kill you?"

"Like I said, I don't think he'll try anything again too soon, and he denied sending the Jotunar to the gym. He certainly never mentioned Ryan. But the default position is that he's always lying."

"And what about Dainn?" Vali asked quietly.

Mist's heart thudded like an iron ball striking a trampoline and bouncing up again. "There's a lot of stuff, Vali. I'll tell you when I feel . . . when I have it all figured out myself."

Vali glanced down, and she knew what he was thinking. But the more she protested, the more he'd believe his guess was right.

"We've done all we can out here," she said. "Dainn told me you were bringing some of your equipment in when you found him. Can you start setting up in the morning?"

Vali glanced at his watch. "It's already three a.m. No point in leaving now."

"Vidarr—"

"Screw Vidarr," Vali said.

She wondered what he'd say if he knew about her recent conversation with his brother. Turning the Spear over to Vidarr was the wrong thing to do. It wasn't just that he'd pretty much coerced her into it. There was something else that bothered her about the bargain. Until she figured it out, she was going to stall Vidarr as long as possible. Or, better yet, tell him she hadn't gotten it back.

It would a dangerous deception, given Vidarr's temper. And she'd have to tell Vali to lie to his own brother. She would be manipulating him the same way she'd manipulated Tashiro.

"Just make sure you don't burn yourself out," she said with a lightness she didn't feel. "I hope we won't have to rely completely on technology to find my Sisters, but right now I don't have any magical solutions."

"Give yourself some time," Vali said. "You just came out of a fight with Loki on his own turf, and I'm guessing you must have worked some pretty major magic to come out of it alive. You'll figure it out." He glanced away with an embarrassed shrug. "I have faith in you."

"You're a good friend, Vali. Keep reminding me, okay?" She looked over their work one more time. "I think I'd better go get that sandwich. Did you get enough to eat?"

He slapped his slightly oversized belly. "A couple of sandwiches?" he said. "You want me to stick around, you'd better be ready to feed me better than that."

"I think it can be arranged."

They went inside. Vali stopped to look over his new workspace again. Mist went into her bedroom, struggling to keep her eyes open and wondering if the garage where the Volvo was supposedly being repaired had made any progress. She suspected that she was going to have to bite the bullet and buy a new car. Or, better yet, a bike. Streetcars and buses just wouldn't cut it now. But how she was going to find the time . . .

Maybe she could offer the owner of the "borrowed" bike enough money that he'd sell it to her and overlook her larceny.

Somewhat cheered by the prospect, Mist took a shower, changed her clothes, and returned to the kitchen and the sandwich Dainn had—she hoped—made for her.

Groceries, she reminded herself, wondering if she could get Vali to go for her. The idea of battling supermarket crowds during the holidays was almost as daunting as another duel with Loki.

Despite Gabi's vigorous protests, Mist sent the teenagers up to bed not long after they'd finished their makeshift dinner. Mist had given the kids only the sketchiest account of what had happened with Loki, figuring they wouldn't need to know too much before they left for good.

"It's time to make a new plan," Mist said once she, Dainn, and Odin's son were sitting in the living room.

"Sitting" not being a very accurate description, Mist thought, with Dainn hunkered on the floor against the far wall and Vali slumped in the armchair by the cold fireplace with his broad, bearded chin resting on his fist. She wasn't doing much better, sprawled out on the couch as if someone had dropped a cartoon anvil on her chest.

"Our first priority must still be increasing your knowledge of magic," Dainn said, his eyes glittering through the black veil of his hair.

"We can have more than one priority now that Vali's with us," Mist said with a wry twist of her lips. "And I can multitask, remember?" She glanced at Odin's son. "Did Dainn tell you I have a super-powered homing signal? He thinks I unconsciously called to Ryan somehow. And I'm going to keep calling until I get a handle on it."

"I'm sorry, Mist," Vali said. "I know you don't want this."

"I didn't mention it before," Mist said, rolling onto her side without lifting her still-throbbing head, "but my convenient little glamour is why Tashiro won't be a problem. I made him forget most of what happened in the gym, except that there was some kind of home invasion and no one was hurt."

Dainn looked at her sharply. He'd been pretty sanguine about the glamour thing before, but he didn't look quite so happy about it now.

"Of course, when Freya's allies show up, we'll have to do a lot more work to keep people from noticing," she went on. "I assume she doesn't want a citywide panic to break out the second they cross the bridges, and it's not going to be that easy to hide an army of swollen-headed Alfar and hard-drinking Einherjar, even in San

Francisco. Dainn, did Freya have a plan about where they're all going to stay, or did she leave that up to you?"

"It was never discussed," Dainn said, apparently fascinated by the worn Celtic design on the carpet.

"Then you'd better discuss it with her soon."

"I will attempt to reach her tonight."

"Good."

The room went very quiet, so quiet that Mist could hear the snow falling outside even over the hum of the heater and the tick of the clock on the mantelpiece. She tried to stay awake. There was so much left to discuss. But her eyes wouldn't cooperate, and after a while she didn't care.

"Mist!"

Someone's hand shook her awake. Mist felt for Kettlingr, remembering too late that she'd left it in the bedroom.

"It's okay," Vali said. He backed away hastily. "That guy Tashiro is at the door."

Mist peered at the clock with blurry eyes. "For Baldr's sake, it's only seven in the morning. What's he doing here? Where's Dainn?"

"Keeping an eye on Tashiro. I don't think he likes the man."

The beast didn't, that was certain.

"I'll talk to Tashiro," she said, self-consciously tucking the tail of her shirt into the waistband of her jeans. She combed her hair with her fingers, wondering what the lawyer would see when he looked at her. There was nothing left of the Lady in her now.

Tashiro was standing in the kitchen, looking around the room as if to avoid noticing the way Dainn stared at him. Dainn had obviously showered and changed into another pair of Eric's pants and an incongruous dress shirt, minus tie, but he didn't look as if he had any ordinary "business" in mind.

He was deliberately trying to find out if Tashiro had really forgotten him.

Mist stepped hastily into the breach and offered her hand to their visitor. "Mr. Tashiro," she said. "I was going to call you, but I didn't expect—"

"Sorry," he said, clasping her hand longer than was strictly necessary. "I know it's early, but I—" He gave her an abashed, charming smile. "The fact is, I thought you might be available to talk about Ryan, and I'd like to get that moving along as quickly as possible."

"Fine," Mist said. "That's great." She waved Vali to her side. "Mr. Tashiro, this is my friend Vali. Vali, Mr. Tashiro."

"Koji," Tashiro said, extending his hand. Vali's was nearly twice the size of his, but Odin's son didn't try to flaunt his superior strength. He let go as soon as he could.

"This is my . . . cousin, Dainn," Mist said, watching Koji's face. "Dainn Alfgrim."

Dainn shot her an unreadable glance and nodded curtly to Koji. "Mr. Tashiro," he said.

The lawyer looked him over with a slight frown. "Have we met before, Mr. Alfgrim?"

They stared at each other like stags sizing each other up for a little autumn jousting. Mist took Tashiro's arm.

"Ryan is in bed right now, Mr. Tashiro—"

"Koji," he corrected.

"Koji. I thought you and I could talk in the living room."

"Of course," he said, meeting her gaze with a little too much personal interest. No, he didn't remember the fight, or Dainn, or what Mist had done to him. But the aftereffects of her glamour were still working, and she hated herself for it.

She wasn't sure if Dainn would try to join the conversation, but he remained outside with Vali. Mist forced herself to relax.

"Sit down," she said, offering Koji a seat in the armchair. "I can light a fire if you'd like."

"Not necessary," he said, "but thanks."

"Okay." Mist sat on the sofa and dropped her hands between her knees. "Here's the situation."

She'd gotten about two sentences into the story she'd prepared for him when she heard the roaring outside on Illinois Street. Her first thought was that Ryan or Gabi had sneaked out of the house and was making off with the borrowed motorcycle.

But it was soon obvious that it wasn't only one bike making the noise.

"Excuse me," Mist said, jumping up from the couch. Vali and Dainn were already standing at the closed front door.

"What's going on out there?" Mist asked as the engines grumbled and snarled like a pack of ill-tempered hyenas.

"Do you remember when we sensed that someone was following us?" Dainn asked.

"Someone followed you?" Vali asked.

"We thought we'd shaken them," Mist said, considering a quick dash to her bedroom for Kettlingr. "If that's who's out there, they didn't exactly try to hide their approach."

"Mortals," Dainn said. "As you once said of the Jotunar, mere cannon-fodder for the Slanderer."

"I guess we'd better find out what they want. Hang on." She jogged to the bedroom, snatched Kettlingr from the bedside table, and returned to the front hall. Holding the knife in a battle-ready grip, she grasped the doorknob with her free hand.

Dainn stepped in front of her. "You are in no condition to confront them," he said.

"I'm in better condition than you are," she retorted.

They locked stares, and Mist saw the flare of the beast in his eyes. But he bowed his head and stood aside. Vali cast him a troubled glance and followed Mist, nearly treading on her heels as she opened the door.

23

A man stood at the curb. Behind him were a dozen motorcycles wreathed in clouds of condensation, each with a rider, male or female, dressed in black leathers bearing embroidered patches with familiar symbols. Some of the riders had removed their helmets, while others remained anonymous behind their visors. They looked like photographic negatives of ghosts sitting for their portraits on the darkest night of the year.

Mist sang Kettlingr to its proper shape. The man, a burly mortal in worn leathers with a knit cap pulled down over his ears, stared at the blade with apparent fascination.

"Ma'am?" the biker said, sweeping his cap from his balding head. "My name is Rick. Rick Jensen. Are you Mist?"

"Who wants to know?" Vali said, straightening to his full, impressive height.

"It's okay, Val," Mist said, pushing him back. "What do you want?" she asked, lifting Kettlingr.

"Uh . . ." Jensen glanced over his shoulder. "If you're Mist, we've been looking for you. We came to help."

"What's going on?" Tashiro asked, joining Vali and Mist. Dainn came out behind him, the shadow of the beast stalking in his wake.

Jensen ran a big hand across his face, clearing away perspiration and melting snowflakes. "Maybe you'd better talk to—"

Before he could finish the sentence, a petite figure wearing a helmet painted with wings on either side strode up behind him. She pulled the helmet off, revealing a cloud of brown, slightly frizzy hair and a delicate face set with a pair of bright, birdlike eyes.

"Mist?" she said.

"Bryn?"

"I was right," Bryn said, flashing white teeth in a surprisingly tanned face. "I knew we had to get to San Francisco, and that it had something to do with one of my Sisters. But I didn't know it would be—"

"But you're—" Mist began.

She tripped over her tongue several times before she finally got it straightened out enough to speak again. "You were dead!" she said.

"I guess I was," Bryn said.

"When I got back to the place where I'd left you, you were gone. I warded your body against animals, so what took you away?"

"Something did take me away, and presumably healed me," Bryn said, "but I never found out who or what it was." She hopped, birdlike, as if she couldn't stand to be still. "Shouldn't you say '*velkommen,*' or don't you have a mug of glogg for an old friend?"

Mist knew she was gaping, but she couldn't seem to close her mouth. "Bryn," she said. *"Venninne min . . ."*

"Do you mind putting that sword down before someone gets hurt?"

Hiding Kettlingr from the view of the men at the door, Mist sang the sword small again, pushed it into its sheath with clumsy fingers, and opened her arms. They embraced warmly. The Valkyrie's head only came up to Mist's shoulder, and there wasn't an ounce of spare flesh on her bones, but her wiry strength was formidable. The fact that she was with a bunch of bikers, and that Jensen had so obviously deferred to her, told Mist that she'd done better than survive since the war.

Bryn wriggled out of Mist's bear hug and stepped back. "You haven't changed at all," she said. "Have I?"

"Not a bit," Mist said. "I just can't believe you're here." She looked over Bryn's head at the assembled bikers. "I take it you're with them?"

"You might say that." Bryn turned to Jensen, who still held his woolen cap clasped between nearly Jotunn-sized hands. "Rick Jensen, my lieutenant." She handed her helmet to him. "I can introduce everyone else later . . . if you're planning to invite us in for that glogg."

"I'll see what I can dig up," Mist said, wishing her vision hadn't gone so blurry. She looked over her shoulder. Vali, Dainn, and Tashiro were all watching intently, and she didn't mean for the lawyer to know anything about what was really going on, especially considering how close he'd come to seeing too much already. "Mr. Tashiro," she called, "I'm afraid I won't be able to talk to you this morning after all. Can we make an appointment for tomorrow?"

Tashiro's gaze snapped from her to Bryn to the bikers and back again. "Is everything okay?"

"These are old friends," Mist said. "If you don't mind . . ."

The lawyer's eyes narrowed, but he went back into the house, returned with his briefcase, and strode to the silver Prius parked a few yards down the street. He obviously wasn't happy about being so summarily dismissed, but Mist had enough guilt to deal with as far as he was concerned. She had already turned back to Bryn when he drove off.

"Who was that?" Bryn asked with a sly smile. "Kind of cute."

"Since when were you interested in men?"

Bryn sobered. "We've got a lot to catch up on."

"You have no idea." She gripped Bryn's arm. "Did you ever see Horja again?"

"No." Bryn glanced away. "What happened to the Cloak?"

No point in telling Bryn about the massacre. "I gave it to Horja to keep along with Gridarvol. I'm sure she still has them."

Bryn said nothing. Mist knew what she was feeling: regret for having had to leave the fight; the loneliness of knowing she had been dead to her Sisters; the guilt of having used the Cloak when she herself had believed doing so was in violation of their covenant with Odin.

She had been right all along.

"You still have Gungnir?" Bryn asked, brightening.

"Yes," Mist said, eager to change the subject. "By the way, were you trying to follow me earlier?"

"That little bar hopper of yours?" Bryn said, glancing toward Mist's unimpressive urban motorcycle. "Sorry if we gave you a scare. You obviously weren't sure if you'd be facing friends or enemies when we showed up, but I didn't realize we were walking into such a bad situation."

"That's one of the things we have to catch up on," Mist said dryly.

"Yeah. Anyway, about that following bit . . . one of my men caught the scent of an elf while we were trying to figure out where to start looking for whichever of the Sisters was in this city. I told him to keep track of it."

"He must have a pretty good sense of smell."

"That's putting it mildly. I think you'll find my friends pretty interesting."

Interesting was a word that had long since lost any meaning for Mist. "You weren't surprised to find an elf in Midgard?" she asked.

"Sure I was. But sometimes you have to go with whatever the Norns throw at you." She stepped sideways to look around Mist. "Is that the elf? He's pretty cute, too."

Mist turned around again. Dainn and Vali were standing side by side, wiry elf and beefy god, both apparently ready to dash to the rescue if Mist felt so much as a swoon coming on.

"That's him," Mist said. "His name is Dainn. But don't mistake him for the usual Alfr."

"I *never* would," Bryn said, widening her eyes dramatically. "You'd never settle for the usual elf. In fact, I thought you didn't like them."

"I don't," Mist said. "The other one is Vali."

"Odin's son?"

"The very same. He's a good guy. His brother, not so much."

"Sounds like we're going to need a few hours to cover all this."

"How many hours have you got?"

"Long as you need us," Bryn said, stripping off her gloves. "That's why we're here, to help, even if we don't know what help you need yet. And don't worry about my people . . . they know the whole background, and they aren't going to think we're crazy."

Allies, Mist thought. It was happening just as Dainn had predicted. She'd already found one of her Sisters without even trying.

Poor Bryn had no idea why she had found Mist so easily.

"Do you have a place to stay?" Mist asked.

"We can set up camp across the street in one of those empty buildings. No one is likely to bother us there."

"I haven't got much in the way of food . . ."

"We brought some stuff, and I can send one of my people out for more."

"Your people . . ." Mist began, wondering how to say it without sounding like an overprotective mother. "There are kids inside, and I—"

"*Your* kids?" Bryn asked with an incredulous lift of her brow.

"Odin's balls, no. Just some street kids who needed a place to stay."

"And they don't know who you really are, and you want us to be careful what we say."

"Yes, but not in the way you think. They actually *do* know. It's complicated. But I was hoping you'd get your people to keep it clean. No foul language. No drinking. No smoking inside. No brawls."

"Jeez, you've been watching too many movies." Bryn sighed. "But you're right, my people can be rough sometimes, even if they wouldn't hurt anyone who wouldn't try to hurt them first. I'll let them know."

Bryn turned to signal to the other bikers, who dismounted and gathered up various packs, duffels, bedrolls, and other equipment. "You mind if we all come in for a while, just to get warm?"

"Of course I don't mind," Mist said, looping her arm around Bryn's shoulder. "And when we get a chance, one of the first things I want to know is how you ended up in a biker club."

"Why not? It's almost as good as riding an elf-bred steed over the battlefield. I can do a lot of pretending that way."

"I don't think you'll have to do much more pretending."

"Glad to hear it. Even life among my Einherjar was getting a little too routine."

Mist stopped. "Einherjar?"

"Didn't I tell you? That's the name we took when I started the club."

Einherjar, Mist thought. The bravest of mortal warriors, who, after death, lived again Valhalla, where they would spend eternity in feasting and fighting. All in preparation for the greatest battle of all.

"I hope they live up to their name," Mist said, "because they might not like what's about to happen."

"They'll stick with me," Bryn said with absolute assurance.

"Will they be willing to sacrifice their lives to save the world?"

"That bad, is it?" Bryn nodded to herself. "They'll like that."

Mist shook her head, and they continued to the door. Vali stuck out his hand, engulfing Bryn's when she took it. He handled her as if she were the small brown bird she resembled.

"Glad you're here," he said gruffly.

"Good to be here." She glanced at Dainn. "*Heil*, Alfr."

He inclined his head, his eyes hooded with emotion Mist couldn't read. "Greetings, Bryn of the Valkyrie."

"A little stuffy, isn't he?" Bryn remarked as they walked past the men into the loft. One by one the other Einherjar followed them, and soon the hall and kitchen were overflowing with men and women removing helmets and setting gear down on every available surface.

Ryan and Gabi were at the foot of the stairs, Gabi's mouth slightly open, Ryan as calm as if he considered the arrival of a dozen bikers to be an everyday event.

Maybe he'd seen it coming.

"Back upstairs," Mist told them.

"But it's time for—" Gabi began.

"Later," Mist said, and they went. Bryn came up beside her.

"What now?" she asked.

"The Einherjar can have the living room for now, if they can all fit in it," Mist said. "There's some Peet's in the fridge, if you want some coffee."

Bryn raised her voice. "Listen up, *huskarlar*. Mist and I are going to have a talk. You can have the living room, but don't make too much noise. There are kids sleeping upstairs. Coffee's on the house."

A couple of the men muttered under their breaths, silenced by a stare from Bryn. One of the women found the coffeemaker. The rest—a hodgepodge of tall, short, thin, husky, large, small—trooped without comment into the living room. Dainn lingered in the kitchen with Vali. Odin's son seemed sanguine enough, but she didn't like the expression in Dainn's eyes.

"Vali, you said you could start setting up your equipment," Mist said. "Dainn, get some sleep."

The elf hesitated. "May I speak to you alone, Freya's daughter?"

Not good, Mist thought, when he started talking that way. "Bryn," she said, "go to the second door to the left down the back hall. We'll talk in my bedroom."

"Freya's *daughter*?" Bryn repeated.

"Just go, Bryn."

The small Valkyrie nodded slowly and backed into the hall with obvious reluctance.

"Gym," Mist said curtly to Dainn.

She turned on the light, trying again to pretend the whole place hadn't been an ocean of blood twenty-four hours ago.

"I didn't exactly appreciate your spilling the beans out there," she said, facing Dainn with a hard stare. "What's so important that it couldn't wait?"

His gaze never left hers. "While you were sleeping," he said, "I attempted to reach Freya again."

"And?"

"I could not find her."

"If Loki sent her away, maybe she needs a little time to lick her wounds."

"You do not understand. There was *nothing*. I had no sense of her presence, no consciousness of the Shadow-Realm where the Aesir reside."

"You're not making any sense."

"I wish I were not." Dainn looked through her as if he saw only the emptiness he was trying to describe. "There was a great silence no voice has ever broken, as if Ginnungagap itself had vanished."

"That isn't possible."

"No." He looked at her again, and she saw what he saw: a negation of all life, a barrenness and desolation beyond words to describe.

Freya couldn't survive in that. No living being could.

"What are you telling me?" she asked. "Are the bridges gone?"

"Yes. Completely gone, not merely closed. And we can only assume that that the Aesir—Freya—can no longer reach us, nor can her allies."

"You mean we're alone," Mist said.

"It may not be a permanent state. But we must go on as if it is."

Mist stiffened her legs, half afraid they might give way beneath her. "If what you're saying is true," she said, "Loki won't be able to get any more Jotunar, either."

"We do not know how many he has left," Dainn said, "but you can be sure that he will soon realize that he, too, is alone. He will certainly redouble his efforts to claim mortal servants. Every Jotunn he can spare will be seeking your Sisters and the Treasures. Without the Aesir, there is no one to prevent Midgard from becoming the kind of world Loki desires. No one but us." He held up one hand, palm cupped toward her as if in supplication. "You must take up a role I know you want no part of."

Mist knew what he was going to say. She'd always figured that Freya wasn't going to be taking direct charge of their mortal allies or distract herself with the day-to-day details of putting together an army that could fight Loki on his own terms.

Dainn had been trying to tell her all along. *She'd* told Loki she was only a foot soldier, even when she'd known her claim had been meant more to protect her own illusions than to deceive him. She just hadn't wanted to accept the obvious truth.

"You must become a leader," Dainn said. "The leader of everyone who fights for Midgard."

"That's crazy talk," Mist said, desperately searching for a way out. "Bryn would be better. She already has followers loyal to her, and—"

"She has only the magic of the Valkyrie," Dainn said. "You are the only one of your kind in this world. The only one who can stand against Loki in single combat."

"With the Vanir magic. But you said I couldn't use—"

"As long as Loki continues to believe that you are in Freya's thrall, he will not risk throwing his full forces against you until he is certain the Lady can be defeated without provoking her to use the Eitr. And when you have learned enough to wield the ancient magic again, it will not matter what he believes."

Mist backed away, raising her hands. "This won't work, Dainn. Look, even assuming we gather enough mortals willing to believe us and risk their lives for their world, we can't have battles in the streets. The only way we can fight Loki is through some kind of guerrilla action, like the Resistance in—" Her vision began to go dark. "Oh, gods. I can't do this. I can't be responsible."

"You can. As a wise man once said, 'With great power comes great responsibility.' You have a clear responsibility, Freya's daughter. One must lead. One must inspire men and women to do deeds they will believe are beyond their capacity, and convince them that their survival depends upon it."

"You don't know," she whispered. "You didn't *see*."

Dainn grabbed her arms, his fingers digging deep into muscle. "Will you pity yourself at a time such as this?"

He had said nearly the same thing to her before, when she had blamed herself for not recognizing who Eric really was. She didn't despise herself any less now.

"I'm not what you think I am," she said. "I never was."

He dropped his hands. His eyes were filled with contempt, but there was no beast lurking behind them. They belonged wholly to Dainn.

"Perhaps you are right," he said, "and this world will fall into chaos because you would not accept the burden of the gifts with which you were born. I will tell your Sister that she has made a mistake, and send Vali home to his brother. The children will be sent away, and I . . ." He closed his eyes. "Loki will kill me eventually, but I believe I can slaughter a few dozen of his Jotunar before he can stop me."

Mist understood. Dainn would let himself go, because he would see no reason to fight any other way. He had been sent to find her, protect her, help her prepare the way for the Aesir. If she gave up, he would truly have no purpose except to kill whatever the beast could hunt down.

That was the choice he had been given: to help her fight for Midgard, or let the beast take him. That was his fate.

His decision, she thought. But Dainn knew her too well. He knew she would blame herself if he became the thing he hated. He knew she understood that what would happen to him was nothing compared to what would become of the people of Midgard: kids like Ryan and Gabi, men and women like the bikers in her living room, the receptionists in Century Tower, the patrons of Asbrew—millions of mortals who didn't deserve what was coming.

Mist knew she had a one-in-a-million chance of stopping it, even if she had every one of her Sisters and thousands of mortals on her side. But the Norns couldn't have revealed her destiny more clearly if they had been spinning the thread of her life right in front of her.

"I recognize you now," Ryan had said. *"You were always there, in the middle."*

He'd just gotten the position slightly wrong.

"Odin-cursed elf," she said. "You always knew you'd win."

When she looked up, Dainn's eyes had changed. There was sadness in them, yes, but there also pride. In her. As if *he* had any right to—

Oh, Hel.

"There's one question you've never answered to my satisfaction," she said.

"Only one?"

She couldn't help but smile, but it didn't last. "Whatever 'exiled' everyone to Ginnungagap during the Last Battle . . . how do we know it won't happen again?"

"We do not. But if there was some force responsible, it has almost certainly long since vanished."

"I hope you're right," she said. "I wouldn't want to have to worry about that on top of everything else."

"Worry only about what you have the power to change," Dainn said. He started toward the door. When she didn't follow, he stopped and looked back.

"Are you coming?" he asked softly.

"Tell Bryn I'm on my way."

He bowed his head as he might to one of the most powerful of elf-lords and walked out of the gym. Mist lingered, looking around the room as if for the last time.

In a way, it was. There wouldn't be any more friendly bouts with lovers followed by a shower and a laughing tumble between the sheets. If Dainn was right and firearms couldn't be used by either side in this war, the weapons displayed on the rack—and all the others she could make—were badly going to be needed, and the gym would become a training ground for warriors.

They'd all have to learn very, very fast.

Turning off the light, Mist went to join her army.

ACKNOWLEDGMENTS

With special thanks to my editor, Lucienne Diver, my husband, Serge Mailloux, and my good friend Geri Lynn Matthews, for their ongoing support and enduring faith in me;

To Mary Kay Norseng, Professor Emerita, Scandinavian Section, UCLA , for her help with Norwegian words and phrases;

To my sister, Lauran Weinmann, for taking me on a tour of San Francisco after all my years away;

To Jeri and Mario Garcia, for their help with colloquial Spanish;

To MacAllister Stone, for her information and advice about blacksmithing.

And also to Genevra Littlejohn, for information about Kendo terminology.